NO WORSE ENEMY

Book One: The Empire's Corps
Book Two: No Worse Enemy
Book Three: When The Bough Breaks
Book Four: Semper Fi
Book Five: The Outcast
Book Six: To The Shores
Book Seven: Reality Check
Book Eight: Retreat Hell
Book Nine: The Thin Blue Line
Book Ten: Never Surrender
Book Eleven: First To Fight
Book Twelve: They Shall Not Pass

NO WORSE ENEMY

THE EMPIRE'S CORPS: BOOK TWO

CHRISTOPHER G. NUTTALL

Copyright © 2012, 2016 by Christopher G. Nuttall

The characters and events portrayed in this book are fictitious. Any similarity to real persons, living or dead, is coincidental and not intended by the author.

All rights reserved.
No part of this book may be reproduced, or stored in a retrieval system, or transmitted in any form or by any means, electronic, mechanical, photocopying, recording, or otherwise, without express written permission of the publisher.

ISBN-13: 9781537411675
ISBN-10: 1537411675

http://www.chrishanger.net
http://chrishanger.wordpress.com/
http://www.facebook.com/ChristopherGNuttall

All Comments Welcome!

DEAR READER

This book is number two in a series that starts with *The Empire's Corps*, currently available as an eBook. You can download a free sample of that book from my website. If you like my books, please review them– it helps boost sales and convinces me to write more in certain universes.

As I am not the best editor in the world, I would be grateful if you email me to point out any spelling mistakes, placing them in context. I can offer cameos, redshirt deals and suchlike in return.

Have fun! And if you want a fifth book, let me know.

Christopher Nuttall
2012

PROLOGUE

The Galactic Empire was dying.
Why? There were a thousand reasons. The Grand Senate's monopoly over legitimate political power. A colossal growth in the bureaucracy that kept the Empire together. Endless delay and procrastination worked into the governing system. Corruption in all ranks of the military, with the possible exception of the Marines. A police force more interested in political correctness than law enforcement. An upswing of interstellar piracy along the Rim and even the inner sectors. Rising taxes that strangled all hopes of creating new jobs and saving the economy. An educational system more focused on rights than responsibilities. And, perhaps worst of all, a rising tide of lawlessness that threatened to overwhelm Earth and the Core Worlds.

Captain Edward Stalker and his Marines were called in to deal with a Nihilist attack on Earth, where the death-worshipping terrorists had seized a city-block. After defeating the Nihilists, Captain Stalker made a single mistake; he told the Grand Senators exactly what had gone wrong and why. The problems that had impeded the response to the crisis had been caused by laws laid down by the Grand Senators themselves. In response, the Grand Senators ordered Captain Stalker and his Marines exiled to Avalon, an isolated world on the edge of the Empire, six months from Earth. It was intended as a permanent exile.

On Avalon, the Marines discovered that the planet suffered from a multitude of different problems. The Planetary Council had trapped most of the population in a stranglehold of debt, there were bandits threatening the countryside, and a growing rebellion – the Crackers - among the people, an insurgency that threatened to topple the government at any moment. Undaunted, the Marines landed and started to operate against the bandits, using that success as a spur to start breaking the Council's monopoly on political power, as well as forming a new army to replace the Civil Guard.

Realising that the Marines might actually succeed in building an army that could secure the planet, the Crackers prepared an assault on Camelot, the planet's capital city. Unknown to them, the Marines had collected the evidence needed to remove the Council and attempt to make peace with the Crackers, a plan that was derailed when the Crackers launched their desperate attack. Although the Marines were surprised and the Crackers achieved many of their early objectives, the Marines and the new Army of Avalon rallied and were able to break the Cracker offensive. In the aftermath, with the Council's removal and the Cracker defeat on the battlefield, a new government was forged that would represent the entire population.

It was then that Captain Stalker received his last message from the Empire. The Rim – including Avalon's sector – was being abandoned. Military bases were being shut down, Sector Governors were being recalled, and the inhabited worlds were left to fend for themselves as best as they could. The Marines would remain trapped on Avalon indefinitely.

Six months have passed since then…

CHAPTER ONE

It should not be surprising that involuntary settlers from Earth often ended up as either slaves or bandits. The lucky ones had endured education that taught them more about their rights than about their responsibilities – or about vital living skills – while the unlucky ones had grown up in the Undercity, little more than feral animals. Put bluntly, the Empire lost the ability to socialise its children.

Indeed, by the time I was exiled from Earth, almost all of the Empire's military and much of its civil service were reporting massive recruiting shortfalls. The educated students they needed simply didn't exist.

- Professor Leo Caesius, *The Perilous Dawn* (unpublished).

"It's quiet," Rifleman Blake Coleman said, over the communications link. "Too quiet."

"Shut up," Lieutenant Jasmine Yamane said lightly. "We are *meant* to be quiet."

She smiled inwardly as they crept closer to the bandit camp, hidden in the Badlands. The bandit leader had been smart – his camp was very well hidden – but he'd reckoned without the Marines. No one would deny that the Badlands were damn near impassable in places, yet they weren't as bad as the Slaughterhouse. Jasmine and her comrades had all graduated from the harshest training camp in the Empire.

The geologists had yet to come up with a good explanation for why the Badlands existed. They were a tangled nightmare of forests, river and lava pools, as well as enough minerals to confuse sensors hunting for targets. There were even places where lava bubbled up from the planet's underground. The best guess was that the Badlands had been the site of an asteroid impact thousands of years before the planet had been settled; the alternative was a botched terraforming project, which was unlikely. There had been no need to improve Avalon when the planet had been settled, not when it was already perfect for human habitation.

"There," Joe Buckley said. He inclined his head towards an outcropping that looked like a tuff of land. The bandits hadn't done a bad job of disguising their lookout; it would have been almost invisible if the Marines hadn't been looking for it. "You see the guy behind it?"

"Yeah," Jasmine answered, studying the position. The bandits wouldn't have based themselves in a place with only one exit; stupid bandits wouldn't have lasted long, even before the Marines had arrived on Avalon. "I'll deal with him. You stay here and watch my back."

She crawled forward, trusting in her camouflage to keep her from being spotted. Up close, it was obvious that the bandits had put some thought into their position; anyone sitting in the lookout should have been able to spot oncoming enemies from a distance. Or they would have been able to see them, if they'd cleared away the foliage. But that would have betrayed them to the orbiting satellites used by the Marines. Quite a few bandit camps had been eliminated since the Battle of Camelot because their occupants had made careless mistakes.

The bandit sitting in the lookout didn't look very competent, but Jasmine checked around carefully anyway before she closed in for the kill. Appearances could be deceiving, as Jasmine herself demonstrated; very few people would have realised that she was a Marine if they saw her out of uniform, or armour. Up close, there was a faint stench surrounding the lookout, suggesting that the bandits didn't give a shit about basic hygiene. Jasmine wasn't too surprised. Unlike the Crackers, who had been offered amnesty after the Battle of Camelot, the bandits had no long-term political objective. They just wanted to have fun. Jasmine pushed her irritation aside as she rose silently to her feet and moved forward. The bandit didn't even realise she was there until she'd cut his throat.

"Got him," she subvocalised into her implant. There had been no time for a battlefield interrogation – and the bandit would have been hanged anyway if she'd dragged him back to Camelot. "I'm going onwards to the camp."

The bandits had built their camp in the middle of the forest, half-hidden in a hollow that would make it harder for orbital observation to pick up on their activities. Jasmine studied it as they crept closer and scowled; the bandits had clearly kidnapped at least one person who actually knew how to build basic huts out of wood and clay. They were rare skills on Earth, which had long since become an entire planet of city-blocks, but quite common on newly-settled worlds. Wood was simply too efficient a building material to ignore.

"I have eyes on hostages," Blake said, suddenly. Jasmine scowled. If the bandits had been alone, she would have called in an airstrike and then cleaned up the mess. "At least five, all young girls. And they're limping."

Jasmine muttered a curse under her breath. The bandits raided the local farms regularly, carrying off food, drink, weapons and women. It wasn't uncommon for them to cripple the girls, just to make sure that they couldn't run away after they'd been dumped in the camp; one camp they'd destroyed had had two girls who'd had their legs amputated by their masters. The girls she could see didn't look as if they'd been treated *that* badly, but they had broken expressions on their faces that made Jasmine wince. They'd had the fire beaten out of them ever since they'd been kidnapped and trapped in a living nightmare.

"Those sick fuckers," Joe breathed. He cleared his throat. "Orders, Lieutenant?"

Jasmine pushed her anger to one side, activating her communicator. "Bring up the rest of the platoon," she ordered. "And then prepare to engage."

She scanned the camp quickly as the remainder of First Platoon closed in on the bandit camp, considering options. If they'd been wearing heavy armour, she would have been sorely tempted just to stand up and walk into the enemy camp, secure in the knowledge that they didn't have any weapons that could touch them. But instead they only wore light armour – and she didn't want to risk causing harm to the prisoners. If they ordered the bandits to surrender and the bandits started firing instead, the prisoners might be caught up in the crossfire. And they *would* open fire. They knew better than to expect mercy from the new government. Why *not* fight?

Jasmine smiled humourlessly. Everything had seemed simpler when she'd been a mere Rifleman.

"Sound off," she muttered, as the platoon got into firing position. She listened briefly to the responses, confirming that her ten subordinates were all in position. "And engage on my command."

There was a shout from the bandit camp. They'd seen something, perhaps one of the Marines as they crawled into position. Jasmine didn't hesitate; she barked the command to open fire as she squeezed the trigger of her own rifle. The bandit she'd targeted, shot through the head, collapsed in a crumpled heap on the ground. Jasmine was already searching for new targets as the Marines wiped out every bandit in sight. The hostages were clinging to each other, panicking.

Jasmine keyed her mike as the Marines inched forward. "GET DOWN ON THE GROUND," she ordered, praying that the hostages would obey. A handful of bandits were trying to fight back, or flee westwards away from the Marines. "GET DOWN AND STAY DOWN."

One muddy hut seemed to be held by at least four bandits, who were shooting wildly towards where they thought the Marines were. It hadn't been designed as a blockhouse, Jasmine noted absently, but it would suffice, as long as the Marines kept the gloves on. She used hand signals to order Blake and Joe towards it, while the other Marines provided covering fire to force the bandits to keep their heads down. Blake used a shaped charge to smash in the wooden door, while Joe charged in, weapon at the ready.

"Two down," Blake reported. "Two others surrendered."

Jasmine nodded. "Secure them," she ordered, as she rose to her feet and headed down into the bandit camp. "And secure the hostages as well."

The girls might have been pretty once, but that had been before they'd spent several months in a bandit camp, where they'd spent the days cooking and cleaning and the nights being raped by their captors. Jasmine's heart went out to them, yet she knew better than to trust them; people did odd things when they were held captive for so long and it was possible that the women had actually fallen in love with their rapists. The human mind was good at twisting itself and inventing excuses to make suffering bearable.

She switched channels as the handful of prisoners were dragged out, searched and then secured, left to wait on the ground while the Marines searched the remainder of the camp. Unsurprisingly, there was nothing particularly interesting about the camp, nor was there a large stash of weapons. The Civil Guard had lost several consignments of weapons before the Marines had arrived, some of which remained unaccounted for, but the mystery wouldn't be solved today. Jasmine, who shared the general feeling that some of the Crackers had hidden the weapons in case the provisional government turned out to be a trick of some kind, was privately relieved. The bandits could have been more than a nuisance if they'd had some heavy weapons.

"Bring in the helicopters," she ordered. The bandits hadn't been foolish enough to build their camp right next to a clearing, but the marines had identified a potential LZ not too far away. Jasmine had had it checked out before they'd started sneaking up on the camp. If someone needed emergency transport back to the medical clinic on Castle Rock, they would need an LZ. "We'll be there in ten minutes."

The former hostages were being helped to their feet by the Marines. They looked badly shocked, even though they were being rescued. Jasmine couldn't blame them; the Marines looked intimidating as hell – *and* they'd secured the girls with plastic ties, just in case. The Marines would have to carry the girls to the LZ, she realised; they'd never be able to walk that far without assistance. Jasmine was used to horror – she'd seen too much of man's inhumanity to man even in her relatively short career – but it never failed to sicken her. How could anyone do that to their fellows?

They wanted slaves and sex objects, she thought, answering her own question. The really sickening part was that the bandits had been amateurs. Some members of the former Planetary Council of Avalon had been truly sadistic little shits, raping children and other helpless victims. And she'd seen much worse in the Empire, back during the nightmare that had enveloped Han, or in the Undercity on Earth.

Blake buzzed her. "The WARCAT team wishes permission to approach," he said. "And the Knights wish to take over the scene."

Jasmine had to smile. The Knights – the newly-raised Army of Avalon – weren't as well-trained as the Marines, but they were learning fast as the former Civil Guardsmen were integrated into their ranks. Captain – no, *Colonel* – Stalker had decided, as Avalon was no longer part of the Empire, to merge the two, knowing that the Civil Guard had a poor reputation. Jasmine had a feeling that the Colonel had some other plan for his Marines, even though a good third of the company had been parcelled out to help the locals. Who knew *what* they could do once they got the tech base set up?

"Tell them they're welcome," she said, finally. They *had* asked for a joint attack on the bandit camp, but Jasmine had vetoed it, pointing out that slipping eleven men close to the camp would be hard enough. Colonel Stalker hadn't overruled her – but then, that wasn't the Marine way. She was the officer on the spot, charged with accomplishing her mission. Success – or failure – would be her responsibility. "Let the WARCAT team take samples from the prisoners before we get them back to Camelot."

"Understood," Blake said. "You think they're going to be hanged *that* quickly?"

Jasmine rolled her eyes as she started to walk to where the prisoners were being mustered. The new government *hated* bandits, for plenty of very good reasons. Every single bandit who was caught alive was either hanged, or sent to work in a very isolated prison camp. It discouraged surrenders, she knew, but she found it hard to blame the new government. They'd suffered too much when the bandits had been allowed to run rampant over the countryside.

"Probably," she said. High overhead, she heard the sound of helicopters. They were noisier than Marine Corps Raptors, but they'd been produced on Avalon, allowing them to save their handful of remaining Raptors. There would be no replacements until their tech base was developed properly. "Prepare the prisoners for their walk."

The WARCAT team acted with practiced efficiency, taking blood samples from the prisoners and uploading them to the planetary datanet for comparison to the records. It seemed a little pointless, but Jasmine had learned long ago that there was no such thing as useless information. Knowing who the bandits were might be useful in the future, or allow them to identify gang members who hadn't been killed or captured during the raid. It also gave them time for the medics to check the girls, verify that none of them were in immediate danger and check their identities too. Their families, if they were still alive, would be very relieved.

"All done," the medic reported, finally. "You can carry them safely."

Jasmine detailed seven Marines to carry the girls, with the remaining five to take point and watch for other bandits, and then led the way back into the Badlands. It never struck her until after an operation that the Badlands were really quite beautiful, if one liked untamed wildernesses. She reminded herself sharply that they were still in bandit country, that they might be attacked at any moment, even though cold logic told her that it was unlikely. The bandits were rarely brave enough to attack Marines. They preferred targets that couldn't fire back.

"If I'm carrying the girl," Blake asked, as they walked away from the remains of the camp, "does that mean I have to marry her?"

Joe snickered. "I would have thought you'd learned your lesson by now," he said. "Women are Bad News."

"Not all of them," Blake said. "They didn't actually kill me."

Jasmine rolled her eyes. Blake had missed the Battle of Camelot because the Crackers had managed to kidnap him two weeks prior to the fighting. One of their female operatives had seduced him, then drugged him, and then somehow transported him out of the city to a hidey-hole where he'd been hidden until after the battle. Command Sergeant Gwendolyn Patterson, the company's senior NCO, had been incredibly scathing about the whole affair, pointing out that Blake had shown very bad judgement. Jasmine was his junior, by seniority alone, but she'd been promoted over his head. At least Blake didn't seem to bear a grudge.

But then, *Lieutenant* wasn't a permanent rank in the Terran Marine Corps. If she fucked up, Jasmine knew, she could be returned to the ranks without any formalities. Ideally, every Rifleman would have a chance at holding the rank for a few months, just to see who would make a good Captain. On Avalon, with only a relative handful of Marines, it wasn't possible to rotate ranks as often as it was on other planets. They'd already started to bend the rules by integrating Auxiliaries into their ranks.

"That makes you damn lucky," Joe said. "Were you borrowing my lucky red shirt?"

"I was too sexy to kill," Blake countered, quickly. "That's why they couldn't kill me."

The other Marines started to chuckle, rather sarcastically. Blake *had* been lucky; it was rare for a Marine prisoner to be left alive for long. Marines had been treated to make it impossible to torture them for information *and* their implants could be tracked, given time, by their allies. Most kidnappers would have killed their prisoner and then vanished.

"Quiet," Jasmine ordered, as they approached the LZ. "Second Platoon is waiting."

Three helicopters were sitting in the clearing, with two more orbiting overhead, weapons at the ready. Few bandits would dare to tangle with an attack helicopter, but Second Platoon was patrolling around the edge of the LZ, just in case. Precautions, her instructors had hammered into her head time and time again, cost very little, certainly less than a helicopter.

There was a brief exchange of signals before they stepped into the LZ itself, confirming their identity, and passed the girls over to the first transport helicopter. Twenty minutes later, they were up in the air, heading back to Camelot and Castle Rock. And debriefing.

Jasmine removed her helmet and ran her hands through her dark hair, cropped close to her skull. Debriefing wasn't going to be fun; being a Lieutenant carried extra responsibilities and few rewards, apart from the credit – and the blame. The rank was supposed to be paid more than a Rifleman, but payment these days was a little skewed. Imperial Credits were worthless on Avalon now and the replacement banking system was still struggling to establish itself. There were places where they used bartering instead of money.

"You'll be fine," Blake assured her. He'd deduced her train of thought, easily. She was hardly the first new Lieutenant to face her commanding officer after an operation. "And then we can go drinking."

"I would have thought you'd learned your lesson about that too," Jasmine said, dryly. The first few months they'd spent on Avalon had included a number of bar fights, before many of the former street gangsters had been either inducted into the Knights or sent to work on the farms. "Besides, I don't feel like drinking right now."

She looked down at Camelot as the tiny city came into view. From high overhead, it looked to be thriving – and indeed, there *had* been any number of improvements since the former Council had been defeated. The damage caused by the Battle of Camelot had been repaired, apart from the ruins of the former Government House, which had been left as a monument to the war. It was easy to forget that the Empire had withdrawn from the sector, abandoning them…

…And that they were completely on their own.

CHAPTER TWO

It was therefore necessary to start teaching the students of Avalon new skills. Both military and civilian. Naturally, there was a degree of makeshift improvising in those early arrangements. Equally naturally, although I didn't see it at the time, was the fact that the youth responded splendidly. The Empire's education consisted of turning out entitled drones. Avalon could not allow itself that self-defeating luxury.

- Professor Leo Caesius, *The Perilous Dawn* (unpublished).

Castle Rock had changed in the six months since the Marines had landed on Avalon. Once a barren island some distance from the capital city, Camelot, it was now a developed military base for both the Marines and the Knights, serving as both training centre and logistics hub for their operations on the planet. The eighty Marines who made up Stalker's Stalkers had been joined by thousands of Knights, many of whom had once been Civil Guardsmen before the Civil Guard had been folded into the Army of Avalon. Looking down from his office, Colonel Edward Stalker could see hundreds of new recruits being put through their paces by the Drill Instructors, before heading to the shooting house to brush up on their weapons skills. Even the washouts would prove dangerous to the remaining bandits on Avalon…

He turned away from the window as Command Sergeant Gwendolyn Patterson entered his office, followed by Lieutenant Jasmine Yamane. Jasmine was young for promotion to Lieutenant, with only limited experience compared to some of the other Marines in the company, but there had been little choice; he'd had to parcel out some of his more experienced officers and men to bolster the Knights. The former Civil Guardsmen weren't completely trusted by the rest of the locals, unsurprisingly. Too many of them had been either corrupt or incompetent. Edward had just fifty Marines – four platoons – as a reserve and it bothered him. At least the bandits were largely broken and on the run by now.

Gwendolyn cleared her throat as Jasmine snapped to attention, issuing a salute that Edward returned gravely. Had he ever been that young? Of course he had – and he'd had the benefit of OCS courses while making his way from Rifleman to Captain. Jasmine was studying hard, under the tutelage of two NCOs and one Lieutenant, but she would never have the formal OCS training provided by the Terran Marine Corps. Being cut off from the Empire ensured that standards would slip. He'd just have to fight to ensure that they didn't slip too far.

"Congratulations on your first command," he said. Jasmine would probably have been absolutely terrified when she'd been out in the field, knowing that she was directly responsible for the lives of her fellow Marines. And it didn't help that she'd been one of them only scant months ago. Normally, a potential officer would have been rotated into a different company. "You did well."

"Thank you, sir," Jasmine said. Edward remembered his own feelings after his first command and concealed a smile. He'd been terrified too, when the excitement wore off and he realised just how badly he could fuck up. "We picked up an update from the Knights; SSE produced nothing, apart from some more genetic traces…"

"That isn't surprising," Edward pointed out, mildly. SSE – Sensitive Site Exploitation – was standard procedure when overrunning terrorist, insurgent or bandit bases, but it was only of limited use when hunting bandits. They tended not to keep records, or operate in large bands, preferring to raid the borders of settlement on Avalon rather than try to overthrow the government. SSE was much more useful when tackling the remains of the Crackers – the ones who had refused to accept the general outbreak of peace in the wake of the Battle of Camelot – but the Crackers were rarely active within the Badlands. "I assume you moved the hostages to the nearest medical centre?"

"The Knights saw to that, sir," Jasmine said. "None of them were in very good shape."

Edward nodded, sourly. The Crackers, whatever else could be said about them, had fought a relatively clean war against the Government, even though the former Council had been trying to enslave the entire planet. They'd been careful to avoid atrocities, knowing that random slaughter would turn the local population against them. The bandits, on the other hand, gloried in their atrocities, using them to spread terror and discourage resistance. Now, with the Marines and the increasingly effective Army of Avalon hunting them – and the local settlers no longer having to hide their arms from the Council – the bandits were in decline. Everyone knew it, including the bandits themselves. They had responded by becoming even nastier to their victims.

"But we put an end to the group's existence," Edward said. The ongoing operation against the bandits had notched up another success – and the Army of Avalon could hold the territory, now that it had been cleared. And the bandits would be driven further into the Badlands. "Did you file a report?"

He grinned openly at Jasmine's expression. As a Rifleman, she wouldn't have been called upon to actually do any paperwork, at least unless the shit had hit the fan spectacularly. Unlike the Army, or the Civil Guard, the Marines tried to keep paperwork to a minimum, believing that it helped reduce unit effectiveness. But since she'd been promoted, Jasmine would have had to handle the paperwork for her platoon as well as actually commanding it in battle. And there was even more paperwork for a Marine Captain…

And considerably less than for a Sergeant in the Civil Guard, Edward thought, in the privacy of his own mind. The regulars were paranoid, insanely so. Every last item of supplies had to be accounted for, up to and including training rounds fired off during exercises. Unsurprisingly, dreading the thought of so much paperwork, unit Sergeants tended to avoid carrying out training exercises…and then wondered why their men couldn't shoot straight. The Marines joked – with black humour – that the safest place to be on the battlefield was where the Civil Guardsmen were supposed to be targeting.

"Yes, sir," Jasmine said, finally. She wouldn't have mastered the tricks for reducing paperwork yet. One of the NCOs would show her, if she didn't work them out for herself. Eventually. Learning the dangers of paperwork was one of the most important lessons for a potential officer. "The report was filed as soon as we landed on Castle Rock."

"Good to hear it," Edward said. "See to your men, Lieutenant, and then stand down for the evening. Third Platoon will be moving up to support the Knights for the rest of the week."

"Thank you, sir," Jasmine said. First Platoon *had* been out in the Badlands for three weeks when they'd finally tracked the bandits back to their lair. "What will we be doing after that?"

Edward had to smile. With fifty Marines on active service, they were mainly running around pissing on fires, backing up the Knights when they ran into trouble as well as serving as a Quick Reaction Force. First Platoon would have the evening off, followed by a few days waiting for trouble. They might have preferred to remain in the Badlands.

"Whatever we have to do, Lieutenant," he said, wryly. He'd been that young too, once upon a time. "Dismissed."

Jasmine saluted and left his office. Edward watched her go, closing the door behind her, and then turned back to Gwendolyn. "She seems to be shaping up fine," he said, pulling the brief report up on his terminal. Jasmine had mastered the laconic style the Marines preferred, thankfully, even if it would never win any prizes for great literature. "Did you hear anything through the grapevine?"

"Nothing bad," Gwendolyn confirmed. The NCOs were intimately involved with grooming potential officers – and could veto promotions that might push someone out of their competence zone. "She definitely had first-mission nerves, but we all get them. And if she survived Han, she can survive anything."

Edward winced. Han had been an overcrowded planet in an overcrowded sector, run by a corrupt government that had constantly refused to read the writing on the wall. And then the government had acted surprised when the entire sector exploded in rebellion, directed against both the government and the Empire. Edward had been a Lieutenant himself on Han when the rebellion had begun, pushed into command of the company when his CO had been killed in the savage fighting. It was humbling to realise that the fighting on Avalon, no matter how devastating it had been to the local settlers, was minor compared to the storm that had raged over Han. The Marines had lost several thousand officers and men; the Civil Guardsmen had been virtually eliminated. And even now the sector was still rebellious.

Or it had been. These days, there was no way to know what was happening in the remainder of the Empire, or even if there still *was* an Empire.

He shook his head at the thought. Once, as a young boy growing up in the Undercity, he'd thought of the Empire as an invincible monolith. But as a Marine he'd learned that the Empire was weakening by the day. There were just too few ships and men to rush around putting out fires, while oppressed communities, planets and sectors were taking the chance to build up their own stockpiles of weapons in preparation for the day they could claim independence and freedom from the Empire. And the Grand Senate, far from realising the danger that threatened to overrun the Empire, had just kept tightening the screws. Didn't they *realise* that they were forcing the Empire's population into rebellion?

Of course they didn't, he knew. They'd been rich, powerful and untouchable for hundreds of years. Why shouldn't they assume that it would last forever? But Earth had been a pressure cooker for centuries and when it exploded, it was likely to start a fire that would burn through the brittle remains of the Empire. It was a bitter thought, but he and his Marines were likely to be better off on Avalon than they would be on Earth when the final collapse of the Empire began.

"Of course she can," he agreed, finally. He looked over at the map of Avalon on one wall. Now that the Crackers had been brought into the government, they had started resettling the street children out on the farms, hoping to reduce the number of starving poor on the streets. It wasn't working too badly, although some of the children had proved rather ungrateful for the chance to actually make something of themselves. They'd had to be moved to penal islands where they could live or die on their own, with neither help nor hindrance from the Government. "And the new recruits?"

Gwendolyn was used to him changing the subject by now. "They're coming along as well as can be expected," she said. That was high praise, coming from her. "Some minor disciplinary problems, a handful unhappy at being away from home for the first time in their lives and none too happy about the lockdown…"

Edward snorted. Now they had some time to breathe, they'd managed to improve the training program for new soldiers – including a three-month period when they would be completely out of contact with their families and friends. It was a taste of what Marines experienced when they left their homeworlds to go to Boot Camp, and then to the Slaughterhouse, but it seemed unnecessary on Avalon. After all, as some of the new Council had pointed out, the Knights weren't going to be deployed off-planet. Edward had countered by saying that the recruits had to develop some independence from their former civilian lives. It hadn't been a pleasant discussion.

"They'll get used to it," he said, dryly. But then, *Edward* hadn't wanted to go back to the Undercity; no one in their right mind would want to go to the Undercity, ever. Most of his fellow Marines felt the same way about their homeworlds. Besides, it could be months between sending a message through a Marine Transport Ship and receiving a reply. On Avalon, it was easy to talk to parents, or friends. "Just keep an eye on the situation."

Gwendolyn nodded, rather drolly. It wasn't an order that needed to be issued. All NCOs went through courses in training new soldiers, even if they didn't intend to become Drill Instructors. They knew what to watch for – and what to avoid. And which recruits should be shown the door as quickly as possible.

"One question did get raised," she said, tapping the map. "How long can we afford to keep raising soldiers?"

Edward scowled. Avalon's economy had been effectively strangled by the former Council – and then torpedoed when the Empire had announced that it would be withdrawing from the outermost sectors along the Rim. Imperial Credits were worthless now, while very few settlers trusted the banks that had been established by the Council. In the end, they'd had to be transferred to Marine control, creating yet another hassle for Edward and his men. But they'd been the only ones everyone on the planet had been prepared to trust.

On the other hand, the Council's defeat had allowed the Governor a chance to remove all of their edicts and laws that had limited any hope of economic development. Avalon was now enjoying something of an economic boom, aided and abetted by some of the tech the Marines had brought with them when they'd left Earth. All of the petty regulations were gone and people were making fortunes, fortunes which they were encouraged to invest elsewhere on the planet. But there had to be limits to expansion and Edward was unsure what would happen when they finally hit those limits. Avalon's population was small – it would have vanished like a drop of water in a bucket if it had been merged into Earth's population – and there were limits to how much the planet could develop for itself.

"As long as we have to, I hope," he said. Between the Knights and the armed settlers, the bandits were being eliminated. So many weapons out in the countryside would create their own problems, sooner or later, but they'd cope with that too. Besides, it might be a good idea to ensure that there was a balance of power between the new Council and the farmers. "Still, we may have to start drawing back soon."

"Which will produce other problems," Gwendolyn pointed out. "We're drawing off the most aggressive of the local youth into the Knights. What happens when we can't take them any longer?"

"We find something else for them to do," Edward said, cursing the previous Council's mentality. God alone knew what they'd been thinking, if they'd been thinking at all. There had been hundreds of thousands of unregistered children on Avalon and many of them had ended up on the streets, where the lucky ones had joined gangs with low life-expectancy. The unlucky ones had had to sell themselves to survive. "There are plenty of farms that need new workers."

Gwendolyn snorted. "That won't suit everyone," she said. "And what about the technical schools?"

"They'll have to make do," Edward admitted. "Just like the rest of us."

It was another problem the previous Council had caused, one that was actually more devastating than the street children and endless debt.

The Empire's educational system had been collapsing for centuries; children on Avalon had never been taught more than reading and writing, if that. They certainly rarely understood how technology actually worked, let alone how to modify and improve it for future development. And if they didn't know those details, who would repair the machines when they started to break? The general technological level on Avalon was primitive and Edward had his doubts that even *that* could have been sustained for more than a few decades after the Empire withdrew from the sector.

The Marines had started technological colleges as part of Edward's plan to preserve as much of civilisation as he could, but it was an uphill struggle. Many of the children were willing to learn – unlike the children in the Core Worlds – yet they were critically ignorant of far too much they needed to know. The Marines had had to distribute too many of their auxiliaries to run basic courses on everything from vehicle maintenance to basic spaceflight technology; if it hadn't been for the agreement with the RockRats, Edward had a sneaking suspicion that they would have to have abandoned space altogether. Maintaining the orbital station, let alone the cloudscoop, would have been almost impossible. And *that* would have doomed Avalon to eventual collapse.

He grinned at Gwendolyn, changing the subject again. "I've got a meeting with the Council in two hours," he added. At least the new Council was more reasonable than its predecessor. "After that, we can review the figures and see what we can do about establishing more farms."

"A meeting with the Council or just with Gaby?" Gwendolyn asked, and laughed at his flush. She'd told him, several months ago, that Gaby Cracker, the former leader of the Crackers, had a crush on him. Edward had been unable to believe it and decided that he was being teased. "You really should ask the girl out, *sir*."

"A meeting with the Council," Edward said firmly, deciding not to rise to the bait. He was probably just being teased, a droll reminder that he was still only human. The Ancient Romans had used to have a slave reminding their Generals that they were only human; Edward, who'd been a young man when he'd first cracked open a book on history, had wondered how many of the slaves had survived the experience. "And then I thought I might inspect the spaceport."

"A very good idea," Gwendolyn said. Like all of the Marines, she had a certain suspicion of anyone handling logistics who wasn't a Marine – or an auxiliary. "Keep the bastards on their toes."

Chapter Three

> If there was a society that seemed almost destined to survive the collapse of the Empire, it was the RockRats. Living in isolated asteroids, mining what they needed from the boundless wealth of space and relying on the Empire for nothing, they believed that they could keep going even when the Empire's civil war collapsed into mass slaughter. And they might have been right. It was our good fortune that some of the RockRats chose to side with Avalon in those early years. Without them, we could not have done what we did.
>
> - Professor Leo Caesius, *The Perilous Dawn* (unpublished).

"You wouldn't believe the view, Jasmine," Mandy Caesius said, into the recorder. "The RockRats simply don't believe in gravity."

She floated in the centre of a tangled forest of strange trees, growing in all directions. The RockRats had burrowed into the heart of the asteroid and hollowed it out, but they hadn't bothered to spin the asteroid to provide gravity – or install a gravity generator. Instead, they'd just planted the seeds in fertile soil and watched to see what would happen. Now, thirty years later, the interior of the asteroid was a jungle that played host to countless birds and insects that seemed to get along just fine without gravity and allowed the RockRats a chance to relax and meditate on the universe. Mandy hadn't been inducted into their religion – it wasn't something shared with outsiders – but she believed that the RockRats worshipped universal harmony. It certainly seemed to make more sense than the strange religions that had run through campus back home on Earth…

No, she reminded herself, *Avalon* was home now. Her father had been exiled from Earth for daring to point out that the Empire was in a state of near-constant decline and his family – Mandy, her sister Mindy and their mother – had been exiled with him. She'd been a right brat about it, Mandy recalled, more concerned with what it would do to her social life than anything else. All of her friends had stopped talking to her after her father had lost tenure and had been forced to leave their home…and if they hadn't been dispatched to Avalon, they would probably have been killed. Now, Mandy looked back on the brat she'd been and shuddered. How *could* she have been so stupid?

She hadn't realised just how ignorant she'd been, even after the near-fatal incident with the sparkle-dust, until she'd started studying at the technical college. And she'd had an academic for a father! It had taken months for her to learn the basics and then move on to practical work; if she hadn't shown some promise, she suspected that she would never have been allowed to leave Avalon and join the RockRats in their asteroid cluster. As it was, she'd had to work hard every day, feeling slow and stupid every time she was introduced to a new concept. The only thing that kept her going was the thought that perhaps her father would be proud of her afterwards.

Her father, and Jasmine, the Marine she'd met and now looked up to as an older sister of sorts.

She raised the recorder to her lips again and continued to speak, dictating the next letter to her friend. They'd all been encouraged to learn to write by hand, something that Mandy found rather uncomfortable after so long using computers, but there was no room on the RockRat settlement for such luxuries. It was something of a relief, although she knew it wouldn't last. The Marines who oversaw the technical schools insisted that they had to keep working on the basics, or else they risked losing competence. Mandy knew better than to argue.

"They're sending us out to the latest mine today," she added, after telling Jasmine about her social life. At least she had friends now, even if they were all driven by a competitiveness that left Mandy wondering how they would have survived on Earth. But then, she'd had opportunities to learn and ignored them; her new friends had been prevented by endless mountains of debt from learning anything useful. "From what they told us, we will be digging up ores that can be used to build new spacecraft for operations inside the Phase Limit…"

"Hey," a voice called, from within the foliage. "Mandy?"

Mandy shut off the recorder and grinned. "Mike," she called back. "Over here!"

Michael Volpe pushed his way through the jungle and out into the clear spot at the heart of the asteroid. He was a handsome young man, although his face bore the scars from a lifetime spent on the streets – and, later, in the Army of Avalon. Someone had clearly thought that he was destined for better things, for he was one of ten young men who'd been added to the technical college's mission to the RockRat settlement, even though he hadn't spent months learning his trade in the college. On Earth, many would have flinched away from him, seeing the military as a pool for losers and sociopaths. She knew better now.

"We're leaving earlier than planned," Michael said, after a quick kiss. They'd been lovers for almost a month. Mandy was unsure of how far it would go, but they were enjoying themselves…besides, he was a much better person than the average teenage boy on Earth. "They want us down at the airlock by 0940."

"Joy," Mandy said, after a quick glance at her timepiece. It was 0920. "And you came to tell me that by yourself?"

Michael gave her the mischievous grin that she was coming to associate with him. "I just thought that we might have time to do something else," he said, pulling himself forward to kiss her. "Even if we don't have time for everything…"

There had been a time, Mandy knew, when she would have dropped everything just to enjoy herself with her latest boyfriend. Perhaps because it had been fun, perhaps because it had annoyed her father, perhaps because it had distracted her from the fact that her life was empty and meaningless…just like the vast majority of the children on campus, back on Earth. Now she knew better…and besides, she did have something to do with her life. She might never be a great engineer – some of the RockRats had forgotten more than the entire class would ever learn – but she did have prospects. There was nothing quite like making something for herself, or keeping a piece of machinery running properly…

She kissed him back and then started to pull herself back through the forest, back down to the tubes that ran through the entire asteroid. The RockRats didn't seem to have much of a sense of aesthetics, she'd once decided; the tubes still looked to have been carved with lasers or fusion torches, as if they'd backed a sublight ship into the asteroid and used the drive to carve out the interior. Later, she'd realised that the very lack of aesthetics was part of the RockRat ethos; unlike the rest of the Empire, they didn't smooth out the world around them. They wanted to be reminded of what they'd done to produce their habitat.

Michael followed her down until they reached the airlock, where one of the RockRat in-system spacecraft was already docked, waiting for the students. The RockRats themselves looked faintly odd to Mandy's eyes; they were inhumanly tall and thin, seemingly so thin that a brief exposure to a gravity field could prove lethal. Mandy knew better – the RockRats had enhanced themselves in ways that ensured they could exist under a standard gravity field, but also in a way that marked them out from the rest of the human race – but she still found them rather creepy. It was just another clue that there was more in the Empire than she'd ever realised, before her father had been exiled to Avalon.

"Check your masks and suits," the RockRat ordered, his dark eyes moving from student to student. "Do you have any problems with your equipment?"

Mandy nodded as her fingers checked automatically. They'd been told to keep their suits on at all times unless they were in a secure compartment – and to have them ready nearby, just in case. After seeing pictures of people who had been exposed, however briefly, to vacuum, Mandy wasn't inclined to argue. Besides, the RockRats had warned that anyone who didn't take care of themselves would be returned to Avalon before the unkind environment took care of them permanently. Space simply didn't care how important – or young – someone was; if they were careless or stupid, they died. The RockRats seemed to approve of this for some reason that didn't make sense to anyone else.

"No," she said, when asked. She checked her mask daily, replacing it whenever the telltales suggested that it might be wearing out. "Everything is fine."

"Then board the ship," the RockRat ordered. "I will fly you to your destination."

Mandy noticed some of her fellow students exchanging sarcastic glances as they filed their way into the ship. The RockRats did seem to love pointing out the obvious – although, as Jasmine had pointed out, sometimes it was better to repeat instructions rather than risk having them misunderstood. Apparently, the Marines did the same; it might have been repetitive, but it prevented accidents. Inside, she allowed Michael to lead her over to a seat near one of the portholes, staring out into the endless darkness of space. It always made her feel small and insignificant. The stars had been burning long before the first human had learned to make fire and would be burning after the Empire and all its works faded away into nothingness.

The Marine Transport Ship that had brought her and her family to Avalon had seemed crude, but the RockRat vessel made it look like the most advanced starship in the Empire. It seemed to have been put together from spare parts, with nothing more than benches for the passengers – although *that* wasn't too surprising. Unlike a starship, or even one of the more advanced in-system ships, it used a small gas drive rather than drive fields or a fusion torch. There was no need for protection against high gravities when there were no high gravities to fear. A dull tremor ran through the spacecraft as it undocked from the asteroid – once the passenger list had been checked, twice – and started to head out to the mining site.

Avalon – like most star systems – had an asteroid belt, allowing the inhabitants to mine for raw materials outside the planet's gravity well. From what Mandy had heard, the original Avalon Development Corporation had planned for a massive economic boom in the sector, hence their decision to spend vast amounts of money on a cloudscoop for HE3. But the Empire had started to retreat from the sector instead and the cloudscoop had become an expensive white elephant. How many of Avalon's problems could be traced back to a single poor financial decision taken by corporate executives thousands of light years away?

The RockRats were currently the only people mining the asteroid belt, although Mandy was sure that Avalon's new government intended to start its own mining operations sooner rather than later. After all, they *were* attempting to encourage as many students as possible to study asteroid mining, as well as the basic technology behind it. Much asteroid mining was done with technology that would have been recognisable to a pre-space society, something that had puzzled Mandy until she'd realised that the simpler the technology, the easier it was to repair if broken. The slow decline in Earth's infrastructure, she'd been told, owed a great deal to the fact that there were just too few technicians trained to maintain it.

Another dull quiver ran through the ship as Mandy forced herself to relax. The RockRat spacecraft were always *slow* – or so it felt, even though they were travelling at a speed she would have found unimaginable on a planetary surface. It would be hours before they reached their destination, and then they'd be expected to start work at once. Months ago, she would have found it impossible to fall asleep on the spacecraft; she'd learned the hard way to bring a book or an entertainment terminal with her. Now, she leaned her head against Michael's shoulder and closed her eyes. A few hours of sleep, even in an uncomfortable position, would leave her in a better state for working on the mine. RockRats kept strange hours…

The shock jerked her awake. A massive *thud* ran through the entire ship, followed rapidly by the alarms sounding in their ears. Mandy reached for her mask automatically, pulling it over her head with practiced ease. Once, she'd regretted losing most of her hair to the demands of space travel, but now she understood just what could have happened to her if her hair had caught in the seal. A faint hiss echoed through the mask as the inbuilt air supply came online, providing several hours of atmosphere for anyone caught outside a pressurised compartment. Faint icons appeared in her HUD, counting down the seconds to the moment when she ran out of air. She glanced over at Michael and saw him looking back at her, his eyes wide with concern. He'd fought in the battles against the Crackers, but here he was just a helpless passenger, unable to do anything to help himself, his girlfriend or the rest of the class. What the hell was going on?

Mandy keyed the intercom in her mask, but heard nothing apart from a hiss of static, followed rapidly by a deafening screech. She turned the volume down hastily, cursing out loud as she glanced around the rest of the compartment, holding up her hands in the signal for communications failure. It took her a moment to realise that everyone else seemed to have had the same piece of equipment failure. That was supposed to be impossible…wasn't it?

The dull throbbing of the drive died away, just as the lights failed. Emergency lighting came on seconds later, illuminating a darkened compartment, a second before another thud ran through the ship. Mandy saw a crack appearing in one bulkhead, where the porthole had allowed the occupants to gaze out into the stars, and realised – to her horror – that the spacecraft was coming apart at the seams. The crack widened as she grabbed hold of the bench, trying desperately to remember the survival lessons that had been hammered into their heads at college. If they were thrown into space, she recalled, the chances of rescue were minimal. Avalon wasn't Earth, with millions of spacecraft cruising around the system. Apart from the RockRats, and the shuttles to and from the cloudscoop, there were almost no ships in the system, ready to pick up unwanted Dutchmen.

She caught hold of Michael's arm as the entire ship started to shatter around them. Great cracks ran through the bulkheads, allowing the remaining atmosphere to blow out of the ship, carrying at least two of the other students out into interplanetary space. Mandy barely had a moment to notice the suits spinning through the air before they were outside and gone. Their suits would keep them alive, but they'd have no hope of rescue. Perhaps they'd open their masks and die quickly; absently, she wondered if she would have the courage to do the same, if she joined them in deep space. She might be about to find out…

I'm sorry, Dad, she thought, numbly. The air was gone, leaving them drifting in a vacuum. There was no sign of any of the RockRats; she looked behind her and saw only a handful of her fellow students, clinging desperately to the remains of the ship. What had happened to them? A disaster, something gone badly wrong, or…what? Had they been attacked? She found herself thinking of Mindy, her sister who wanted to be a Marine, and her mother, who wanted to be a social climber. Would they mourn her when she was gone? Or would they cling to the hope that she was still alive?

She felt another quiver running through the ship and looked up. Two figures were standing in the largest crack, both wearing combat armour. For a moment, she found herself wondering if the Marines had saved them, before catching sight of the decorations emblazoned along the side of the armour. Marine armour was designed to blend in with its surroundings, she knew from Jasmine; these men wore armour designed to terrify. One of them had shark-like teeth on his mask, the other had an idealised male form – complete with genitals – painted on his armour. There was no sign of their faces, hidden under the masks.

Pirates, she realised in horror. Piracy was an epidemic problem in some sectors, but she hadn't thought that there would be much near Avalon. Why would there be? It wasn't as if the interstellar combines ran massive shipping lanes through the sector. There was literally nothing to attract pirates on Avalon. Attacking the RockRats was rarely profitable…

All of the horror stories ran through her head. Pirates looted, raped and destroyed, all along the Rim. Perhaps she should kill herself…her hand was halfway to her mask before Michael caught it. His expression was grim, but seemed to suggest that there was hope. Mandy could only pray that he was right.

One of the pirates stepped forward, caught a student by the arm, and pushed him forward, towards the crack. The other pirate caught him and propelled him outside, into space. Mandy stared, unable to believe her eyes. Were the pirates simply spacing their victims? No, she realised a moment later, as she and Michael were picked up and pushed towards the crack. There was a spacecraft out there, waiting for them. They tumbled through space until they reached a third pirate, who caught them and shoved the captives into another airlock. Inside, a fourth pirate pointed a weapon at them. Mandy had bare seconds to recognise that it was a stunner before the universe went away in a blue-white flash of light.

CHAPTER FOUR

The regeneration of Camelot was a difficult task, yet it was one that had to succeed. Put simply, the city played host to hundreds of thousands of unemployed and unemployable people who had to be placated, or they might riot. Matters were not helped by the fact that it was often very difficult to get a job – at least a legal job – as much of the salary would have to go to debt servicing. The previous Council dealt with the problem through doling out a limited supply of food and ensuring that there was always enough alcohol to meet their requirements. Its successor had to do a better job.

This was accomplished though several different methods. Young street thugs were invited to join the Knights and put to work well away from the city. Others, including mature adults, were helped to set up smaller farming settlements of their own. And those who proved unable to cope with a non-criminal lifestyle were eventually isolated on penal islands. The result was a slow decline in the unemployed urban population.

- Professor Leo Caesius, *The Perilous Dawn* (unpublished).

"I really think that Blake should have an armed escort," Joe Buckley said, nodding towards the corner of the room. "We don't want to see him kidnapped again."

Jasmine rolled her eyes. After her meeting with the Colonel, the remainder of the platoon had insisted on taking her out to drink anyway – and, to be honest, she'd felt like a drink. These days, the Red Light District was one street on the edge of Camelot, a considerably cleaner environment than the one they'd impacted on when they'd arrived. Blake and some of the other Marines who spent all of their off-duty time chasing women might complain, but Jasmine found it a much better place to relax. Besides, the prostitutes were paid properly for their services and the pimps who'd once abused them had been dispatched to penal islands or work camps hundreds of miles from the city.

"I think that would cramp his style," she said, finally. "We'll just keep an eye on him from a distance."

She'd given Blake strict orders not to leave the Red Light District, no matter who he was with. It wasn't as if there was a shortage of rooms for brief sexual congress above the bar. She'd watched with some amusement as a group of recruits from the Knights, holding their first pay-checks in their hands, had come into the bar, where they'd been pounced on by the staff. They wouldn't remain solvent much longer, Jasmine knew; she just hoped that they'd consider what they got in return worthwhile. At least this bar was relatively friendly. She'd been in bars that would have taken some cleaning to deserve the term *shithole*. And ones where she'd wanted to wear a full set of combat armour.

Koenraad Jurgen sniggered, unpleasantly. "I think we should go with him," he said. "Can you imagine us all standing round the bed, carrying our weapons, as we…"

"Yes, I *can*," Jasmine said. "Would *you* enjoy having people watching you?"

"He'd be limp for a week," Joe put in, dryly. "Or else he'd be bragging about it for a week afterwards." He snickered. "Did he ever tell you about the time on Han we went into a bar…?"

Jasmine shook her head, bracing herself for another exaggerated story.

"Well, we'd been told that we should keep our weapons with us at all times," Joe said, grinning. "And Rifleman Lucas – he bought the farm on Han – was assigned to carry the Overcompensator. I don't know why he thought he should take it off base, but no one wanted to argue about it…"

"I don't believe it," Jasmine said. The CSW-34 – nicknamed the Overcompensator by the Marines who used it – was a massive piece of kit, so large that there were Marines in powered combat armour who had difficulty using the weapon. There was nothing like it for laying down hot plasma death and discouraging enemy soldiers from coming too close, but it wasn't exactly designed for carrying on a bar-crawl. "He had to be insane."

"That's what we all thought," Joe said. "But Lucas refused to be parted from his gun, so we went down to the bar and ordered beer. And Lucas starts chatting up this really hot girl who just happens to be working the bar that night."

He chuckled. "And she takes one look at the Overcompensator and says that she isn't going to be riding on *that*," he concluded. "And Lucas looks at her and practically wets himself laughing. And *then* – and *then* – he tells her that his *real* weapon is much bigger. And then she says that she ain't going to be riding on him at all."

Jasmine shook her head as she realised that that was the punchline. "I think I'm not drunk enough for that to be funny," she said, after a moment. The one good thing about being posted to Avalon – apart from the fact it wasn't Han – was that Avalon actually had good beer. None of the local breweries had realised that they could sell the troops horse-piss and they wouldn't actually complain, at least not yet. "Pass me another beer."

"Of course, My Lady and Mistress," Joe said. "It will be my honour to serve."

He sauntered off to the bar before Jasmine could think of a crushing retort. She hadn't really understood what it meant to succeed to command of the platoon until it had actually happened – and why the officers were transferred to a new unit when they were promoted. The rest of the platoon still thought of her as a fellow Rifleman, rather than as an officer; they couldn't help being familiar. There was no way she could keep her distance from them, as the manuals on how to be an officer demanded, when they'd been with her from the moment she'd graduated the Slaughterhouse and joined the company on Han. Even if she were to be transferred to a different platoon, she'd still be with Marines who *knew* her.

"So," Koenraad said, after a long moment, "did that man ever get back in touch with you?"

Jasmine shook her head. Four weeks ago, she'd met a man in a bar and struck up a friendship – which had come to a crashing halt when he'd realised that she was a Marine. It was annoying to know that she'd worked just as hard as any of the male Marines to qualify from the Slaughterhouse

– women were expected to do just as much as the men, or quit – and yet male Marines seemed to find it easier to find sexual companionship. Just because she could have snapped the man's neck with one hand didn't mean that she was an inhuman killer. But men didn't seem to like the idea of strong women.

"I knew it," Koenraad said. "Maybe you should date someone from the Knights…"

Jasmine glared at him. "If I wanted advice on my sex life, I would have asked for it," she snapped, finally. She regretted it almost at once, but it was too much to deal with right now. "And what about that girl you met over in Pendragon?"

"She wanted to meet with me the next time she visited Camelot," Koenraad said, complacently. "I hear she has a brother…"

Jasmine bit down the response that came to mind and shook her head, just as Joe returned with the beer. "Thank you," she said, gratefully. "How many people did you have to push aside to get it so quickly?"

"They saw the uniform and let me through," Joe said. "These people actually *like* Marines."

"Too true," Koenraad said. "The girl I'm dating was *delighted* to be able to tell a friend that she was banging a Marine."

Jasmine nodded. Avalon had largely detested the Civil Guard – and, to be fair, they'd had a point. Their CO had only been able to call on a handful of units that actually knew how to fight, nowhere near enough to fight both the bandits and the Crackers. And the goddamned Council hadn't helped; they'd deliberately kept half of the Civil Guard neutered while preparing the other half to serve as their enforcers. It had been the Marines who had beaten the bandits, given the corrupt half of the Civil Guard the boot and paved the way for a peace deal that had ensured that Avalon would have a chance to grow again. The Marines were popular on Avalon, something that rarely happened on the Core Worlds, where the military was despised, or feared, or outright hated.

One of the books she'd read – on the Captain's orders, to help prepare her for higher command – had speculated that the Marines formed a state within a state. Retired Marines – there was no such thing as an ex-Marine – tended to marry their fellow retired Marines, or to bring their wives and children up on the Slaughterhouse or one of the other planets in the restricted system. It was possible, the writer had continued, that one day the Marines would start acting on their own behalf, rather than that of the Empire. They'd effectively be an insular civilisation in their own right. Jasmine found the concept a little daunting – they'd been trained to bear in mind, at all times, that they were the Empire's rapier – but if the Empire collapsed completely, who knew what would happen?

We won't, she told herself, rather sourly. They were thousands of light years from Earth, a distance that had been daunting even before the Empire had withdrawn from their sector. *Anything* could be happening on Earth, or on the other side of the Empire, and they'd never know about it. Or perhaps they'd only know about it when the victorious side in the civil war roared out of Phase Space, intent on restoring the Empire's authority along the frontier. Or maybe the civil war everyone knew was coming – apart from the populations of the Core Worlds – would be averted somehow, and everyone would live happily ever after.

She shook her head, dismissively. The only way to avert outright civil war would be the Grand Senate giving up some of its power. That wasn't going to happen.

"Speaking of dating, I think that Blake just got shot down," Koenraad said. Jasmine turned her head in time to see the girl stamping off, with a downcast Blake heading back towards their table. "Hey, what happened, stud?"

"It turned out that she wanted a long-term relationship," Blake said, as he sat down. "Can you imagine it?"

Jasmine joined in the general laughter. "At least she didn't kidnap you and interrogate you," she said, finally. It would be years before Blake lived that down. "Count your blessings."

"But at least I got a fuck out of the whole deal," Blake said. "A soldier who won't fuck won't fight."

"And a soldier…and so on, and so on and so on," Jasmine said, rolling her eyes. "I think that…"

Her communications implant buzzed in her ears, sounding the general recall. "That's a muster," she said, as she stood up and dropped a credit chip on the table. The others followed her to their feet, already triggering implants that flushed the remains of the alcohol from their bodies. Whatever had happened had to be urgent, or they wouldn't have been summoned back from leave. "We're heading to the nearest helipad."

She keyed her implant to call in as they ran out of the bar and started to head down towards the closest pickup point. Camelot was tiny compared to the vast megacity that covered most of Earth's surface, but it would take too long to get back to the spaceport, even if they wore battlesuits or hired cars. They'd have to call in for pickup and hope that there was a helicopter – or a Raptor – close enough to serve.

"General orders," the dispatcher at Castle Rock said. "Report back to base; I say again, report back to base."

Jasmine frowned, thoughtfully. That sounded as if someone was calling a drill, rather than an emergency muster in response to a problem. And yet it was rare to call a drill when a unit was just coming off its patrol rotation and going for some well-deserved R&R. Perhaps the Command Sergeant had thought that they needed to be shaken out of their complacency, or perhaps…

She shook her head. No doubt they would find out soon enough.

Castle Rock didn't have a real spaceport, even though they'd had to land shuttles on the island once or twice. Accordingly, control over operations in near-Avalon space was routed through the planetary spaceport, although Edward was grimly aware that their ability to influence events away from the planet was minimal. Avalon had almost no orbital defences at all; the heavily-armed orbital weapons platforms that protected wealthy worlds were years beyond their ability to manufacture. It wasn't too surprising – the Imperial Navy had been called upon to intervene on Avalon years ago, and it might have had to do it again – but it was irritating. He knew exactly what would happen if a hostile cruiser appeared in orbit, ready to drop Kinetic Energy Weapons on the planet below.

He picked up the headphones as soon as he entered the operations centre and waited as patiently as he could for the spaceport staff to brief him. The original spaceport staff had been largely withdrawn as Avalon declined in importance, leaving a handful of staffers behind who'd had to train up promising youngsters from Avalon. Like the rest of the arrangements on the planet, there was a degree of improvisation that sometimes made it hard to get things done in a timely manner. Edward was uncomfortably aware that the IG would have a few sharp things to say about it if they ever conducted an inspection. But then, the IG was on the other side of the Empire's rapidly shrinking boundary.

"Colonel," a female voice said, finally. "We picked up an emergency alert from the RockRats seven minutes ago."

Edward nodded, impatiently. "And what did it say?"

"They report…sir, they report that their transport ship was attacked and presumed destroyed," the voice said. "They don't have the ships to go after the hostile vessel."

Edward felt cold ice running down his spine. He'd known it would be bad, but he'd hoped – prayed – that it had just been an accident. There had been no way of knowing just how long Avalon's isolation from the rest of the settled galaxy would last, yet he'd dared to assume that they would have a year or two before they had to resume contact with nearby worlds. That assumption had just bitten him on the behind, hard.

"Understood," he said. He couldn't blame the RockRats for not being inclined to give chase. Their clans possessed thousands of starships, but the ones isolated in the Avalon System had nothing capable of standing up to a hostile starship. There was a good chance that the pirates would continue to ignore the RockRats – the rest of their society gave serious grudge and would never allow the pirates to escape – yet that wouldn't be enough to preserve Avalon.

"Did they take any visuals of the hostile vessel?" He asked, thoughtfully. "Anything at all?"

"Yes, sir," the voice said. "The attacked ship transmitted an alert before it was cut off by the hostile vessel."

Jammed or destroyed, Edward thought. He pushed the sinking feeling in his chest to one side. "Patch them through to me," he ordered, aloud. "And then start running them through the analysis computers – see what they can pull from the records."

He pulled his terminal out of his belt pouch and studied the records as they popped up on the screen. The RockRats hadn't been expecting trouble and their in-system ship was hardly built to put up a fight. There were only a handful of images, all showing a starship that appeared to be an elderly design of Imperial Navy destroyer. That probably didn't mean anything; the design was over three hundred years old and most of them had either been scrapped or sold onwards to private interests. Some of them had probably been pirates. Edward had once heard that if former Imperial Navy starships were broken down into their component pieces, the level of piracy would drop sharply. But the Navy beancounters wanted to recoup as much of their costs as possible. Who cared where the ships ended up as long as the beancounters got their cut of the profits?

"They were attacked," he said, as Gwendolyn entered the compartment. A quick check revealed a list of names, everyone who had been on the doomed flight. There was no reason to assume that the pirates – if they were pirates – had killed everyone, but the last blip of information had reported total hull collapse. That suggested that the pirates might have overestimated the force needed to bring the ship to a halt. And then...? There was no time to speculate.

He keyed his communicator. "Attention, all personnel," he said. "Case Omega is now in effect; I say again, Case Omega is now in effect."

"I'll take control of the evacuation," Gwendolyn said. Case Omega assumed that Castle Rock was going to come under KEW attack – and end up being destroyed from orbit. If Edward had been running the pirate operation, that was exactly what he would have done. The Marines were just too dangerous to leave alive. "Are you going to speak to the Council?"

Edward nodded. There was really no choice, even if he *had* met the Council earlier in the day. He glanced at his timepiece; it was almost midnight, local time. They'd be in bed and asleep. Looking back down at the list, he realised that there was a name he needed to visit personally. He had to inform the Professor that his daughter was missing before the media informed him – and everyone else.

"We'll have to wake them up," he said. If nothing else, flying so many helicopters out of the bases near Camelot would alert them that *something* was up. "I'll speak to them personally – in the meantime, I want you to get

First Platoon prepped for orbit and inserted into the orbital station. I've had an idea."

"Yes, sir," Gwendolyn said. "Good luck with the Council."

"It isn't the Council I'm worried about," Edward admitted. "It's the Professor."

CHAPTER FIVE

> The old Council had effectively consisted of the richer citizens, who gamed the political system in their favour. Unsurprisingly, it was utterly unpopular with the rest of the population. The new Council attempted to be a compromise between the various different factions on the planet; Empire-loyalists, Crackers, farmers, city-dwellers…everyone was supposed to be represented. It was a cumbersome arrangement, but it worked well enough to prevent a repeat of the civil war.
>
> - Professor Leo Caesius, *The Perilous Dawn* (unpublished).

Earth never slept, Edward recalled, as the Raptor settled down on the lawn of what had once been Wilhelm Mansion. Camelot…did; outside the Red Light District and the hospitals, most of the city went to bed in the darkness and almost all activity came to a halt. It felt odd, after the more established cities on a hundred different worlds, but Edward had come to welcome it. But now, with helicopters flying away from the bases and heading out into the countryside, everyone would know that *something* was wrong. Rumours would probably be spreading already.

Wilhelm Mansion was the largest surviving building in Camelot, after the battle that had devastated the city centre. It had been built by Carola and Markus Wilhelm, the richest and most ambitious members of the former Council, who had dreamed of ruling the planet as its King and Queen. They'd come far too close to succeeding before they'd been arrested and dumped on a penal island, along with many of the gangsters and bandits they'd tried to use as servants and allies. Edward had studiously resisted the temptation to check up on them; several thousand miles from any other settlement, the only people they could hurt were their fellow criminals. Shaking his head, he disembarked from the Raptor and walked towards the mansion's doors. They were guarded by a pair of Knights wearing combat armour passed down from the Marines.

The building itself was incredibly ugly, at least in his considered opinion, and it was difficult to see how anyone had missed the fact that it was intended to be a fortress. A team of armoured Marines would have had no difficulty breaking in, but a mob could be kept out by a handful of snipers and the armoured walls. Edward passed through the security check and walked through the corridors, smiling at the bare spaces on the walls that had once housed tacky artwork. Now, the building played host to most of the civil servants who kept the government working, as well as a handful of Councillors who hailed from outside the capital. The remaining Councillors lived in the city, as did the Governor himself. They had been reluctant to live permanently in Wilhelm Mansion. Edward found it hard to blame them.

He passed through another security check and into the newly-designed Council Chamber, where most of the Council was already waiting for him. There were twenty-one Councillors in all, seventeen of them seated around the table. They had been elected into power by the population in Avalon's first free vote – the original Council had been elected by those who had no debts to repay, which was a tiny percentage of the population – after much political wrangling. The Governor - Brent Roeder – was, technically speaking, the voice of the Empire, but the Empire had abandoned Avalon. There had been more time wasted over the question of giving the Governor a voice in local politics than anything else. In the end, the Governor had been given the chair while Gaby Cracker, the former leader of the Crackers, had been elected President. It was inefficient, but at least it had produced a workable compromise.

The Councillors looked tired, he noted, as he took the seat at one end of the table. Edward's own position was rather ill-defined, something that had happened more by accident than through deliberate planning. As the military commander of both the Marines and the Knights of Avalon, he had a seat on the Council, but he was technically subordinate to the civilian officials. At the same time, the Marines were sworn to the Emperor personally, rather than the elected civilians, which was at least partly why the Grand Senate hated and feared the Terran Marine Corps. If they went decades without resuming contact with the Empire, Edward suspected, the Marines were likely to fade into the Knights, all the more so as they lacked the facilities for training and enhancing new Marines. And on that day, something precious would be lost.

"Colonel," Gaby Cracker said. She looked, as always, very young for her role, but Edward knew that the fiery redhead had a working brain and was genuinely devoted to Avalon. Her grandfather, Peter Cracker, had led the first rebellion against the government, a rebellion that would have succeeded if the Imperial Navy hadn't dropped KEWs on his advancing army, crushing it under superior firepower. Edward sometimes wondered what the old man would have made of their new government. "What's happened?"

Edward would have smiled, if the situation hadn't been so grave. On Earth, at least outside the Marines, there were endless formalities before a meeting could begin, starting with an oath to the Emperor. No wonder so little got decided – or left in the hands of the bureaucrats – when the formalities could take longer than the meetings themselves. On Avalon, most of the formalities had never had a chance to take root – and Edward hoped that they never would. Besides, Avalon was too small for the formalities and most of the Council knew their fellows outside of politics.

"We have a major problem," he said, bluntly. "Two hours ago, a RockRat transport was attacked by a vessel of unknown origin."

Gaby looked shocked; she, at least, understood the implications. Apart from Avalon itself, and the RockRats, there were no other settlements within the system. Even the cloudscoop was little more than a makeshift structure orbiting the largest gas giant. An attack on anything within the system had to come from *outside* the system, suggesting...what? The last they'd heard from outside Avalon had been that the Empire was pulling out, leaving the Rim to its own devices. They hadn't even seen a tramp freighter since then.

But if someone had raided the system, what did that mean? Pirates, intent on taking anything that wasn't nailed down, or a political entity that intended to climb to power in the wake of the Empire's departure? Or perhaps the destroyer they'd seen was just an armed merchantman; it would hardly be the first merchant ship to turn pirate when confronted by a defenceless target. Edward honestly wasn't sure which one was more likely, but one fact was clear; Avalon had something that both pirates and other political entities would want very badly. HE3 was the backbone of the interstellar economy and Avalon, unlike most planets in the sector, possessed a working source of fuel. They'd do whatever it took to capture the cloudscoop.

One of the other Councillors leaned forward. "Colonel," he asked, "what happened to the people on the transport?"

"We don't know," Edward admitted. The RockRats had notified Avalon that they were dispatching a shuttle to search for the wreckage – and survivors – but Edward wasn't hopeful. He'd seen the wrecks of enough starships in the past to know that disasters in space were rarely survivable. "It's possible that they might have been taken by the raiders."

"And then...what?" Gaby asked. "What will they do to them?"

"It depends on who they caught and what they actually want," Edward said. It wasn't a very helpful answer, but there was no way to know – yet – who had captured their people. Pirates might rape and then kill their captives, unless they were worth a considerable ransom; someone else might have other ideas. In their place, Edward would have interrogated any captives to discover the political conditions on Avalon. "At the moment, we have to assume the worst. The raiders intend to invade and occupy this star system."

"We'll fight," Julian Rufus said. He tossed Edward a challenging look. "We held off the Empire. We can hold off these newcomers too."

Edward kept his face expressionless, even though the Crackers had been beaten in the Battle of Camelot. He had never quite understood the relationship between him and Gaby Cracker; at times he seemed to be in love with her, but at other times he seemed to think that she was too conservative. The Crackers might have become part of the political process, yet Julian apparently felt that they'd compromised too much. Edward had sensed that his election to the Council – his father, regrettably, had refused to stand for office – promised trouble in the future. Sooner or later, there would be a major clash between the old and the new on Avalon.

"The situation is different," he said, instead. Julian had a brain too, even if it had been shaped by a life on the run. "The former Council wanted to rule the planet; that alone limited what it could do to the population. A pirate ship that wants tribute could simply take up position in orbit and drop rocks on our heads until we submitted and gave them whatever they wanted. They are not likely to be deterred by an insurgency on the planet's surface – and we couldn't touch them from the ground."

It was a classic problem, older than the Empire itself. Boosting something – anything – to orbit required a great deal of energy, energy that was easily detectable from high overhead. A starship with a proper sensor suite could see missiles incoming and either evade them or shoot them down with point defence, while launching KEWs against targets on the ground. The Empire had rarely based defences on planetary surfaces, knowing that they were effectively useless. They could be taken out by an invading starship from well outside their own range.

"Right," Julian said. He didn't seem convinced, which was odd; Peter Cracker's rebellion had been stopped by KEWs launched from orbit. "And what are they likely to want?"

Edward scowled. In the days when the Empire had been strong, ready and able to respond to any emergency, pirates had found it hard to get any real traction. But now, with law and order breaking down, piracy had rapidly become epidemic. Edward had seen the remains of colony worlds hit by pirates, raided for food, drink and women, or other worlds forced into effective servitude by the threat of overwhelming force. The Imperial Navy no longer had the ability to provide protection against pirates, so the locals made what accommodations they could with the bastards, even if it meant feeding them and selling their daughters into slavery – or worse. They had no other choice.

"They'll want the command codes for the cloudscoop," Edward said, after briefly outlining what other colony worlds had experienced. "That will give them an excellent long-term position for dictating terms to half the sector."

He saw the Councillors exchanging glances and smiled, inwardly. The fusion reactors that provided most of the colony's power were very efficient, and there was a considerable stockpile of fuel established in underground bunkers, but it would run out eventually. Avalon had a cloudscoop to replenish its stockpiles, yet it was rare for any colony world to have a cloudscoop until its space-based industry grew much larger. Most colony worlds simply had HE3 shipped to them by massive tankers, none of which would be running any longer.

How long would it be, he asked himself as the Councillors started to argue, before the other worlds in the sector began running short of fuel? Years, definitely, particularly if they had no space-based industry of their own. The early colonial investments always included a large stockpile of fuel, as well as the farming equipment needed to ensure the colony could feed itself as quickly as possible. They certainly wouldn't want to be shipping bulk foodstuffs across interstellar distances. But what would happen when the fuel ran out? They'd fall back on more primitive technologies, if they had the time to produce them. Offhand, Edward couldn't think of any standard colony world that had bothered to include non-HE3 power sources. The only ones that might survive the Empire's fall without noticing were the ones that chose to follow a deliberately primitive lifestyle.

The Governor tapped the table and silence fell. "As interesting as the long-term implications of us possessing a cloudscoop are," he said, "we do have a more immediate problem. What exactly are we going to do about this new threat?"

Gaby looked over at Edward. "Colonel, do you have a plan to deal with the newcomers?"

Edward hesitated. In truth, he had half an idea at best, one that could easily get First Platoon killed, followed rapidly by the rest of the Marines. But the alternative was contacting the newcomers and offering surrender – and hoping that they merely wanted to establish their own hegemony over the sector rather than looting, raping and burning. Surrender wasn't in his nature; years ago, one of his Drill Instructors had claimed that surrender was in the Marine Corps lexicon, but only as something the enemy did. Marines could be tired, wounded and very near death, yet they kept going.

"I'm working on it," he said. At least the Council understood the need for operational security. "Our problem, right now, is that we need to start dispersing our military forces and civilian population as quickly as possible."

"Out of fear of bombardment," the Governor said. "Do you think we can get most of the population out of Camelot in time to matter?"

Edward scowled. It would have been impossible on Earth, or any major settled world, but Camelot had always been a relatively small city, even before the new Council had started encouraging people to move out to the farms. They did have contingency plans to move large numbers of people away from the settlements that would be visible from orbit, if they had time to make them work. The city might have lacked the teeming multitudes on Earth, but it also lacked Earth's public transportation system.

"I think we have to start now," he said. If the newcomers were pirates, with all the bad intentions that implied, dispersing the population might be the only way to save them. "And we need to take control of the situation before rumours start to spread."

The Council debated the issue quickly; unlike Earth's politicians, they could come to a decision without requiring days of debate, as well as requesting further study just to delay proceedings. Edward had the professional officer's contempt for politicians, but he had to admit that Avalon's Council seemed to be better than most; they certainly understood the limits of their own power, an awareness that was lacking in the Grand Senate. He answered a handful of questions, made comments when the situation required it, and listened gravely as Major George Grosskopf outlined the evacuation plan. The Council hadn't been entirely happy with Edward keeping him on active duty – he might have been a competent and clean officer, but he'd led the Civil Guard before the Marines arrived – but they seemed willing to forget the past for the moment. Besides, George did know what he was doing.

"We have an evacuation list of children and people in vitally important positions," George explained. The Council had never reviewed the evacuation plans; the original plans had started with politicians and the wealthy first, but the rewritten plans left politicians in the city until the rest of the population was evacuated. It was an advantage of Avalon's more open government that Edward hadn't appreciated until it had actually happened. "With your permission, we will start buzzing the people to be evacuated first now."

Edward nodded, impatiently. Avalon's small cadre of trained workers – everything from plumbers and builders to spacecraft designers – would be among the first to be evacuated, along with the children. Losing someone with genuine experience in actually building something would hurt; the old Council had never focused on building up a wealth of experts in any category, even planet-side construction. Edward had often wondered what they'd planned to do if – when – the Empire withdrew from the sector. Carola Wilhelm, at least, had understood the likely outcome of the ongoing crisis gripping the once-proud union of human worlds.

"I need to leave these matters in your hands," he said, finally. George could handle it; with the Council's authority, he would have command of the Knights based near the capital and the local police force. The police were civilian – without any of the training that should have been given to the Civil Guard – but they took their duties seriously. And besides, they were responsible to the local population in a way the Civil Guard had never been. "I have to pay a call on the Professor."

Gaby nodded as the debate came to an end. "We'll see to the evacuation," she assured him. "Keep us informed of the situation."

Edward saluted and left the chamber, linking back into the Marine communications network as he strode back towards the Raptor. There was no change; the deep space monitoring system, such as it was, reported no sign of unfriendly starships lurking near Avalon. Edward, who knew that the system was primitive compared to the systems that guarded Earth, wasn't reassured. Given time and some reasonable precautions, a starship could probably slip into orbit without being detected.

He sighed as he ordered the Raptor to return to the spaceport, without him. It was the moments *between* action that he dreaded, the times when he could do nothing but worry. He'd given all the orders he could; now, while his subordinates turned his wishes into actions, he could only wait and consider what might go wrong. There was nothing he could do any longer to affect the outcome of events. All he could do was wait.

There was a cab outside the gates, dropping off one of the missing Councillors. Edward hailed the driver and asked him to drive to the nearest residential zone. The Professor lived there, along with his wife and younger daughter. And Edward had to tell them that his older daughter was missing, presumed dead.

CHAPTER SIX

By Imperial Law, every settled world – certainly those settled with loans from the Empire's Colonisation Department – had to have an orbital station for easy transhipment of goods. Avalon's was, in fact, much larger than the standard required by law, yet another white elephant caused by the ADC's unfounded belief in the sector's coming economic boom. Perversely, this was actually a great advantage to us when we started returning to space, once we had secured the planet's surface.

The standard structure of these stations included…
- Professor Leo Caesius, *The Perilous Dawn* (unpublished).

"It's beautiful," Jasmine breathed.

"It sure is," Blake agreed, serious for once. Down below, the blue-green orb of Avalon hung in the endless darkness of space. Jasmine could see white flecks in the planet's atmosphere – clouds forming over the unsettled continent – and wondered, idly, if Avalon would ever have something big enough to be seen from orbit with the naked eye. "Earth just can't compare any longer."

Jasmine nodded. Earth had once been like Avalon, but now humanity's homeworld was a grey world, covered with the towering city-blocks that made up the megacities. If the technology that supported the human population – the algae farms that produced food and drink, the fusion reactions that provided power – ever failed, Earth's decline would be unstoppable. Hell, there were places on Earth's surface that were badly contaminated by industrial accidents, where the population effectively lived in spacesuits or protective armour. If the infrastructure ever failed, Earth's population would fall sharply, almost immediately. They could never go back to living off the land.

She couldn't understand why the Grand Senate didn't seem to realise that they were living on top of a ticking time bomb. Earth's authorities expelled everyone who was caught committing a crime – even something as minor as speeding – as well as encouraging emigration, but it was nowhere near enough to dampen the population boom. Millions of new children joined Earth's teeming population every month, far more than could ever be removed from the planet. The only solution that might work was forced contraception, perhaps lacing the tasteless algae glop the average citizen ate with something to stop them breeding, but the Grand Senate didn't seem willing to order it. It made no sense to her; she'd thought her own homeworld was rigorously controlled – and controlling – until she'd seen Earth. Humanity's homeworld was dying and no one seemed to care.

"You think we might have to do something clever?" Joe asked. First Platoon had drawn their space combat armour the moment they'd received the order to board the shuttle and boost for orbit; now, all they could do was wait while the shuttle made transit to the orbit station. Jasmine had always hated the moment of vulnerability while they were in a flying tin can – she'd had to bail out of a Raptor during the Battle of Camelot – but there was no choice. Combat suits couldn't fly to orbit, not yet. "This could get really bad."

Jasmine winced. The list of students who had been on the transport and either killed or kidnapped had been uploaded into the command network, and she'd seen – to her horror – Mandy's name. She would never have believed that she could have come to like the girl, even to care for her, not when they'd first met. But they'd become friends, of a sort, and she'd encouraged Mandy to study engineering and space construction technology, knowing that it would be vitally important in the future. She might as well have signed Mandy's death warrant with her own hands.

Blake and the others had known the risks when they went to Boot Camp. Any recruit who had thought that Marine training was a game would have been shorn of that notion by the Drill Instructors, in their first encounter with the terrifying hat-wearing figures who would dominate their lives for the next three months. Jasmine would always feel guilty if they died under her command, but they'd volunteered for service in the Marine Corps. Mandy hadn't volunteered for anything in her life, up until the moment she'd decided to go to the technical college. And it might just have placed her in the firing line.

And maybe I should pray that she's dead, Jasmine thought. She hadn't had to board the wrecked ships left behind by pirates, but she'd seen photographs and read the reports – and worked her way through hundreds of simulations. Pirates knew that they were dead when – if – the Imperial Navy caught up with them. It made them savage, willing to do *anything* to their captives. Jasmine had saved Mandy from a situation that could easily have turned into rape, but this time she'd been hundreds of thousands of miles away from the girl. This time, Mandy would have to survive by herself.

The pilot's voice buzzed through her implant. "Orbit Station is coming into view," she said. "Hands off cocks and on with socks."

Jasmine didn't smile at the standard joke, a tradition that dated back thousands of years. Had she *always* gotten nervous before a mission? But as a Rifleman, her duty had been to follow orders and look after herself, not command other Marines in combat. This time, she could lose people… but that was always going to be true. Not for the first time, she considered reporting to Colonel Stalker that she could not handle it and requesting a return to the ranks, before pushing the thought aside in some irritation. She was the best-qualified Marine to take First Platoon, or so she had been told, and walking away from her duty wasn't in her nature. Besides, one rule the Marines *did* share with every other military service was simple; if you turned down a promotion, you would never be offered another one.

Orbit Station came into view slowly as the shuttle drifted up to the airlock. It was a boxy structure, mostly composed of modules that had been shipped in from the industrial node several dozen light years away. Now, a handful of RockRat-produced modules had been added, expanding the space available for storing goods and equipment. Jasmine remembered assisting her superior officers to take as much as they could from Earth, before they bid farewell to humanity's dying homeworld. Given enough time, she knew, they could build an entire tech base from scratch. If the pirates – or whoever the newcomers were – gave them the time...

"Armour up," she ordered, as the shuttle docked with the station. There was no reason to suspect trouble, but Marines were trained to be careful. Besides, they had to convince the station manager and his family to leave the platform before the newcomers arrived – if they did arrive – and wearing battle armour might help. "Blake, Joe; you're on point."

"Understood," Blake said. She heard the calm competence in his voice and allowed herself a moment of relief, even though she felt as if she should be taking point herself. The point man always had the most dangerous job, being the person who would be shot at first if there was an ambush waiting for them. "Joe can watch my back."

"You'll have to pay me to watch your back," Joe muttered, as they stepped into the airlock. Jasmine had to swallow the urge to tell them to stop bantering and get on with it. The airlock hissed closed behind them and she braced herself. If there *was* an ambush waiting for them, it would be sprung now, when the Marines were cooped up in the shuttle.

"Airlock opening," Blake reported. Jasmine accessed the live feed from his armour and smiled in relief when she saw the young girl waiting for them past the inner airlock. "One person waiting for us, Morag Campbell."

"Trust you to know her name," Joe said. "Just remember, she isn't old enough to fuck yet and the CO will roast your ass if you even look at her sideways..."

"That will do," Jasmine snapped. Like most orbiting stations – and small establishments in space – orbit station was operated by a family, one that had ties to the RockRats or the planet below. Their exact legal status was somewhat disputed – they had a contract with the ADC, which had folded along with the corporation itself – but they'd stayed on the station anyway. No one seemed inclined to chase them away. "Ask Morag where her father is."

"She says that he's in the control compartment," Blake reported. Orbit station was really too small and immobile to have either a bridge or a command centre. "And she welcomes us to the station."

"Good," Jasmine said. She opened the airlock and stepped through into the station, followed by the remainder of First Platoon. The little girl's eyes opened wide as she took in the armoured Marines; like many children raised on isolated stations, she was slightly agoraphobic. She probably wouldn't have seen so many people tramping through the station since the Marines had arrived, almost a year ago.

Jasmine removed her mask and knelt down beside her. "Hi," she said, with a smile. The girl responded with a shy grin. "Can you take us to your father?"

She'd met Douglas Campbell before, back when they'd first arrived at Avalon. He was a tall, powerfully-built man, almost certainly with some genetic enhancement in his family's bloodline. The Empire tended to frown on such enhancement – apart from those who were in the military, or wealthy and powerful enough to ignore the law – but the RockRats used it regularly, as did most of the other families that lived permanently in space. Humanity was ill-adapted to survive in low gravity without heavy exercise. Genetic engineering was the only realistic alternative.

"I heard about the attack," Campbell said, without preamble. Jasmine rather approved. He would have made a good Marine. "Do you really feel that you can deter an attack on this station?"

Jasmine took a moment to consider her reply. Orbit Station was almost completely defenceless – and the two makeshift plasma cannons the crew had rigged up wouldn't even scratch the paint of a military starship. Even a civilian craft coated with a layer of ablative armour would be able to shrug them off, while a single missile would blow the station into a great deal of expensive debris. If the enemy simply fired on the station from a safe distance, they were all dead – and there was no point in trying to hide it from him. But on the other hand…

"We have a plan," she said, and tried to project as much confidence as she could into her voice. They *did* have a plan, but it would depend more on luck than judgement. If anyone other than Colonel Stalker had come up with it, Jasmine would have had little faith in its success. "However, we need you to move your family off the station."

Campbell scowled. "The kids aren't ready for life on a planet," he said, crossly. "Can I send them out to the RockRats?"

Jasmine hesitated before answering. "They are at risk," she said. If the plan failed, or even if it didn't work *in time*, Orbit Station might be destroyed. "You can send them down to the planet for a few days, maybe two weeks. They won't be harmed."

"But they will be scooped up by the meddlers," Campbell said. "I won't have them stamped into drones…"

It took Jasmine a moment to realise what he meant. Earth and the Core Worlds had meddling bureaucrats whose only purpose seemed to be ensuring that all children went to the same schools, where they were taught little of any value and far more about their rights than their responsibilities. Jasmine hadn't realised just how free her homeworld had been until she'd learned that, on Earth, childcare could be used as a way to punish political opponents of the regime. *Anyone* could be declared an unfit parent and have their children taken away, perfectly legally. The RockRats kept their distance from the Core Worlds out of fear that their lifestyles would be meddled with by the bureaucrats.

"Avalon doesn't have any meddlers," she said, dryly. Even the old Council hadn't bothered to build up a Department of Child Services – and *that* was ironic, as Avalon could actually have used such a department. Coming to think of it, if they did their job properly, the Undercity on Earth wouldn't have been such a teeming mass of darkness and despair – and hatred. "Look, I swear to you, upon my honour as a Marine, that the children will be returned to you, even if I have to launch an armed raid on the Council Chamber."

Campbell smiled for the first time. "I'll hold you to that," he said. "Do you want the command codes for the station?"

Jasmine nodded. "We have to get ready," she said. "Please ensure that the children get aboard the shuttle. The craft will be leaving as soon as possible."

Professor Leo Caesius had once been an academic on Earth before he'd made the mistake of questioning the true state of the Empire. His downfall had been rapid and would have killed him if the Commandant of the Terran

Marine Corps, one of the few people who was aware of the crisis, hadn't seen to it that he and his family received protection and eventual transport to Avalon. Edward had come to like the older man on the long journey to their new world, where the Professor had found himself assisting the formation of a new government – and teaching the children about what had killed the Empire. His wife, a social climber of no small ambitions, had been rather less amused. The couple were not precisely separated, but Edward had heard that Fiona Caesius had been seen with other men.

He found himself pacing in Leo's study as the maid went to fetch the Professor. It was tradition in the Marine Corps that the unit's CO had to visit the family of any deceased Marine, even though it could be years before the visit could be made. Edward had only had to do it twice and it never got any easier. And *this* particular person hadn't even been a Marine. Mandy should have been safe, even if she had been living in a very unforgiving environment. It was quite likely that Leo would blame Edward for his loss.

That's funny, he thought, bitterly. I can face the enemy without panic, but I want to run from this study and flee into the city…

He looked up as Leo entered the room, wearing a tattered dressing gown that had seen better days. "Captain…ah, Colonel," he said. The last time they'd spoken, they'd planned out a History and Moral Philosophy course for the city's students. "It is really rather late…"

"I'm afraid so," Edward agreed. For once, he found himself indecisive. How should he approach the issue? "I'm afraid I have bad news."

The blood seemed to drain out of the Professor's face. "It's Mandy, isn't it?"

Edward hesitated, and then nodded. "Her transport was attacked," he said. "She is missing…"

"She might still be alive," Leo said. "I…I only got to know her again and…"

His voice tailed off. Edward caught his shoulder and guided him towards the sofa, feeling a moment of pity for the academic. Mandy had been a brat until one of Edward's Marines had taken her in hand, guiding her towards a more promising career and a life that would be more fulfilling. And Leo had had a chance to get to know his daughter again.

"She might," Edward agreed. He kept the thought that Mandy might be better off dead to himself. She was young, and attractive, and alone. The pirates would be tempted to use her, abuse her and then kill her. "We don't know for sure."

"But why?" Leo demanded. "Why would anyone want to kill her?"

"It could have been the first shot in an invasion of this system," Edward said. In some ways, he was hoping that was the case. The newcomers were obviously sneaking around, rather than just charging into high orbit and demanding surrender. It would give him some time to prepare to meet them. "Or it could simply have been a random raid."

Leo shook his head. "I'll have to tell Mindy…my god, I'll have to tell Mindy. And Fiona."

Edward didn't envy him. Mindy was still too young to join the Knights – she'd expressed her desire to join the Marines, but they didn't have the training facilities on Avalon to produce new Marines – but she was working hard. There was a tough mentality inside the girl who had been raised among Earth's middle classes. Fiona, on the other hand…Leo's wife would blame him, as she'd blamed him for everything else that had happened in her life. Didn't the woman realise that she was better off on Avalon than Earth?

"They might demand money," Leo said. He looked up at Edward. "Will we pay?"

"It depends on what they want," Edward said. Imperial Credit chips were useless on Avalon now, but they might still be usable further in towards the Core Worlds. Or they might want food and fuel. Edward knew that standard policy was to refuse to pay ransoms on the grounds that paying merely encouraged the bastards to do it again, yet that might not be possible. They were a long way from the Imperial Navy. "We'll have to see what they want."

Leo started to shake. "I had a lecture planned for tomorrow," he admitted. "I thought…"

"Cancel it," Edward urged. On the Slaughterhouse, there were trained officers to help grief-stricken parents through the darkness that lay ahead. Here…there were none. He knew that he should find Leo something to do, something that might keep him busy, but he couldn't think of anything. "Cancel it and stay with your daughter."

"You'd better go now," Leo said, after a long moment. Edward understood and rose to his feet, just before Leo caught his arm. "You *are* going to catch them, aren't you?"

"Yes," Edward said, flatly. He understood exactly what Leo meant. "We *will* catch them."

CHAPTER SEVEN

There is a very old saying that runs "luck is like government; you can't get along without it, but only a fool relies on it." In many ways, that saying reflects the problem with both the Empire and the successor states that arose in the wake of its slow withdrawal from the Rim. Put simply, without a government acting as a reasonably fair referee, the strong will always bully and oppress the weak – BUT if the government is given too much power, it will become the strong itself and bully its citizens. Striking a permanent balance between too much and too little power – and then expecting it to work indefinitely – is impossible. It is tempting to conclude that, if the Empire's population had paid more attention to its government, the Grand Senate would never have amassed the power to rule the Empire and start it on the slow course to eventual collapse.

In pirate societies – a term that was often expanded to cover all of the post-Empire societies along the Rim – it was much simpler. There, without any of the Empire's benefits as well as its disadvantages, it was the Rule of the Strong. This was extremely unfortunate for anyone caught up in their grasp...

- Professor Leo Caesius, *The Perilous Dawn* (unpublished).

"Mandy!"

Mandy groaned, trying to pull herself out of a morass of pain and dizziness that threatened to push her back into the darkness. She'd had a nightmare, hadn't she? They'd all had nightmares after their first briefing on how to look after themselves in space – and after the instructor had told them that all he was telling them only applied if they were near life-support equipment. Otherwise…

"Let's face it," he'd said. "If you're not close to life support equipment, bend over and kiss your ass goodbye."

And there was pain around her wrists, and a cold breeze on her body, and…

She opened her eyes. "You're awake," Michael said, in relief. Mandy's neck hurt, as if she'd fallen asleep on one of the RockRat transports while leaning against him, but she managed to look over at him. He was naked and his hands were cuffed to a metal pipe…it struck her, suddenly, that it wasn't a dream. "I thought I might have lost you."

Mandy tried to move her hands, only to discover that the pain around her wrists was another pair of handcuffs. Someone had cuffed her hands behind her back and used a third cuff to secure her to the metal pipe. She pulled at it in the hopes that it was weaker than it looked, but discovered that it was simply too strong to break. And she was naked too. The suits they'd been told to wear at all times, along with the masks that might save their lives if the shit hit the fan, were gone. A shallow cut on her chest suggested that her captors, whoever they were, had used a knife to cut her clothes away from her body. It struck her that they could have done something else to her while she was stunned, but there was no way to know. They could have raped her…

She pushed the thought aside as quickly as possible, trying to peer around the darkened compartment. It was solid metal, not unlike the module they'd stayed in while on Orbit Station, but clearly designed to hold prisoners. The only source of light was a single glow, high overhead, casting a cold merciless light down on them. In the darkness, she could see the shapes of at least two other people, also cuffed to the bulkhead. It was impossible to make out their faces, but she heard at least one groan.

Somehow, she managed to find her voice. "What…what happened?"

"They stunned us," Michael said. "I assume they stripped us while we were out of it."

Mandy nodded, despite the throbbing pain in her head. He'd recovered quicker than her, but then stunning would have been part of his training. Repeated stunning conferred some limited immunity, if she recalled correctly, or it could just have been nonsense repeated by students back on Earth as they planned protest marches in support of the Cause of the Week. Her mother had never allowed her to join one of the protests, no matter how she'd whined and pleaded and eventually thrown tantrums. In hindsight, it might have been the sole smart decision her mother had ever made for her.

"I need a drink," she said. Her throat was dry and felt raspy. "What happened to the others?"

There was another groan from the darkened corner. "I don't know," Michael said. "I'm sure they caught more than four of us."

Mandy blanched. There had been ten students in all, not counting the RockRats…how many RockRats did it take to operate a transport ship? She'd seen two students falling into space…that left eight, not four. Or had others died and she hadn't noticed? It was alarmingly possible. Or had their captors merely separated them…in which case, why had they left her with Michael?

Perhaps I shouldn't complain, she thought. *At least I have a friend with me.*

A chink of light appeared in the bulkhead, so bright that Mandy half-closed her eyes to protect herself. Someone marched into the cell, carrying a bottle of water in one hand and a strange-looking tool in the other. He stopped in front of Mandy and knelt down beside her, his eyes surprisingly kindly. It dawned on her that he was as much of a captive as herself, even if he was trusted to some extent. He lifted the bottle of water and held it up in front of her lips. Despite her thirst, Mandy hesitated.

"Come on," he said. "If I wanted to poison you, I wouldn't have to resort to trickery to do it."

Mandy shivered. His voice didn't have an Avalon accent, or anything she recognised from Earth. They could be hundreds of light years from Avalon by now…absently, she wished she knew more about interstellar transport. Her first and last interstellar voyage – the trip from Earth to Avalon – had been conducted in stasis. Six months had gone by in the blink of an eye. Reluctantly, she allowed him to place the bottle against her lips and sucked greedily. The water tasted completely clean, purified in a starship purification plant. There was no hint of planetary life forms at all.

"Good," the man said, after he'd attended to the others. "The Admiral will wish to see you soon. When he does, I advise you to be polite and very obedient. He may have a use for you."

Mandy and Michael exchanged glances. *The Admiral?*

"If you're not useful, you'll go into the pool," the man said. His voice darkened as he looked at Mandy. "You really do not want to go into the pool."

"I'm sure we will be useful," Michael said, quickly. "We're both training to become spaceship engineers."

Mandy blinked in surprise, and then smothered the reaction desperately. If their captors knew that Michael had military experience, if they knew that he'd fought in the war against the Crackers, they'd throw him out an airlock rather than risk keeping him alive. They couldn't risk letting the pirates to know the truth. Michael would just have to pose as an engineer until they could figure out a way to escape.

"That might be useful," the man said. He stood up, looking down at them. Mandy looked back and saw numb hopelessness in his eyes. "And you two, over there, should make yourselves useful too."

The bulkhead door closed behind them, leaving the four captives alone. Mandy raised her voice as she looked into the shadows, trying to see the other two captives. "Who's there?"

"Dave," a male voice said. Mandy remembered him – one of the street children who had had more practical experience with stolen vehicles than Mandy had had with legal vehicles – and allowed herself a moment of relief. "But Shelia isn't in a very good state. I think she hit her head badly."

There was another groan, underlying his words. Shelia had been smart and funny and one of the few real friends Mandy had made on Avalon. Mandy twisted lightly, trying to see her friend, but it was impossible to make out much in the darkness. She rather suspected that the groans weren't a good sign. The Empire's medical science could work miracles, yet Shelia's captives weren't rushing to get her into a stasis pod. Mandy tried to recall all she'd learned about head injuries, before realising that it was futile. Everything she knew about medicine came from bad entertainment programs back on Earth.

She wanted to take Michael's arm to draw support, but she couldn't move her hands. Instead, she had to settle for inching closer to him and pressing against his body. His eyes were grim and worried; he knew, just as well as she did, what was likely to happen if their captors discovered what he'd been. Hours seemed to pass as they huddled together, before the bulkhead doors opened to reveal two more men. They marched over to Dave, released him from the pipe and pushed him towards the door.

"Shelia needs help," Dave started. "She…"

One of the men punched him in the stomach, hard. Dave doubled over, gasping for breath, just before he was dragged away and the door closed behind him. Mandy heard another groan from Shelia's direction and shivered, wishing that she could get closer to her friend. An attempt to slip along the railing failed when she found herself caught by one of the railings that connected the pipe to the bulkhead. Another series of hours seemed to go by – it couldn't be more than thirty minutes, she told herself – before the bulkhead doors opened again, allowing the men back into the cell. There was no sign of Dave. They dragged the unresisting Shelia out of the cell – for a moment, as her face was illuminated, Mandy saw a slack helpless expression – and then vanished again.

Her turn came next. Mandy stayed quiet as they unhooked her from the railing and pulled her to her feet. Her legs felt cramped after so long in the cell, but she forced herself to move anyway, unwilling to give them any excuse to lay hands on her. Outside, they pushed her through a crowd of men who leered and catcalled as they saw her nakedness, although they didn't try to touch her. Mandy wished she'd kept her hair long enough for it to dangle over her breasts, preserving what she could of her modesty. But it probably wouldn't have mattered.

Concentrate on what you're seeing, she told herself, firmly. *And keep calm.*

She thought she was inside a starship, from the omnipresent background hum she recalled from the Marine Transport Ship. The bulkheads were plastered with a logo she didn't recognise; a snake curled up, ready to spring on its prey. None of the men looked like real soldiers or Marines, she decided; their shipsuits were patchy and frayed. Only a few of them even seemed to be wearing fully-protective garments. And *all* of them carried weapons, ranging from the small pistols she'd been taught how to use at the technical college to rifles that reminded her of the ones the Marines carried. A handful even carried edged weapons and looked fully capable of using them.

The men fell away as her escorts glared at them, pushing Mandy up the corridor and through a long series of passageways that seemed completely unmarked, apart from the snake logo. She rapidly lost track of where she was in relation to the cell, although it probably didn't matter. Her hands were cuffed and she was escorted by two burly men – and she had a feeling that falling into the hands of the other men wouldn't be any safer. Her mind was starting to swim – partly through hunger and partly through fear – when they stopped in front of a large airlock and opened it. Mandy felt a brief moment of panic – they were going to *space* her – before logic reasserted itself. They would hardly space *themselves*.

Inside the airlock, there was a single large cabin, about the same size as a RockRat family room. A man stood in front of a holographic display, his hands clasped behind his back; as he turned to face Mandy, she realised that he had no hair and one of his eyes was missing, leaving behind an empty socket. It looked almost as if it had popped out only minutes ago, even though she *knew* that had to be impossible. He wore a long black cloak that covered a set of body armour and a belt carrying several different weapons.

"I am the Admiral," he said. His accent was just as unfamiliar as the previous man's accent. "I lead this fleet. One day, I will be Emperor."

Mandy stared at him. He *had* to be joking…and yet, she could tell that he believed every word he was saying. She tried to find her voice, only to discover that she had absolutely no idea what to say. What did one say to a madman with the power of life and death over her? If she'd studied more history, as her father wanted…she'd probably have still found herself speechless. He *had* to be insane.

"I took you from your previous life because it was time for you to come and serve me," the Admiral continued. Thankfully, he didn't seem to be expecting a response. "You will never see your home again."

Mandy felt a cold flash of panic, which she struggled to fight down. If they were under Phase Drive, they could be anywhere by now…and a starship was little more than a grain of sand on a giant cosmic beach. Even if the Marines set out to find her at once – and she knew that Jasmine would come looking, if she could – they'd never be able to track down the Admiral and his ship. And what if he had a *real* fleet? The Marines didn't have anything more than a few in-system ships and a handful of shuttles.

"You have two choices," the Admiral said. His remaining eye gleamed with fanatical determination as Mandy shrank away. "You can convince me, now, that you can be useful to me, that you will be a good member of my crew. Or you can go to keep my men entertained, as your friend has already gone."

Mandy blanched. Shelia...what would they do to her? Mandy's imagination provided too many possible answers. The catcalling the men had made as she'd been paraded past them suggested several others. And Dave? What had happened to Dave? She didn't dare ask.

"Convince me," the Admiral ordered. "Now, if you please."

The mockery in his voice stung. "I am a technical student," Mandy said. "I was working with the RockRats when you kidnapped us, but I was ready to take the tests for maintaining starship systems and components and..."

She thought about mentioning her father's work on Avalon, before dismissing the thought. Either the Admiral wouldn't be too interested, or he'd be *very* interested indeed. The cloudscoop alone might keep his fleet operating for years to come.

"We could always use more engineering staff," the Admiral said, after a long moment. He looked her up and down, his eyes lingering her bare breasts. "And are you willing to bet your life on your competence?"

Mandy swallowed. "Yes," she said.

He slapped her, hard enough to send her staggering to her knees. Through a wave of pain, she could barely make out his next words. It was something about showing proper respect to her commanding officer...the pain made it hard to focus. A strong hand fell on her shoulder and pulled her back to her feet, despite her dizziness. If her guards hadn't moved in to support her, she knew that she would have fallen back to the deck.

"You will address me as *Sir*," the Admiral said. Mandy nodded quickly, desperately. "And now you will go to your cabin, where you will rest until you are called. My engineer has leave to beat you if he feels that you are not performing…and if you are *incapable* of performing, you will be thrown to the men. I assure you that will not be pleasant."

"Yes, sir," Mandy said, quickly. "I won't let you down."

"Good," the Admiral said. He barked orders to the guards, who started to drag Mandy back out of the cabin. "Get some sleep. You will need it."

This time, there were no men in the passageway gaping at her as she was hustled down and into a tiny cabin, barely large enough to house a bed. They undid the handcuffs, shoved her into the compartment, threw a box of something after her and then closed the door. A quick check revealed that it was locked, or impossible to open from the inside. Mandy rubbed at her cheek, wondering if he'd knocked a tooth loose. It didn't feel that way, but how could she be sure?

She picked the box off the deck and looked inside. There was a small collection of ration bars – she'd been assured that the algae-based food was universally awful – and a single empty cup. Looking around the compartment, she found a spigot of water and a single tattered shipsuit. It stank, so badly that she almost would have preferred to go naked, and there was a hole in it just over where her heart would have been. She didn't want to know what had happened to the original owner.

Carefully, she nibbled at the ration bars, before lying down on the uncomfortable bunk and closing her eyes. A deep feeling of helplessness welled up inside her and she started to cry, unable to keep the tears from flowing. Where was she? Where was Michael? And what would happen to her?

And would she ever see home again?

CHAPTER EIGHT

I invite you all to imagine, if you can from your lofty perch, what it was like on Avalon, just after the first attack on the transport ship. We had barely grown used to considering ourselves alone in the universe – we were no longer part of the Empire, for better or worse – and suddenly we were no longer alone. Who was out there? Who was threatening us? It will not surprise you to know that fear and uncertainty ran through the body politic. We had beaten the bandits, come to terms with the Crackers, and then started to build a new nation.

But what was happening to us now?

- Professor Leo Caesius, *The Perilous Dawn* (unpublished).

"I'm afraid the media want an interview," Gwendolyn said. "Do you want me to tell them to go to hell?"

Edward nodded. The sun was rising over Castle Rock, rising on a world that had just realised that everything was going to change yet again. They'd managed to start getting the first people on the list out of Camelot before the news broke, but as more and more people were informed it was inevitable that the media would pick up on it. Avalon's media was nowhere near as tame as the media on Earth – where reporters knew their place as servants of the Grand Senate – and it couldn't be relied upon to be sensible, even if it did have more common sense than the average chicken. And he didn't have time for an interview.

"Tell them that I'll speak to them as soon as possible," he said, as another flight of helicopters roared overhead, heading back to the mainland. The latest batch of recruits had already been dispatched to the emergency base near the Badlands, along with most of the training staff. Moving the heavy equipment would take longer. Thankfully, they'd taken the time to spread out the stockpiles, even though that risked losing one or more of them to bandit attack. "We don't have the time right now."

Gwendolyn smiled. "And probably never will," she added. Both of them had been surprised by the local media. It was more honest than the media on Earth, at least after the old Council had been defeated, but it was also more inquisitive. At least it didn't repeat propaganda put out by one Grand Senator or another without actually bothering to do basic fact-checking. "Lieutenant Hawking sends his compliments and reports that his company is ready for operations in Camelot if necessary."

"Let's hope they won't be needed," Edward said, shortly. Camelot didn't seem to be panicking, but there was a definite sense of unease as the Knights tried to run the evacuation. They'd always meant to rehearse the process, yet they'd never gotten around to it. Moving even a few hundred thousand people was tricky and it would have disrupted everything else – and made the Council very unpopular.

He shook his head. Emergency precautions and exercises were always unnecessary – until the day they became necessary. People always bitched and moaned about them, even Marines, who really should have known better. But now that there *was* a crisis…maybe they could carry out more drills afterwards, once the crisis was over, before everyone forgot why they were important. And they could work on distributing more people around the countryside.

Absently, he picked up his terminal, which he'd linked directly into the orbital monitoring system. The shuttle carrying the children from orbit station had landed and the children had been rapidly transported to one of the smaller farming settlements, where they would remain until the emergency was over, one way or the other. There was no reason to assume that the smaller farms would draw fire unless they were dealing with raiders who would wreck an entire planet for the hell of it. Edward had seen the result of raider attacks, but even they had never wrecked entire planets. It would have left them without any future source of food, drink and women.

But terrorists might destroy the entire biosphere, he thought. It had happened in the past. He'd been in Boot Camp when a subset of the Nihilists had used orbital bombardment to wipe out an entire planetary population, slaughtering millions of people in the name of their death-loving creed. And yet, the Nihilists were rare outside the Core Worlds. It wasn't likely that they would come all the way to menace Avalon.

There was no sign of any activity outside the planet's orbitals, but that meant nothing. Monitoring the RockRats alone was difficult from such a distance – the limited speed of light alone ensured that most of their data would be hours out of date – and a starship operated by a competent crew could sneak up on the planet without being detected. The spaceport staff had always meant to build a better orbital monitoring system, but they'd never had the time or equipment. Edward had concentrated more on producing weapons and equipment for the military. Hindsight suggested that that might not have been such a great decision.

"I have the latest reports from the FOBs too," Gwendolyn added, after a moment. "They don't report any major upswing in bandit activity."

"That's good," Edward said. "Remind the platoons to prepare to disperse if I send the order. The FOBs may well be noticeable from orbit."

He'd worried that the bandits would have links to the newcomers; if he'd been trying to take the planet, building up an intelligence network would have been his first priority. In theory, it should have been impossible for anyone to land on the planet without the Marines spotting them, but in practice Edward knew that there were gaps in the surveillance system. A skilled team of Marines could almost certainly land on the planet without being detected.

"Of course, sir," Gwendolyn said. Her tone suggested that he was nagging – and repeating himself, issuing the same order time and time again. But then, it was her job to point out whenever he was starting to harass his subordinates. "They're ready to disperse on command."

Edward nodded. The Marine Corps disliked the idea of pinning its officers and men in one spot, rather than taking the fight to the enemy, but there was little choice. Random sweeps through the Badlands would only stumble on bandit camps through sheer luck; meanwhile, the bandits might be raiding the towns and villages they were meant to be protecting.

Instead, Edward had placed platoons of Knights – backed up by one of the Marine platoons – near threatened locations, allowing the military to respond quickly to any incursion. It was helping to mop up the bandits, but it was a long slow process. Counter-insurgency always was.

"Right," he said. "And…"

His terminal started to bleep, followed rapidly by his communicator. "This is Stevenson," a voice said. "Colonel, we're picking up a starship on approach vector. Class and weaponry uncertain as yet."

Edward looked down at the terminal's display. The newcomers were playing it carefully, although there was a frightening *lack* of care in their approach that worried him. On one hand, they were moving forward slowly, hoping that he'd reveal any surprises he had before they got too close to escape; on the other hand, they weren't trying to hide any longer. It seemed very likely that the newcomer commander no longer really believed that Avalon might pose a threat.

"We're on our way to the command centre," he said, standing up and heading for the door. "Keep us informed."

The newcomer showed up clearly on the main display, a single red icon surrounded by pop-up boxes representing the analysis computer's best guess at its capabilities. It was impossible to be entirely certain, but the general tonnage of the intruder suggested a light cruiser, rather than the destroyer that had attacked the RockRat transport. *That* definitely didn't bode well; one ship might be within their capability to handle, yet two or more might be impossible. A standard Imperial Navy tactic was to keep one or more ships in reserve, under stealth, to see what happened. The newcomers might have learned their tactics from the Navy.

Or they might be former Navy, he thought. The Imperial Navy had been a bloated bureaucracy for so long that few people really knew how many ships and men were actually in service. Going by the official fleet lists alone, the Imperial Navy should have had no trouble meeting its responsibilities, but Edward had heard – unofficially – that the fleet lists were at least an order of magnitude greater than the reality. Starships vanished all the time; who was to say that they hadn't become pirates, or petty warlords, or…there were just too many possibilities.

"We can't pick up any trace of another ship," Colonel Kitty Stevenson reported through the communicator. She was Imperial Navy Intelligence, rather than a line officer, but she had been the best qualified person to put in charge of the spaceport, as well as internal intelligence. The Imperial Navy traditionalists would have been horrified at the breach in protocol; Edward found it hard to care. "The newcomer doesn't seem to be sending any signals, but they could be lasing someone outside our detection range…"

"Understood," Edward said, calmly. "Inform me the moment you have a positive identification on the ship's class."

The hours ticked away as the intruder came closer to the planet. Edward sat down in his chair and forced himself to be patient, feeling – again – as if he'd been promoted too far too fast. He was a Captain – he *still* thought of himself as a Captain – trained to lead his men into battle, not to serve as the overall commander. But he had no choice, but to watch from safety as his subordinates went into danger. Shaking his head bitterly, he considered hailing the newcomer, before dismissing the thought. Hailing the intruding ship would reveal too much about their space-based observation systems.

Did they know they'd been detected? It was impossible to tell. Passive sensors were impossible to detect by definition and the spaceport staff had been careful not to sweep the intruder with active sensors. On the other hand, they weren't trying to hide any longer – and in their place, Edward would have assumed that he'd been detected at once. He found himself running through possible scenarios in his mind; the intruder intended to intimidate them, the intruder was trying to distract them from another starship, the intruder was just stupid…there were too many possibilities there, too. The only reassuring thought was that there shouldn't have been any need to try to be subtle. Avalon's orbital defences were effectively non-existent.

And maybe they don't know that, he thought. It might explain the slow approach. If they knew that a company of Marines had been abandoned on Avalon, would they expect some orbital defences as well?

He looked over at one of the operators. "Time to orbit?"

"Thirty-seven minutes, assuming they don't change their course and speed," the operator reported. The enemy ship was already within weapons range of the planet, assuming they didn't really care about accuracy. KEWs were cheap; anyone with access to space and a basic fabricator could produce as many as they wanted from an asteroid or two. "They're starting to sweep space with radar pulses."

Gwendolyn looked over at him. "Well," she said, "at least they won't think they're undetected now."

Edward nodded. It didn't take a mil-grade sensor to pick up radar pulses – and they could be detected from outside their active reception range. The intruder had just announced its presence for all to see. It wouldn't be long before they started hailing the planet…

The minutes ticked away until the intruder was nearing high orbit, altering course slightly to enter orbit over the settled continent. That didn't bode well, Edward decided. They'd clearly obtained *some* intelligence on Avalon…

They probably downloaded the planet's records from the Imperial Library, he thought, dryly. It would hardly be the first time that 'intelligence' had been freely available, if someone had thought to look for it. The Civil Guard's intelligence analysts had often repackaged data from the Imperial Library, or corporate records, by slapping a security classification on it and claiming that it was the result of extensive intelligence-gathering operations. At least Imperial Intelligence generally did a better job.

"Incoming," the operator snapped. Edward's eyes flew back to the display as a red icon broke away from the intruder, lancing into the planet's atmosphere. The projected endpoint was only seventy kilometres from Camelot, in the Mystic Mountains. They'd be able to see the flash and hear the impact in the city. "Time to target, three minutes and…"

Edward accessed the live feed from one of the FOBs. The Mystic Mountains were home to the Mountain Men – hermits who chose to remain isolated from society – and a handful of the more irreconcilable Crackers, forcing him to leave a small detachment of Knights near the foothills. It was a major hassle – he would have preferred to deploy those soldiers elsewhere – but there had been little choice. Now, he watched through their sensors as a streak of light hit the mountain's peak, always hidden among the clouds, and sent shockwaves running through the region. Anyone caught underneath dislodged rocks would be dead.

"Impact," the operator said. "I couldn't get a very good read on its force, sir, but it seems roughly identical to a standard-issue KEW…"

"Don't worry about it," Edward advised. There was no reason why the intruder couldn't simply keep experimenting with different sizes of KEW until they found one that worked, if they even bothered to try. The Imperial Navy might have a KEW-standard, but it was hardly a requirement they needed to follow. "Send the dispersal signal to the FOBs."

The intruder came to a halt over Camelot and waited. Edward waited too, knowing that there was nothing else they could do. Seconds ticked away, forcing him to monitor progress as his men dispersed into the countryside and the Council headed to their underground bunker – although he doubted that it would provide much protection if the intruder wanted to kill them. The Imperial Navy had invested billions of credits in producing weapons designed to crush bunkers, but a handful of KEWs would have the same effect – at least, if one wasn't worried about civilians caught in the line of fire. He was pretty sure that the intruders would have a frightening lack of concern about civilians, if they were prepared to bombard the planet almost at random.

"They're hailing us," the operator said.

Gwendolyn leaned forward. "The entire planet, or the Council, or what?"

"The signal is being relayed from orbit station through the laser link," the operator said. "I don't think it can be picked up on the planet directly."

Edward frowned. That suggested that the intruders were trying to keep their demands a secret – even though they'd already given up on keeping their *presence* a secret. It could be a tactic to put pressure on the Council, or it could be an attempt to keep the general population from knowing what they wanted until it was too late. Either was possible.

"Let's hear it," he said. "What do they want?"

The voice was completely atonal, almost certainly computer-generated. *That* was a fairly standard pirate tactic; they knew just how far the Imperial Navy would go to hunt them down, so they concealed their identities as much as they could. It never boded well for anyone taken prisoner by the pirates; if they *knew* they had someone worth ransoming, they would take precautions to prevent them learning anything about their captors, but anyone else would almost certainly never see freedom again. Unless they were rescued by the Imperial Navy…

"We hold the high orbitals over your world," the voice said. "You are ordered to surrender and submit yourself to our rule. We hold the entire sector in our hands. If you refuse to surrender, we will bombard your planet until you submit – or die."

Edward looked over at Gwendolyn, who looked back in equal puzzlement. Pirates making demands on planets normally wanted food, drink and women. Edward had been considering a contingency plan for slipping a handful of female Marines onto the shuttles in the guise of unwilling victims. But a demand for complete surrender? *That* was odd, unless someone was making a bid for power. Or trying to confuse the defenders.

"You will provide us with the following items," the voice continued. "A complete list of your resources. The names of your governors, who will rule your world in our name. A complete list of everyone on your planet with spacefaring experience. We will be dispatching armed soldiers to occupy your orbiting station; you will surrender it without a fight. Any resistance will be met by punitive strikes against your population, followed by us repeating our demands publicly."

And causing a panic, Edward thought.

"The Council is calling," the operator said. They'd taken pains to establish secure land-links from Castle Rock to Camelot, even if they had been expensive. There was no way they could be detected from orbit. "They want to know what they should do."

Edward silently blessed his own foresight. "Tell them that we are rolling the die," he said. If this went wrong, the entire planet might be lost. But the alternative was slavery – and certain death for the Marines. "Sergeant, contact Lieutenant Yamane. Inform her that she is cleared to proceed."

"Understood," Gwendolyn said. She keyed her terminal, sending a single message up the laser link to orbit station. If she had her own doubts about the wisdom of this course of action, she kept them to herself. "Message sent."

"And now we wait," Edward said.

He sat back, wishing that he was in orbit. Despite the risks – and they were colossal – it was better than sitting on the ground, watching helplessly as his Marines went into battle. But all he could do was watch, and wait, and pray.

CHAPTER NINE

Marines are expected to be the most well-rounded soldiers in the Empire. A Marine Company may find itself serving on a planet's surface, or in deep space. As such, Marines are trained extensively for operations in all possible locations. Those who fail the training program cannot be given their Rifleman's Tab…

…As might be expected, the training process is the hardest in the military. Those without the dedication and drive that makes a Marine will find it a foretaste of hell.

-Major-General Thomas Kratman (Ret), *A Civilian's Guide to the Terran Marine Corps.*

Jasmine felt, as she took her first step out into space, the sense of awe and complete insignificance that always gripped her when she spacewalked. Space was vast; the planet below seemed huge, but it was tiny compared to the vastness of the local star, let alone the entirety of space. On such a scale, a single Marine didn't even register. A starship wasn't even a speck of dust in God's eye. She pushed the old terror to the back of her mind – she'd had to learn to overcome it at the Slaughterhouse – and drifted forward, using the gas jets mounted on her suit to propel herself. A moment later, the rest of the platoon followed her into the inky darkness of space.

The enemy ship had positioned itself some distance from the station, as if it expected the station to be carrying weapons that could threaten it. Jasmine wasn't sure if the intruders were just being paranoid, or if they had picked up some bad intelligence somewhere, but it hardly mattered. It was a lucky break and the Marines would need every one of those they could get. The suit's sensors reported that the intruder was sweeping space with radar pulses, locating and tracking every piece of junk in orbit around the planet, but its radar shouldn't be able to pick up the combat suits. They were stealthed specifically for operations in space.

And if we're wrong about that, she thought, in the privacy of her own mind, *we're all dead.*

Being a sitting duck was never the Marine way, or so she had been told. Even when in friendly territory, they'd been trained to take precautions against surprise attack. But in space, there was no choice. There was nothing that would shield them against enemy weapons if they were spotted; they'd be wiped out in seconds if the pirates noticed their presence. Jasmine took a deep breath as they drifted closer to the pirate ship, wondering – absurdly – if she would even notice before they fried her. Laser weapons propagated at the speed of light; plasma cannon blasts weren't too far behind. Detection would mean certain death.

Up close, the pirate ship was a hulking mass of metal, painted black. That was odd for pirate ships, particularly the ones that couldn't hope to pass for civilian vessels. They tended to paint their ships in intimidating colours, although Jasmine had never been able to see the point. Most of their victims would never have the chance to see their naked hulls before it was too late. She kept a sharp eye on the gravity sensors as they drifted closer, watching for any sign that the enemy ship was deploying gravity shields. It was lucky that no one had ever managed to come up with a protective bubble that surrounded the entire ship, or their planned stunt would be completely impossible.

Her HUD flickered a message in front of her eyes. Ship class identified; Casanova-C CL (Assault). Standard weapons platform…

Jasmine smiled in relief. They'd had no trouble in identifying the basic hull – light cruiser designs followed the same pattern, ever since naval technology had stopped advancing – but the interior could have followed a dozen different designs. The *Casanova-C* design, if she recalled correctly, had been a stopgap construction program to produce a light cruiser suitable for raiding and convoy escort, one that should have been replaced with a more specialised design. But the tightening budgets had kept them in service for centuries after they were first designed, as well as forcing the Imperial Navy to sell hundreds of them to outside interests. Who knew where this particular cruiser had originally come from? There were no identifying marks on the hull that would allow them to identify its original designation.

There didn't seem to be anyone on the hull, she saw, as the Marines drifted closer and finally came to a halt, hovering just over the metal. Standard procedure was to use magnetic fields to attach themselves to the hull, but that might have set off alarms inside the ship. The Marine Transport Ships certainly monitored their own environment very closely; there was too much at stake to risk assuming that the pirates wouldn't do the same. Instead, she led the way towards the airlock she knew had to be there, an emergency maintenance hatch that would be difficult to seal. Most space technology was standardised and had been so for centuries. She doubted the pirates would have bothered to change much. They rarely showed that much concern for their ships.

She held up her hands, using them to signal the rest of the platoon. A single radio signal, even a microburst, would be too risky near the enemy hull. Blake and Joe moved forward to cover Brains as he drifted up to the airlock, looking for the access point. Imperial Law demanded that all airlocks be manually accessible from the outside, just in case someone punctured their suit and had to get into the ship's atmosphere in a hurry. It was why naval vessels posted guards at all airlocks, even though it was very difficult to board a ship while it was under way. But it was tradition and therefore couldn't be changed.

Brains held up his own hands, signalling that he was about to disconnect the airlock system from the rest of the ship. It would be too much to expect that opening the airlock wouldn't sound an alarm; the Imperial Navy took a dim view of airlocks that opened without an apparent reason. But if they could disconnect the warning system…Brains reached inside as the Marines tensed, bracing themselves, and pulled out the component inside. A moment later, working with desperate speed, he opened the airlock. Inside, there was barely enough room for two armoured Marines.

Jasmine led the way inside, followed by Joe, who covered her as the airlock hissed shut. Pirates were notoriously sloppy at maintenance, but only a complete idiot would remove the basic safety precautions built into standard airlocks, including the one that prevented one door from opening while the other was still open. Jasmine lifted her rifle as the second door opened, her suit's sensors noting the presence of a standard atmosphere, surprisingly clean for a pirate ship. She'd heard stories of Marines who'd boarded pirate ships to discover that the pirate crews had defecated in the passageways and urinated in their own cabins, not to mention leaving dead bodies scattered everywhere. Not all of the stories were exaggerated…

Two men turned to stare at the Marines as they stepped out of the airlock and into the passageway. One of them reached for a weapon, just before Jasmine triggered the stunner built into her rifle and sent both men tumbling to the deck. A quick inspection of their outfits revealed that they weren't wearing shipsuits, let alone carrying protective gear. She dreaded to think what a Marine Sergeant would have said about such carelessness when approaching a hostile planet. They might have been prisoners…no, prisoners wouldn't be carrying weapons.

The airlock hissed open again, revealing two more Marines. Jasmine used her hands to order them to take up positions at the end of the corridor, pulling up the plans for the *Casanova*-C design in her HUD. The semi-intelligent system was already comparing what the suit's sensors were picking up to the standard plans, looking for places where the pirate crew might have reconfigured the interior. Jasmine had heard horror stories about ships that had been reconfigured by crews that hadn't known what they were doing – and she wouldn't trust a ship that had been reconfigured by pirates – but there were plenty of civilian yards that would take pirate gold to reconfigure their ship and then keep their mouths shut.

She smiled as the remainder of the platoon entered and started issuing orders. Two of the Marines would remain at the airlock, protecting the tactical nuke they'd brought with them. Detonating it on the hull would have damaged the ship; detonating it *inside* the hull would completely vaporise the vessel. It was a poor second-best to capturing it intact – and it would wipe out the entire platoon along with the pirates – but there was no choice. If the pirates managed to defeat the Marines and remain in control of their vessel, they could exterminate the entire population of Avalon.

Brains and three other Marines would head down to Engineering, where they would capture the compartment and hack into the vessel's computer network. The pirates weren't foolish enough to leave the computer network open for anyone to access; they knew what a dedicated hacker could do to the network. Besides, unless this pirate gang was really unusual, their commander would probably want to keep control of the network for himself. It would help to discourage his subordinates from trying to take over by sticking a knife in his back.

Jasmine led the way up the corridor towards the bridge, watching for other pirates. The interior of the ship looked *old*; she was silently relieved that her mask covered her nose, even though it didn't look as bad as the stories suggested. No pirates attempted to block their way as they inched through what should have been a set of shared cabins for junior crewmen – all of them appeared to be locked, oddly – and reached the elevator shaft. The entire system appeared to be non-functional, something else that puzzled her. If they could maintain the Phase Drive and the life-support systems, why couldn't they maintain the elevator?

They want control, Blake signalled to her.

Jasmine nodded in understanding. The light cruiser was tiny compared to a battleship, but the pirate commander would probably want to limit his crew's mobility as much as possible anyway. How could *anyone* run a starship like that and expect to survive a battle with an equal foe? But then, pirates shied away from warships, even warships operated by the more comic-opera self-defence forces. Even a small destroyer, manned by a competent crew, could take out a pirate cruiser.

Their combat suits were too bulky to allow them to slip up the Jeffries tubes, so they had to take the ladders. There, they encountered several more pirates, all heading down towards the lower levels. Had they detected the airlock opening and passed it off as a glitch? It was possible, she decided as they stunned the pirates, but surely anyone that stupid wouldn't be capable of running a starship for very long. The Marines were trained to treat all alarms as the genuine thing, even if the perimeter sensors had a long history of sounding false alerts. A single genuine intrusion that was ignored could be completely disastrous.

She heard the sound of shouting up above and knew that they'd lost the element of surprise. There must have been other pirates at the top of the ladders, in position to see their comrades fall stunned. Jasmine launched a set of remote probes from her suit, activating the full combat network and linking into Brains' group. The network would have been detected by enemy sensors if they'd activated them, but there was no longer any point in refusing to use it. Her HUD updated rapidly, filling out the internal chart of the ship's innards. There didn't seem to be any real surprises, apart from an interior airlock that had been pulled out completely and junked.

Someone high overhead was a quick thinker. He took up position and started to fire down the ladders, trying to keep the Marines back long enough for reinforcements to arrive. Blake stepped forward, fitted a grenade to his rifle, and fired it up the shaft, timing the detonation perfectly. Jasmine ran up as soon as the grenade exploded, firing at anything that moved. A pirate had been turned into bloody chunks by the explosion, which had also scorched the paint on the bulkheads. The remainder of the material looked unharmed.

"Move," she sent, as the remaining Marines followed her. Three pirates seemed to be running forward, two of them wearing body armour. Cursing – the body armour would deflect the stun bursts – she flicked the switch on her rifle and opened fire with armour-piercing bullets. Blake readied a plasma rifle – there were battlesuits designed to deal with standard bullets – but it wasn't necessary. Both pirates staggered backwards, dead the moment her bullets passed through their skulls. "Up to the bridge."

Brains updated her; the pirates had started to seal Engineering, but not quickly enough to prevent the Marines from breaking in and opening fire with stunners. The fighting had rapidly become hand-to-hand – no one would fire automatic weapons in an engineering compartment if they had any sense – and that gave the Marines an advantage. Brains was already trying to hack into their computer core, but he was finding it slow going. The Imperial Navy might have standardised everything, with certain weaknesses and access points hardwired into the systems, yet the pirates had apparently added their own improvements. Or, more likely, whoever had owned the ship after the Imperial Navy had decommissioned it. The self-defence forces tended to dislike the idea of the Imperial Navy being able to regain control of its former ships.

The pirates had extensively modified Officer Country, the living compartments belonging to the five senior officers on the ship. They'd welded in heavy barriers, in some cases binding them directly to the bulkheads, and positioned heavy weapons, as if they'd expected to have to defend themselves against their own crew. The Marines paused long enough to regroup and then started to use explosive charges to knock down the barricades. A handful of pirates attempted to duck into the cabins to hide, just as the main lighting flickered and failed. Brains notified her a second later that he'd triggered a security flag and most of the command network had simply shut down. Jasmine wasn't too worried; the Marines could fight in the dark and the pirates wouldn't be able to bombard the planet, at least until they regained their network. She sent a signal back to Avalon, requesting reinforcements, and led the thrust that cleared the remainder of the corridor. Ahead of them, the airlock leading to the bridge was sealed shut.

"Get the debonder," she ordered. Blake hurried to obey. The airlock door was solid, made out of hullmetal, as was the bulkheads surrounding the bridge. In theory, the bridge – buried in the heart of the ship – should have been the last place to be destroyed, although Jasmine had always questioned that theory. Take out Engineering and the weapons, and the ship would be effectively helpless. "Break down the airlock."

The debonder hummed to life, weakening the molecular bonds that held the airlock together. It was difficult to use it on the external hull – it was simply too thick for the debonder to work quickly, while setting off all kinds of alarms – but it should work on the airlock. Unless, of course, the pirates had set up a countering field. If so, they'd simply have to cut all of the command lines into the bridge and wait for the pirates to run out of atmosphere and suffocate to death. That could take a while.

Jasmine drew back as the airlock crumbled into dust, just as the pirates started shooting through the gap. The Marines returned fire, launching stun grenades into the bridge and jumping into the compartment as the pirates reeled back. Only a pair of them seemed to be wearing proper armour and they were both quickly dispatched by bursts of plasma fire; the others, caught up in the stun bursts, were twitching on the deck. Jasmine strode over to the main command chair, flipped open the protective box covering the Captain's personal console, and plugged a link from her suit into it. Computer experts down on Avalon would work through the network to gain control and check for any unpleasant surprises.

"We have reinforcements on their way to you," Captain Stalker said, through the communications network. It wouldn't take more than twenty minutes for the shuttle to dock with the pirate ship, allowing Second Platoon to join them. They'd be able to help with the mopping up. "How many prisoners do you have?"

Jasmine checked the HUD records quickly. "We have five on the bridge and we have stunned seventeen so far – none of them are actually restrained. There may be others somewhere else on the cruiser"

There were commanding officers who would have bitched about that; protocol demanded restraining prisoners, but there hadn't been time. Captain Stalker, thankfully, understood.

"Once Second Platoon joins you, sweep the remainder of the ship for prisoners and prepare them for transfer to the surface," he ordered. "Once the ship is empty, we can set the analysts loose on it and see what they can pull from the computers."

Jasmine nodded. She'd forgotten that her friend was missing, in the excitement of boarding the enemy ship, but if Mandy was still alive the contents of the ship's databanks would be the best hope they'd have of finding her. Carefully, she passed the orders on to the rest of the platoon; now they held the sensitive parts of the ship, they could wait for reinforcements before taking the rest of her. They'd just have to hope that the pirates couldn't trigger one of the warheads on the missiles, assuming they'd already bypassed the safeties that were supposed to prevent them from detonating inside their mothership.

"Understood, sir," she said. She couldn't resist a grin. "The ship is ours!"

CHAPTER TEN

The Empire has always devised the laws concerning the treatment of prisoners-of-war to suit itself; unsurprisingly, as the Empire has always been massively more powerful than any of its possible opponents (and, in its later years, there were no other multi-system powers). In particular, pirates, insurgents and terrorists are almost inevitably rated as illegal combatants who can be interrogated, tortured and shot out of hand, without trial.

Naturally, it is hotly debated if this is actually a good idea. Enemy combatants do not surrender if they believe they will be killed afterwards. Further, at least when dealing with peer powers, mistreating one side's captives will encourage retaliation by the other side against its own POWs. Marines must therefore use their wide latitude to strike a balance between several different issues, including that of operational security and the safety of Marines who may be captured later in the operation…

…In fact, we may want to grant legal status to insurgents who don't act in a manner designed to bring death and destruction to their own people…

-Major-General Thomas Kratman (Ret), *A Civilian's Guide to the Terran Marine Corps.*

"They don't look very impressive, do they?"

Edward shrugged at Gwendolyn's comment. Pirates were never very impressive once hauled out of their ships and held in the sunlight. Most of them tended to be cowards, brave when carrying weapons, but unwilling to fight when facing an armed opponent. Looking at them, it was no longer possible to believe that one of the other planets in the sector was starting its own empire. They were unmistakably pirates, complete with a mixture of outfits, poor medical care and craven attitudes. According to Second Platoon, who had rounded up most of the survivors and escorted them to Castle Rock, some of them had already started trying to sell out their comrades while they were being shackled.

"No," he agreed. "But we will pretend to take them seriously, for the moment."

The pirates – there were fifty-two captives in all – would be separated from their comrades and interrogated one by one. Most of them were probably low-ranking scum without any real connection to the greater pirate community – pirates knew to maintain at least some operational security, or the Imperial Navy would have wiped them out long ago – but they could still provide intelligence. If nothing else, they could identify the senior officers among the captured pirates, allowing the interrogators to focus on those who might be able to tell the Marines something useful. Some of them would probably have implants designed to make it difficult to interrogate the bastards, but there were ways around them. The interrogator just had to be clever.

He watched as the prisoners were hustled across the landing field towards the penal block. Avalon didn't keep many prisoners; those who were arrested and tried were generally sent to work camps or penal islands once sentence was passed, unless they were sentenced to death. Technically, Edward had the legal authority to execute all of the pirates – and they knew it. If they'd talk, however, he was prepared to deal. On a penal island, they wouldn't be able to hurt anyone but themselves.

The surprise had come when Second Platoon had swept the living quarters on the captured vessel. They'd discovered seven young women – the oldest couldn't be more than twenty – whom the pirates had apparently kept as sex slaves. The Marines had restrained them anyway, just in case they'd developed an affinity for their captors, but had sent them for medical attention rather than transporting them down to the surface with the rest of the prisoners. Edward had skimmed the preliminary report and felt thoroughly sick. All of the girls had been raped repeatedly, as well as being beaten by their captors. Three dead bodies had also been discovered, their throats cut by their masters. How could *anyone* do that to their captives?

"The Council would like to know what you've pulled from the ship," Gwendolyn said, after the prisoners had shuffled their way into the penal block. "I thought we hadn't pulled anything from their databanks yet…?"

"Nothing," Edward confirmed. "Kitty is on her way up there now, along with three other analysts with some computer experience. We'll have to see what they can get for us."

He had to smile. At least some of the Council had seriously considered trying to deal with the pirates, before they'd discovered the truth. Making links with an interstellar power near Avalon would have been very useful, both for the planet's economic development and their own security – and career prospects. But it seemed that there was no such power, and once the records of what the Marines had found on the ship became public, those Councillors would wind up looking like fools. It was a pity, Edward decided, that Julian hadn't been one of them. The pirates made the bandits who had tormented Avalon look kind and civilised.

They walked after the pirates into the penal block and watched as the interrogators began their work. The first test was simple enough; once the pirates had been wired to a lie detector, they were asked for their names and origins, which were then compared to the records they'd sent to Avalon before the Empire had withdrawn from the sector. Edward wasn't hopeful that would yield anything useful, but it did help to provide a baseline for fine-tuning the lie detectors. It also allowed the interrogators to start building up a picture of who had held what position on the pirate ship.

Steadily, the network started to build up in the main interrogation room. As Edward had suspected, most of the prisoners were deliberately kept ignorant, but a handful were senior officers. One of them – the one the Marines believed had killed his sex slave rather than risk having her recovered – was actually the third-in-command of the ship. Edward had asked why the tactical officer – who would be third in the chain of command on an Imperial Navy starship – would be off the bridge and discovered that the pirate was actually the Captain's bodyguard and security officer. Apparently, he was completely loyal to the Captain, but Edward had his doubts. The preferred method of promotion in the pirate world was knifing one's superior in the back, literally.

His lips quirked into a smile. How very much like the Grand Senate.

"He wants to deal," the interrogator reported. He was a Marine auxiliary wearing a bloodstained apron intended to intimidate the prisoners. There was no need to use physical torture just yet. "But he insists on dealing with someone senior."

Edward nodded and allowed the interrogator to lead him into the interrogation chamber. The prisoner was cuffed and shackled to a chair, so solidly that even a boosted Marine in full battle armour couldn't have hoped to escape. He was a rat-faced man with eyes that flickered nervously from side to side, as if he was looking for salvation he knew he wouldn't find. Edward knew his type well; brave enough in packs, willing to do absolutely anything to a helpless victim, but a coward when confronting someone stronger than him. And he had to know what the Marines could do to him – what they *would* do to him, if he failed to strike a deal.

"Who…" The prisoner coughed and started again. "Who are you?"

Edward studied him for a long thoughtful moment. "Colonel Stalker, Terran Marines," he said. He didn't miss the prisoner's flinch. Marines had a good record for hunting down and exterminating pirates. "Convince me that you can be useful and your life will be spared."

The prisoner swallowed hard. "I want guarantees…"

"And I want proof that you can be useful," Edward said, shortly. He looked over at the interrogator. "Does he have an implant?"

"Yes, but it's an old design," the interrogator said. "We can probably break it."

Edward looked down at the prisoner, who cringed back. "You heard the man," he said. "We can break your implant. Even if we fail, we'll inflict staggering pain on your mind, perhaps kill you outright. It's very easy to cause a brain spasm by messing around with an implant."

He kept his face carefully blank as the prisoner glanced around, unwilling to meet Edward's eyes. The Empire's standard practice for dealing with new kinds of anti-interrogation implants was to take the implanted person to a lab and start experimenting, looking for a way to break it. It was a process that tended to go through experimental subjects very quickly – whoever was designing the implants kept developing new designs – but they were all sentenced to death anyway. If they died broadening the Empire's knowledge base, perhaps allowing the next attempt to succeed, no one would care.

"It's your choice," he said, slowly. "Tell us what we want to know, or we'll see what we can do with your implant."

There were other ways to pressure someone with an implant. The system would destroy the carrier's brain if it sensed that he was being tortured, or drugged, but it had its limits. Hunger was often as good a means of torture as any, or thirst. Edward could wait for the man to crack – and someone as cowardly as their prisoner would probably not hold out long enough for the implant to notice and take him out.

The prisoner looked up at him, finally. "What do you want to know?"

"Tell me about your ship and crew," Edward said. "What did you hope to achieve by coming here?"

"We were running out of fuel," the pirate said, finally. Edward concealed a flicker of humour. With the Empire's withdrawal from the sector, fuel shipping would have broken down completely. "The ship was too badly damaged to make a skimming run through a gas giant's atmosphere and the processor never worked properly. We were seriously thinking about finding a planet we could invade and just settling there. Everyone knew that it was just a matter of time before the Captain did it, or he was killed and his successor took us to our final resting place."

He took a breath. "We called in at an asteroid settlement, looking for fuel," he continued. "That's when we met the Admiral. He offered us fuel and food and supplies; in exchange, we had to work with him as his allies. The Captain decided that we didn't have a choice. We made the deal. The Admiral gave us a new XO and sent us here."

Edward's eyes narrowed. "The Admiral?"

"We don't know much about him," the prisoner confessed. Edward took a sharp look at the lie detector, which was still showing a green light. "He…he told us that he intended to build an empire, that we could work with him or be removed. And then he led us here on a raiding mission and then left, leaving us orders to take control of the planet."

"Which you failed at, rather spectacularly," Edward pointed out. There were hundreds of questions that needed to be asked, but he had one he wanted answered first, if possible. "Did you take prisoners from the transport you attacked?"

"I think so," the prisoner admitted. "We weren't allowed to see them; they were transhipped to the Admiral's personal vessel and taken out of the system. I think the Admiral wanted to recruit them if possible; we were told we could find our entertainment on Avalon, once we took the planet."

"You mean you intended to rape your way through the planet's female population," Edward said, coldly. Just how many crimes did this man have on his soul? "Here's the deal we will offer you."

He leaned forward, until he was staring right into the prisoner's eyes. "You will answer all of our questions, fully and completely, without trying to lie," he said. "If you have information we haven't asked about, you will volunteer it. In exchange, we will send you to an island where you can live out the remainder of your life, however long that is. If you break the agreement or try to lie to us, all bets are off and we will try to break your implant's protection. Do you understand me?"

The prisoner nodded, meekly. "Start running through the questions," Edward ordered the interrogator, as he turned to the door. "And keep me informed."

He'd have to read the reports very carefully. The interrogators would record everything for the analysts, who would read it and propose new questions for the next session. It could take weeks to drain a prisoner of everything he knew, even a completely cooperative prisoner, and they'd have to be careful. The 'Admiral' could easily have lied to his reluctant subordinates and their captive would repeat his lies as truth. Unfortunately, the lie detector that could tell the difference between a lie someone believed to be truthful and something that was objectively true had yet to be invented.

Outside, he met Gwendolyn and two other interrogators. "Most of the prisoners were deliberately kept ignorant," she said, passing him a datapad. "A handful might know something useful."

Edward skimmed the datapad quickly. A few questions was all that it had taken to establish that most of the prisoners knew nothing useful. Later sessions would piece together how they'd joined the pirate crew, although Edward suspected he knew the answer. The interstellar shipping community had its seedy side – and crewmen in poor financial situations would often find themselves sinking into crime, eventually moving to a pirate ship and becoming outright pirates. And once they'd been tainted, they would never be able to return to civilisation. It was a story as old as crime itself.

"Keep working on them," he ordered, returning the datapad to the interrogators. They'd ask other questions, just in case one of the pirates had managed to slip something past their captors. "Did you hear anything from the inspection team?"

"Only that the engineers were astonished the ship didn't blow up under them," Gwendolyn informed him as they stepped back outside. The sun shone down brightly, causing Edward to shield his eyes after the darkness of the penal block. "Apparently, their basic maintenance left a great deal to be desired."

Edward scowled. The Imperial Navy had been reporting recruitment shortfalls for centuries, all concentrated in the categories – skilled technicians – where they were desperately needed. Accordingly, most components for starships were black boxes, ones that could be inserted into the right places without the maintenance crew actually knowing what the boxes *did*. In some ways, it made life easier, but it was a false saving. The ignorance of many of the crews could be very dangerous, particularly on ships that had been cut off from the Empire.

On the plus side, the ships were very rugged. Even a poor crew could keep them going, as long as they didn't run out of supplies. And even if they did, components could be cannibalised from other ships, or even civilian vessels. The Navy's components, designed to a far higher standard than the average civilian component, were in great demand among civilian shippers.

"I wish I was surprised," he said. "Did they have any idea how long it would take to restore the ship to operating condition?"

Gwendolyn threw him a sharp look. "You plan to take the ship and wage war on the pirates?"

"I don't think we have a choice," Edward admitted. "If this…*Admiral* really exists, if he really thinks he can build his own empire, he's going to want the cloudscoop. The prisoner didn't mention the scoop at all, which is odd…"

"Unless the Admiral plans to take it later, once they get the command codes off us," Gwendolyn said. "Odd that they didn't demand them from the start."

Edward nodded. He *hated* working blind; hell, they'd had better intelligence when they were fighting the Crackers. Just what were they dealing with? A pirate with delusions of grandeur or someone who thought that they could actually build their own empire? If the latter, might he *want* cooperation from Avalon's Council? But if that was the case, why had he sent a pirate crew who would gleefully have inflicted vast sufferings on a civilian population? He keyed his terminal and sent a message back to the interrogators, to ask them to find out what the Admiral had ordered once the high orbitals were taken and secured.

"We'll see what we can pull from the databanks," he said, finally. His communications implant buzzed before he could say anything else. "Stalker."

"Colonel, this is Sadie," a voice said. She'd been one of the Marine Auxiliaries who had received a field promotion to combat medic. Technically, she should have been returned to the Slaughterhouse to run through the Crucible again, but it was impossible. At least she already had most of the Marine-issue implants. "I've just had a look at the body of the ship's XO – sir, this guy was heavily implanted."

Edward blinked in surprise. "How heavily implanted?"

"Heavily, sir," Sadie said. "Some of the blasted things have melted down, but I can see traces of enhanced strength and resilience, as well as something that seems to be an advanced neural link – I'd say that he was a Cobra, if there were any Cobras left."

"Odd," Edward mused aloud. Cobras had been enhanced soldiers from several hundred years ago, but they'd been replaced by Pathfinders and Force Recon. They weren't genetically-engineered; they certainly couldn't reproduce and expect their children to have the same improvements. "Do you think he was in stasis?"

"Impossible to say," Sadie said. "It's possible that someone might have preserved a set of Cobra implants and the facilities to use them."

"This just gets better and better," Edward said. "I'll be heading to Camelot in a couple of hours to brief the Council. Please bring whatever you have by then with you."

"Yes, sir," Sadie said. "I'll be there."

"Cobras," Gwendolyn said, thoughtfully. "I always wanted to know if I could take one."

"Don't wish too hard," Edward said. "You might get your wish."

CHAPTER ELEVEN

As the renowned sociologist Kimball Kinnison pointed out, the pirates have actually evolved a culture of their own – although they wouldn't see it that way. Put simply, the pirate culture is based on the rule of the strong; those too weak to defend themselves, or to build up a following, remain at the bottom of the heap. This has dire implications for the 'losers;' they can be raped, tortured and killed at will by their superiors. The only hope for survival is to ally themselves to a powerful patron…

…However, the pirate culture does not admit of a strong leader. The very nature of interstellar travel makes it easier for subordinate Captains to break free, given a chance. Any group effort must proceed with the cooperation of everyone with power, which can sometimes be as simple as knowing more about engineering than anyone else..

-Edward E. Smith, Professor of Sociology. *Pirates and their Lives.*

Mandy had no idea how long she'd slept before she heard the sound of someone tapping at the hatch. She felt an odd moment of disorientation as she sat up in the bunk, wincing slightly as she bumped her head into the ceiling. The trainees had received more than enough lectures on how the Empire worked hard to cram as much as possible into a tiny space, but hearing about it was different from actually experiencing it. There just wasn't enough room in the cabin to swing a cat.

She clutched at the ragged blanket as the hatch started to open, revealing a gray-haired man whose features seemed oddly immobile. It took her a moment to realise what must have happened to him; impure rejuvenation drugs still worked, but they tended to inflict damage on the recipient's nervous system. Or something like that. The man looked younger than her father, yet he could easily be a great deal older. His eyes, however, were sharp and utterly uninterested in her, apart from how she could help him. He wore a black uniform with a silver star on his right shoulder. On his belt, he carried an assortment of guns, knives and something that looked like a short coil of rope.

"You may call me Vane," he said. Like the rest of the pirates, he had an accent she couldn't place. "I was informed that you are an engineering student?"

"Yes, sir," Mandy said carefully. It beat whore, she'd told herself in the night. "I was in training when you took me…"

"I am this ship's Chief Engineer," Vane informed her. "You will be working directly for me. Get out of bed and turn around, facing the wall."

Mandy hesitated, before realising that she didn't really have a choice and obeyed. She heard the sound of something rustling before a strand of rope cracked across her back, followed by a tearing wave of pain that drove her to her knees. Mandy found herself on the deck, screaming in pain; every inch of her body seemed to have turned red hot, burning its way into her very soul. And then the pain just vanished, leaving her staring at him in horror.

"This is called a neural whip," Vane said, recoiling the device she'd taken for rope. "It is really the most economical torture device ever invented. While it is used, the target feels horrific pain, but there are almost no after-effects. It takes months of torture before permanent damage is inflicted on its target."

His eyes met hers as she pulled herself to her feet. "If you fuck up, I will use this on you," he added. "If you prove unable to learn, or don't know enough to be useful, I will throw you to the men. Do you understand me?"

"Yes, sir," Mandy said. Her entire body was shaking, although she couldn't tell if it was through shock or outrage. She felt almost as if she'd caught a nasty cold and her entire body was electric and sensitive. "I understand."

"Good," Vane said. He looked her up and down, considering. "I think the first thing you need is a shower" – Mandy was suddenly uncomfortably aware that she *stank* – "and then we can get down to engineering. Follow me."

Mandy obeyed, stepping out of the cabin and into the ship's scarred corridors. "Anyone with a silver star on their shoulder is a superior officer," Vane said, as they walked down a flight of steps and into a washroom. "Do whatever they tell you to do, without arguing. They have leave to whip you if you refuse to obey. Anyone else…you're welcome to fight them off, if you can."

"Oh," Mandy said. A moment later, she realised what he meant and blanched. "I…"

Vane snorted. "Wash as quickly as you can," he ordered, "and then we can go down to engineering."

Mandy wanted to linger for hours under the hot stream of water, even though she was still wearing the tattered shipsuit, but she didn't want to irritate Vane. No wonder everyone obeyed their officers, if the alternative was being whipped like that. But Captain Stalker didn't have to whip his men to enforce discipline…she couldn't imagine any of the Marines being whipped for disobedience. But then, *she* hadn't wanted to come on board the pirate ship, while the Marines had volunteered for service with the Marine Corps. For all she knew, the remainder of the pirate crew had been shanghaied too.

A hot stream of air dried her skin and – feeling human for the first time in far too long – she allowed him to lead her down into the engineering compartment. There was a guard outside, who saluted as Vane approached, before taking a long hard look at Mandy. Mandy winced, all too aware of just how much flesh the tattered outfit showed off, before realising that the guard was in charge of preventing intruders from entering the engineering compartment. The pirates wouldn't want just anyone accessing the heart of their ship.

"She can enter with me or another of the senior monkeys," Vane said, to the guard. *Monkeys* was slang for engineers, Mandy recalled, something the RockRats had used to make fun of the trainees. It's origin was somewhere lost in the mists of time. "If she's on her own, restrain her and summon me."

Mandy swallowed hard as they passed through another heavy airlock and into the engineering compartment. The Empire's designs all followed the same basic pattern; looking at the Phase Core, right in front of her as she entered the section, convinced her that she was onboard a heavy cruiser. Long strands of solid power conductors led to the four fusion reactors that kept the ship going, which were in turn linked to the ship's fuel tanks. The entire compartment was heavily armoured, ensuring that a disaster with the ship's drives wouldn't take out the entire ship, while making it harder for any outside vessel to disable the ship's drives and bring her to a halt.

The engineering compartment was neater than the rest of the ship, or at least the parts she'd seen as she'd been dragged through the ship's innards. But then, that made a certain kind of sense; careless or messy engineers didn't tend to live very long. The best of them, she'd been told, had been trained to pay careful attention to detail, as well as keep all of their tools and spare parts comprehensively organised. Leaving tools and components scattered everywhere was asking for trouble. She saw a handful of other engineers as she was led through the compartment, into the side room that served as the chief engineer's office. It was evident that he spent as little time in the office as possible.

"Take a seat," Vane ordered, as he studied a situation board on one of the bulkheads. It looked as though one of the ship's fusion reactors was fluctuating – and that another simply wasn't working at all. Mandy had been taught that attempting to repair a damaged fusion reactor was an exercise in futility, but that had been before the Empire withdrew from the nearby sectors. The pirates might have no choice apart from trying to repair the complex and fragile piece of equipment.

Vane turned back to her and dropped a single component in her lap. "Tell me," he said, "exactly what you would do with that?"

Mandy hesitated. The component was a black box…no, she knew what it was. She'd seen enough of them during her training. "You plug it in to reroute power," she said, finally. "If you add it to a computer node, you can ensure that the node has enough power to function…"

Vane nodded and fired another question at her. Mandy braced herself as she answered that question, and the next, and the next…it seemed she was being given an exam. A handful of her answers were wrong and Vane painstakingly corrected her, but he seemed pleased enough with the others, although it rapidly became clear that Mandy had less hands-on experience than he would have liked. One answer had him threatening to whip her again before pointing out that trying to reconfigure the drive fields while the ship was in motion was likely to cause an explosive backlash. The ship should have had safeties to prevent such a backlash, but from Vane's response, she had the feeling that the pirates had disconnected half of the safety systems. She'd been told that the Empire massively over-engineered its ships, yet removing the safeties didn't strike her as a good idea.

She was sweating by the time Vane finished her exam, feeling her stomach growling its hunger. Vane didn't seem to notice; he paced back and forth in the compartment, muttering to himself in a language Mandy didn't recognise. Most planets taught their populations Empire Standard as well as their local language, assuming that they managed to preserve a separate tongue at all; it had never occurred to her that using a second language would make an effective code. But then, most spacers would have access to some form of translation software.

"You are not prepared for work on the main power systems," Vane said. Mandy wasn't surprised, although she *was* disappointed. Given time, she was sure she could figure out how to wreck the entire ship from engineering. "Fortunately, there is no shortage of other work that requires a trained technician. The waste disposal and hydroponics facilities, for example."

Mandy shuddered. She had never realised just how much forethought had to go into building space stations and starships, at least until her first visit to Orbit Station. Space wasn't a planet; everything from the atmosphere to the crew's biological wastes had to be carefully handled, or simply removed from the environment. Orbit station had processed the crew's wastes and dropped the remainder into Avalon's atmosphere. Starships tended to shoot anything that couldn't be recycled into the nearest sun.

"Follow me," Vane said. He stood up and led her towards the door. "I strongly suggest that you do not go running around the ship on your own. Some of the crew will consider you a potential target."

Mandy shivered as they walked back into the engineering compartment – and stopped dead as she saw Michael, on the other side of the chamber. He was being interrogated by another engineering officer, presumably one of Vane's subordinates as he didn't have a silver star. Mandy wanted to call to him, particularly when he looked up and saw her, but she didn't quite dare. Who knew *what* would happen if the pirates ended up believing that they had trained together? But surely it was too late to prevent them from getting that impression?

Vane stopped in front of a hatch and opened it, revealing a Jefferies tube. Mandy followed him up inside the tube, allowing herself a moment of relief as the hatch clanged shut, cutting off the noise from engineering. Instead, she could hear a dull thrumming sound echoing through the entire ship, louder than the sound she recalled from the Marine Transport Ship. The pirate ship – it struck her suddenly that she didn't even know the ship's *name* – wasn't a healthy ship at all.

"This ship is called the *Sword*," Vane said, as he climbed through the tubes. The gravity field pulled at her as she climbed up a ladder leading up to the upper levels, leaving her feeling tired and dizzy. "The Admiral uses it as his flagship and so it must be kept in pristine condition."

Mandy glanced at him, sharply. It didn't take an expert to realise that the ship was *not* in pristine condition. As they approached the network of pipes that made up part of the ship's plumbing system, it became increasingly obvious. Hundreds of components had been allowed to decay, wires hung down from the ceiling – presenting a hazard to life and limb – and at least one of the pipes had started to leak. She wrinkled her nose against the stench, realising just why the pirates had given her this job. If she accidentally killed herself, it would only be a small loss to the pirate crew.

Bastards, she thought, as they came to a halt underneath the main set of piping. The damage was much more extensive here, to the point where human wastes had begun to rot away the surrounding area. Starships were designed with considerable redundancy – losing the entire compartment wouldn't cripple the *Sword* – but it might be lethal if they ever went into battle against the Imperial Navy. Going to full power might suddenly reveal *all* of the ship's little problems.

"Tell me," Vane said, with suspicious politeness, "how you would fix this problem?"

Mandy grimaced. The smell alone made it hard to think properly. It would be nice to find a shortcut, but she had the idea that the only real solution would be to fix the piping and then start repairing all of the power conduits, one by one. If she stopped the *cause* of the problem, she could then take the time to mop up the damage...

But if she did, would she not be helping the pirates?

The thought nagged at her mind. Mindy, her sister, had probably been taught what to do if she were ever taken prisoner. *Mandy* had never expected to face an enemy POW camp, let alone involuntary servitude. And if she helped the pirates, would she be charged with piracy when – if – she returned home? What would the Marines say if they discovered that she'd helped the pirates maintain their ship? What would *Jasmine* say if she found out the truth?

But the alternative was being whipped, or worse.

"Deal with the damaged processors first, then start fixing the mess," she said, finally. A normal starship would have internal monitoring software that would allow the maintenance crews to target the most heavily-damaged parts of the network, but she rather doubted that the pirate monitoring software would be working properly. "And we'd need gas masks."

Vane laughed, the first glimpse of humour she'd seen from him. "You can have one," he said, dryly. "I'll take you to lunch and then you can get to work. And while you're eating, you can decide what else you need for your task."

Lunch consisted of a stew so unpleasant that ration bars would have been preferable. Mandy ate it in a crowded dining compartment, uncomfortably aware of the eyes mentally undressing her as she ate her meal. The pirates looked a rough lot, probably made more unpleasant by the food and drink rations; almost all of them were male. Only two women appeared to be full members of the crew and they looked worse than the men. Another woman, seated at an isolated table, seemed to be having real problems eating her stew. It wasn't until she turned to look at Mandy that Mandy realised that the woman's teeth had all been removed, making it impossible for her to chew her meal.

"She had too much pride," Vane said, by way of explanation. "Eventually, they knocked out her teeth to make it impossible for her to bite when they used her."

Mandy swallowed hard to prevent herself from throwing up. The very thought was horrifying, and disgusting, and…it could happen to her. Or to any of the others, come to think of it. For all she knew, the pirates kept male sex slaves too. The woman looked beaten down, her exposed flesh showing marks from where she'd been hit, time and time again. It was just too unpleasant to contemplate. Even the bandits hadn't been so nasty to their captives…

But how would you know? She asked herself. You spent most of your first months on Avalon in a haze of bitterness and loneliness…

Vane stood up. "What other pieces of equipment do you want for your task?"

Mandy dragged her thoughts back to the matter at hand with an effort. Vane had timed the visit to the dining compartment perfectly, she realised, giving Mandy a glimpse of what awaited her if she failed to please her new masters. It was a very convincing argument, she had to admit; she didn't want to end up a brainless piece of meat, servicing men until she died.

"A pump, a storage tank, a gas mask and some tools," she said, slowly. She'd have to empty out the septic tank to clean it. *That* wasn't going to be pleasant. Absently, she wondered how the pirates managed to survive in such an unhealthy atmosphere. Surely, they knew the concept of basic hygiene if nothing else. "And perhaps a direct link to one of the recycling chambers."

Vane nodded and led her from the compartment. Mandy followed him, silently resolving to be the most loyal minion the Admiral could hope for, until she got a chance to escape. And then she would do whatever she could to stop the Admiral in his tracks. And if she could help the poor slave girl, she would do that too.

Carefully, she eyed Vane's back and considered where best to stick the knife.

CHAPTER TWELVE

> We had known, of course, that there were other planets in the sector. Avalon was far from alone, even if it was out along the Rim. But the five light years between Avalon and the nearest other inhabited world might have been an impassable gulf, as far as we were concerned. Without a starship, reaching it was impossible.
>
> But others, sadly, did have starships.
>
> - Professor Leo Caesius, *The Perilous Dawn* (unpublished).

"The good news is that we captured the ship largely intact," Kitty Stevenson said. The Imperial Navy officer looked tired and worn. "Unfortunately, we didn't manage to secure their database."

Edward frowned. "They took out the main database?"

"They didn't use it," Kitty clarified. "The engineers say that they stepped the entire thing right down and replaced it with a portable system from a different starship. That system is now dust, leaving us without any navigational data for tracking the pirates down."

"I see," Edward said. "So we don't know where they came from at all?"

The thought made him scowl. Imperial Navy starships recorded a great deal of data about their surroundings at all times, starting with enough information on the nearby stars to allow their past voyages to be reconstructed, even if the main database had been lost. Indeed, one of the tests posed to analysts was to have them reconstruct a ship's course, condition and crew status from the recorded data. But if the pirates had stepped the entire system down, there would be little data for the analysts to work from.

"I'm not sure about that," Kitty admitted. "We *did* interrogate the pirates at some length and we know quite a bit about their operations. Including, I should add, a planet they have effectively taken over."

Edward nodded as he led the way into the Council Chamber. "You can brief the Council," he said, flatly. "And then we'll have to decide what to do with the information."

Thankfully, the new Council didn't waste time with formalities. Edward was permitted to speak at once. "We captured the pirate ship," he said, without preamble. "A number of pirates were taken prisoner and interrogated. The news is not good."

He nodded to Kitty, who stood up. "The prisoners all claim to work for someone called the Admiral," she said. "According to them, the Admiral is a pirate warlord who believes that he can build an empire of his own in the wake of Earth's withdrawal from this sector. They knew very little about his forces, but they do believe that he has at least seventeen starships under his command, including a hard core of ex-Imperial Navy warships. He also seems to have access to a source of fuel, although we are unable to guess at its nature."

Edward nodded, thoughtfully. It was possible to use a starship to skim gas from a gas giant's atmosphere, to mine fuel from lunar rock or even to process it from water. A cloudscoop was massively more efficient, but they had their limitations – and they were sitting ducks, easy targets for anyone with a missile and bad intentions. There was no reason why a handful of pirate ships couldn't keep supplying themselves with fuel indefinitely.

"The Admiral apparently gave them orders for dealing with us after we surrendered," Kitty continued. "Everyone with technical experience was to be dispatched to one of his bases, where they would be put to work maintaining his fleet; Avalon itself would be responsible for supplying his fleet with food, fuel and…entertainment. If we refused to cooperate, we would be hammered from orbit until we gave in and accepted defeat. In short, the Admiral believes he can build an empire and there is very little in the sector to stop him."

"But you took their ship," Julian pointed out. "Surely you can do the same to any other ship?"

"What we did rather depended upon the advantage of surprise," Edward said, before Kitty could answer. "The pirates could have had another ship watching from a safe distance, one that would have recorded what happened to their first ship and then slipped out of the system. We cannot count on getting so lucky again."

"Besides, the next squadron he sends here might be bigger," Kitty added. "Even three ships would be difficult to board and storm at the same time."

She cleared her throat, continuing the briefing. "According to the pirates, their last port of call – at least, the last one they can identify for us – was Elysium," she said. "I'm afraid that they are currently holding the planet in bondage."

"The planet of the nomads?" Gaby asked, thoughtfully. "What do they have to offer the pirates?"

Edward had wondered that himself. Elysium had started life as a fairly normal colony world, but – not too unlike Avalon – it had developed in an unusual direction. The Empire had wanted to transport a number of minority populations away from the Core Worlds and had selected Elysium as their destination, believing that the debris-rich system would one day be a jewel in the Empire's crown. But the population, not all of whom were willing to become cogs in the Empire's machine, had started regressing to hunter-gatherer clans, rather than concentrating on their economic development. The Empire had found it hard to deal with the clans – after all, they weren't actually *rebelling* – and Elysium had been largely abandoned, even before the Empire had pulled out of the sector completely.

The last report the Marines had received – the compressed datafiles from the Commandant of the Marine Corps – had noted that the few remaining corporations had pulled out of the system completely, leaving a small nexus of RockRats alone. Anything could have happened in six months, but he rather doubted that the RockRats could have built a cloudscoop or anything else the pirates could use. Perhaps the Admiral had just selected Elysium as his first target to test the concept. It wasn't as if the planet could fight back.

"Food, drink and women," he said, bluntly. He looked around the room, wondering which way the different Councillors would jump. "Our only option is to go on the offensive."

Gaby leaned forward. "Do you even know where to attack?"

Edward scowled. Without proper sensors, one star system was very much like another – and the pirates had taken basic security precautions to conceal the location of their hidden base. The prisoners all agreed that it had been a settled asteroid – there were millions within the Empire, or past the Rim – but they didn't actually know *where* it was, and searching at random was unlikely to produce a definite result. Indeed, even if they did pick the right star system, they would have to get very lucky to locate the asteroid base. It would be easy for the pirates to hide it from passive sensors.

"Elysium," he said. He had to smile at their reactions. "Right now, we know that there is a small detachment of pirates on the planet's surface, and in orbit. We can get to them using the pirate ship and take them out. And then we might be able to capture someone who knows something more useful."

"Might," Gaby repeated. "And what happens if the Admiral's fleet returns to this system while you're gone?"

"We lose control of the orbitals," Edward admitted. He hesitated, and then pressed on. Civilians often had to have things explained to them that any military officer would understand instinctively. "If we sit here, with a single captured starship, we lose. They *need* the cloudscoop; they will eventually return to the system, expecting the pirates we captured to have secured it for their use. At that point, we will be snookered. We have to take the offensive now, while we have a chance."

Julian looked down at his hands. "How many other worlds does the Admiral have under his control?"

"We're uncertain," Kitty said. "Some of the pirates gave us different answers, but they all believed that they were telling the truth. The worst case is seven other worlds, none of them more advanced than Elysium itself. I think they may have been leaving the more advanced worlds for last."

It sounded reasonable, Edward thought, but he didn't believe that it was true. The Admiral needed the cloudscoop more than anything else; indeed, if Edward had been running his campaign, he would have targeted Avalon *first*. There had to be something else going on…or maybe the Admiral had a vast stockpile of fuel for his early operations. Every intelligence analyst in the Empire knew the dangers of over-analysing data…

"I have a question," one of the older Councillors said. He had been elected by a farming community near the Badlands, one of the ones that had been at the mercy of the bandits until the Marines had arrived. "Why should we risk ourselves to help the other worlds? What did they do to help us when we needed it?"

Edward winced. The hell of it was that the Councillor had a point. Avalon's Governor had been begging for help for years before his understrength company had arrived on the planet, during which time the bandits had run riot and the Crackers had carefully prepared their forces for a final battle to determine the planet's future. But then, none of the other worlds could have done much to help, except perhaps sending mercenaries to fight beside the Civil Guard, and that would have been expensive.

"I can show you the records from the WARCAT team's survey of the ship, if you like," Kitty said sharply. "The pirates committed all sorts of atrocities against their prisoners – and they would have committed them on Avalon, if they had managed to beat off the Marines. We recovered datachips containing recordings of some of their other antics. One chip records the rape, torture and murder of a girl who couldn't be older than ten…"

"I know how unpleasant some people can be," the Councillor snapped at her. "God knows, I saw enough of what the bandits did to my people. I just don't see why we should divert our forces to Elysium when we have enough problems at home."

"I wasn't planning to send any of the Knights," Edward said, quietly. "They're not trained for operations in space. I intend to take three Marine platoons and a handful of engineering technicians to help run the ship."

"Leaving us defenceless," the Councillor said.

"There will be two full platoons and the Knights left behind to hold the line," Edward said, refusing to allow himself to become angry. "And the single ship we have – in very poor condition – will not be able to provide much resistance if the pirates return to Avalon. Having her well away from the planet might be more useful than keeping her in orbit."

"It is true that the other worlds in the sector gave us no help when we needed it," Gaby said. Edward saw her smile and grinned inwardly. Gaby had been on the other side during the war and wouldn't have *wanted* the Governor receiving help from other worlds. "On the other hand, we do not want the Admiral as a neighbour – and we could use friendly relations with our other neighbours. I believe that we should send what help we can."

"I have a better idea," the obstructive Councillor said. "Why don't we ask the Empire for help?"

Edward sighed. "The last we heard was that the Grand Senate had closed down the Midway and Trafalgar fleet bases," he said. "Assuming that the Jutland fleet base remains active, it will take at least a month to get there with the ship we captured and another month for any help to return to the system. And that assumes that the base CO has a squadron at his disposal that he is willing to send so far from his sector."

He scowled. "And even when Midway was active, the Empire was reluctant to send any ships as far out as Avalon," he added, grimly. "I don't think that we can count on the Empire for help…"

Julian gaped at him. "But the Admiral wants to build his own empire…"

"The Empire was never very willing to confront problems along the Rim," Edward admitted. It was no coincidence that most of the horror stories about pirates, insurgents and outright rebels came from the Rim. Concentrating a major fleet presence at the edge of the Empire was expensive, time-consuming…and tended to be futile. The pirates tended to move to other sectors, or simply wait until the warships had to return to their bases. "We cannot expect them to do anything about the Admiral."

His scowl deepened. Even in its reduced state, the Imperial Navy could smash any pirate fleet with ease, if it could be concentrated against the pirates. But the Navy's commanders had been reluctant to get their ships scratched for decades; he remembered the dark days on Han, when the Imperial Navy ships had refused to support the troops on the ground out of fear of the defences the rebels had managed to put into orbit. Quick action might have halted the slaughter long before it got out of hand.

"We vote," Gaby said. "All those in favour of dispatching a mission to Elysium?"

Edward counted the votes quickly. It was closer than he had hoped, but enough Councillors had voted in favour to allow the mission to proceed. Silently, he went through his basic concept of operations as the Councillors chatted about other matters, deciding who was going to accompany the captured starship to Elysium. First Platoon would be going, by right of conquest; Third and Fourth Platoons would probably be the best to accompany them. Fourth Platoon in particular had a number of veterans of operations in space. If they hadn't been on deployment when the RockRat base had been attacked, he would have sent them to orbit station instead.

"There's another issue that should be addressed," Governor Brent Roeder said. "Should we seek to make closer ties with Elysium, if we succeed in liberating them?"

Edward wondered, absently, just how much it must have cost him to make that statement. The Governor had been resolutely loyal to the Empire and had only reluctantly accepted the reshaped Council after the Battle of Camelot. No doubt part of him had expected the Empire to complain about the outcome and blame the man on the spot. Governors were important people, but their careers depended upon patronage from the Grand Senate and the new Council had no ties at all to the Empire's political masters. It would be much harder to exploit Avalon in future.

"I think so," Gaby said, finally. "Even if they can't do much to help us now, in the long run…"

There was a long pause as they considered the possibilities. The Marines had brought a massive infusion of technology along with them to Avalon. Given enough time, Avalon would start producing its own starships, particularly now that the Empire's restrictions on industrial growth were a non-issue. The RockRats had even noted that it might be possible to start producing their own ships within a year.

And then…Edward could understand the temptations facing the Council. If the Admiral could dream of empire, why couldn't Avalon build up its own network of allied and subordinate worlds? If nothing else, a multi-system political entity would be in a better position to negotiate with the Empire than a multitude of isolated systems. Making alliances with the populations of the other worlds in the sector might be the first step towards building a better union.

It was a thought that nagged at him, in the darkness of the night. He was sworn to the Empire and the Emperor, the ideal of unity that had saved the human race from wars that might have exterminated it. In the Empire's Golden Age, they had wanted to bring every world into the Empire, believing that it was for the best. And now…he was watching as the Empire crumbled and the first successor states began to arise.

The discussion took longer than the argument over sending help to Elysium in the first place, but eventually Professor Caesius was chosen as Avalon's representative to Elysium. Edward wasn't sure if that was a mercy or not – he hadn't seen the Professor since telling him that his daughter was missing, presumed dead – yet he had to admit that there were few other people who could do the job. The Professor had considerable experience in dealing with people from different backgrounds; after all, he'd taught on Earth, where students came from all over the Empire.

It was a relief when the meeting finally ended and he could walk out of the building, back towards the spaceport. Camelot still felt largely deserted; the Council, unsurprisingly, had decided not to start moving people back to the city just yet. There was no way to tell when the next hostile starship might arrive and announce its presence by firing on the city. In the long run, Edward knew, they'd have to build some planetary defence stations for themselves, or Avalon would be permanently vulnerable. But they'd have to build starships too.

It's too soon, he thought, sourly. Given five years, they could have turned Avalon into a nexus of starship construction. But they'd barely had six months. *It's far too soon.*

Shaking his head, he linked into the command network and started to issue orders. Third and Fourth Platoons would make their way to orbit, where they would be joined by a small army of technical experts and everyone they could find with starship experience. The preliminary report suggested that the pirate ship would require weeks of work to render it safe, but they didn't have weeks. They would have to carry out basic maintenance on the way to Elysium.

Oddly, he found himself smiling. After the complexities of fighting the Crackers and building a new government, hunting down pirates should be simple. And then they could all be legally exterminated.

CHAPTER THIRTEEN

> Given what flowered from it, many people find it hard to believe that it all started with a single starship that threatened to explode under its new owners at any moment. When I think about the risks we took, I start to shake, even many years after the event. Not that I thought about it at the time, really; after Mandy's disappearance, I cared nothing for my own survival. Being on an explosive starship might just have provided a way to end it all.
>
> - Professor Leo Caesius, *The Perilous Dawn* (unpublished).

"You do realise you get to rename the starship?"

Jasmine turned to see Kitty Stevenson entering the compartment. The Imperial Navy officer had always rubbed her the wrong way, if only because Imperial Intelligence and the Imperial Navy had blundered badly on Han. Technically, Kitty wasn't in her line of command – Marines answered to their own officers, rather than to the Imperial Navy – but there was such a thing as showing respect to other officers.

"You commanded the mission that captured it," Kitty explained, when Jasmine lifted her eyebrows. The hours since they had captured the ship had been hectic; they'd taken the prisoners off the ship, along with their slaves, and then vented the entire ship to exterminate the bugs that infested the lower levels. After *that*, they'd started working on the ship's systems, trying to bring it back to full working order. "Tradition says that you name it."

"The *Horny Goat*," Blake suggested. "Or what about the *Desirous Dildo*?"

"I am *not* going into battle on a ship called *Dildo*," Jasmine said, shaking her head. "And why would we want to name a ship after you?"

Blake laughed. "But just think about all the kids who will have to read about this mission in their history books," he said. "Don't you want to give them a laugh?"

Jasmine snorted, although she did have to admit that the thought was appealing. But then, how many historical starships could the average person name? There were far too many people on Earth who believed that Neil Armstrong had captained the first starship to travel beyond the speed of light, rather than the starship being named after Armstrong, who had actually been the first man to walk on the moon. And then there was *Dauntless*, which had been the flagship of the Imperial Navy during the Unification Wars, and *Harrington*, which had been the most successful starship at hunting down pirates…how many others were even remembered? Hadn't the Professor once said that a galaxy that forgot its past had no future either?

"Maybe something simpler," she said, as she turned back to their work. It seemed that there wasn't a single part of the ship that hadn't been damaged in some way, either through mistreatment or simple avoidance of maintenance. The Civil Guard's worst units certainly didn't bother to maintain their own weapons, although that wasn't a mistake that the Marines made themselves. Back on the Slaughterhouse, they'd been shown exactly how easily their weapons could become degraded through lack of cleaning and maintenance. And then they wouldn't be fit for combat.

"Choose something soon," Kitty said, as she turned to leave the compartment. "We're planning to leave in six hours."

Jasmine watched her go and then pulled out another strand of corroded wire. "Perhaps the *Shithouse*," Blake added, dryly. "Or the *Thunder Box*. Or…"

"I think you'd ensure that it wasn't suitable for children," Jasmine said. The less said about thunder boxes, the better. "Maybe we should just call her the *Dancing Fool*."

Blake made a show of rolling his eyes. "That isn't quite as…amusing," he objected. "And the kids wouldn't understand."

"It might encourage them to look it up," Jasmine countered. Carefully, she finished pulling out the wire and started to replace it, carefully logging each step. "And then they might decide to follow in his footsteps."

"Maybe," Blake said. "But *Shithouse* definitely fits this ship."

Jasmine couldn't disagree. She knew how hard it could be to do basic maintenance, day in and day out, but anyone who spent their lives in space *had* to understand the importance of keeping their equipment working. Those who didn't normally ended up dead; if the Imperial Navy hadn't designed its ships to be so forgiving, the pirates would probably have killed themselves by now. At least they hadn't managed to destroy the internal monitoring system, thankfully. It could be used to point the repair crews to the areas that needed immediate attention.

She'd been on long operations into the bush, back on the Slaughterhouse and later on Han – and Avalon. No one emerged from one of those feeling clean, but the pirates hadn't seemed to care at all. The stink, thankfully, had been blown away when the atmosphere had been vented and the entire ship had been frozen, yet she knew that wouldn't last. They'd have to spend hours washing the deck among other things, just to make the ship safe for habitation. If they hadn't had boosted immune systems, she would have worried about catching diseases from the ship's interior.

"I was told that one of the pirates was a Cobra," Blake said, changing the subject. "Do you think there might be more of them out there?"

Jasmine straightened up and looked down at her work before answering. "I suppose it is possible," she said. Cobras didn't have biological enhancements; they were enhanced in labs, all of which were supposed to have been shut down. No one knew where the pirate Cobra had come from, or if there were more of them out there. "Maybe someone set up a whole production line out along the Rim."

"Maybe." Blake agreed. He grinned, nastily. "I always wanted to know if I could take one of them."

"You only wanted to know if you could once there was a chance you might encounter one outside simulations," Jasmine corrected him. They'd all faced heavily-enhanced opponents during basic training, where the enhancements could be simulated to a far higher level than was possible in reality. She still remembered being tossed around the training field by a simulated warrior – called a Draka for reasons lost in time – before realising that it was a trick. They hadn't been *meant* to fight the Draka hand-to-hand. "Who knows? Maybe you *could* beat one..."

"Unless it happens to be a young and sexy Cobra," Joe said, as he entered the compartment. "Aux-Lieutenant Delacroix's complements, Lieutenant, and would we be so kind as to check out our quarters and make them safe for habitation?"

Blake grinned. "And what exactly did you do to piss off Layla so badly she sent you up here as a messenger boy?"

"I volunteered," Joe said. Jasmine and Blake exchanged disbelieving glances. "I heard that Third and Fourth are coming to join us and I wanted to make sure that we got the best sleeping quarters on the ship."

"The ones that only stink of urine, as opposed to urine and shit?" Blake asked. "Or perhaps the ones that will probably electrocute us all if the ship goes to full power?"

Jasmine shook her head. "Honestly," she said. "It's like dealing with a mob of adult children. Does it really matter which set of quarters we get? We're going to be jammed in so tightly that we'll be glad of the chance to go on a suicide mission."

Joe nodded. "The Lieutenant was saying that about half of the quarters on this ship are going to have to be sealed up completely," he said. "If we had a proper shipyard..."

"And while we're wishing, I'd like an entire squadron of modern warships and a full division of Marines," Jasmine said, as she headed towards the hatch. Blake and Joe followed her. "I think we just have to make do with what we've got."

Marines were used to bedding down in uncomfortable positions. On bases, or transport ships, Marine platoons were given a set of barracks and told to organise themselves; on FOBs, sleeping quarters could be as simple as a roll of bedding under the stars, or a cold stone floor cleared of all traces of its former occupants. Jasmine had long ago grown used to sharing her sleeping quarters with men, even men who weren't her fellow Marines. Someone – a particularly stupid member of the Civil Guard – had tried to slip into her bedding on Han and she'd stuck a knife in him. Even so, the quarters on the pirate ship were truly unpleasant.

The basic sleeping facilities were standardised, but a quick check revealed that the washrooms didn't work and the sonic showers were inoperative. All of the bedding the pirates had used had been taken out of the compartment and dumped into the planet's atmosphere, which was something of a relief. She didn't want to have to use bedding that had last been used by unsanitary pirates. The remainder of the platoon arrived and started working on clearing the remaining bunks, before ordering new bedding from the planet's surface. Compared to the clockwork precision of a division of Marines embarking on a transport ship, their preparations were laughable. It wasn't a pleasant thought.

But then, the Marine Corps had plenty of experience boarding its own starships. They had never practiced converting a pirate ship into a transport before…

"They say that the bedding is on the way," she said. Marines travelled light; Jasmine had been a Rifleman when she'd left Earth and she hadn't had a large baggage allowance. Besides, they weren't leaving Avalon forever. "And plenty of ration bars."

"I'm sure there are laws against cruel and unusual punishments," Blake grumbled. "What did we do to deserve ration bars?"

"Hey," Joe pointed out. "You want to rely on this ship's food processor?"

Blake scowled, but had to admit that Joe was right. The better food processors almost invariably produced tasteless slop; the worse designs produced food that was technically nutritious, yet tasted appalling. And the pirates probably hadn't bothered to maintain their food processors any more than they'd maintained the rest of the ship, even though it helped keep them alive. Jasmine had heard that the engineers had taken one look at the life support systems, specifically the air scrubbers, and almost fainted. The pirates might have been on the verge of killing themselves simply through polluting their own air.

His communicator buzzed. "This is Stalker," the Colonel said. "Did you select a name for the ship, Lieutenant?"

Jasmine nodded, although she knew that her superior couldn't see her. "The *Dancing Fool,* sir," she said. "I thought it was appropriate."

There was a long pause. "Acceptable," the Colonel said. "I will have the ship renamed just before we set out on our mission."

"Good choice," Joe said, softly. "It might just remind us that we need to be daring."

"Yeah," Blake said. "But come on – can you imagine the ship being called the *Horny Goat?"*

The Dancing Fool had been a Marine, back in the days of the Unification Wars, one of the rare heroes who had actually done almost everything they said he'd done. Jasmine hadn't been sure if she believed the stories of his exploits when she'd been taught about them on the Slaughterhouse, but he had been an inspiration to her and the rest of her class. His missions had been the stuff of legends, with him just smashing his way through obstacle after obstacle and never giving up, even when he seemed to have overreached himself. They just hadn't made men like him after the Empire was solidly established.

And now they were going to need more men like him.

"I'd prefer not to think about it," she said. "And we have to prepare for departure."

"This ship doesn't smell very healthy," the Professor said.

"It isn't," Edward said, shortly. It had been barely two days since he'd seen Professor Caesius, but he was profoundly shocked by the change in his friend. The Professor hadn't looked so withdrawn when he'd been evicted from Earth for questioning the state of the Empire. "You really don't want to know what the pirates were doing for their own entertainment."

"I believe I can guess," the Professor said. He looked over at Edward, grimly. "Is there any news?"

Edward hesitated, just long enough for the Professor to notice. "I don't know anything for certain," he admitted, finally. The Professor had a right to know, but he didn't want to raise the man's hopes. "They did have orders to take prisoners and…Mandy was an engineering student. She would be *useful* to them."

"Useful," the Professor repeated. "You know, I was so proud of her when she finally started to work."

"I know," Edward said, gently. The old Mandy had been a teenage brat, plain and simple, someone who had bitched and moaned about being forced to move to Avalon. But she'd improved and turned into someone with real promise…and her sister might make a good Knight. "What did your wife have to say?"

"She blamed me for Mandy's capture," the Professor said. Edward noticed that he didn't refer to his daughter as *dead*. "If I hadn't been exiled out here, she said, Mandy would have lived a full and happy life on Earth…at least until the Undercity exploded and Earth collapsed into a nightmare."

Edward nodded in understanding. The average citizen of the Empire had no idea of the storm that was already pressing against the establishment. They saw the Empire as strong and didn't see the weaknesses underneath, or the cracks running through the military and bureaucracy that would eventually tear it apart. All they saw was the endless bounty of the Empire – and forgot that it had to be paid for, by someone. The Professor's calculations of what would start happening, soon enough, were horrific. How could anyone *not* believe that the Empire was in serious trouble?

But maybe Earth's fall would be delayed long enough for Mandy to live out her life. If so, it would take place during her children's lives. Edward wouldn't bet one credit on anyone's chances of surviving in the middle city as the hordes raged up from below; the middle classes were deliberately kept disarmed, just to keep them from posing a problem to the Empire's rulers. The Fall of Earth would be an orgy of looting, rape and slaughter on an utterly unprecedented scale.

He led the Professor up through the ship's passageways – none of the internal elevators were working – and onto the bridge. The pirates had taken out half of the original consoles and replaced them with cannibalised items from several other ships, including a helm console that had evidently been taken from a freighter. Edward was surprised that they'd even been able to get it to work; the engineering crews had suggested that the pirates had had the help of a genuine shipyard, perhaps one of the civilian yards that were happy to do work without asking too many questions. Or maybe they had a secret shipyard somewhere out along the Rim.

Kitty Stevenson was working on one of the consoles when they entered, but she stood up to welcome them. "The ship should be ready to depart on schedule, sir," she reported. Technically, she was the vessel's commander – they didn't have many people with the right qualifications – but Edward was her superior officer. Naval protocol hadn't really been designed for such a situation. "We're just loading the rest of our supplies now."

The Professor leaned forward. "How long will it take to get to Elysium?"

"Roughly nine days," Kitty said. "We could do it in four, but I'd prefer not to press the drive too hard until we have a better idea of its condition. Right now, a single fluctuation in the drive core and we'd be drifting in interstellar space for the rest of our lives. And, of course, once we get there we're going to have to sneak into the system."

"Which may be difficult," Edward put in. Starship sensors were tuned to watch for starships coming out of Phase Space along the Phase Limit – and they dared not assume that the pirates would have neglected their sensors badly enough for them to slip in without being detected. The only sure method of sneaking into the system was to drop out of Phase Space some distance from the Phase Limit and crawl into the system at sublight speed. "And then we have to deal with the pirates."

"And anyone else who might be in the area," the Professor said. Edward gave him a sharp look, and then nodded. Who knew *what* the Admiral might be doing with his ships? "Do we have any idea what we will be facing?"

"No," Edward admitted, reluctantly. He *hated* operating blind. The fog of war had swallowed up everything more than a short distance outside Avalon's atmosphere, ensuring that they would never truly know what was out there, waiting for them. It had been so much easier operating on Earth, where the finest units in the Imperial Navy were based. No pirate would be able to get close to *Earth*...

"Of course not," the Professor said, when Edward said that out loud. "They're all in the Grand Senate."

Two hours later, the *Dancing Fool* groaned into life and headed towards the Phase Limit. Edward sat on the bridge, watching grimly as the technicians checked and rechecked the systems, noting down critical components that required inspection or immediate replacement. Given a completely free choice, he would have preferred to scrap the light cruiser completely, but they didn't have any other starships.

"I don't think they ever wanted to fight a warship," Kitty said. "We can barely get one-third of this ship's rated speed out of its engines. Even a merchant skipper could probably outrun her if he got a head start."

"Let's just hope that our target comes to us," Edward said reluctantly. A plan that depended upon the enemy doing something stupid was a plan designed to fail. "At least they can't cause an entire planet to disappear."

CHAPTER FOURTEEN

Why did the Empire find it so hard to deal with the crisis? Every one of my students who looks at the problem comes up with a different answer. The Empire's leaders, on Earth, didn't realise that they had a problem. The Empire's leaders didn't want to admit that they had a problem. The Empire's leaders didn't want to share power, or start breaking down the established interest groups that were facilitating the crash, or... all of those theories are valid.

But the core reason, I think, was more fundamental. Imagine a single man walking through a desert. That man can change his path at will. Now imagine a massive army doing the same; for the army, changing course is difficult and even dangerous. The chaos caused by changing its course may even be worse than staying on the same path.

This, in short, was the true problem of the Empire.

- Professor Leo Caesius, *The Perilous Dawn* (unpublished).

"Yuk," Mandy muttered.

It had taken her four days to empty the tanks, clear the pipes and clean the interior of the tube of the waste that had spewed out of the damaged system. Four days, during which she'd stunk to high heaven of piss and shit and things she didn't want to think about; four days when the pirates had pointed and laughed at her from a distance as she worked. At least none of them had wanted to touch her during that time, thankfully. The stench would keep the most ardent lover away from her.

Fixing the interior sanitation system hadn't been that difficult, once she'd cleaned it out and replaced a handful of the damaged pipes. She was at a loss to understand why it had gotten so badly jammed up in the first place, until she'd seen some of the things the pirates had been jamming into the tubes. Back on Avalon, they'd been warned that the waste disposal system had its limitations – and orbit station's engineers had maintained the system properly. The pirates had never bothered to actually maintain the interior of their ship.

Once the tube had been cleaned, she started making a list of components that needed to be replaced. Vane had made it clear that she wasn't to start fiddling with the ship's internal power conduits without supervision, but there was no other way to fix the mess. She found it hard to understand his paranoia – the worst she'd been able to figure out how to do was burn out the entire compartment, which wouldn't take out the entire ship – unless he was afraid that she would come across as a better engineer than himself. What would the Admiral do if he decided that Mandy was capable of taking Vane's place?

Nothing, she thought, sourly. She had once heard of the concept of Stockholm Syndrome, even though she had no idea which planet Stockholm had been; prisoners tended to develop an affinity for their captors, something that would easily become loyalty or lust. Mandy cursed her own foolishness as she looked upon the work she'd been so proud of a moment ago, knowing that she'd helped the pirates in their quest to establish an empire for the Admiral. And if they thought she was a superb engineer, they'd just find a way to get more blood on her hands.

She considered, briefly, offering to maintain the missile warheads, before dismissing the thought as absurd. They'd never let her work on the warheads – and besides, she didn't know how to detonate them inside their mothership. It hadn't been covered in the courses she'd taken in the technical school. On the other hand, if the pirates were maintaining and launching the missiles themselves, sabotaging them couldn't be that hard.

Shaking her head, she completed her list and studied it thoughtfully. The original designers of the heavy cruiser had put a dozen different systems in the small compartment, which meant that a problem with one system might spread to others. That had puzzled her until she'd decided that the Imperial Navy had expected its people to do actual maintenance and there wouldn't be a problem as long as everything was maintained properly. Besides, only trained engineers were supposed to have access to the tubes.

Vane wasn't going to be happy when he saw her list. She was going to need to replace fifty-seven components outright, some of them very hard to find outside Imperial Navy warships. Some of them might be repairable, but Mandy knew that repairing them was beyond her skill; she doubted that anyone short of a fully-trained engineer could repair the damaged components. It would be much better to throw them all in the recycler and break them down into material to produce new components. If the Admiral genuinely intended to produce his own empire, he'd need a shipyard and industrial node of his own, sooner rather than later.

She glanced up sharply as she heard a hatch opening in the distance. In theory, only the engineers and the senior staff were supposed to be able to enter the tubes, but the ship's internal monitoring network was so badly damaged that she doubted that any of the locks would hold against someone who really wanted in. And who knew what that person would want? She reached for a long crowbar she'd been using to pry away at damaged components as she heard someone crawling their way towards her, just before Michael's head popped out of the tube. Mandy was in his arms, despite the smell, before her mind had quite caught up with what was happening to her.

"I thought you were dead," she said, feeling tears pricking at the corner of her eyes. She hadn't seen Michael since that fateful first day. "I thought…"

She stared as he flinched back from her touch. "Are you all right?"

"My engineering education wasn't as good as it could have been," Michael said. But he hadn't had *any* real education…Mandy realised, suddenly, that he'd been whipped. Badly. "I don't have many of the skills they need."

"My God," Mandy said. "What are they doing to you?"

Michael grinned, but there was no true humour in his eyes. "Right now, they have me mopping the decks," he said sarcastically. "I managed to break two different components instead of inserting them into the right position and…and then I inserted the wrong component into the wrong place. Vane was not happy."

Mandy could imagine. Imperial Navy components were designed to be tough, but inserting the wrong one into the wrong place could burn them out. Or worse. *She'd* been taught to check everything before doing any maintenance work; Michael hadn't had any specialised engineering training at all. His military service had involved components and vehicles that were a great deal easier to maintain than a starship.

"You have to work harder," she said, nervously. Michael was the only real friend she had on the *Sword*. What would happen to her if he was thrown out of an airlock? "I don't think they have room for freeloaders."

Michael leaned closer, until his lips were almost touching hers. "Do they have any internal monitoring systems at all?"

Mandy hesitated. "I don't know," she admitted. It stood to reason that the Admiral – and his senior officers, she assumed – would want to monitor the crew. On the other hand, she wouldn't have trusted the internal network to do anything, not with the casual damage the pirates inflicted on it every day. "I don't think the system works very well."

"Our duty is to find a way to get back to Avalon," Michael said. He looked around the compartment, seeing the signs of Mandy's hard work. "We're not meant to *collaborate*."

Mandy felt a hot flush rising to her cheeks. "Do you really think we have a choice?"

She glared at Michael until he lowered his eyes, and then pressed on. "It won't matter in the slightest if we refuse to work," she added. "If we do, they will simply dispose of us and keep going. We have to appear loyal until the right time."

Michael nodded, slowly. "I may not be alive much longer," he said. His movements were oddly twitchy, worrying Mandy. Vane had implied that a person could be whipped for days without causing any lasting damage, but that was just physical damage. What sort of damage would be inflicted on a person's mind? "If that happens, I need you to remain alive and stay ready."

He reached into his belt and produced a pair of knives. "Take these and stick them in your clothing," he said, as she stared at him. "You said they'd taught you how to use a knife?"

Mandy took the knives, puzzled. "How did you get them?"

Michael grinned. This time, she saw true humour on his face. "The pirates are very much like a street gang," he said. "I used to run with one on Avalon...well, I was close to one. I never really wanted to be a full member, but..."

He shook his head. "The footsoldiers at the bottom talk trash constantly and jostle each other for precedence," he added. "I chatted to a few of them, learned a little more about how they operate – and eventually managed to get my hands on the knives. Betting is pretty damn risky if you don't have anything to bet with, but I won."

"Thank God," Mandy said. Her mind caught up a moment later. "They let you win *weapons* in a betting match?"

"Only knives," Michael said. "They wouldn't let me bid for an automatic weapon; from what they were saying, we will only be allowed to have them after there is blood on our hands."

Mandy scowled. The Imperial Navy drew no distinction between those who joined the pirates of their own free will and those who were shanghaied onto a pirate ship. Once someone became an accessory to piracy, they were dead when the Imperial Navy caught up with them. And it was quite possible that if they ever returned to Avalon, they would be charged with piracy and executed. On the other hand, Colonel Stalker would know that they'd had no choice, wouldn't he?

And tell me, a voice whispered at the back of her mind, *quite what he will say after you do something that kills innocent people?*

"I've been poking around the ship while swabbing the decks," Michael added. "There are some compartments they won't let me enter, but plenty of sections are almost completely empty – and useless. A ship like this should have a crew of nine hundred; I think there isn't any more than three hundred pirates onboard at most."

Mandy nodded, feeling another hint of shame. *She* hadn't done any investigating while she'd been working. Perhaps she could stop working early each day and explore the tube network before going to eat, or being escorted back to her cabin. They still locked her in every night.

"We'll have to keep comparing notes," she said, instead. "I've...I've missed you."

"Me too," Michael admitted. He walked back to the tube and started to scramble into it. "I think you'd better watch your back. You have been noticed."

Mandy was still mulling over his words when lunch hour rolled around and she found her way out of the tubes. This time, she took the chance to explore other parts of the tube network, trying to see how it all went together. Vane hadn't provided her with any internal diagrams, yet *Sword* didn't seem to be too dissimilar to the ships she'd studied in technical college. She'd dismissed those classes as a waste of time – they were never going to be able to work on a battleship – but now she saw their value. It was easy to extrapolate much of *Sword's* interior from the other ships.

There was no sign of Vane in the engineering compartment, so she left the datapad in his office and walked out, heading for the dining compartment. Michael didn't seem to have made much of an impression on the decks, although mopping the entire ship would take months for a single person. Mandy hoped desperately that he would be fine, that the pirates would decide that better hygiene was worth the hassle of keeping him alive; there was no way that she wanted to be alone on the pirate ship. And then a hand caught her collar as she walked past a door, pulling her into a compartment.

She started to struggle as a pirate shoved her to the deck, only to have her head banged against the hard metal. His weight pressed down on her, his hand on her throat, slowly choking the life out of her body. Mandy fought for breath, struggling as best as she could, and then realised that he was trying to force her to surrender to him. Somehow, she managed to relax as his hand moved to her shipsuit zipper, pulling it open. A moment later, she recoiled as she felt his hand on her breast.

The sound of heavy breathing grew louder as her captor tugged at her pants, trying to pull them down. He seemed to be halfway drunk, she decided; his coordination didn't seem to be very good at all. Panic bubbled at the back of her mind – this was worse than her near-disastrous experience on Avalon, without a Marine to come to the rescue – and she fought it down savagely. She was *not* going to allow him to do *anything* to her. And he hadn't noticed the knives.

"Lie still," he ordered. His voice definitely sounded drunk. "I'll do all of the work."

Mandy shuddered at the stench of alcohol from his mouth. "I can make it better," she said, trying to sit upright. How drunk was he? Drunk enough to believe her if she promised to cooperate? His hands tugged her pants down to her ankles, making it harder for her to move her legs. "I can suck you and…"

She forced her face to stay calm as he opened his pants, revealing his erection. Taking her chance, she kicked him as hard as she could, right in the groin. He doubled over, gasping in pain as a uniquely male agony raged through his system, hitting the deck between Mandy's legs. Somehow, she managed to pull herself free and up to her feet, looking down at him rolling on the deck. The blood-red look in his eye promised revenge, in the future. And there was no one to help her on the pirate ship, no one who could and would help her.

On Avalon, she could have handed him over to the new police force, who would have sent him to the work camps or a penal island. Earth's more progressive view on crime would have had him exiled to a colony world instead. But on a pirate ship…she recalled Michael's words and shuddered. It was just like a street gang. The strong dominated and bullied the weak – and he'd thought of her as weak. And now it had become a matter of pride.

Slowly, as if she were in a daze, she drew the knife and advanced forward. She had never killed before, not in her entire life. Jasmine, on the other hand, had killed hundreds of people; bandits, insurgents and rebels. Had she ever killed anyone with a knife? Mandy had never asked her. The old Mandy had looked down on the military, both out of contempt for their profession and – although she would have never admitted it to anyone else – fear of violence. But she'd learned hard lessons since.

Rage flared through Mandy and she stabbed down, sticking the knife into the pirate's back. How *dare* he try to rape her? She'd been a child of Earth – she'd lost her virginity as soon as she could, like so many other children of her generation – but no one had ever entered her without her consent. Blood flowed from the pirate's back as she withdrew the knife and then stabbed down again and again, splattering red bloodstains on the remains of her shipsuit and the deck. The pirate shuddered one final time as her knife slashed across his throat and then lay still.

Mandy stared for a long moment, feeling the madness draining away from her mind, and then threw up violently. She'd killed him…desperately, she started to stagger forward, out of the compartment, just before tripping over her own shipsuit. The pain of hitting the deck helped her mind to focus; somehow, she managed to cover herself before opening the hatch and escaping, leaving the dead body for someone else to find. God alone knew what the Admiral would say if he knew what she'd done. It crossed her mind that she'd left traces of her DNA in the cabin for any halfway competent inspector to find, but she found it hard to care. Her entire body was shaking with delayed shock.

It was hard to walk to the washroom, but thankfully it was deserted. Mandy staggered into the shower and turned on the taps, allowing warm water to wash the blood away from her body. And yet she could still feel his touch on her, a mark that would never fade away. Even the fact she'd killed him wouldn't stop him from tormenting her for the rest of her life. Carefully, she washed and dried the knife too, cleaning away the blood. Taking care of her weapons had been one lesson that she had absorbed with great eagerness.

Once she was clean, she pasted a smile on her face and went to eat. No one said anything to her as she chewed her stew before going back to work. No one said anything at all, even after the day had ended. Had they not found the body? Or did they simply not care? The man she'd killed had just been another piece of shit, someone recruited from the dregs of society and easily replaced.

And that thought frightened her most of all.

CHAPTER FIFTEEN

Repeat after me: Train, Fight, Train, Fight, Train, Fight.

That is the life of a Marine. We train hard, pushing the limits as much as we can, when we are not actually fighting the enemies of the Empire. Can't hack it? Do yourself and us a favour and don't even think about staying in line. Go back home and consider yourself lucky, for escaping the shame of failing publicly. In Boot Camp, we separate the potential Marines from the wannabes, from those who mean well but cannot handle it.

-Introductory Speech, given to prospective recruits entering Boot Camp.

"I think we need better passageways," Blake said. "Or a bigger ship."

Jasmine nodded. A Marine Transport Ship was massive, with enough room to allow several companies to exercise by running through the ship's corridors. The *Dancing Fool* was too small to allow the Marines to exercise properly, even if only one platoon at a time tried to run. If there had been more time, they could have brought more exercise gear, but there hadn't been time.

"Maybe we can build one later," Jasmine said. The run hadn't pushed her or any of the others to the limit. She certainly wasn't even gasping for breath. "Or maybe we should just go back to doing push-ups or cleaning the decks."

There was a chorus of good-natured groans. Five days in the small starship had taken its toll, even though the Marines were used to sleeping in cramped confines. There was nothing to do but exercise and run simulations that were based on their best guess of what they would encounter on Elysium. And, of course, assist the crewmen in repairing the damaged ship. At least it smelled better after the decks had been washed and scrubbed thoroughly.

Back in their compartment, the Marines stripped down their weapons and started to clean them, even though they hadn't been using the weapons on the *Dancing Fool*. Jasmine had stripped down her weapon so often that she could have done it in her sleep or blindfolded, one of the tests she'd had to undergo at the Slaughterhouse. Carefully, she took it apart and put it back together, once she'd cleaned the different components of the weapon. It would be in perfect condition for when she would need it.

They'd all read the files on Elysium, but everything they had was at least six months out of date. Jasmine had tried to extrapolate from what they had to guess what they might see when they reached their destination, along with the other Marines, yet they'd come up with so many different possibilities that there was no way to know for sure. Blake was already running a betting pool that Jasmine, as an officer, wasn't supposed to know about. The favoured theory seemed to be that Elysium's government, an ad hoc affair at the best of times, had simply melted away. And then the pirates had simply taken the high orbitals and started dictating terms.

Jasmine wasn't so sure. Elysium had plenty of debris in-system, enough asteroids and comets to fuel a healthy industry – and to make a planetary impact inevitable, sooner or later. There were no shortage of records about what happened to planets unfortunate enough to be hit by asteroids; the planet's inhabitants would have to be absolutely insane to abandon all of their space-capable technology. But then, the inhabitants wouldn't have been able to afford something that could stand off the pirates as well as rogue asteroids. It was quite possible that the pirates were now running a protection racket, trading food, drink and women for protection against asteroid impacts. And perhaps threatening to speed up the process if the locals refused to pay.

She finished putting her weapon back together and slung it over her shoulder. Marine Corps regulations called for Marines to carry weapons at all times, unless they were in serious trouble. It had always astonished her to discover that the Civil Guard never allowed its men to carry weapons until they were actually going to fight, which meant that they would be unarmed if the enemy managed to launch a surprise attack. At least seven *thousand* Civil Guardsmen had died on Han because the rebels had managed to catch them by surprise. It seemed insane…although, given the quality of the average recruit to the Civil Guard, perhaps their superiors had a point. Jasmine had known Civil Guardsmen who were more likely to take shots at her rather than the enemy.

Her implant buzzed. "First Platoon has access to the shuttles now," the Sergeant said. Jasmine nodded; while her platoon had been running around the ship, Third Platoon had been working on their shuttle. "We've uploaded the latest simulations into the shuttle's computers."

Jasmine grinned. "Down to the shuttles," she ordered, as soon as the Marines had finished cleaning their weapons. Blake seemed to be taking longer than usual to finish his task; she made a mental note to watch him the next time he carried out the exercise. They'd been trained to strip down the weapons and clear blockages as quickly as possible – they might have to do it under fire one day – and they couldn't afford delays. "We have servicing to do and simulations to complete."

Colonel Stalker had warned her that the Marine Assault Shuttles were irreplaceable, at least for the next two or three years. They'd been designed to a very high standard by the Terran Marine Corps and produced on the Slaughterhouse, rather than farmed out to the Imperial Navy's production nodes. It wasn't entirely surprising – each of them cost twenty times as much as a standard shuttle and the bean-counters kept looking for ways to cut costs – but right now it meant they couldn't produce any more if they lost any in combat. They hadn't been able to deploy them into the maelstrom of the Battle of Camelot for fear of Cracker HVMs.

At the time, Jasmine had wondered if the CO had made the wrong call. As a Lieutenant, with responsibility for the weapons, supplies and other equipment used by her platoon, she understood what had been going through his mind. It was far easier to produce new Raptors than it was to produce Assault Shuttles, while the Assault Shuttles weren't designed for precision operations. She shook her head as the platoon opened the hatches and started to scramble into the craft. They had to check it out thoroughly before they could start running the simulations.

The Assault Shuttle was a boxy design, one that starship-spotters across the Empire considered crude and badly deformed. Jasmine had always considered that conceit amusing; the Assault Shuttle might look crude, but it was very effective. It was heavily armoured, allowing Marines a chance to survive a missile hit that would take out a standard shuttle, and carried enough weapons and decoys to allow it to provide support for Marines on the ground. She still remembered a flight of shuttles coming to the rescue on Han, back when the company had been trapped in a residential block and threatened with extermination. The rebels hadn't even realised that they were under attack until it was too late.

"Check the flight box," she ordered Blake, as she climbed into the shuttle. Everything on the shuttle would be checked at least twice, by two different Marines. It was alarmingly possible for tiredness to cause someone to make a mistake and miss something important, but two checks should reveal any surprises. "And then pull up the simulation and get ready to load it into the system."

"Understood," Blake said, as he took the pilot's chair and sat down. "Hey – we have a red light. Some idiot forgot to put the weapons pod in the right way round."

Jasmine smiled. It wouldn't be the first time some senior officer had altered the shuttle's configuration to see if he could catch the Marines out. Everything had to be checked, and checked again, even if they *hadn't* done anything since they'd left Avalon. But a weapons pod inserted the wrong way? *That* didn't need a physical check to identify. The internal monitoring systems had picked it up right away. Chances were that the seemingly simple alteration had a nasty sting in the tail.

"Check it, carefully," she ordered. "And then check the rest of the shuttle, even more carefully."

Joe walked back out of the shuttle and inspected the weapons pod. "They just inserted it badly," he said, as he studied it. Weapons pods required at least two Marines to move properly. "Looks like someone tried to do it wearing powered armour, rather than…ah."

Jasmine glanced up, sharply. "Ah?"

"*Ah* is never good," Blake said. "Joe? What have you found?"

"I think we were meant to shove it into its proper place," Joe said. "But they left a grenade inside; one shove and it would have detonated. We could have blown ourselves up."

Or, more accurately, received a tongue-lashing for carelessness from the Colonel, Jasmine thought, ruefully. Being blown up might be preferable. "Can you remove it?"

"Yep," Joe said. There was a brief pause. "It was a training grenade, all right."

"Glad to hear it," Jasmine said, dryly. "Check the rest of the weapons pod anyway, and then slot it into place."

"I bet it was Mike from Third who thought of that trick," Blake said, as they started to check the rest of the shuttle. "He always was a practical joker."

"Yeah," Joe said. "We should prank him back, Lieutenant."

Jasmine managed – somehow – to avoid rolling her eyes. Playing pranks on each other was a long-standing Marine tradition, but it was only open to Riflemen; as a Lieutenant, she was expected to set a good example. The nasty part of her mind remembered waking up to discover a snake in her bedding – Mike had caught it outside the FOB and sneaked it inside – and considered revenge, before deciding that Mike had probably been following orders. They weren't spared the need to train just because they were heading into a combat zone…

The list of surprises grew longer as the platoon finished checking the shuttle, although Mike had apparently run out of imagination after leaving a second grenade under one of the seats. It had been far harder at the Slaughterhouse, where they'd been given a set of plans and told to put a shuttle together out of a small pile of components; it had taken several hours for the recruits to realise that they'd been given the wrong plans. The Drill Instructors had been scathing, pointing out that if they'd checked the components they'd been given against the plans they would have discovered that several components were missing. And the next set of plans had been out of date.

"I think that's everything," Jasmine said, finally. Keying her communicator, she called the Command Sergeant and reported in. Mike would have kept a list of everything he'd done and Sergeant Patterson would compare the two. Anything missing from Jasmine's list would be grounds for a sharp lecture from her superior officer. She recited the entire list, concluding with the seat that had been loosened from where it had been bolted to the deck. That could easily have been disastrous if the shuttle had had to go to full emergency power. "Sergeant?"

"You appear to have found everything," Sergeant Patterson said, after a pause long enough for Jasmine to start to worry. "Please inform me when you are finished with the simulation."

"Understood," Jasmine said, and broke the connection.

The rest of the platoon was already donning their armour, ready to run the simulation. It wasn't perfect, not like the training fields in the Slaughterhouse or even exercises on Avalon, but it would have to do. Smiling, Jasmine donned her own suit and activated the simulation. A moment later, the shuttle appeared to be punching its way into a planetary atmosphere, despite increasingly heavy fire from the ground.

It probably wasn't what they were facing on Elysium, she knew, but the Slaughterhouse had taught her that hard training made the missions easier. And that easy training got people killed on operations.

"Catching up with your paperwork?"

"I should really hire a scribe," Edward said. He rubbed his forehead as he looked down at the datapad. If there was no hope of ever returning to the Empire, part of his mind wasn't sure why he should keep doing the mountain of paperwork that came with command of a Marine company. Why bother, that part of his mind asked, if no one would ever read it? But even if they didn't return to the Empire, surely their descendents on Avalon would look at the files. "There's just too much to do."

Gwendolyn snorted. "That's why I became a Sergeant," she said. "Less paperwork."

Edward nodded. In theory, there was supposed to be little actual paperwork; the last thing the Marines wanted was for their officers to spend more time filing papers than working with their men. As always, practice was different, particularly when he was responsible for the

Knights as well as for the Marines. Marine Generals *did* have staffs to handle the paperwork; right now, Edward wished he'd established one for himself as well. But that would have been a step too far.

He signed his certificate to a document and uploaded it into the message buffer. It would be sent to the Marine command network once they returned to Avalon; thankfully, it wasn't anything that required immediate attention. He'd left officers behind with authority to act in his absence, but…but he felt guilty for leaving Avalon, almost as if he had left the planet unattended. Perhaps he should have handed the *Dancing Fool* to someone else and stayed on Avalon himself. Not that it mattered; right now, there was no time to change his mind.

"As your Command Sergeant, it is my duty to tell you when you are spending too much time in your office," Gwendolyn said, firmly. "Right now, you need some exercise or you will wind up as flabby as that family from Rowdy Yates block."

Edward shuddered, remembering. The adults of the family had been so overweight that they needed special vehicles to help them get around, while the children had already had their lives ruined by their parents. How could the fatties even have kids, he'd wondered at the time, and didn't they realise that their children were too fat to live? Edward had honestly never considered the possibility of winding up with spinal damage caused by overeating until then. Even the Empire's medical science had limits.

And if the Marines hadn't arrived, the fatties would have been unable to run and escape the Nihilists…

"You've talked me into getting up," he said. The 'office' had once belonged to the pirate commander; Edward had seen the videos the WARCAT team had taken before they'd removed the pirate's gear and felt sick. What was it about pirates that they felt the need to be as uncivilised as possible? But then, they had already cut themselves off from civilisation. The Empire could only kill them once, after all. "Fancy a match in the ring?"

Gwendolyn grinned. "How did you guess?"

Edward followed her down into the sparring compartment and rapidly changed into shorts and a shirt. All of the Marines were expected to be experts in hand-to-hand combat, and then to keep those skills sharp, whatever else they were doing. Edward had been told that being personally lethal was more character-building than simply carrying weapons; it was something he hadn't truly understood until Han, where weapons had been passed out to a downtrodden population that had promptly started to use them to slaughter their tormentors. They'd then started slaughtering everyone else…if the Crackers had won the war, would they have started fighting each other too? Rebellions never seemed to survive actually winning the war.

"You're rusty," Gwendolyn said, after three minutes of inconclusive sparring. She threw a kick that forced Edward to jump back sharply, just in time to prevent her landing a blow on his chest. "I really should have taken you out and sparred with you before this."

Edward gritted his teeth and struck back, realising that she was right. Too long in his office, all of his offices, had sapped his skills and dulled his edge. He'd told himself that he could afford to miss a training and exercise session or two, but he'd just kept making the same excuses time and time again. Of course, a Major General would have done the same…

But he would have had more subordinates, Edward told himself, as Gwendolyn hit him in the shoulder. And he would have had more people he could trust without needing to watch them carefully.

He dodged one blow, only to have Gwendolyn close in and knock his legs out from under him. Edward tumbled to the deck and rolled over, just before Gwendolyn managed to land on top of him. She was slighter than him, and probably weaker despite the enhancement, but she had him in a death-lock. A quick motion could snap his neck, something that would kill him without immediate medical attention. Edward sighed and lay still. He hated to lose to anyone.

"We are going to spar every day," Gwendolyn informed him. "And you are going to practice everything."

Edward scowled, but nodded. It *was* her job to tell him when he wasn't up to scratch, even though it involved a level of familiarity the Civil Guard would never have tolerated. Besides, he might have to lead his Marines back into battle and to do that he would have to be as fit as anyone. Leadership was more than just having the rank, he'd been told;

leadership was being able and willing to do anything he might ask his subordinates to do.

"Four days to Elysium," Gwendolyn said. "I think we *might* be able to sharpen you up by then. Might."

Edward didn't bother to reply.

Chapter Sixteen

It is a fundamental principle of interstellar law, at least before the days of the Empire, that you have jurisdiction over only as much space as you can physically control. In order to do this, you must have the strongest military presence in the area and the ability to patrol that region of space. Naturally, this led to plenty of wrangling in the law courts over precisely what constituted physical control. Did a single leaky patrol boat suffice? The Empire, naturally, claimed jurisdiction everywhere, even in systems where there was a pre-existing self-defence force. Enforcing this was a difficult task for the Imperial Navy.

Given the inherent limitations on technology, this was a major problem when the Empire started its long decline and fall.

- Professor Leo Caesius, *The Perilous Dawn* (unpublished).

"Ten seconds," Kitty Stevenson said. "Nine…eight…"

Dancing Fool shuddered violently as she dropped out of Phase Space, five light hours from the system primary. Edward hung onto his chair as the vibration grew stronger – he thought he could hear the entire hull creaking alarmingly – before it slowly faded away into nothingness. At such a distance, well outside the Phase Limit, their arrival should have gone unnoticed. Only the most advanced systems bothered to scatter early-warning satellites along the Phase Limit.

"I think we made it," he said. On the main display, Elysium's primary star appeared in front of them. "Did the ship survive?"

"Barely," Kitty said, after a long moment of studying the readings. "If the Phase Drive wasn't built to be so tough, I think we would have lost it then."

Edward scowled. One of the other disastrous possibilities that had been discussed intensively was losing the Phase Drive while in transit, or in the Elysium System. If that happened, they would be stranded, unable to return to Avalon or even signal for help. Thankfully, they seemed to have avoided that possibility, but they still had to get back to Avalon. Running a ship into the Phase Limit while in Phase Space was not a recommended way of returning to normal space.

"Keep an eye on it," he said, finally. "Any contacts within sensor range?"

"Nothing on active sensors, sir," Aux-Lieutenant Delacroix reported. "We're drawing in passive observation data now."

Slowly, the display built up in front of them. The Imperial Navy fought under handicaps that puzzled the Marines, handicaps imposed by the laws of nature themselves. Passive sensors could pick up a fusion burn two light hours away from their ship, but by the time they picked it up the information would be two hours out of date. The ship they detected could have changed course, or deactivated its drive; they wouldn't know until they drew closer. Fighting in deep space was more complex than fighting on the surface of a planet. The fog of war enveloped everything.

"Five planets, plenty of asteroids and other junk," Delacroix said, finally. "No gas giant, sadly, or this system would be worth more than Avalon."

And the ADC might have colonised it instead of Avalon, Edward thought. "Any trace of technological presence?"

"Nothing so far," Delacroix said.

"That doesn't prove anything," Kitty pointed out. There was an edge in her voice, but it took Edward a moment to understand why she was annoyed. Of course; he'd started barking commands on her bridge. No Captain would tolerate that for a second. "At this distance, it would be sheer luck if we picked up anything from a stage-one colony."

Edward couldn't disagree. Systems like Earth, with thousands of starships, orbital colonies and inhabited worlds, produced plenty of radio noise. Star systems with only one inhabited planet and a very small presence in space produced almost nothing. Avalon hadn't produced much, even before the new Council had started building telecom landlines as a security precaution – and a job creation program. Elysium might be silent; it didn't mean that there was anything wrong.

He sat back in his chair as Kitty continued to study the display. "I suggest we proceed with our original plan," she said, finally. "It will take nearly a day to slip up to the planet, but it will make detection very unlikely. And then we can start launching the remotes further into the area."

"See to it," Edward said.

He looked back at the display. There was something oddly beautiful about any star system, particularly one that had been largely untouched by mankind. But then, on such a scale, the works of humanity were almost unnoticeable. Once, the Empire had talked about producing Dyson Spheres, about shrouding entire stars in material. Such projects had never made the jump from concept to reality. It was almost a shame, in a way. It would have given the human race something to dream about once again.

Waiting was never easy, but he forced himself to sit back and meditate on the value of patience. The hours ticked away slowly as *Dancing Fool* crept further and further into the system, every passive sensor straining for a hint that someone else was out there, watching them. Crewmen talked in hushed voices, even though they *knew* that no one would hear them in the soundless vacuum of space. Third Platoon remained on alert while First and Fourth Platoons concentrated on their sleep, resting for the time when they'd have to go into battle. And then the display chimed an alert…

"We have a contact," Delacroix reported. "It looks like a fusion-drive ship, probably a RockRat vessel. Judging from the burn, it appears to be heading away from the asteroids."

Edward frowned as Kitty and her crew sought to make sense out of the inflow of information. The RockRats were unlikely to be helping the pirates, willingly at least, but what *were* they doing? Were they being forced to comply, or were they trying to keep their distance from the Admiral and his men? He briefly considered using a laser communicator to hail the RockRats and ask for an update, but it was too great a risk. If the RockRats were being forced to help the pirates, they might reveal the presence of the *Dancing Fool* to their new masters.

"I wonder if they're actually planning to flee the system," Kitty mused. "That trajectory isn't aligned on any actual destination."

"Could be," Edward agreed. There were Slowboaters who lived out their lives on giant interstellar arks, moving between the stars at STL speeds. He had always considered them insane, but if the RockRats had no other choice perhaps they could launch an STL mission to another star. They could easily outfit a fusion-drive starship with stasis tubes to preserve them during the long years in interstellar space. "If so, where are they going?"

"Several different destinations," Kitty said. She shook her head. "They don't stand a chance."

Edward nodded. Once, years ago, he had studied the wars that had broken out when the Phase Drive was first invented. The drive didn't give its possessor any tactical advantages inside the Phase Limit, but it did allow them to operate on an interstellar scale for the first time, combining the resources of several star systems against one. If the Admiral managed to establish his empire, the RockRats might arrive in their new system to discover a reception committee waiting for them. On the other hand, perhaps the Admiral might forget over the years.

Kitty turned back to the helm console. "Keep moving us inwards," she ordered. "And prepare to launch the first remotes."

The display updated again as they advanced towards Elysium, the planet slowly coming into view. It was a blue-green sphere, very much like Avalon, although the planetary biology was more active than Edward's new homeworld. The briefing files had noted that the local plant and animal kingdoms had managed to merge with the plants and animals transported from Earth, something that was actually rare in the Empire. It was rather more common for the imported wildlife, being of hardier stock, to overwhelm the local environment. There had been entire protest movements against 'ecological imperialism' in the Empire at one point, he recalled, none of which had come to anything. It was rare to find a planet with native wildlife that fulfilled *all* of humanity's requirements.

"Launch the first remotes and cut the drives," Kitty ordered, finally. Unlike a planet-side object, *Dancing Fool* would continue to drift towards the planet on a ballistic trajectory. "Let's see how much we can scope out before we alter course."

Edward leaned forward as the first remote sensor platforms were launched towards the planet. With her drives and sensors stepped down to the bare minimum, *Dancing Fool* should have been almost completely undetectable; the remote platforms were so stealthy that even the best sensors in the Empire had difficulty tracking them at point-blank range. Whisker-thin lasers allowed them to send their readings back to their mothership. Back on Earth, the bean-counters would have complained about deploying so many remotes, if only because the remotes cost millions of credits per deployment, but he didn't have to worry about that now. Preserving the lives of his men – and the *Dancing Fool* – was more important than pleasing bean-counters on a far-distant world.

"Picking up two structures in orbit," Delacroix reported. "And three freighters."

"Interesting," Edward mused. What did Elysium have that might interest merchant skippers? The only things he could think of offhand was food, drink and women. "Are they under power?"

"I don't think so," Delacroix said, after a moment. "Their drive systems are definitely stepped down; they're not even emitting IFF beacons."

"How terribly illegal of them," Kitty observed, with a quick grin. Imperial law ordered all merchant ship to broadcast an IFF signal at all times, particularly when they were in a crowded set of orbitals. Statistically speaking, collisions were unlikely, but it only took one stroke of bad luck to cause a disaster. "Do you think we should arrest them?"

"Later, maybe," Edward said. The two orbital platforms were coming into visual range of the remotes. One of them was clearly an orbital station, comparable to the one orbiting Avalon. The other…? "Can you identify the other orbiting structure?"

"I'm not certain, but I think it's an Orbital Bombardment System," Delacroix said, after a moment. "The orbit it's in would eventually allow it to target any part of the planet – and it doesn't intersect the orbit of anything else at all. Assuming it's comparable to a *Hades*-class system, anyone underneath is going to know that they've been kissed."

Edward scowled. *Hades*-class OBS systems were intended to keep rebellious planets quiet while the Marines and the regular army amassed a force to spank them. The automated systems tracked any sign of hostile activity and fired on it, dropping KEWs from orbit right onto the targeted coordinates. They were feared because, being automated, the system had no hesitation in firing on targets that happened to be in the middle of a densely populated city. Edward would have given a great deal to have five minutes alone with the man who had designed them, and the Grand Senators who ordered them deployed.

Kitty had a different question. "They didn't mount weapons on the orbit station?"

"I don't think they have anything beyond lasers," Delacroix said. "Wouldn't they be worried about someone taking over the weapons and turning them on the pirates?"

"Probably," Edward said. "Can you pick up anything from the planet itself?"

"Some minor encrypted communications," Delacroix reported. "I'm afraid that breaking them is probably beyond this equipment."

She paused as the remotes slipped into orbit. "But I think I can tell you where the pirates are based," she added. "There's a set of heavy armour located near Elysium City."

Edward studied the information as it flowed into the main display. The Admiral's forces had apparently occupied the city, with the OBS overhead to make any attempt at evicting them a bloody failure, and then started issuing orders to the rest of the planet. That, at least, was fairly standard policy in the Empire too, although the heavy armour was a surprise. Most military units would use combat armour rather than tanks.

"Probably cheap mercenaries," Kitty suggested, when he said that out loud. "They don't want to go to the expense of producing combat suits, so they build tanks instead. You don't need to design a tank specifically for one person."

Edward couldn't disagree, but the presence of the forces on the ground posed a major problem for his Marines. Standard procedure would be to drop KEWs on them from orbit, but that ran the risk of unacceptable civilian casualties. Edward was too practical a man to believe that collateral damage was completely avoidable – only a politician or a reporter could be so stupid – yet he refused to countenance it if there was any other option. The Marines would have to go down to the surface and deal with the mercenaries directly.

"Check the rest of the planet," he ordered, as he started to draw up a loose plan of attack. "Let me know if you find other enemy outposts on the surface."

He would have been surprised if they found any – garrisoning the surface of an entire planet was pointless and wasteful when one held the high orbitals – but he knew they had to check. It wouldn't be the first time some amateur strategist had caused problems for the professional military simply by not knowing what to avoid. Right now, though, the real problem was dealing with the OBS; as long as that was in orbit, the pirates could simply threaten to bombard the entire planet. Once it was taken out, it was quite possible that the Marines would find themselves joined by outraged locals.

"I think there are a handful of smaller detachments on patrol," Delacroix reported, after the remotes had skimmed over the entire planet. "There's also a large base here" – she tapped a position on the map – "that seems to be quite some distance from any local settlement."

"Curious," Edward mused. She was right; there wasn't a local settlement for several hundred miles. It was quite possible that the locals didn't even realise that the pirate base was *there*. And that meant…what? Did the pirates intend to keep a reserve of mercenaries some distance from the civilians, just in case there was a planetary uprising, or did they have something else in mind? "Are you sure it's a *pirate* base?"

"If it belonged to rebels, they'd have destroyed it by now," Delacroix pointed out. "We could simply bomb it from orbit ourselves, once we dealt with the OBS."

"True," Edward said. He studied the final update and then keyed his communicator. "All Marines, report to the briefing compartment immediately. We have an operation to plan."

He looked over at Kitty. "Is there any sign at all that we might have been detected?"

"None," Kitty said, flatly. "If they had detected us, they'd probably have brought up their active sensors and the OBS weapons pods."

Edward nodded. "Keep us here," he said. "As long as we remain undetected, we should have the advantage of surprise."

The pirate commander had used the briefing compartment to store supplies for his crew, rather than putting it to its proper use. Unlike the rest of the ship, it wasn't really a chamber of horrors; Edward's Marines had simply emptied most of the supplies into the hold and then cleaned it up a little. The original projector was long-since gone, but Edward had never liked them anyway. It was all too easy to get more concerned about presentation than actually carrying out the mission.

"We will use a kinetic strike to take out the OBS system," he said. A projectile would be accelerated to near-light speed and hurled at the OBS from a safe distance. The pirates would only see it coming when it was too late to stop. At that speed, the impact would shatter the structure completely. "Once the OBS system is gone, First Platoon will land on the planet here" – he tapped a location near the city – "and advance to take out the mercenaries. Third Platoon will secure the orbit station, while Fourth Platoon will split up and secure the freighters."

He paused. "We don't know the situation on the ground, so there's no way of knowing just how much help you will receive from the inhabitants," he continued. He'd thought about trying to insert First Platoon first, but it was just too risky. Moving a shuttle, even a Marine Assault Shuttle, through the atmosphere could be detected; the pirates might pick up something and sound the alert. "Assume the worst; there's no local resistance at all and you're completely on your own."

"That's good," Blake Coleman said. "No pressure, sir."

Edward gave him a sharp look. "These mercenaries have tanks and we must presume that they won't hesitate to endanger civilians," he continued. "Take them out as quickly as possible, unless they surrender, in which case take them into custody. We'll broadcast an offer to let them keep their lives if they surrender, once we reveal ourselves; they may give up if they think there's a way out."

He looked around the room. Mercenaries could be very good, well-trained and experienced, or very bad – and there was no way to know what they were dealing with until the shit hit the fan. On the other hand, mercenaries weren't fanatics and would usually surrender if there was a way to keep their lives. They were generally only loyal to their pay – and there was no way to spend it if they were squashed by the Marines.

"There's an entire planet of helpless civilians here," he concluded. "We have to save them quickly, before it's too late. Man your shuttles."

He returned their salute and watched as they filed out, remembering the days he would have led the company into battle. Now, he still had to watch and wait…shaking his head, he turned and headed back to the bridge. The timing had to be absolutely perfect…

…Or the entire operation could end in disaster.

CHAPTER
SEVENTEEN

The Empire generally disliked and distrusted mercenaries, which didn't stop it making use of them. All mercenary companies were expected to abide by a set of codes imposed by the Empire and ruthlessly squashed if the codes were broken; unsurprisingly, companies with political connections were able to skirt the letter of the law with more aplomb than those without. By the time of the Empire's decline and fall, there were some very well armed mercenary companies operating in the galaxy…

…The most specific restriction was that mercenaries were not to use either planetary bombardment weapons or weapons of mass destruction. It was a restriction that would be flouted many times as the Empire fell.
- Professor Leo Caesius, *The Perilous Dawn* (unpublished).

"I always get the bloody shakes before a drop."

Jasmine kept her mouth closed as Sergeant Chester Harris leaned over towards Joe and told him to shut up. The shuttle was gliding towards the planet, propelled by gas jets that should have been impossible to detect, an experience that always made her feel nervous too. A single hit would vaporise the entire shuttle, along with Jasmine and her platoon. Forcing a landing on a planet could be immensely costly.

She'd been on the ground during the uprising on Han, so she'd been spared taking part in the relief operation mounted by the Marine Corps – and the Army. The rebels had controlled enough of the planetary defences to make the landing operation extremely hazardous for the soldiers, with dozens of shuttles blown out of the sky as they entered the planet's atmosphere. If it hadn't been for the Imperial Navy providing fire support, the entire operation might have failed spectacularly. As it was, hundreds of thousands had died in the operation. It wasn't a reassuring thought. Stalker's Stalkers simply didn't have the manpower to force a landing on a defended world.

They shouldn't have the firepower to stop us, she told herself. But she didn't really believe it. A single HVM could take out the entire shuttle, if they were foolhardy enough to fly over the city or one of the other mercenary bases. And then the whole operation might fail. Captain Stalker would have to threaten orbital bombardment to bring the mercenaries to heel, causing a stand-off that might be resolved by the arrival of more pirate ships. She pushed the thought out of her mind as her implants linked into the shuttle's passive sensors. Some Marines preferred not to know what was outside the ship – being helpless didn't sit well with any of them – but Jasmine had always believed that it was better to know the worst. Besides, it helped avert the claustrophobia some people suffered in the shuttles.

The planet's orbital space was nearly empty, thankfully. Elysium's settling corporation might have planned to turn the world into an industrial node, but they hadn't had time to set up more than a handful of facilities before the Empire had pulled back from the Rim. There was little space junk in orbit, nothing that would force them to alter course sharply enough that they might be detected. The shuttle should be out of sight from both the orbiting station and the OBS before it reached the planet's atmosphere, but they were still trying to be sneaky. It was quite possible that the mercenaries, like the Marines on Avalon, had placed stealthed sensor satellites in orbit around their world.

"Seven minutes to atmospheric insertion," the pilot informed them. Shuttle pilots were Marine Auxiliaries rather than full Marines, but they earned and deserved a great deal of respect from their passengers. On Han, far too many pilots had bought the farm when their shuttles had been targeted as they tried to escape the planet's atmosphere after their Marines had dropped from the shuttles. "No sign of active sensor sweeps."

Jasmine nodded. The shuttles were designed to be hard to pick up, even with active sensors, but they weren't cloaked. They simply lacked the power to mount a cloaking device, which meant that they *could* be detected – and if they were detected, there would be no choice, but to go to full military power and pray they could evade incoming fire long enough to drop the Marines onto the planet. Or back off, leaving the enemy aware that their defences were being probed. She reminded herself, sharply, that this world wasn't Han. They shouldn't have any problems actually landing on the surface. The tricky part would be advancing on the city.

The Empire had prided itself on sharing information about colony worlds, but it had been six months – perhaps longer – since the files on Elysium had been updated. It hadn't taken more than a quick glimpse at the orbital observation records to confirm that the locals had improved their capital city, altering it to the point where the Marine files were effectively useless. There were always limits to what one could learn from orbit – a point often forgotten by Imperial Intelligence – and they'd have to bear in mind that they could be misinterpreting the data. Jasmine brought the live feed up in her HUD and studied it, feeling her heartbeat starting to pound in her ears as they drew closer to the planet. The tension seemed unbearable.

"Hurry up and wait," Blake said, cheerfully. He sounded calm. How the hell did he sound so calm? "What else do we do for a living?"

"That reminds me," Joe said. "I haven't had my pay packet in six months."

Jasmine scowled at him, although the expression would be hidden behind her helm. "You get paid in Avalon money these days," she reminded him. He was trying to distract them all from the thought of the coming drop. "Imperial Credits are damn near worthless."

"But I'm sure they'd pay you in them if you asked nicely," Blake added. He chuckled. "You won't be able to *spend* them, but…"

Jasmine shook her head as the timer ticked down. By law, Marines – and everyone else who served the Empire directly – were paid in Imperial Credits, which were usable everywhere, unlike currencies belonging to individual planets. It helped bind them to the Empire, or so Jasmine had heard, and it kept local currencies from becoming too prominent. But right now, with the Empire effectively gone, Imperial Credits were worthless. The Marines had to be paid in Avalon's own currency or nothing.

There were a handful of Marines gathering all the credits they could – in the hope that one day they would get back to the Empire – but Jasmine suspected that they were wasting their time. The value of the Credit had been falling even before the Empire had withdrawn from Avalon.

"Two minutes to insertion," the pilot said. Jasmine checked her straps quickly, again. They'd gone through simulations of what would happen if they weren't careful – and they never ended well. "The ship is about to engage the OBS."

Jasmine nodded. One way or another, the mercenaries were about to discover that *someone* was out there, ready to engage them. And then the shit would hit the fan.

———

"The shuttles are nearing their targets now," Kitty said. She looked over at Edward, sharply. "Do I have permission to engage the OBS?"

Edward studied the display, wishing – once again – that he was out with his Marines. He should be in the shuttle heading to the planet, sharing the danger, not remaining behind in safety. But he was in command and he couldn't risk his life…he scowled, inwardly. Maybe they would encounter more senior officers later on, officers who could take overall command while he returned to his old position.

Or maybe you should just man up and deal with it, he told himself. *This is getting old.*

"You may fire at will," Edward said. As a Rifleman, he would have cracked jokes; who, for a start, was Will? The joke was pathetic and yet it was almost tradition. Now, he didn't have that luxury. "Take the bastard out."

Kitty tapped a command on the tactical console. There was a brief pause as the magnetic accelerator came to life, sucking in power, a second before it propelled the projectile down the tube and out into space. The projectile, emitting nothing, should have been completely undetectable until it struck its target. Even if they had a radar sweep underway, Edward doubted that they could react in time to save themselves. The whole concept – sniping from the shadows – had never failed to chill him. It could be used against Avalon's orbital stations just as easily.

"Projectile away," Kitty said. On the display, the projectile's course lanced towards the OBS system. "Time to impact: thirty-two seconds."

Edward forced himself to watch. A ballistic course was predictable; the projectile would keep moving in a straight line until it hit its target. There was no need to mount a tracking beacon on the projectile to know where it was...even if it wasn't something that sat well with him. He was too used to fighting on the ground, where courses were unpredictable...

"Ten seconds," Kitty said. "No sign of detection. Five seconds..."

The projectile struck the OBS system. Edward watched as the station tore itself apart, feeling a moment of pity for anyone on board. Their world would have shattered without the slightest moment of warning. The crew wouldn't be in shipsuits, if the crew of the *Dancing Fool* had been anything to go by; the ones who survived the first impact would be flung out into space, to die without an atmosphere to breathe. They were either mercenaries or pirates – he was unwilling to accept that the Admiral was anything else – yet did they deserve to die like that?

Just ask their victims, he thought, and scowled.

"Send a signal to the shuttles," he ordered. The planet's occupiers would know they were there now, naturally. No one would have missed the explosion that wiped out the OBS. "Order them to go to full power and advance on their targets."

One shuttle brought up its drives and headed right towards the orbital station. Edward had feared that the pirates would have mounted weapons on the station's hull, giving them some additional firepower to call upon if necessary. The Marines had braced themselves to bail out of the shuttle and fly towards the station in combat suits, but no enemy fire reached out towards the shuttle as they approached. Edward fought the temptation to issue orders, rather than trusting the Marines on the shuttle to handle it, shaking his head in dismay. He'd never understood why so many senior officers were micromanagers until he'd been promoted.

The burden of command, they called it, often without knowing what it actually meant. An officer was responsible for his men, but also for the performance of his unit. Success would have a thousand fathers; failure belonged solely to the officer in command. It was a hard task, balancing the welfare of his men with the need to succeed in his mission, and far too many officers erred too far in one direction. They either cared more about their career than about their men or the other way around. The Marines tried to avert it by insisting that all officers had to have been Riflemen first, but even the Corps had problems. They too insisted that an officer had to take responsibility, both for the mission and for his men.

"Broadcast the demand for surrender," he ordered, as the shuttle started to launch Marines towards the station. It felt odd to be offering pirates their lives – even though he'd made the deal before – but there was little choice. If the pirates decided to fight to the death, they could wreak huge damage on the planet before they were wiped out. The mercenaries might take a more practical stand, yet who was really in command? "And then move us into position to provide fire support if necessary."

"Signal from shuttle three," Delacroix reported. "They're boarding the freighters now. The ships appear to be completely unmanned."

Edward and Kitty exchanged glances. It was rare for a starship to be left completely unmanned, unless it was in the shipyard or docked at an orbital station. There were certain bureaucrats who delighted in seizing unmanned ships, claiming that they were abandoned – and then demanding a huge bribe to restore the ship to its rightful owners. Edward's first platoon had been placed on alert to respond to a riot caused by such an act, before the local governor had backed down and fired the bureaucrat. It was very rare to have any local governor act in such a wise manner. Normally, they backed up the bureaucrats.

"No resistance from the station," she added, a moment later. "The pirates are willing to surrender – sir, they had three dozen *children* on the station as hostages."

"Have the medics look at them once the pirates are secured," Edward ordered. He wasn't too surprised. The pirates would have wanted hostages to keep the planetary government in line, as if the mercenaries wouldn't have been enough to keep the world under control. But they probably wouldn't have been. Edward had found it hard to fight the Crackers to a standstill with a far larger and more capable force under his command. "Did they keep any of the original crew on the station?"

"Uncertain as yet," Delacroix said. "They're still searching the rest of the station."

Edward nodded, fighting down the surge of impatience. It was easy to forget that military operations took time. The Marines would secure everyone on the station – just in case the pirates tried to pass themselves off as ordinary staff, or the hostages had developed Stockholm Syndrome – and then search the entire structure. It was large enough for the search to take nearly an hour.

"Understood," he said.

He forced himself to sit back and relax. Matters might have been out of his hands, but his subordinates knew what they were doing. They would just have to be trusted to get on with it.

"Going to full military power," the pilot snapped. The shuttle hummed to life and jerked forward, seconds after the OBS unit had been destroyed. Jasmine felt the sudden spurt of acceleration – the internal compensators in Marine shuttles were stepped down, allowing them to feel changes in the craft's course and speed – and braced herself as the shuttle roared towards the planet's atmosphere. "They don't appear to be bringing up any sensors."

But they don't need them now, Jasmine thought. The shuttle was still stealthier than the average civilian craft, but someone with sufficiently good passive sensors could pretend to be a hole in space while slowly drawing a bead on the Marine craft. *Or they could be ready to fire on us from the ground.*

She linked into the communications network and tried to pull up a picture of what might be happening on the ground. Jasmine knew – as well as anyone else who had endured surprise attacks from enemy forces – just how quickly a situation could go from peaceful to absolute chaos. The real question was just how quickly the mercenaries would react. Marines were trained to react rapidly and attempt to regain control of the situation, but how quickly would a mercenary unit react? It depended on too many factors they knew nothing about – did the mercenaries carry weapons at all times? Did the locals harass them constantly? And just how experienced were they?

"Picking up some heavy communications chatter, all encrypted," one of the analysts said, into the network. "We are unable to decrypt it immediately."

Jasmine wasn't too surprised. Theory stated that decrypting the enemy's communications systems would produce useful intelligence that could be used at once, but theory somehow never accounted for the time it took to break their encryption and then process the new intelligence. In practice, it rarely produced anything useful, unless the enemy were careless. Broadcasting a message, encrypted or not, revealed the location of the transmitter. It could also be the location of a careless enemy CO.

"Entering the atmosphere," the pilot said. "Here we go…"

The shuttle began to rock violently, sending the Marines lurching backwards and forwards in their seats. Jasmine swallowed hard as the shaking grew worse, the pilot taking them into the atmosphere as fast as possible, levelling out over the sea. She'd had nightmares about being trapped in an unpowered shuttle until it hit the ground, back when she'd first been practicing combat landings. There were people, brave in many ways, who couldn't endure parachuting to the ground, let alone orbital insertion from an Assault Shuttle. And she'd once been told that a specialist who had been attached to a Marine unit had had to be pushed out of the aircraft. He'd been too scared to jump.

She winced as the shuttle shook again. Incoming enemy fire would have been preferable, she told herself. Linking back into the shuttle's sensors, she saw them coming in over land, heading right towards Elysium City. The designers had placed the city at the mouth of the River Jordan, where it met the sea, allowing the locals to develop their seaborne commerce. It was cheaper than vehicles – and had the advantage of being easier to maintain.

"Picking up sensor sweeps from the mercenary base," the pilot said. Red flares of light appeared in Jasmine's HUD. "They're locking onto us. Launching decoys…now."

Jasmine nodded. "Brace yourselves," she ordered. "Jump!"

Her suit jerked as the straps suddenly went taut, pulling her towards the shuttle's hatch. A moment later, she was thrown out of the shuttle and started tumbling towards the ground, followed rapidly by the rest of the Marines. The decoys would create the impression that hundreds of Marines had spilled out of the shuttle and even though the mercenaries would know that was impossible, they'd still have problems sorting out the real Marines from the decoys. Besides, they were still largely out of weapons range.

"Launch the drones," she added, as they fell. "There's no point in hiding now."

CHAPTER EIGHTEEN

> Speed is the key to Marine operations. Why? Because we are almost always outnumbered by our enemies, who may also possess superior firepower. Speed and operational skill, therefore, become our key advantages over our foes. Those require junior officers to be capable of noticing fleeting opportunities and moving to take advantage of them.
>
> -Major-General Thomas Kratman (Ret), A Civilian's Guide to the Terran Marine Corps.

"They're moving the tanks further into the city," the operator warned, as Jasmine landed in the midst of a field and glanced around, looking for trouble. In the distance, there was a burned-out farmhouse and a handful of stray animals. She'd seen enough destroyed farms on Avalon to realise that it hadn't been destroyed very long ago, but the animals were a surprise. Sheep would normally be butchered by the bandits, rather than just being abandoned to wander.

"Understood," she said. She'd hoped that the enemy would come out of the city, to meet the Marines in the open field, but she'd known that it wasn't likely to happen. Tanks were much bigger targets than Marines in powered combat armour and if they exposed themselves, Colonel Stalker would drop KEWs on their heads. Their only hope for bleeding the Marines lay in forcing the Marines to fight them on the ground. "Do we have any ID on their commander just yet?"

"Negative," the operator said. "They're scattering their communications; I think they've also adapted part of the city's communications network to help them. We can't identify a commander from their unit."

Jasmine nodded. A stupid enemy would have been too much to hope for. "We'll advance to contact then," she said, as she signalled the rest of the platoon. They'd spread out, looking for trouble. "Keep monitoring the tanks, but watch for other surprises."

She broke the communications link and glanced at her Marines. "Move out."

Marine combat armour could allow its wearer to jump huge distances in a single bound, or run faster than a cheetah. Jasmine also knew that jumping exposed them to enemy fire, while running too fast could mean running right *into* a problem before it had time to register. Spreading out, the Marines started to move towards the city, watching the drones and remotes as they advanced. Like most stage-one colony worlds, Elysium's road network left something to be desired. It was more suited to horses and carts than modern warfare.

Avalon's road network had been the same, apart from the parts where the Crackers had fixed IEDs to deny the Civil Guard easy use of the roads. They'd snarled up the logistics, even though they'd been careful not to risk too many civilian lives. Jasmine had heard of operations on planets where the enemy literally hadn't given a damn about their own people, as long as they impeded the Empire's troops. How could *anyone* act like that?

They skirted a small hamlet that appeared deserted, apart from a single house at the edge of the tiny village. Jasmine briefly considered attempting to pump the inhabitants for information, before dismissing the thought. They had to try to unseat the mercenaries before they dug into the city. The enemy force did have some HVMs – they'd downed a couple of drones and narrowly missed a remote – and she had to assume that they had other weapons too. Chances were they'd be trying to prepare bargaining chips for negotiation.

Unless they know that they have help on the way, she thought. She hadn't been given the standard exams for potential officers, let alone sent to OCS, but Colonel Stalker and his officers had forced her to work through hundreds of exercises, some on paper and some out in the field.

Only an idiot would rely on interstellar shipping schedules being kept – even without malice, it was easy for a schedule to slip – yet if the mercenaries knew that a warship was going to visit the system within a week, they might try to hold out that long. Or they might want away from the Admiral and his crazy dreams, even to the point where they would bargain with the Marines. But if that was the case, she asked herself, surely they would have surrendered by now.

She linked into the standard communications channel and heard Colonel Stalker's message, identifying the attacking force and calling upon the defenders to surrender. It was the best offer they were likely to get; as collaborators with pirates, they could normally expect nothing more than immediate death. A penal island had to seem preferable. No doubt the mercenaries would want to leave with their guns, equipment and starships, but Jasmine knew that they wouldn't be allowed to go. The Marines needed those ships.

"Picking up a handful of microburst transmissions from the next village," the dispatcher reported. Jasmine's HUD lit up with the location of the hidden transmitters. The drone overflying the village suggested that there were at least a platoon of mercenaries inside the village, along with four vehicles that looked like converted local stock. Jasmine wondered absently if they hated using such simple vehicles, like the more prestigious Imperial Army regiments, or if they were grateful for something that was so easy to maintain. "Do you want to engage?"

Jasmine scanned the map quickly, and then nodded. "I think there's no choice," she said, grimly. They could avoid the village, but that would leave the mercenaries in their rear. She linked back to the platoon and started to issue orders. One fire team would advance directly into the village, while the other two would flank the enemy positions from left and right, respectively. "Bring up the complete network, now."

The Marines ran forward, moving almost as one entity, watching for the enemy. Jasmine smiled to herself in relief as five mercenaries were detected, firing towards the Marines as soon as they appeared in front of them. Most of them were armed with simple assault rifles, rather than plasma cannons or anything that would pose a threat to the Marines, something that puzzled her. They had to know that they were outmatched…why didn't they surrender? One by one, the enemy were picked off, save for a younger mercenary who threw up his arms in surrender. He was luckier than he deserved, Jasmine realised. Blundering forward like that, he could have been taken for a suicide bomber and shot down by one of the Marines before they realised that he was trying to surrender. Thankfully, suicide attacks tended to be carried out by fanatics, rather than mercenaries. The latter wanted to live to spend their money.

"Sweep the village," she ordered, as soon as the firing stopped. There was no time to be gentle; the Marines moved from house to house, kicking down the doors with armoured feet and checking on the inhabitants. Most of them appeared harmless, although the Marines confiscated any weapons they found until they knew that the owners were not going to fire on the Marines. "And see what the prisoner can tell us?"

She didn't want to watch as Sergeant Harris fired questions at the prisoner, but there was no choice. An officer, she'd been told, couldn't just give a distasteful order and then walk away, leaving her juniors to carry it out. The prisoner didn't know very much; apparently, he'd been a new recruit when the Empire had withdrawn from the sector, without any actual stake in the mercenary company. All he really knew was that he and his platoon had been told to keep the village – which controlled the access road to the capital – firmly under control.

"Lieutenant," Blake said, through the communications network, "I think you're going to want to see this."

Jasmine left the prisoner with Harris and walked around to where Blake was waiting, outside a church. Her suit's sensors detected the faint aroma of smoke as Blake pushed open the door, revealing a handful of dead bodies, all young women. Jasmine pushed her shock to the back of her mind and examined them as clinically as she could. They'd been killed by a grenade someone had hurled into the building.

"Their slaves," Blake said. There was a grim note to his voice. Like most of the Marines, he considered himself a protector of the weak and helpless – and the women in the building had been helpless when they'd died. Jasmine had seen the story before, over and over again. Their captors had killed them to prevent the Marines from saving their lives. "They just killed them."

Jasmine saw one of the locals peeking out of his shattered door and waved to him, inviting him to join them. He was a middle-aged man, prematurely aged like many of the farmers on Avalon, looking at the Marines as if he couldn't decide if they were saviours or more tormentors. Jasmine had a sudden vision of what life must have been like before the Unification Wars, where borders had changed weekly and hapless settlers had found themselves caught in the middle of the fighting. And those who had backed the wrong side, or collaborated too early, had found themselves being slaughtered when their planets changed sides once again.

Comics had joked about it, in the centuries of peace that had followed the establishment of the Empire. The jokes didn't seem so funny now.

"They brought them from the city," the man explained. "There wasn't anything we could do for them…"

"I understand," Jasmine said. She forced her rage back into a corner of her mind. There would be time for punishment and recriminations later. "Do you have links to any local resistance?"

The man looked at her for a long moment. "Maybe," he said. "I…"

Jasmine cracked open her helm, allowing him to see her face. "We're Terran Marines, here to liberate your planet," she said. She couldn't blame him for being cautious, but there were limits. "Do you know how to contact the resistance?"

"I can pass on a message," the man said. "What would you like me to tell them?"

Jasmine considered, briefly, and then passed him one of her spare wristcom units. "Tell them to use this to contact us," she ordered, as she closed her helm. "And then we can arrange to work together."

Leaving the prisoner in the hands of the locals – with strict orders not to kill him – the Marines resumed their advance towards the city. Jasmine barely noticed the beauty of the countryside, which became more settled as they closed in on Elysium City, as she wondered if they'd wasted too much time in the village. But, if they hadn't stopped, they wouldn't have realised just how many crimes the mercenaries had committed against the locals. And they might not have been able to make contact with the resistance. There *was* a resistance, she knew; the mercenaries wouldn't have needed so many outposts, or to burn farmhouses, if someone wasn't fighting.

Elysium City wasn't much larger than Camelot, she realised as she studied the updating map, but it might be a tougher nut to crack. The prefabricated buildings that made up the heart of the city were composed of starship hullmetal, while the remainder of the city seemed built out of solid stone quarried from further up the coast. Unlike Camelot, which had sprawled out for miles around the first landing site, Elysium City seemed remarkably compact. The analysts were still trying to decide if the planet had deliberately built an under-populated city or if the planet's ethos had changed since the Empire had withdrawn from the sector.

On the edge of the city, there were a handful of large warehouses. Jasmine was familiar enough with Camelot to guess that they stored food to keep the city fed; feeding even a small city took thousands of tons of food every day. The mercenaries had taken control of them right from the start, probably using food distribution as another way to keep the rest of the population in line. They wouldn't have found it as easy as Avalon's former Council had, Jasmine suspected; Elysium's biosphere contained plenty of plants that humans could eat, with a little preparation. Normally, food from other worlds was unsatisfactory at best, but not on Elysium. They'd been told that the planet's development corporation had had high hopes for introducing new kinds of food and drink on Earth, before the Empire had abandoned the planet.

"Incoming fire," Blake snapped, as red lights flared up in Jasmine's HUD. "I say again, incoming fire!"

"Scatter," Jasmine snapped. Her HUD identified the source of the missiles; a MLRS unit hidden near the warehouses, protected by a handful of tanks. The firing didn't seem to be very accurate, as if the mercenaries weren't entirely sure where they were, but it hardly mattered. They'd forced her unit to scatter. "Engage the missiles as they come down."

She allowed her suit's inbuilt weapons to fire on the incoming missiles as the Marines moved faster, heading up towards the warehouse complex. The ground shook as a handful of missiles detonated, but thankfully none of the Marines were harmed. Ahead, Jasmine saw a tank moving out to engage them, hull-mounted weapons spitting brilliant flickers of plasma fire towards the Marines. That was the true danger, she knew; Marine combat suits were tough, but superhot plasma would burn right through them. As one, the Marines hit the deck.

"Deploy Hornets," she ordered. The suits launched a spread of tiny missiles, each heading right towards the tank. They wouldn't be enough to damage it – the tank was armoured to the point that it could withstand intensive plasma fire – but it would distract the tank's crewmen. "Blake, Joe; plasma grenades."

The remainder of the platoon spread out, providing cover by firing on the tank with their own plasma weapons. Unsurprisingly, the tankers refused to be pulled too far from the warehouses, knowing that a single KEW would be enough to vaporise them. Instead, they just kept spraying fire towards the Marines, hoping for a single hit. Jasmine wondered, absently, if they knew how few Marines they were facing, before deciding that they would know that only one shuttle had entered the atmosphere. There couldn't be more than twenty Marines at most.

Blake advanced rapidly, crawling on the ground, as the other Marines distracted the gunners. As soon as he got into range, he activated his grenade launcher and fired a grenade right at the tank, striking the vehicle's side armour. The plasma grenades generated a far hotter stream of plasma than any plasma cannon, if only because the containment fields didn't have to be maintained to avoid burning the operator. Jasmine saw the tank's gun barrels flare with brilliant white fire, a moment before the hulk simply stopped moving. The crew would have been incinerated without ever knowing what had struck them.

There was no time to delay. The Marines kept moving forward, firing on the mercenaries as they revealed themselves. Half of them seemed to be running back into the city, the other half seemed intent on trying to keep the Marines back long enough for the other tanks to get into position to engage the Marines. Jasmine kept one eye on her HUD, watching as the enemy tanks moved forwards slowly, wishing that she had some proper fire support. A handful of missiles would be very useful right now.

"I see the tanks," Blake said. He'd reached an observation position, just in time to see the next tank appear and start firing towards the Marines. Jasmine linked into his suit and peered through his sensors, and then cursed. The next tank appeared to be Imperial Army surplus, tougher than anything they'd faced so far. "There're three of the brutes."

"Covering each other too," Joe added. "I don't think that we can sneak up on these guys, boss."

Jasmine would have smiled – it was the first time anyone had called her *boss* – if the situation hadn't been so serious. The tanks were holding a position the Marines needed to occupy, but they couldn't dislodge them without using KEWs, which ran the risk of causing massive civilian casualties. And their onboard antiaircraft systems would more than suffice for taking out the shuttle if she ordered the pilot to launch an attack run.

And then she glanced at her HUD's city plan and smiled as the solution struck her. "Keep them pinned down," she ordered the first fire team. The tankers couldn't move very far, or they'd risk exposing themselves. "They're right on top of a sewer."

"I think they have *us* pinned down," Blake grumbled. The waves of plasma fire from the tanks were coming far too close to wiping out the Marines, even though most of the platoon was digging their way into the dirt. "I move from here, they get me…"

Jasmine nodded as she led the third fire team back, away from the warehouses and down towards a point where the sewer should be close to the ground. Selecting a HE grenade, she launched it at the right location and allowed herself a moment of relief when the grenade exposed the sewer. Navigating through it in combat suits wasn't easy, but once they'd found the right location it was simple enough to place a dozen plasma grenades in the right locations, before withdrawing as silently as they'd come. As soon as the fire team was out of the sewers, Jasmine sent the detonation command…and watched in awe as a towering pillar of white fire wiped the tanks out of existence.

"We got them," Blake said. The last tank had been left a lifeless hulk. These tanks had been melted, almost completely. The warehouse had caught fire and the flames were threatening to spread rapidly. "I think we got them."

"Secure the warehouse," Jasmine ordered, quickly. At such temperatures, almost anything flammable could catch fire. If there were civilians trapped inside the building, they had to be liberated immediately. "And then prepare to advance…"

"This is Stalker," the Colonel's voice said. "Hold position; I say again, hold position."

Jasmine blinked in surprise. "Sir?"

"They've contacted us," the Colonel said. "They have hostages."

CHAPTER NINETEEN

> If you want to know which side in any war is the good side, find out which one takes hostages, uses civilians as human shields and terrorises its own people. That side is inevitably the one that isn't good; defeating it may be bloody, but it is infinitely preferable to letting it win. Their willingness to see their own people harmed bodes ill for their future if they win their war.
> —Major-General Thomas Kratman (Ret), A Civilian's Guide to the Terran Marine Corps.

"My name is General Garth," the mercenary commander said. He'd hailed the *Dancing Fool* as soon as First Platoon had started destroying tanks. "I wish to negotiate."

Edward studied the commander thoughtfully. The Marines should have had a complete list of registered mercenary companies, but – unsurprisingly – there was no record of a General Garth. Given how close they were to the Rim, it was quite possible that Garth had never bothered to register. It was unlikely that anyone would notice as long as he didn't try to take up a contract on an inner world.

Garth was a short man, with a boosted muscular structure that suggested a heavy-world origin. His head was completely hairless; one eye had been replaced by an artificial eye that rotated independently of his remaining natural eye. Edward suspected that had to be deliberate choice on his part; it was easy enough to replace a missing eye with the Empire's medical technology. But the overall effect, combined with the blood-red uniform, was fearsome, at least to someone who didn't know how to fight. Edward had a feeling that Garth was trying too hard.

"I am Colonel Stalker, Terran Marine Corps," he said. Garth would have already seen his uniform, of course, although he might have wondered why a Marine was on a half-wrecked ship. "Surrender your men now and you will live…"

"I'm afraid that's not good enough," Garth interrupted. "Right now, my men and I are dug into the main city – and we have hostages. If you try to dig us out, those hostages will be killed."

Edward scowled. He *hated* dealing with people who took hostages. Right now, thousands of people were fleeing the city for an uncertain safety in the countryside, but the mercenaries were doing their best to keep a handful confined in the city. The Marine Corps knew better than to think that all hostages could be recovered safely – the hostage-takers had too many advantages – yet Edward didn't want to lose a single one. It went against the grain.

"You have to know that you're not going to win this," he said, calmly. "We control the high orbitals; Elysium City is already emptying. You can kill your hostages, but if you do, we'll kill you. There isn't any way out, unless you surrender. You'll get to keep your lives."

He watched Garth, trying to read the man. What were his people thinking? Would they stick a knife in his back and surrender, or would they go down fighting? Did they even know that their boss was negotiating with the Marines? Garth was using a standard channel, without encryption, but Edward had never heard of anyone monitoring standard channels unless it was specifically part of their duties. Imperial Law required all starships, space stations and military bases to monitor the channels constantly; mercenaries on the ground could not be expected to follow that law.

"Only to go into prison," Garth said. One thing about penal colonies held true; they were *always* the final destination for their unwilling colonists. The Imperial Navy fired on all craft that tried to land without permission, usually without bothering to ask questions first. "We don't want to do that."

Edward looked at him, rather sardonically. "You would rather die?"

"We can wait until you offer us better terms," Garth said. "Do you know how long it will be until the Admiral sends another ship here? Of course you don't."

"Right," Edward agreed. Looking at the report from the boarded freighters, it was clear that one of them had been adapted to carry the mercenary company's equipment. The other two looked to have been taken as prizes at some point and brought to Elysium. There was no clue as to what had happened to their original crews. But it did suggest that the Admiral wasn't in regular contact with his occupation force.

"On the other hand," Edward added, "if we do have to withdraw from this system, we'll bomb you before we go."

"And kill the hostages," Garth pointed out. "I think we will wait."

His face vanished from the display. "Damn," Edward said, out loud. He'd been told that the key to conducting negotiations was to remain firm at all times, but it didn't seem to have worked very well. Garth was right, in a sense; sooner or later, the Admiral *would* want to check up on Elysium. The hostage situation had to be resolved before then. "Analysis?"

"He has a voder implanted in his mouth, distorting his voice," the analyst said. "That's a fairly standard precaution among people who live on the fringes, sir; they don't want people being able to determine their truthfulness from their voice. But we believe that he's under a great deal of stress. It's possible that his own followers will overthrow him when they realise that they're caught in a trap."

Edward, who already knew that, scowled. "Is there anything useful you can draw from his words?"

"Nothing," the analyst admitted. "But sir, if he knew that there was a starship on the way, surely he'd try to stall as long as possible."

"Perhaps," Edward said. He scowled, considering the possibilities. Unfortunately, that one made a great deal of sense. If the Admiral *did* have a starship scheduled to arrive at Elysium, Garth might be right to try to hold out, relying on his human shields to cover his ass. He might think that Edward was bluffing when he'd threatened to bomb the city before withdrawing from the system, or he might believe that the Admiral's ship could sneak up on the *Dancing Fool* before she could escape. "Options?"

"We could broadcast a message on their channel, directly to his people," Kitty offered. "They might not know that he's playing with their lives."

Edward considered it, briefly. It *might* work – if the reports of atrocities on the surface were accurate, the mercenaries would be desperate for *someone* to get them out of the line of fire – but Garth might have too firm a grip on power to be removed so easily. And if it failed…

"We're going to have to take them out," he said, and winced inwardly. It was going to be costly. "Move Fourth Platoon down to the surface to reinforce First Platoon. The freighters can take care of themselves for the moment."

"Understood," Gwendolyn said.

Jasmine watched, as dispassionately as she could, while hundreds of thousands of people fled the city. Elysium City had a larger population than they'd appreciated, partly because the mercenaries had ordered most of the citizens to cram themselves into the heart of the city rather than spreading themselves out into the empty buildings. Now, the civilians were running for their lives, heading outside the city in the hopes of avoiding being caught in the line of fire. They might escape the fighting, Jasmine knew, but she doubted they would escape the privation that was to come.

The Marine Corps prided itself on trying to take care of civilians and most operations were conducted with an eye to supporting the locals, as well as keeping them away from the fighting. It was good policy, she'd been taught; if local civilians could be convinced that the Marines were actually there to help them, they would volunteer the sort of intelligence the Marines needed to carry out precision strikes on their enemies. But, as always, theory was easier than practice; the Marines were normally only sent in when the shit had hit the fan and the Empire's other servants had convinced the locals that the Empire was only out to exploit them. After a few years of Earth-appointed governors milking them for all they were worth, the locals were normally rebellious and the Marines faced an uphill struggle.

"We don't have the field rations for them," Blake said, quietly. Even his irrepressible nature had been dimmed by watching the tide of humanity. "How do we feed them?"

Jasmine shook her head grimly. They'd never considered bringing enough ration packs to feed an entire city's population, nor did they have the shipping to transport them if they had considered it. She'd already sent one fire team to secure the remaining food warehouses, but looters were now on the streets, stealing food from the handful of shops that the mercenaries had allowed to remain open. The Marines just didn't have the numbers to secure them, even though she'd given orders that looters were to be shot on sight.

"We just have to see what the farms can offer," Harris said. Jasmine didn't know him as well as the rest of the platoon – he'd been in Sixth Platoon before it had effectively been disbanded, transferring into First Platoon to give her an NCO who wasn't so familiar with her – but there was no doubting his competence. "If they're anything like the farmers on Avalon, they'll have stashed away plenty to eat in a dozen different places."

Jasmine nodded. It was certainly something to check, although she had a feeling that extracting the food from the farmers would be difficult. But then, on Avalon, they'd been forced to work by the old Council and had resisted savagely; here, the oppressors had been outsiders. Would they help their fellow locals? Or would they put their own families first?

But then, it was easy to draw substance from Elysium's biosphere. Perhaps she was worrying over nothing.

The Marines had stopped just outside the cluster of prefabricated buildings that made up the heart of the city. Inside, the mercenaries were still holding out, using a handful of smaller tanks to keep their hostages firmly trapped. Jasmine had ordered drones and remotes to quarter the area, but after losing a handful of microscopic spies she realised that it was effectively useless. The mercenaries had cleared enough space around their complex to make any frontal attack suicide. They'd have to go underground…

If they didn't think to block the sewers, Jasmine thought, sourly. They'd used the sewers once, alerting the mercenaries…if they knew, of course, what had happened to their tanks. If they knew to watch for intruders in the sewer system, the Marines would walk right into a trap. The alternative was to drop in from high overhead…it might work, if the mercenaries weren't watching for flyers. But if they were detected, they would be blown out of the air within seconds.

"Fourth Platoon has landed outside the city," Colonel Stalker informed her. Jasmine allowed herself a moment of relief. Reinforcements would be very helpful. "You will continue in command until Lieutenant Faulkner is appraised of the situation."

"Understood," Jasmine said. Part of her had hoped that Faulkner would assume command at once, but that wasn't the Marine way. The person who knew what was going on outranked the person who didn't. It was a lesson the Marines had learned the hard way – and the Civil Guard never had. "Colonel, I think we're going to have to try to get in through the sewers."

She outlined her reasoning as the Colonel listened. "Sir," she concluded, "we're not going to be able to get combat armour through the sewers we have listed on the chart."

"Yes," the Colonel agreed. He didn't sound any happier than Jasmine felt. "See if you can round up some local technicians and start asking questions. They might be able to provide some proper intelligence."

Jasmine nodded and checked with the platoon. A number of civil officers had identified themselves to the Marines, once they'd realised that they weren't being attacked by a different group of pirates. They appeared to believe that the Empire had returned to the sector and Jasmine hadn't had the heart to tell them otherwise. Instead, she met up with them in an office building and checked their plans of the underground network, comparing them to the ones the Marines had brought with them. Unsurprisingly, the network had been expanded since the last update.

"We sealed off this section," a local engineer explained. "They were still landing, so we hoped that we could hide it completely from their gaze, allowing us to hide weapons right under their noses. If they'd pulled their ships out of orbit, we could have retaken the city."

"Apart from those damned tanks," another official pointed out. He'd demanded protective custody before anything else, apparently in fear that his fellows would lynch him as a collaborator. A number of locals had already been killed, or had their heads shaved, for working too closely with the occupiers. Apparently, the latter had slept freely with the mercenary soldiers. "How would we have stopped them?"

Jasmine held up a hand before the argument could get to blows. "It doesn't matter right now," she assured them. "All that matters is getting into the sewers and using them to break into the complex. Now…how much can you tell me about the complex itself?"

Slowly, inch by inch, they put together a chart of the government complex. Not unlike many other early colony worlds, it consisted of five massive conical dumpsters that had been dropped from orbit by the first colonists. Normally, they would have been retired and then broken up for scrap metal once the colony was on its way to success – Avalon's dumpsters were long gone – but Elysium had never bothered to retire them. Jasmine couldn't tell if that was caused by the fact that half the population seemed to have become hunter-gatherers or if the planet's governors had simply found better things to do with their money. Now that Elysium had been abandoned by the Empire, the money to build a better home for the government would have to be found on the planet itself. There would be no influx from the rest of the sector.

"The governor used to live here before he left us," the engineer explained, tapping the centre dumpster. "After that, it was abandoned until the bastards arrived and took control of the complex for themselves. At first, they allowed the council to keep meeting normally so we'd keep producing food for them…"

He shook his head. "And then they just took hostages and started issuing orders directly," he added. "Children from the wealthiest people in the city are held as prisoners within the complex."

Jasmine scowled. Child hostages were the worst of all. "What did they actually want from you?"

"Just food and drink," the former collaborator said. "They ordered us to produce a considerable amount every two months; it would be picked up by a starship, which then took it somewhere beyond our ken. They never asked for anything else; they did attempt to round up people with experience of working in space, but hardly anyone came forward and they never pressed the issue."

Interesting, Jasmine thought. They'd shown every sign of wanting to press that demand on Avalon…had they thought that Elysium's spacers had left with the governor? Or had they been less desperate for personnel? Or…what? Maybe they hadn't intended to be so harsh on Avalon, assuming that the spacers would be more cooperative if they believed their homeworld was safe. Or maybe she was just over-thinking it.

"They did keep every prostitute on the planet in business," the engineer added, sourly. "And they sometimes seduced girls, or pressured them into bed…"

Jasmine shook her head. On Avalon, girls had been forced into prostitution through simple poverty; it had been the only way to stay alive. Elysium would have had the same problem, probably worse as the Marines hadn't been there to force the colony to start preparing for existence without the Empire. But then, they could take food from the planet's biosphere…

"Tell me," she said. "Do you know when the next shipment was supposed to be dispatched?"

"Going from past experience, another week from now," the engineer said. "But their timing was never very good. Why?"

"I've had an idea," Jasmine said. Sending them back to the holding area outside the city, she studied the plans until Lieutenant Faulkner entered. "Sir?"

"You get to call me Tom now," Faulkner reminded her, dryly.

Jasmine flushed; Faulkner had been a Lieutenant since before she'd received her own Rifleman's Tab. He'd been marked down for possible promotion to Captain before the company had been exiled to Avalon and would probably wind up commanding a regiment of Knights. Calling him anything other than *sir* seemed absurd.

"I assume command," he said, smiling at her flush.

"I stand relieved," Jasmine said, gravely. She pointed to the plans of the sewer network under the complex. "I think I have an assault plan worked out…"

They discussed it briefly, comparing notes and thoughts. Getting in would be straightforward, particularly using the parts of the network the locals had managed to hide. After that, General Garth would need to be captured or killed – and then his subordinates would need to be forced to surrender. One possibility was trying to get the hostages out before continuing the attack…it might be possible, if they were lucky.

"We don't have a complete list of hostages," she concluded, finally. She'd started asking the locals to help her compile one, but so many people were missing that it was impossible to tell if they were hostages, hiding out in the countryside or dead. "We could get half of them out and lose the rest."

"I'll keep Fourth Platoon here, on guard," Faulkner said, tapping the map. "You lead First Platoon through the sewers. It was your idea."

Jasmine grinned. "Me and my bright ideas," she said. "You don't want it for yourself?"

"As soon as they know you're there, we'll be coming in mob-handed," Faulkner reminded her. "That's going to be the most dangerous part of the operation."

"Yeah," Jasmine said, reluctantly. It was dangerous – and not just for the Marines. Civilians could be caught up in the firing line. "Don't fuck up."

CHAPTER TWENTY

An ancient piece of military wisdom runs "in difficult ground, press on; on hemmed-in ground, use subterfuge; in death ground, fight." A counterpart to that wisdom advises commanders always to leave the enemy a way out. This may seem absurd, until one realises that an enemy with nothing to lose is one who will fight to the death.

This is the fundamental problem facing the Empire's stance on piracy. If the pirates are always sentenced to death, they will fight – but merely imprisoning them doesn't provide sufficient punishment for their crimes…
-Major-General Thomas Kratman (Ret), *A Civilian's Guide to the Terran Marine Corps.*

The children were restless again.

Eric Hazelton looked at the little mites, sleeping on the hard metal floor on rough bedding, and felt a hint of guilt and pity. He hadn't signed up to take hostages and bully children. It was worth risking his life to escape from the mining colony where he'd been born, but bullying children? There was no way he could convince himself that he was doing the right thing. He hadn't really been given a choice, however, and he knew exactly what Garth would do to him if he showed too many scruples. Scruples were for mercenary companies that weren't in danger of being stranded on a very hostile planet.

Silently, he paced through the room, wondering if they would ever get off the damned world, or if the children would survive their confinement. Now that the planet was being attacked by another force, it wouldn't be long before the government complex itself was attacked – and the children were horrifyingly vulnerable. Eric had nerved himself up to refuse to obey any orders to kill them – they were *children* – but Garth had plenty of sociopaths under his command. *They* wouldn't have any problems killing the children, and then Eric himself. He would have deserted Garth if he had anywhere to go, yet he knew that there was no escape. Deserting Garth and running into the countryside would only deliver himself into the hands of the resistance. They'd kill him in a truly horrific manner and leave the body for Garth's men to find.

He took a look at a pair of little girls, huddling together for warmth, and started to turn back towards the far side of the compartment. A moment later, he felt a pair of strong arms wrapped around his throat, just before a sharp knife sliced through his skin. Eric realised, in a final moment of awareness, that he'd finally escaped Garth's madness, before falling into darkness…

Jasmine hated to kill the mercenary in front of the children, some of whom had been woken by the thud as the man's body hit the ground, but there was no choice. The vision of what could happen when – if – a grenade went off inside the compartment had haunted her as soon as she'd realised where the hostages were being kept. Sneaking through the sewers had been unpleasant, but it was nothing compared to risking the lives of children…

"Get the kids out of here," she subvocalised. The rest of the platoon had already taken up position to cover the kids, but she needed to get the kids out before the shit *really* hit the fan. So far, the mercenaries didn't seem to have realised that they were there, yet she knew they'd cotton on sooner rather than later. "Hurry!"

The kids had a bad case of Stockholm Syndrome, she realised, as the local volunteers started chivvying them towards the hatch. Or maybe it was just the stench drifting up from the sewers below. Most of them kept staring at the body, or at the armour-clad Marines as if they thought the Marines were monsters. Jasmine watched them go, praying that they would have time to get the children out before it was too late. It took seven minutes to get them all into the sewers.

"Let's move," she muttered. According to the locals, Garth had set himself up in the former President's suite. Jasmine wasn't too surprised. Mercenaries weren't often as loyal to one another as the Marines, even though most of their leaders did have experience in a proper military. But no one had been able to find Garth's file, if he had a file. "Follow me."

Blake's voice was too quiet for unenhanced ears to hear, but the communications network picked it up easily. "Why didn't they have more guards with the children?"

"I don't think the children could have escaped that airlock," Joe pointed out, as they reached the top of the ladders. There was a solid airlock in front of him, utterly impregnable if all one had was bare hands. "Besides, Garth might also have been trying to *protect* the children from his own men."

Jasmine grimaced. Everyone knew that soldiers and spacers developed new concepts of beauty after long voyages, even if they weren't totally perverse. Some of the kids were definitely approaching adulthood. And besides, mercenaries weren't anything like as disciplined as *real* soldiers. Some of them might be interested in children, or had perhaps even joined up to avoid being arrested and executed for child abuse. Or maybe Garth was just being careful and she was over-thinking it. They'd find out once they'd won the fight.

"Get the charges on the airlock," she ordered. It wouldn't stand up to the shaped charges the Marines used to blow their way through obstacles in their path. "Hurry."

Blake slapped the two charges in place and then ducked backwards for cover. Jasmine braced herself as he sent the detonation command, blowing the airlock out of the bulkhead and right into the compartment beyond. Her audio-discrimination program picked up a scream from outside as a massive piece of flying debris knocked down a mercenary, followed rapidly by shouts of alarm. The Marines plunged through the gap where the airlock had been and opened fire, trying to take out all of the mercenaries before they could recover. Two threw down their guns and surrendered; a third was badly injured, unable to offer any resistance. The remainder either fled or died.

Jasmine keyed her communicator. "We've been detected," she said. Garth would have to be deaf to avoid hearing the explosion as they blew through the airlock. "It's time for you to come in from the outside."

Absently, she wondered just how good Garth was at coping with chaos. He'd have one threat *inside* his command centre and another one coming in from outside. If he pulled his men back to deal with the former, the latter would secure the outside and trap him, holding him helpless. But if he didn't pull his men back, Jasmine's team would catch and kill him. The safest course of action would be to abandon the complex entirely, if he could. Was there a way out of the President's suite that didn't show up on the plans?

She led the way up the stairs, firing at the mercenaries as they sought to slow the Marines down. They wore body armour too, she noted; good enough to block stun bolts even if they couldn't protect their wearers from armour-piercing bullets. Garth seemed to agree that his men should be armed at all times, although the weapons weren't very good by Marine standards. It was quite possible that they'd spent most of their funds obtaining and maintaining the tanks that had provided the heavy firepower. Jasmine wasn't used to having to actually *pay* for her equipment, but she had bartered with supply officers in the past and the principle was the same.

The complex rocked alarmingly as a missile landed too close to the structure. Her HUD notified her that Lieutenant Faulkner and Fourth Platoon had begun their assault, firing on the remaining vehicles the mercenaries had landed on the planet. *Dancing Fool* had moved into position to support them, shooting down a handful of rockets that the mercenaries had tried to fire out at the Marines – or at the city. The update stated that there was no way to know where the mercenaries had been aiming, if they *had* been aiming. They could easily have simply intended to fire at random.

Jasmine jerked back as a stream of plasma fire burned down from high overhead. The top of the stairs, leading into the President's suite of rooms and offices, was blocked by a pair of mercenaries wearing powered combat armour and carrying plasma cannons. Blake threw a pair of grenades up at the mercenaries, only to see their suits take out the grenades before they could detonate. A moment later, they started throwing grenades of their own back down the stairs, forcing the Marines to scramble out into the nearest corridor for cover. They'd been stalled.

Blake held up his plasma cannon. "We could melt through the stairs," he suggested, quickly. "Or…"

"Melt through the ceiling," Jasmine agreed. She checked the plans and located the spot under where the mercenaries were standing, and then detailed four Marines to open fire. So much plasma fire in one spot would have burned them, without armour, but there was no choice. The only alternative was to pull out and allow the complex to be struck by another missile, which would mean abandoning the objective of taking Garth alive and forcing him to surrender his men. "Open fire."

The interior of the dumpster wasn't built with the same hullmetal as its exterior. Jasmine watched with cold anticipation as metal started to run like water, a moment before the ceiling started to collapse and one of the armoured troopers fell through, right on top of the Marines. He had no time to react before three separate Marines fired on him, streams of superhot plasma burning through his armour and killing him instantly. His companion managed to jump backwards, only to slam his helm into the ceiling and fall back to the boiling deck. A moment later, he lifted his hands in surrender.

Jasmine ordered two Marines to watch him – they couldn't force him to take off his armour until the compartment cooled – and led the rest of the platoon into the President's suite. Outside, it was as plain as any starship; inside, there was an astonishing amount of luxury, reminding her of the Wilhelm Mansion on Avalon. Her experience suggested that anyone who obtained a position of political power would start using it to enrich themselves, or at least ensure that they had the best of everything; Elysium's rulers had apparently been no different. The carpet looked to have been imported from the Core Worlds; unsurprisingly, it was also starting to smoulder from the heat.

There was no sign of Garth in the antechamber, or the President's office. Jasmine saw a handful of weapons and papers lying on the desk and checked them quickly, but Garth himself seemed to be absent. She wondered if he might have abandoned his people to fight and die to cover his escape, even though it seemed futile. Where would he go to hide from the locals? They knew their world and they wanted revenge…

Maybe he thinks that the Admiral will save him, she thought, as they moved from room to room. The locals had suggested that the next shipment of foodstuffs was expected to leave in a week; maybe Garth thought he could hide out until then. Or maybe…she heard the sound of someone moving in the next room and tensed, using hand signals to motion Joe and Koenraad forward to cover her. There was someone inside…

She raised her voice, activating the loudspeaker. "Garth," she snapped. "There's no way out. Your men are captured or dead. Give up or we'll hand you over to the locals!"

There was a long pause, followed rapidly by a burst of plasma fire that burned right through the bulkhead. Jasmine jumped to one side, relying on the suit's muscles to throw her out of the line of fire, just before a red light flashed up in her HUD. She felt as if the world had just exploded around her; Koenraad had taken a hit, right in the chest. A bullet wound in the chest might not have been fatal, but plasma fire caused massive trauma as well as heavy burns. He was dead the moment it burned through his suit. Jasmine stared in horror, almost freezing, as the suit hit the deck and lay still. She'd seen death before – Marines weren't invulnerable, or immortal – but he was the first person who'd died under her command.

"Get in there," she snapped, forcing her anger and rage into the back of her mind. She couldn't afford to allow it to drive her. "Now!"

Blake fired a pair of stun grenades into the compartment – the plasma fire had destroyed most of the bulkhead – and followed them in, weapon at the ready. Garth had been hiding behind the bed, balancing his plasma cannon on the sheets as he fired on the Marines. Blake fired several shots back and then ducked for cover, forcing Garth to swing the cannon around to fire on him. Jasmine took the opportunity to fire two shots at Garth, one striking the mercenary in the shoulder and the other striking the plasma cannon. She yelled a warning to Blake as the containment field collapsed, releasing a storm of white-hot plasma. For a long moment, she could have sworn she saw Garth's form wrapped in blinding light, an instant before it faded into nothingness. The flames scorched the entire suite, forcing the Marines to step back before the deck melted. They were barely in time to escape.

Jasmine keyed her communication. "We have a KIA," she reported, bitterly. Her first death…how did Colonel Stalker live with himself? How many Marines had died under his command? "Rifleman Jurgen, KIA; I say again, KIA."

"Understood," Colonel Stalker said.

If the Marine had been injured, they would have moved Heaven and Earth to get him into a stasis tube, where he would have been frozen until the medics had time to treat him properly. But there was nothing they could do for him now and they knew it, apart from preserving what remained of his body for burial. Jasmine felt sick as she realised that *she* would be responsible for handling the funeral.

But there was no time for grief now. "Sweep through the rest of the complex," she ordered, grimly. She hoped, for their sake, that any remaining mercenaries were smart enough to surrender. Her platoon was in a murderous mood. "With Garth dead, they know they don't have a hope."

Colonel Stalker was already broadcasting to the mercenaries as Jasmine reorganised her platoon and started to sweep down through the rest of the complex, telling the mercenaries that their leader was dead and that the locals were coming to kill them. Their smart choice – the only one that would keep them alive – was to surrender to the Marines. It seemed to be having some effect, Jasmine decided, as a handful of mercenaries appeared with their hands in the air. The Marines kept a sharp eye on them anyway; it only took one bastard faking a surrender to start a massacre.

"We took seventy and a half captives," Lieutenant Faulkner reported. "One of them had his legs blown off."

Jasmine groaned at the weak joke. Added to the mercenaries captured by Jasmine's platoon, they'd taken one hundred and ten captives in total – but she was fairly sure that most of them were just ignorant grunts. They probably wouldn't know anything useful, although they'd be desperate to please the Marines. The alternative was facing outraged locals…

We should leave them here, part of her mind whispered. They killed a Marine!

She pushed the thought to the back of her mind. The Marine Corps took prisoners, when the prisoners were ready to surrender. It was good policy, she'd been told time and time again; people who believed that they wouldn't be killed if they surrendered were more likely to surrender than those who thought the Marines would simply kill them when they gave up. And yet one of her Marines was dead…she wanted to kill them all, to burn them down, to avenge a man who'd been her friend as well as her comrade and subordinate.

But he wouldn't have wanted me to do that, would he?

The prisoners were rapidly corralled in a park and guarded by a fire team of Marines, allowing Jasmine and her platoon a chance to go back and recover Koenraad's body. A combat medic had already arrived, but only to pronounce Koenraad dead and start making the preparations for his funeral. Jasmine gently pushed her aside and picked up Koenraad's suit by the arms, allowing Blake to take the legs. They'd carry him back to the shuttle themselves.

"There's nothing more costlier than a battle lost," one of her instructors had said, "than a battle won." Jasmine hadn't understood him at the time; she hadn't understood him at all until now, until she'd lost a man under her command. The taste of victory, of proving that Terran Marines were the best of the best, had been soured by the loss of one of their men. She *knew* that the mercenaries had to be feeling worse, but she didn't really believe it. How *could* she?

Two new shuttles from the *Dancing Fool* were landing in the city, one carrying Colonel Stalker and the representatives from Avalon, the other carrying half of Third Platoon, coming to reinforce the Marines on the ground. It didn't look as if the orbiting station had provided any resistance to the Marines, thankfully. Taking the station intact would be immensely useful in the future. She paused as Colonel Stalker emerged from the shuttle and walked over to Jasmine, stopping in front of Koenraad's body. It hurt him as much as it hurt her, she realised. He'd never come to accept losing Marines in combat.

"You did well," he said, very quietly. "Well done."

"Thank you, sir," Jasmine managed. "I…does it get easier?"

The Colonel understood. "No," he said, sadly. "It never gets easier."

CHAPTER TWENTY-ONE

Liberating Elysium was the first step towards building a replacement for the Empire. Not all of us were comfortable with the thought, of course, but it had to be done. The Empire had failed and if we were to keep something of civilisation alive, we could not fail. However, this left us with a problem. The agreements we reached with other colony worlds had to be ones that we could all live with.

That wasn't going to be easy.

They say that compromise is a dirty word. There's a very good reason for that.

- Professor Leo Caesius, *The Perilous Dawn* (unpublished).

"I was sorry to hear about your man, Colonel."

President Bone had been the third or fourth in the line of succession to the Presidency of Elysium – Edward wasn't sure he understood the system very well – before the mercenaries had arrived and taken over the planet. Bone had been in hiding, moving from nomad group to nomad group, trying to keep some semblance of the pre-invasion government intact. He'd succeeded about as well as could be expected, but he'd known that he was fighting a losing war until the Marines arrived. Now, perhaps, Elysium could breathe free.

"Thank you," Edward said. He had rarely had time for politics on Earth – which was partly what had gotten him into trouble and exiled to Avalon – while he seemed to spend half of his time on Avalon wrestling with local politics. "And I was sorry to hear about your loss too."

"My children are safe," Bone said. His family had become hostages too, but his wife had been killed before the Marines arrived, officially for trying to escape. Edward suspected that the truth was far darker, but none of the prisoners they'd taken seemed to know what had happened. "I think that's all that matters right now."

He leaned forward. "Apart," he added in a nastier tone, "from the fact that you are keeping the prisoners. We want them handed over to us."

Edward winced. He'd been expecting that demand, but it didn't make it any easier to deal with. The Marines had accepted surrender – and that gave them a responsibility to look after their prisoners, as long as the prisoners behaved themselves. He couldn't fault the locals for wanting to execute each and every last member of the mercenary unit, but the Marines had to keep them alive. Besides, the interrogators were already drawing what they could from the prisoners; even if they didn't know specific details, they knew enough to allow the analysts to put together a better picture of what was happening outside the Avalon System.

"We took them prisoner," Edward said. "We cannot let you kill them."

Bone's eyes flared. "Do you know what they did here?"

"Yes," Edward said, flatly. "I know what they did."

There had been no time for a WARCAT investigation, but they hardly needed one. The mercenaries had behaved better than the bandits on Avalon...which wasn't saying very much. They'd taken girls as slaves as well as hostages, they'd looted from the local population – and they'd fired on civilians, either to scare them or merely for amusement. The Admiral had been scraping the barrel when he'd hired Garth and his men...Edward had privately wondered if they'd been sent here so they couldn't cause trouble elsewhere. After all, the Grand Senate had followed the same reasoning when they'd exiled Edward and his men to Avalon.

"Then you must understand that we want justice," Bone snapped. "They have to *die!*"

Edward took a breath. "I understand how you feel," he said, as gently as he could. "But if we start killing our prisoners after they surrender, no one else will surrender to us."

The thought made him scowl. Compared to the Civil Guard, or even the Imperial Army, losing just one Marine was miraculous. But every

Marine was easily worth at least ten regular soldiers and losing even one of them weakened his force considerably. When he considered that he had *started* with an understrength force in the first place…he'd already had to parcel out too many Marines to shore up the Knights of Avalon. He couldn't afford to lose any more Marines.

Edward held up a hand before Bone could say anything else. "We will take them off the planet and drop them on a penal colony," he continued. He decided not to mention that the penal colony was an island on Avalon, several thousand miles from civilisation. It would only upset the President. "You will never have to see them again."

"I must protest, officially," Bone said. He looked down at the floor for a long moment, and then back up at Edward. "What do you intend to do now?"

"I'm working on it," Edward said. The teams inspecting the three freighters they'd captured had confirmed that two of them were common tramp freighters, presumably hijacked by the Admiral's ships, while the third had served as Garth's transport vessel. It wasn't configured for Marine operations, but it was better than anything else they had. "The pirates are supposed to show up in a week for their next shipment."

Bone's eyes gleamed. "And you intend to give them a hot reception?"

"Something like that," Edward said. Maybe they could board and storm the second pirate ship, then pull navigational data from the ship's hull. Without it…they were interrogating the mercenaries, but none of them seemed to know anything useful, like where the Admiral was based. "After that, we will have to decide what to do next."

He looked over at the President. "Did you get any response to your broadcast for anyone with space experience?"

"Plenty," Bone told him. "Hundreds of them signalled in already – and there will be more, once word spreads."

Edward had to smile. Elysium's strange nomad culture had absorbed hundreds of spacers, looking for the simpler life. They hadn't really realised what it meant until the Empire withdrew from the sector and the Admiral's pirates turned up, demanding submission and surrender. Now there was a chance to go back into space, they were willing to take it, even if it did mean working with the Marines. At least the problem of trained manpower was about to go away for a while.

"Look for other people with skill-sets we can use," he added. "Technicians and engineers, teachers and researchers…anything we can use to rebuild the tech base the Empire no longer offers us. God alone knows how much time we have."

Bone leaned forward. "Until what?"

"Until what we have already falls apart," Edward said. "How long do we have before our gear wears out?"

It wasn't a pleasant thought, but it had to be faced. Anyone with any sense knew that *everything* wore out. Weapons, starship components… even basic tools. If they failed to set up a production line to replace everything that was slowly wearing out, civilisation would eventually start to crumble along with the worn-out components. The RockRats survived so well because most of what they produced was very basic, easily maintained and sustained. It would be possible to support Avalon's current situation almost indefinitely. But it would leave them completely defenceless if – when – someone turned up with bad intentions.

And the Admiral had already started to threaten Avalon.

"Very well," Bone said. He settled back in his chair – he'd stayed in his old office, as the President's former office had been melted down to slag – and smiled. "In exchange for our human capital, we shall be wanting a regular shipment of HE3…"

Edward smiled back. "The Professor will handle all such negotiations," he said, quickly. It would give the poor man something to do, rather than worrying about his daughter. "And I believe that he also intends to offer you an alliance."

Bone considered it. "My people may not be interested in another alliance," he pointed out. "The Empire certainly didn't treat us very well. How do we know that you won't do the same?"

"Perhaps I should let the Professor explain," Edward said. He reached for his wristcom. "With your permission…?"

"On the face of it, a centralised authority has much to recommend it," the Professor said. "There are no arguments about who is actually in charge, while the government is – at least in theory – capable of taking everything into account before making decisions. Unfortunately, such a system is remarkably inefficient even when restricted to a single planetary surface. It is completely inefficient when dealing with something the size of the Empire."

Edward nodded. It took six months to get a starship from Earth to Avalon. If he'd wanted to request new orders from the Grand Senate, before the Empire pulled out, it would have taken a year for his message to reach Earth and a reply to be sent, assuming that it was sent immediately. By then, whatever crisis had required new orders would have either blown over or exploded in his face. The Empire had tried to cope with the problem by appointing governors to entire sectors, but it hadn't worked very well. Sharing out power just wasn't how the Grand Senate did things.

It got worse, even when deliberate malice wasn't involved. The Grand Senate could and did stamp on the colonists, insisting that they followed laws made on Earth, laws that weren't made for their benefit. Some colonies had been restricted from becoming anything other than a purely agricultural settlement, because having a new industrial world would upset the Core World corporations. Others had been stripped of their natural resources, or had specific legislation drawn up by corporate-backed Senators that restricted their ability to control corporate behaviour on their territory. And then the Grand Senate wondered why so many worlds were rebellious, requiring the military to put down the revolts at staggering cost.

"The Empire isn't evil," Edward had been told, back when he'd been a Rifleman and had his first exposure to the way things worked. "It's just bloated and stupid."

The Professor leaned forward. "We believe that true strength is to be found in a federal system," he continued. "By leaving local authority with the locals, it will be easier to deal with localised problems by coming to a mutually acceptable solution, rather than having a solution imposed from high overhead."

"It sounds good," Bone agreed, thoughtfully. "But how would this work on an interstellar level?"

It definitely sounded good, Edward agreed silently. He'd encouraged the Professor to think about the best way to create a new interstellar alliance, something that could unite the sector against the Admiral, and he'd done a fairly good job of devising something that might work. It would have to be tried, of course, and tested; theory was all very well, but Edward knew better than to take theory for fact. The only way they'd know for sure was through practical experience.

But it would *have* to work better than the Empire. On Earth, the complexities of the Rim sectors were simply not visible. The Grand Senate judged without any real awareness of the facts on the ground, either through listening to corporate representations or simply assuming that the problems were the same in all cases. But the Grand Senate had had massive firepower at its disposal to try to enforce its rulings. Edward knew that Avalon didn't even begin to have the firepower to keep the sector in line.

"Each star system would be responsible for its own internal government, provided it stayed within certain limits," the Professor said. He'd written out a Bill of Rights that – he claimed – made more sense than the thousands of rights 'guaranteed' by Imperial Law. "The systems would elect a single representative to an interstellar parliament, which would be responsible for issues like building a military and handling relationships with other powers. And there *will* be other powers, Mr. President. The Empire will leave a great many successor states in its wake."

Edward's wristcom buzzed. "Colonel," Gwendolyn said, "one of the interrogators just turned up something interesting. He would like you to see the prisoner."

"Understood," Edward said. He could leave the Professor trying to convince Bone of the wisdom of joining the planned interstellar alliance. Edward had spent hours on the *Dancing Fool*, attacking the Professor's concepts as savagely as he could, forcing him to tighten up the weaknesses. Perhaps Bone could spot other problems, perhaps not…besides, his entire planet had just had a lesson in why some kind of interstellar authority was necessary. "Excuse me, gentlemen."

There were no formal interrogation chambers on Elysium, so the prisoners were being isolated in a handful of buildings and interrogated in one of the shuttles. Once they were interrogated and certified useless, they were moved to one of the freighters, which would be sent directly back to

Avalon. The prisoners would be transported to a penal island, while the Avalon Council would receive a complete report on the Battle of Elysium. They'd also receive the first wave of experts recruited from the nomads.

"This woman was Garth's whore," Gwendolyn explained, as Edward met her outside the shuttle. "She says she knows something we need to know, but wants to make a deal."

"Everyone wants to make a deal," Edward muttered. He accessed the shuttle's internal sensors and studied the woman. She'd been cuffed to a metal chair, an experience that should have been more than a little disconcerting, but she seemed surprisingly calm. "Calm, isn't she?"

"She may have been through some form of Conduct After Capture course," Gwendolyn said. "Or she might just have had to put up with Garth."

Edward snorted. Conduct After Capture was one of the most dreaded parts of the Slaughterhouse's extensive training, schooling Marines in what they should do if they fell into enemy hands. Marine Regulations allowed them only to admit their name, rank and serial number, but everyone knew that any captured Marine would be put through hell by his captors. They might be drugged, or tortured, or simply mistreated; the savagery of the Conduct After Capture course was meant to reflect it. And it succeeded remarkably well.

Pity the course doesn't start with an intended seduction, he thought with a glint of humour. It started by having the recruits rousted out of their beds in the middle of the night, beaten if they tried to fight, and then being thrust into the interrogation cells. *Blake Coleman might have been more careful...*

He looked over at Gwendolyn. "Is she prepped for resisting interrogation?"

"We're uncertain," Gwendolyn admitted. Edward gave her a sharp look. "Her body chemistry is messed up; the medics think she's actually addicted to a couple of drugs – it may have been how Garth controlled her. We shoot her with truth drugs and she might sing like a canary, or her heart might burst."

Edward nodded. Drugs were a recurring problem in the Undercity on Earth – and almost everywhere else in the Empire. The producers often kept their workers addicted to their product, making it hard for them to leave or seek help. It was simple enough to tailor a drug to a specific person – and, once they were addicted, the withdrawal symptoms would kill them. Or, for that matter, just giving them a basic drug that did the same. There was a planet where addicts were sent, where they could produce their own drugs. God alone knew what had happened to it now that the Empire was crumbling.

"Then we'll talk to her," he said, and stepped into the shuttle. The girl looked up as he entered the makeshift interrogation room and introduced himself. "I'm Colonel Stalker, CO."

His heart went out to the girl as he saw her clearly. She was painstakingly thin, her body badly bruised; he couldn't tell if the bruises had been caused by Garth, or merely poor health. Her eyes were dull, her hair long and lanky, seemingly on the verge of falling out. His first guess, he suspected, was correct. She *was* addicted to something.

"I need Dust," the girl said, without preamble. "And I don't want to be with them."

Edward frowned. Dust – Sparkle Dust – was hardly the worst addictive drug in the Empire, but if the girl had been a regular user...

"We can help you overcome the withdrawal symptoms," he said, after a moment. There had been some Dust-producers on Avalon, but they'd been rounded up and dumped on a penal camp. Chances were that someone had taken their place, yet they'd been very quiet. "What do you have to offer us in exchange?"

"Garth never trusted the Admiral," the girl said. Her body was starting to shake, either through fear or the onset of the first symptoms. Edward couldn't remember how long it took for Dust Mites – addicts – to go into withdrawal. "He thought that the Admiral would betray him, eventually. So he let the man have command of the navigation systems on the ship, but he left sensors on the hull. I know where those records were stored."

"I see," Edward said, fighting down the urge to laugh. Maybe naked human eyes couldn't identify stars, but it would be simple to locate the Admiral's base through running the sensor records through the computer files. "And where is that?"

The girl looked down at the deck. "Take me out of this nightmare and you can have them," she said. "I just want to be free of this curse."

Drama, Edward thought, crossly. But then, Dust's effects could certainly be considered a curse…

"Very well," he said, making up his mind. The medics could put the girl in stasis while they prepared a course of treatment for her that would take her off the Dust. "Where did he put the records?"

"On the ship," the girl said. "He didn't leave them in his cabin, because he thought the Admiral would have it searched. They're hidden in the tubes."

Edward allowed himself a smile, afterwards. Perhaps the lead wouldn't pan out, but if it did…they'd know exactly where to go next. And the Admiral would have no reason to expect that they were on their way.

CHAPTER
TWENTY-TWO

Marines are a brotherhood – and if you don't know what that means, you will never be a Marine. They live together, work together, play together…if you are a Marine, you have thousands of brothers. Marines from different units slot together, seeking out each other's company when on leave; they even end up retiring to homes on the Slaughterhouse where they can be with other retired Marines.

And when a Marine dies, his or her brothers mourn his passing. But they also celebrate; they celebrate the fact that he was once one of them and that he died well, serving the Empire and placing himself between his people and war's desolation. There can be no finer way to die.

-Major-General Thomas Kratman (Ret), A Civilian's Guide to the Terran Marine Corps.

Every Marine learned about the traditions of the Terran Marine Corps, in exhaustive detail. Jasmine knew why Drill Instructors wore specific hats, the importance of the Rifleman's Tab and every other tradition, bar one. No one knew who had first started the Death Box tradition, or why. The silence was so profound that Jasmine knew that some Corps historians believed that it was deliberately covered up by the Commandant at the time. Others believed that the tradition had been developed spontaneously, without a single originator. Jasmine wasn't sure which one she believed.

The Death Box was small, barely larger than Jasmine's hand. By tradition, every Marine had one, leaving them behind on the ship or

FOB when they went out to battle. If they died in battle, then – and only then – was the box opened, by the senior survivor from the unit. It contained the Marine's last wishes and letters to his friends and family; the boxes could never be opened until the Marine was dead. Tradition demanded it.

Koenraad had left his box on the *Dancing Fool*, along with every other Marine on the ship. Jasmine had had it shuttled down to her as soon as the fighting stopped and she got a moment to relax, even though her body refused to calm down. Her mind kept replaying the awful moment when Koenraad had been shot down, over and over again. She'd seen horror – she'd seen worse horror, including the deaths of other Marines – so why did that vision keep tormenting her? But then, Koenraad had been under her command. Every other death wasn't on her hands. She looked down at her hands and wondered if she should be seeing blood.

You did everything right, fool, she told herself.

She had – and it hadn't mattered. Koenraad had died, doing what he loved. Jasmine knew that she should be glad of that, if nothing else, but it still tore at her as she twisted the box, pressing the Rifleman's Tab against its inbuilt sensor. No Marine ever lost his Tab until he died, whereupon it was returned to the Slaughterhouse. They were never passed on to other Marines.

The box clicked in her hands as the lid opened. Inside, she found a single datachip, a pair of gold pips Koenraad had been awarded by the Slaughterhouse for coming first in both parts of the Crucible, and a folded scrap of paper. Opening it, she found a scrawled set of lines, written in oddly imprecise handwriting. It took her a moment to realise that the language was from Koenraad's homeworld…she'd have to have it translated, just in case it was instructions for his body's disposal. She couldn't speak it herself and it wasn't loaded into her implant. No doubt that would have changed if they'd ever been sent to his homeworld to fight.

Shaking her head sadly, she slipped the datachip into the reader. A moment passed, and then the first message scrolled up in front of her. Koenraad had requested burial on the world where he fell, with an unmarked grave. It wasn't an unusual request among Marines, although several of the ones who had fallen on Avalon had requested burial on the Slaughterhouse, or interstellar space. The former were frozen, waiting until the day contact was re-established.

The second message detailed the disposition of his property. His savings, such as they were, had been donated to the company fund, his handful of possessions were to be distributed among the rest of the platoon. There was no mention of any other donations, but then Marines always travelled light. They just didn't have the rack space to carry vast amounts of junk with them. If Koenraad had property back on his homeworld, his last wishes made no mention of it.

Jasmine barely glanced at the final three messages. One was intended for someone – a girl, probably – on Avalon and would be delivered when the *Dancing Fool* returned home. The other two were marked as being for his family; Jasmine had no idea when *they* would be delivered. The Marines did what they could to ensure that all such messages were delivered – and it was up to her to write to them, to tell them how their son had died – but it might be years before they heard the news. Koenraad's last chance to write to them would have been before they left Earth. Had he written to his family? Jasmine had no way to know that either.

Standing up, she pocketed the chip and dropped the Rifleman's Tab into the Death Box, before sealing it again. The box would be stored until they had a chance to send it back to the Slaughterhouse, where it would be used to inspire new recruits. Jasmine had spent enough time studying the boxes – and the Tabs – back when she'd been a recruit, learning about the men who'd worn them. In the future, would the Marine Corps endure?

We're the Empire's attack dogs, she thought, as she left the compartment. *What will we do without the Empire?*

Two hours later, she stood with the rest of her platoon on a grassy knoll and watched as the body was lowered into the ground. Some planetary authorities were reluctant to have Marines buried on their soil, even if the Marines in question had died trying to save them, but Elysium's government had raised no objections. They'd even offered to provide a preacher and anything else the Marines needed for the service, an offer that had been tactfully refused.

Jasmine took a breath as they started to bury Koenraad's body. "Koenraad joined the Marines at eighteen years old and aced Boot Camp," she said, out loud. It was her duty now, even though it was one she would have gladly passed on to someone else. "At the Slaughterhouse, he did very well, graduating as a full Crucible First. His assignment to a front-line combat unit was a sign of future greatness in his career."

She winced at the memory of her own Crucible. There were two parts to the test, one faced by the prospective recruit completely on her own, the other faced as part of a team. Coming first in both parts – the only way to earn a Crucible First – was difficult; even for the Marines, it was very rare. Koenraad should have gone far; hell, he should have been promoted instead of her. If he'd been in command, would he have lived and Jasmine died? Or would he have still met his death on Elysium?

"On Farnsworth, he served with distinction; on Han, he saved many lives, including mine," she continued. "On Avalon, he fought bravely and well against the Crackers, helping to pave the way for a sustainable peace. Here, he helped save an entire world from slavery. We will miss him."

She bent down, picked up a piece of soil and threw it into the grave. She'd messed it up, she was sure; how could she encapsulate Koenraad in a handful of words? Everything she'd said didn't even begin to encompass him. He'd been smart and funny and sardonic…and she was going to miss him terribly. And he would probably laugh at how badly she'd spoken about him after he'd died.

"Koenraad was a friend," Blake said, into the silence. "He saved my life on Han twice, and once on Avalon, but that isn't what I remember about him. I remember him coming up with a completely insane plan to prank an entire company, back when we were sitting on Han before the rebellion exploded in our face. We slipped into their HQ and started rigging their communications system to issue completely silly orders. I think they cottoned on when their CO sent an order for the best blowjob artist on the base to come and service him at once."

There were some chuckles. Jasmine had been the FNG – Fucking New Girl – at the time, but she remembered hearing about it…and about the icy lecture that every Marine in the company had received about the dangers of fiddling with communications systems. Pranks might have been part of the tradition – and they'd been hit with their own pranks the following week – but there were dangers. And a month later, Han had exploded into violence and half the Marines she'd only just been starting to befriend had been killed.

Blake put his own piece of soil into the grave. Joe stepped forward. "Koenraad was supposed to be my mentor when I joined the company," he said. "He saved me from no small number of embarrassing mistakes while I found my feet, as well as saving my life when the shit finally hit the fan. But what do I remember about him? Which memory sticks in my mind?

"We were all on a Raptor, trying to respond to the first reports of massive civil unrest on Han," he continued. "One moment, everything was fine; the next, some bastard has taken a shot at us with an HVM and we don't have time to react before we get hit. I remember the hatch springing open and Koenraad hurling me out of the Raptor, jumping after me himself seconds later. And then we ended up stuck in a small house, trying to keep ourselves alive until reinforcements could get through to us. There were howling mobs everywhere, baying for our blood. We knew that we couldn't hold out forever.

"It was Koenraad who took command, Koenraad who organised us into holding out for hours before making a daring escape. The mob didn't catch us; we ended up making our way back to the base, meeting up with our reinforcements halfway here. And when we met them, do you know what Koenraad said to them? He asked them what they had been doing while we'd been fighting for our lives? Playing with their cocks?"

There were some chuckles. Joe tossed dirt into the grave and then stepped back, allowing the rest of the platoon to tell their own stories. Jasmine listened; some of the stories she'd known, or she'd been a part of, others were new to her. She'd been luckier than Joe on Han, although not lucky enough to avoid being there. The slaughter had been shocking, yet she had a grim feeling that it would be nothing compared to the slaughter to come. Mandy's father had said that Han might have been the first battle in the fall of the Empire. Jasmine suspected that he was right.

As Koenraad had requested, there was no headstone to mark his grave. Instead, the Marines scattered seeds on it, so that flowers would grow. Koenraad's homeworld had believed in the cycle of life – she had never been sure that Koenraad had been a true believer – but she had a feeling that he would have appreciated it. Elysium would have a future, at least in part thanks to Koenraad's sacrifice.

She looked up at the darkening sky and shivered. Out there, the Admiral was still alive – and he had Mandy. Jasmine had asked the interrogators to check if any of their captives knew what had happened to her, but she suspected that it was nothing more than a waste of effort. Mandy's capture had been months after the Admiral had moved in on Elysium. But, on the other hand, they did have a rough location for one of the Admiral's bases. They could go after him.

And we will, she thought, *as soon as we deal with their supply ship. And finish the wake.*

"This way," she said. Organising the booze was *also* part of the Lieutenant's job, although Blake and Joe had offered to handle it for her. She wasn't sure if they'd offered because they felt sorry for her, or if they distrusted her taste in beer. And it was her responsibility. "I had them set up a tent for us."

She heard the sound of thunder in the distance as night fell over Elysium. The locals, at least, hadn't asked too many questions when she'd ordered several dozen bottles of beer and a tent, although she had no idea of the quality of the beer. For the moment, they were ready to do anything they could for the Marines, thankfully. It wouldn't last – it never did – but she would take as much advantage of it as she could. Inside the large tent, there were chairs and crates of beer bottles, without any glasses. No one would use them anyway.

Jasmine took one of the crates of beer and started to pass them to the rest of the platoon, leaving one for herself. It was part of the old tradition of Marine officers serving their men food before they went into action, although she would have happily foregone this part. Popping open the bottle's lid, she held it in the air and waited for silence.

"Koenraad," she said, simply. "May he rest in peace."

The Marines drank. It wasn't bad beer, Jasmine decided after a moment, although it wasn't quite as good as the beer on Avalon. Or maybe she'd already grown used to thinking of Avalon as home. Marines were normally shuttled around from trouble spot to trouble spot, without being given a chance to put down roots, but they'd been effectively stranded on Avalon for nearly a year. Even now, with a handful of starships at their command, they would never see Earth again. Why *not* put down roots?

They tell us that we are part of a brotherhood, and we are, she thought sourly. *But we may never see the rest of our brothers again.*

She took another swig of the beer and watched as the bottles, one by one, were emptied rapidly. The locals would probably be astonished to see the Marines in the morning, when they would be walking normally; their enhanced bodies swept alcohol out of their bloodstreams before it got a proper grip on them. It simply wasn't possible for a Marine to get drunk.

Which probably doesn't explain why we still drank beer on Earth, she thought, as she picked up a new bottle. *The beer there should have been poured back in the horse.*

She felt a little better the following morning, when they were woken up at 0900 by Command Sergeant Patterson – they'd fallen asleep in the tent – and sent for a long run around the city. Elysium City looked much better in the cold light of dawn, even though the locals were clearing up the rubble and burying bodies. Apparently, according to the command network, they'd started dumping the bodies of the mercenaries in the nearby bog. That didn't seem like a great idea to Jasmine, but she kept her peace. The locals had probably had enough of newcomers from space telling them what to do.

As soon as they returned to the spaceport, they were ordered to board one of the shuttles for the flight back to the *Dancing Fool*. The Marines bitched about it, but they all knew the score; they couldn't stay on Elysium much longer. Jasmine saw a few dozen locals boarding various shuttles as well, all signing up to join the effort to build up the tech base on Avalon, where the extra manpower would be very welcome. If only they had some extra firepower too.

Blake evidently agreed with her. "You think they can outfit one of those freighters with weapons?"

"I doubt it," Joe said, as they strapped themselves into their seats. "You can cram as many weapons as you like into a freighter hull, but they'd be wallowing whales compared to any real warship. No real speed, no real ability to manoeuvre, let alone turn on a dime…"

"Still, you could give some unwary pirate a real shock if you outfitted one of them as a Q-ship," Blake countered. "And *pirates* aren't going to be going around blowing potential prizes out of space at maximum range."

The shuttle lurched to life as the argument continued. Jasmine suspected that Blake was right; piracy operated according to economic laws and blowing ships up at random simply wasn't profitable. The pirates had to capture the ship and her cargo, then get it to someone who could fence it to people who were willing to buy it and not ask too many questions. Thanks to the Empire's restrictions on economic development, there was a whole black market set up along the Rim. Planets on the brink of starvation weren't going to ask where their suppliers had picked up their goods, not when their lives were on the line.

"I think the Grand Admiral forgot to ask your opinion," Joe said. He chuckled. "Should I send him a message with your suggestion?"

"You could send it to Colonel Stalker," Jasmine said, before the argument could turn into a fight. "He'd certainly be interested – and Blake's right, it might work."

The thought made her smile. Pirates also wanted to spend their ill-gotten gains, which meant that sneaking up to something that *might* be a Q-ship wasn't their idea of fun. And there would be no way to be certain that the ship *wasn't* a Q-ship without inspecting it, which would mean getting into weapons range. And *that* would be unfortunate.

Her smile widened. *Very* unfortunate for the pirates.

CHAPTER
TWENTY-THREE

Pirate ships do not have the hierarchy of military warships, nor do their commanders have the support of the establishment against disobedience or death. A pirate captain's position is always at risk from an ambitious subordinate. Unsurprisingly, the senior officers form patronage networks where they offer their protection and support to juniors in exchange for services. Discipline, therefore, is maintained with the lash – or, in the modern world, the neural whip.

-Edward E. Smith, Professor of Sociology. *Pirates and their Lives.*

"Hey."

Mandy looked up, alarmed. She had taken to spending her lunch breaks in a hidden compartment in the ship's vast innards and she hadn't realised that someone knew where she relaxed. The entire crew knew what she'd done to her would-be rapist, but they hadn't said or done anything to her. In a way, she was waiting for the penny to drop.

A grinning face looked at her from the hatch. Ha – if he had any other name, she'd never heard it – was young, no older than Mandy herself. And he was completely psychotic. She'd seen older pirates flinch away from him, or keep one hand on their weapons when they were in his presence. Just looking into his eyes made her feel sick; Ha was a person who wouldn't care how badly he was hurt, as long as he hurt his target too. She had the feeling, going from one of her father's lectures, that Ha had actually joined the pirates at a very young age and grown up in a culture where strength was the key to survival and violence the only way to gain respect.

"Hi," she said, trying hard to hide her nervousness. Ha's grin told her that he wasn't fooled; he *knew* the effect he had on people and liked it. "What do you want?"

"Vane says you're to go to engineering at once," Ha said, as he pulled himself through the hatch. "He wants you there."

"Oh," Mandy said. She looked down at the ration bar and forced herself to take one final bite, washed down with a swig of water. Vane had made her fix one of the water processors too – the pirates had allowed it to decay – and after that she'd been able to draw bottles of water for herself. The processor had really just needed cleaning, but she'd strung it out as long as she dared. "I'm on my way."

"Nice little place you have here," Ha observed, in a manner that reminded her of a friend's irritating little brother. "Shame if something happened to it, or to you if you were here."

He reached out and patted her rear end as she tried to walk past him, grinning unpleasantly. "Maybe we could come to some arrangement," he added. "I can be very accommodating…"

Mandy saw the look in his eyes and couldn't help herself. She fled, driven by absolute terror, his laughter following her as she pulled herself through the tube. Her body felt dirty where he'd touched her, worse than the pirate who'd tried to rape her. He'd merely wanted a quick and unwelcome fuck, or so she told herself. Ha would happily torture her to death for his own amusement. And he was so intimidating that she wouldn't be able to fight if he decided he wanted her.

Ha didn't follow her through the tubes, but he was still in engineering to greet her when she finally arrived at the big airlock. Inside, several other members of the engineering crew were also waiting, having been summoned by their superior too. Mandy hadn't really been able to talk to them; some of the engineers gave the impression of being as twisted as the other pirates, others seemed to be trapped in their own private hells. From what little they'd said, the Admiral had forced them to participate in terrible deeds, leaving them with the knowledge that they'd be killed if they ever made it back to the Empire. Few of them had realised that the Empire had withdrawn from the sector.

Mandy found a place to wait and looked around for Michael. She hadn't seen much of him in the days since she'd killed the rapist. The pirates didn't seem to be trying to keep them apart, but their working shifts were apparently different and she assumed that – like her – he was locked into his cabin when the time came to sleep. It wasn't easy to tell if the pirates trusted them or not – they'd be fools to trust complete newcomers – but so far she hadn't been able to find a way to sabotage the ship. Certainly, she hadn't found anything worse than the damage caused by neglect or disrepair.

She looked up as Vane entered the engineering compartment, followed by a pair of black-clad men, the Admiral's personal enforcers. They seemed isolated from the rest of the crew, a silent presence on the bridge and in the other vital compartments, ready to intervene if one of the officers decided to stage a mutiny. Their bodies looked oddly misshaped, suggesting that they'd been given some illicit enhancements. Jasmine had been enhanced at the Slaughterhouse and yet she looked little different from any normal human adult, apart from being extremely muscular. These men would stand out almost everywhere, except perhaps on a RockRat colony. Or Earth, where pointing out physical differences was considered extremely rude.

"We are approaching Haven," Vane said, without preamble. Mandy felt the excitement running through the crew. She'd heard them talking about Haven as a place for some R&R, although she knew little else about it, leaving her to wonder if it was a planet or asteroid. "You will all be granted shore leave" – there was another mummer of excitement – "but there is a matter we need to deal with first."

He nodded to one of the Admiral's enforcers, who opened the hatch for Michael to step into the compartment. Mandy felt her eyes go wide with horror as she looked at her boyfriend. His hands were cuffed in front of him and a chain had been wrapped around his feet, making it hard for him to move at anything above a snail's pace.

"This piece of shit claimed a competence he didn't have," Vane said. "We tested him and discovered that his engineering skills were minimal. All he is really good for is washing the decks."

There were some nervous chuckles at his words. "I do not tolerate failure," Vane said, as silence fell again. "I do not tolerate people who claim too much. We have wasted rations on this…*person* while he has proved himself completely useless. You have been brought here to witness his punishment."

Mandy swallowed hard, unsure of what to do. But what *could* she do? Draw her knife and stab everyone in the compartment? The Admiral's enforcers would kill her, or stun her and then throw her to the crew. She caught sight of Ha, watching the scene with an unholy gleam in his eye, and fought back an urge to throw up. Maybe she could just slip away, if there was nothing she could do…Jasmine would have found a way, she was sure. But Mandy couldn't see anything she could do.

The enforcers pushed Michael against the bulkhead and held him there. A moment later, Vane struck him with the neural whip. Michael screamed in pain as the whip lashed his bare back, time and time again. Mandy looked away, trying to block out the sound, only to discover that some of the pirates were watching her. What would they say if they knew that she and Michael had been lovers? She wanted to run, but there was nowhere to go…

It felt like hours before the whipping finally stopped. Michael collapsed to the deck, his entire body twitching as if he were having a fit. How much punishment did it take to cause permanent damage? Surely, if they'd wanted to kill him, they would have just pitched him out the nearest airlock…no, she realised grimly. It was worse than that. Vane – and the Admiral's enforcers – had wanted to use Michael as an object lesson for the crew. And *then* they'd kill him.

They picked up his body and carried it back through the hatch, into one of the sealed sections of the ship. Mandy watched them go in numb horror, catching sight of Ha's face as he turned and left the engineering compartment. The bastard had drawn sexual pleasure from watching the torture, Mandy was sure; his expression was that of a man who'd just had a deeply satisfying orgasm. She felt sick and stumbled, as if the entire ship was shaking around her, before she gathered herself. Michael was depending on her to do *something* to save his life, but what? What did she have to bargain with?

She watched as Vane issued a few minor rebukes, including whipping another crewmember twice for being drunk on duty, and then headed back to his office. No doubt the Admiral would want a report, if his enforcers hadn't told him what had happened already. Mandy hesitated, unsure of what *she* should be doing, and then followed Vane to his office. He looked around and saw her as he reached the hatch, gave her an oddly quizzical glance, and then stepped inside. After a moment, Mandy followed him. The hatch hissed closed, trapping her in his office.

"He was useless," Vane said, by way of explanation. "The quality of engineering students on your planet is very low."

Mandy flushed. It wouldn't do any good to explain that Michael wasn't really an engineering student; if they'd known what he really was, they would kill him out of hand. But they might have come close to killing him anyway, or damaging him permanently. There were just too many possibilities…surely, someone as tough as Michael could last longer than someone like her.

"He was a newcomer to the class," she said, which was technically true. "Please don't kill him."

"He's a waste of resources," Vane said, coldly. "We don't have the resources to waste."

Mandy was tempted to point out that the pirates threatened their own lives every time they damaged part of the life support system, but she suspected that it would be useless. Vane was determined to get rid of Michael, either because he was no use to the ship or because Vane suspected Michael's true nature, or…no, that couldn't be right. They'd have killed Michael by now.

"He is my friend," Mandy said, desperately. "Surely there's something else you can do."

Vane studied her for a long moment. "What do you have to bargain with?"

Mandy thought – briefly – of her mother, and then pushed the thought aside. She did have something to bargain with, if she was prepared to lower herself so far. Being raped would have been preferable to selling her body to the highest bidder; rape was not consensual by definition, while prostituting herself…but Michael's life depended on it. If the price for saving his life was allowing Vane access to her body, then it was a price she was prepared to pay.

"Me," she said, finally. "I can offer you myself."

"Really?" Vane asked. "And what do you have in mind?"

Mandy flushed. He was going to force her to spell it out, either to make her suffer or simply because he wanted to be clear on the bargain. If it was a bargain…what recourse would she have if he cheated her? The remaining prostitutes on Avalon had some legal protections, but there was no such thing on a pirate ship. On the other hand, she told herself, if she did this and Michael died anyway, she would stick a knife in him and to hell with the consequences.

"You can have me," she said, fighting down the embarrassment that almost held her frozen. She'd been a typical child of Earth, but she'd never offered herself to another in such a cold-blooded manner. How, she wondered with a sudden desperate intensity, did prostitutes handle it? "Here, or in your cabin, or anywhere…as long as you let him live."

Vane made a show of stroking his cheek. "I cannot keep him on this ship," he said. Mandy wondered if he was about to refuse her, no matter what she offered. Maybe he was too old to be interested in women. "But I can arrange for him to be left on Haven, rather than being sold into slavery or simply pushed out of an airlock. After that, he'd be on his own."

His eyes met hers. "How does *that* sound?"

Mandy swallowed, hard. She didn't know enough about Haven to know if that would be better for Michael, but there was no other choice.

"It sounds workable," she said. "And I want to talk to him before he leaves the ship."

Vane smiled. "You can keep your side of the bargain first," he said. For a second, his face twisted into a leer. "Strip."

It was harder than she had realised to undo her shipsuit and step out of it in front of his triumphant gaze. Harder still to go on her knees, unzip his pants and take his cock in her mouth. Hardest of all to lie back and allow him to enter her, to feel him moving inside her while doing her best to fake enjoyment of his efforts. Afterwards, she felt dirty, even worse than when she had almost been raped, or touched by Ha. Vane's hands ran over her body, marking his claim, before he stood up and passed her the remains of her shipsuit.

"I'll arrange for you to be able to see him," he said, as Mandy dressed. There was nowhere to wash, or to clean herself. She'd just have to endure until she got to the washroom and had a chance to shower. "And then you can say goodbye to him on Haven."

Mandy couldn't stop replaying it in her mind as she walked out of engineering, wondering just how many of the other engineers now knew that she had lowered herself to become a whore. The compartments were solid, built to be soundproof, but Mandy wouldn't have bet good money on them keeping out *all* sound. She'd groaned and moaned at the right times, hoping that it was good enough to fool him. Who knew who might have heard their loveless copulation?

The washroom was unoccupied, thankfully. Mandy stepped inside and allowed the water to cascade down, over her face. No matter how she scrubbed, she couldn't wash his touch off her body. If she closed her eyes, she could feel his fingers running over her breasts, or reaching down to stroke between her legs. The thought was sickening…suddenly, as if she could no longer control it, she stumbled over to the toilet and threw up. What had she done?

You are a whore, she thought she heard her mother say. *My eldest daughter is a whore.*

"And you're a gold-digger, Mom," she said, angrily. She didn't realise that she'd spoken out loud until she heard her own voice echoing back. "You betrayed Dad because you couldn't get your wealth and power with him…"

Later, feeling cleaner on the outside, if not on the inside, she was escorted into one of the sealed compartments on the ship. The Admiral kept some prisoners to himself, she'd been told, and Michael had apparently been stuffed into one of those compartments. Mandy said nothing as Vane kissed her, and then pointed her at one of the hatches. Opening it, Mandy saw Michael chained to a bench, his entire body still twitching. He no longer looked healthy.

"Michael," she said, as the hatch closed behind her. "Can you hear me?"

Michael looked up, his eyes disbelieving. "Mandy?"

"They're going to abandon you at Haven," Mandy said. She was *not* going to tell him what she'd done to save his life. What would he think of her if he knew? "You have to be ready for that…I don't know how long you have."

One of Michael's hands reached up to take hers. He was twitching badly, as if he were coming off a drug. There was no sign of any physical damage, but then there never was with a neural whip. One of the pirates had told her how whips were used to keep slaves working without actually damaging their bodies. Most resisters thought better of it after they'd been lashed once or twice. And Michael had been lashed dozens of times.

"I don't know either," he said. His voice was different too, no longer as confident as she remembered. The man who'd earned medals in a dozen different skirmishes with the Crackers was broken. And then he smiled weakly at her. "My head feels as though there's a grumpy old Mountain Man living in it."

Mandy stared at him. "You're making *jokes*?"

"Hurts when I cry," Michael said. "What happened?"

"Never mind that," Mandy said, flatly. "I need you to get better, so you won't die on Haven. *Please…*"

"Tell me," Michael said. "What is there left to live for?"

Mandy winced. Hadn't *he* been the one telling her that they would have to watch and wait for the opportunity to make the pirates regret ever kidnapping them? But that had been before he'd been whipped so badly that it might have caused permanent damage.

She placed her lips close to his ears and whispered a single word. "Revenge."

"I hope you're right," Michael said. He twisted his head and kissed her on the lips. "Do whatever you can, understand?"

Mandy nodded and stood up, unwilling to let him see her crying. Instead, she walked out of the hatch and out into the corridor, where Vane was waiting for her. The Chief Engineer smiled at her, as if to remind her that he'd kept his word, and then led her to the sealed hatch.

"Oh, and gather your stuff," he ordered. Mandy felt her heart sinking before he had even finished his orders. She knew where this was going. "You're going to be sleeping in my cabin from now on."

She eyed Vane's back as he walked away, leaving her behind. Whatever it took, she vowed to herself, she would make him regret everything he'd done to her – and Michael.

Chapter Twenty-Four

> Tramp freighters were disliked by the big interstellar corporations, simply because they forced the corporations to keep their shipping prices down. They retaliated by means of semi-legal syndicates and legal harassment, often pushing the Grand Senate to pass laws that restricted the operations of independent shippers. Unsurprisingly, most of the tramp freighters drifted out to the Rim, where the laws were less strict. Unfortunately, there were also more pirates waiting for them…
> - Professor Leo Caesius, *The Perilous Dawn* (unpublished).

"Colonel?"

Edward's eyes snapped open. As a young Marine, he'd learned to sleep when and wherever he could; even as a Colonel, he still managed to snap awake instantly when called. One hand reached for the pistol under the pillow before he remembered that he was in his cabin on the *Dancing Fool* and it was unlikely that they were being boarded. Keeping the weapon within reach was another old habit that he'd kept, even though he knew it worried civilians. Not everywhere he slept was safe.

He rubbed the side of his head as he activated his implanted communicator. "I'm here," he said. There had been too much organising to do on Elysium, as well as loading volunteers onboard the freighters and lying in wait for the pirate supply ship. "What do you have?"

"One ship just sent an IFF pulse to us," Kitty reported. "The files we recovered from Garth's ship identified it as the supply ship."

Edward swung his legs over the side of the bunk and stood up, carefully. He was used to living in quarters civilians might find claustrophobic, but he was tall enough to crack his head on the ceiling the first night he'd slept in the cabin. Reaching for his uniform trousers, he pulled them on, followed by his jacket and shipsuit. The supply ship was probably not a warship, but it was quite possible that she had an escort. After all, there were pirates running through the sector.

"Good," he said. They'd been waiting nine days, as the supply ship was apparently overdue. "Do we have any more details yet?"

"Not at this distance," Kitty informed him. "She was halfway to the planet before pinging us; we can't make out more than her drive field. The sensors think that she's a medium freighter, but we don't really know anything for sure."

"I'm on my way," Edward said. He could have gone back to sleep – it would be at least four hours before the pirate ship reached engagement range – but there was no shortage of paperwork to do. Besides, he wouldn't be able to sleep, knowing that the shit was about to hit the fan. "Alert the planetary government and warn them to keep transmissions to a minimum. We don't want to tip our hand too soon."

He opened the hatch and stepped out into the corridor. Kitty had claimed the cabin closest to the bridge, but Edward had taken the one next to it, a few seconds from the hatch leading onto the command deck. On an Imperial Navy starship, there would have been an armed Marine standing at the hatch, permanently watching for trouble; Edward had decided that there was no point in continuing the tradition on the *Dancing Fool*. There were only Marines and a handful of spacers onboard anyway.

The hatch hissed open as he pressed his fingers against the sensor, revealing the cramped interior of the bridge. Kitty was sitting in front of the main display, studying a holographic representation of the star system, with a single ominous red dot approaching the planet from outside the Phase Limit. Backtracking the vessel's course, Edward suspected that the ship had actually come in from further out along the Rim, but it was impossible to be sure. It would have been simple for the ship's crew to come in from a different angle, just to confuse any watching sensors.

Not that it really matters, he thought, sourly. He might not be a naval expert, but even he knew that there were thousands of stars that could have been the ship's previous location. Pirate bases were rarely established in inhabited star systems, which left only a few thousand possible suspects. And there was no way to know how far the ship had travelled, or how many other stars it had visited along the way. The best trackers in the Imperial Navy had only been able to provide rough guesses, at best, and it was as much a matter of luck than judgement.

"The crew of the orbiting station report that they didn't have to send any kind of signal back," Kitty said, quietly. "We don't know if Garth had his own signalling system."

Edward nodded as he took one of the seats and settled down to wait. The pirates had held Elysium by force, which suggested that they would be careful about approaching a potentially hostile world. Standard procedure in the Imperial Navy was to exchange signals and make sure of each other's *bona fides* before entering weapons range – even an armed freighter could do a great deal of damage if it had the advantage of surprise. But so far the pirate ship hadn't bothered to demand a response from Garth or anyone else on the planet. It was…odd.

"I'd like to move out to intercept the ship," Kitty added. "If they do intend to demand any codes from us – and I think they will – the sooner we get into intercept position, the better."

"Make it so," Edward said. Kitty was right – and it would have the advantage of keeping any combat well away from the planet. "The command is yours."

He watched as the *Dancing Fool* left orbit and headed towards the freighter, using the pirate cloaking device. It wasn't perfect, according to the engineers, but it should be enough to fool civilian-grade sensors. That wasn't a guarantee of anything – out on the Rim, most traders wanted military-grade equipment if they could get it – yet the pirates didn't seem to be using active sensors. It was almost as if they didn't quite believe that the Empire was gone.

But we don't really believe it either, he thought. *Why else would we spend so much time trying to uphold law and order?*

The main display sharpened as they came closer to the pirate ship. It was a *Taurus*-class medium freighter, a design that had originally been produced for the Imperial Navy, centuries ago. Although it was bulky, a good third of that bulk was made up of engines, allowing the freighter to move at a speed that wouldn't shame a proper warship. The design had been intended to stay in the line of battle with the Navy's battleships, either because they might need to resupply while moving at high speed or to draw missiles away from the capital ships.

"I think they never bothered to replace the drive," Delacroix said. "She still reads out as a standard *Taurus*."

"It would be tricky without a proper shipyard and plenty of money," Kitty reminded her. "The people who designed this ship wanted something for the military, remember?"

Edward nodded. Most civilian craft were designed to be easy to disassemble, repair and upgrade. Military starships were modular too, but their heavy armour plating and internal security measures made it harder to upgrade them without a great deal of effort. The *Taurus* design shared the weaknesses of both military and civilian designs, neither fish nor fowl but some unholy combination of the two. On the other hand, the design was known for being robust and had been quite popular with the Navy – and civilians, once the Navy had started selling them off.

He leaned forward. "Is she armed?"

"Unknown," Delacroix admitted. "There's no way to know what weapons a converted civilian ship might be carrying until she opens fire, or we board her."

"The original design carried a handful of point defence pulsars," Kitty added. "They were often outfitted with command datalink as well, although I don't think they ever saw action as part of a fleet. Someone could have easily bolted missile pods to the hull if they wanted to give them some additional punch."

Edward scowled. "When do you want to intercept her?"

"Here," Kitty said, pointing to the display. In some ways, springing an ambush in space was identical to springing an ambush on the ground. The trick was to wait until the enemy couldn't retreat and *then* open fire.

"We should be in position to chase her down, whatever she does after we announce ourselves."

"Right," Edward said. He keyed the command network and spoke briefly to Lieutenant Faulkner. Fourth Platoon had performed well in the Battle of Elysium, but their real role was boarding spacecraft and they were about to get their chance to do it again. "We wait."

He felt an odd flicker of *déjà vu* as the pirate ship came closer, before forcing himself to relax. They'd done the same when the *Dancing Fool* had approached Avalon, but that had been different. The *Dancing Fool* had been in a position to destroy much of the planet if the trap had been sprung too early, while the pirate freighter ahead of them could do nothing to harm Elysium. It was possible that they would simply surrender as soon as they realised that they were under the guns of a warship.

And it is equally possible that they will try to destroy themselves, he reminded himself. *Who knows what the Admiral might have planned for?*

The interrogations hadn't revealed much in the way of specifics about the Admiral's operations – apart from the location of one of his bases – but they had provided the intelligence officers with a great many factoids that they'd pulled into a picture. According to them, the Admiral didn't have anything more than a ramshackle force, although that would certainly change, given time. It might explain why he had been so timorous in approaching Avalon, or avoided leaving a warship at Elysium; he simply didn't have enough ships to risk losing any of them. Edward knew better than to take everything intelligence officers said for granted, but it certainly *sounded* as though it made sense. Two warships would have made it impossible for the Marines to defend Avalon.

And yet…surely the cloudscoop was worth the risk involved in trying to seize it?

"We're in position," Kitty informed him. "Decloaking…now!"

The pirates obviously *hadn't* detected them, or they would never have come so close without trying to alter course. Edward watched dispassionately as their drive fields flared with power, trying desperately to get them out of weapons range before it was too late. But it was already too late. Kitty tapped a switch and a single missile roared out of the tubes, detonating a bare kilometre from the pirate ship's hull. They'd know that they'd been kissed.

"This is the Imperial Navy," Kitty said, keying her console. "You are under the guns of a warship. Surrender now and go to a penal colony, or die. There are no other choices."

Edward braced himself. If the pirates *had* stuffed weaponry into the ship's hull, they were about to find out the hard way. No converted civilian ship could match a warship; their best bet was to open fire at once and pray. Not that it would save them, unless they'd managed to invent some hellish new missiles. They would just be kicking and scratching on their way to the gallows.

"They dropped their drive," Delacroix reported. "I think they're surrendering."

"We surrender," a voice said, over the standard communication channel. "Don't shoot – we surrender."

"Marines are on their way to board your vessel," Kitty said. She glanced at Edward, who sent the command to Fourth Platoon. Their shuttle disengaged from the *Dancing Fool* and started to head towards the pirate ship. "They will take command of your ship. Any resistance or attempts to destroy sensitive data will be met with deadly force. Your crew will be transported to a penal colony to begin their sentence."

Edward watched as Fourth Platoon's shuttle approached the pirate ship. These moments were always nerve-racking for everyone involved; he'd heard of pirates who, knowing that they would be executed, had waited for the shuttle to come close and then fired on it. The Imperial Navy had blown those ships away seconds later, but it hadn't been in time to save the Marines from being vaporised. There were Marines who believed that all boarding action should be done in combat armour, rather than shuttles. They felt that it made it harder for treachery to bear fruit.

"Docking now," Lieutenant Faulkner said. It didn't get any easier. Pirates who were about to be captured and shipped to a penal colony might do something desperate – and they might have weapons that would be effective against powered armour. "The airlock is opening."

Edward watched through the live feed as the Marines entered the ship. A number of crewmen seemed very glad to see the Marines, claiming to have been forced to work by the pirates. The Marines restrained them anyway, just in case; they'd be injected with truth drugs later and interrogated to clear their names. If found innocent, Edward decided, they'd be offered a chance to help with the starship building program on Avalon. Or perhaps asked to run the new ship as it headed to its next destination.

"We secured the ship and shut down the main computer," Lieutenant Faulkner reported, finally. "Ninety-seven captives, thirty-two claiming to be shanghaied crewmen from other ships. Sir, no sex slaves at all."

Edward frowned. That was *odd*. Pirates normally had no hesitation in kidnapping girls from colony worlds and using them as sex slaves. Almost every pirate ship the Marines had boarded over the years had had a handful of slaves onboard, broken by months or years of mistreatment. And when the girls got too old and broken, they were dumped into space and new ones installed in their place. Edward had once heard of a romance novel about a girl who'd been kidnapped by sexy pirates. The writer hadn't had the slightest idea what she'd been talking about.

He looked over at Kitty. "They didn't have time to eject them into space?"

"We would have detected it, unless they did it before they knew we were there," Kitty pointed out. "And why would they have bothered?"

"Get the prisoners over to the freighter," Edward ordered, tabling the question for now. "We need to know where they were taking the supplies – and why. Everything else can wait."

―――――

"Crawford," Kitty said, an hour later.

Edward scowled as he studied the star system in the display. "I've never heard of it," he admitted, reluctantly. He'd accessed the files on other planets in the sector, back when they'd been assigned to Avalon, but Crawford had never even been mentioned. "Where is it?"

"Officially, it's unsettled," Kitty said. "The planet had an ecological collapse hundreds of years ago; right now, Crawford is pretty much one huge desert. I checked the files; apparently, the terraforming institute considered attempting to reshape the planet, before deciding that it would be too much effort for too little return. Unofficially, according to the prisoners, there's a thriving black colony there."

"A black colony," Edward said, thoughtfully. "Why did they settle the planet instead of the asteroids?"

Legally, colonisation was only permitted with permission from the Empire. Black colonists settled worlds – and asteroids – without bothering to ask permission, either because they wanted somewhere to hide or because they couldn't afford the bribes to get an entire star system signed over to them. They were often religious cultists, looking for a place to build their own paradise, or political dissidents trying to live without the Empire. There was no shortage of hidden colonies along the Rim.

"I'm uncertain and we don't really have time to speculate," Kitty said. "Our prisoners say that the settlers managed to build a small industrial base on the planet, one that the pirates have taken over. They've destroyed the farms; the supplies from Elysium are meant to keep the workers on Crawford alive – and dependent. Colonel, if we could get our hands on that industrial base…"

Edward nodded. Black colonists were often targeted by pirates – and worked with them, just as often. Crawford's population, on the other hand, would probably have had enough of the Admiral's goons by now, if only they could break the stranglehold the Admiral had on their planet. Edward had to admit that it was a neat trick. The Admiral had made shipping foodstuffs across interstellar distances profitable.

And if something happened to go wrong, those poor bastards on Crawford would starve, he thought. What would happen to his plan then?

"Tell the locals to start loading the supplies into the freighter," he ordered. "We are going to have to follow up on this before we can go to the pirate recruitment centre."

"They're not that far apart," Kitty pointed out. "The Admiral might have known about Crawford because it had links to other black colonies."

It was possible, Edward agreed. Black colonies could certainly trade with other colonies, particularly if they had managed to establish an industrial base. But doing that risked detection, either by the Empire or by less scrupulous rebels and pirates. Ironically, if Crawford had built up a defence force instead, it was likely that the Empire would simply have ignored it. And then it would have been in a much better position to survive the Empire's decline and fall.

"See what else the interrogators can pull out of the prisoners about Crawford," he said, "along with whatever else they can tell us about the Admiral. It won't be long before he notices what we're doing – and then it will become a great deal harder to operate."

"Yeah," Kitty said. "And do you intend to storm his HQ with three platoons of Marines?"

"I have a plan," Edward assured her. It just wasn't a very good one. "We're going to pretend to be mercenaries."

CHAPTER
TWENTY-FIVE

In a very real sense, the pirates themselves are just the tip of a whole iceberg of illegal operations. The loot the pirates take from their victims must be sold onwards to people who can use it, eventually selling it to colony worlds and populations who are unwilling to ask too many questions. The middlemen, in this case, are the inhabitants of hidden colonies – mainly asteroids – that have no qualms about dealing with pirates. Sometimes this is because they need the pirates as much as the pirates need them, sometimes this is because they were founded on a creed of resistance to the Empire.

Unsurprisingly, finding one of these bases is extremely difficult. The pirates work hard to conceal their locations. Often, only a couple of people on each pirate ship will know where to go. Even if one base is located, it may not lead to the next.

As such, they represent places where pirates can relax.

-Edward E. Smith, Professor of Sociology. *Pirates and their Lives*.

Haven seemed a fairly typical asteroid colony, as far as Mandy could tell. The glimpse she'd had of it through a porthole had suggested a rocky asteroid, hollowed out by generations of asteroid miners who had then gone on to bigger things, leaving their caves behind for the pirates to occupy. The RockRat colonies had been far more elegant than Haven, she decided as she walked through a long corridor, keeping one hand on her knife and the other on the small lump of cash she'd been given by Vane. There was something crude about the pirate settlement, as if it wasn't really intended to be permanent.

The great caves the miners had dug were crammed with people, all drinking, dancing and whoring the night away. Half of *Sword's* crew were on the asteroid, looking for entertainment; if Mandy hadn't wanted to accompany Michael to the asteroid, she would have tried to stay behind on the pirate ship. But then, the alternative was spending more time in Vane's bed. She hadn't realised that their bargain meant that she'd be his for the rest of his life, or until he tired of her, but there was no choice. God alone knew what he would do if she said no.

Michael had given her one last kiss and then told her to leave him to find his own way through the asteroid, pointing out that it would be dangerous for them to be seen together. Mandy hadn't wanted to go, but he was right. After Michael had been kicked off the Admiral's ship, he wouldn't be allowed to talk to any of her crew. Mandy had seriously considered deserting and trying to stay on the asteroid, only to realise that it might be jumping from the frying pan into the fire. Haven was rougher than the worst parts of Camelot, perhaps even rougher than the Undercity on Earth.

She peered through a curtain into a dining room and saw dozens of crewmen eating, drinking and watching a stage show where a dozen naked women danced around poles. Mandy flushed as soon as she realised what the women were doing, even though she'd done far worse just to keep Michael alive. Shaking her head, she walked away from the entertainment section and into the market cave. There, there were dozens of different stalls, selling loot the pirates had captured from various starships. One of them held datachips that promised hours of pornographic entertainment, or bootleg copies of the latest films and books from inside the Empire. Others sold ration packs, basic equipment, or weapons. Mandy walked over to the last stall and examined what the seller was offering, wondering if she had enough money to purchase a gun. And if she did, would she be allowed to keep it?

"That one is called the Killer," the seller said. He grinned at her, showing that he was missing several teeth. "The bullets are designed to expand as soon as they are inside the body, helping to ensure an immediate death. She's got one hell of a kick, but believe me, she's worth it."

Mandy picked up the gun, frowning slightly at the weight. The weapons she'd worked with on Avalon had been much lighter – but then, they'd been designed for women. And they'd been warned that shooting someone didn't guarantee death, even if you shot them in the head. Mandy had been told more about the different types of gun than she'd wanted to remember, information that she *should* have remembered. It would have been very helpful right now.

"How much?" She asked. A thought struck her and she cursed herself. "How much for the gun *and* the bullets."

"Couple of hundred neo-credos," the seller said, with another grin. "But I can throw in a holster in exchange for a blowjob."

Mandy glared at him, which made him laugh and her flush. Did she have a sign on her back saying *whore*? Or that she'd allowed a man to fuck her to save her friend's life? Or, given how many wolf-whistles she'd attracted on Haven, was it just another example of someone trying to press their luck? There was no way to know.

"You couldn't afford me," she said, spitefully, and reached for the lump of cash she'd been given. Vane had told her that the pirates received salaries, but she hadn't realised that it applied to her as well. But then, she *was* working for them. "A couple of hundred, you said?"

The seller nodded as she counted out the cash. She wasn't entirely sure how pirate economics worked, but they did seem to have evolved a replacement currency for the Imperial Credit, although she had no idea *how*. If she'd paid more attention to her father's lectures on basic economics, she might have understood what she was seeing; it was quite possible, she decided, that they'd simply designed their own. But then, if the Admiral did intend to create his own Empire, he'd have to have some kind of unified currency.

"A very good choice," the seller said, as he handed over the gun and ten clips of ammunition. "I suggest test-firing it on the range, so that I can make any adjustments you might need."

Mandy nodded and followed his pointing finger towards the firing range. It was bigger than the one she recalled on Avalon, crammed with pirates firing all kinds of guns towards holographic targets. Jasmine had told her that firing ranges were good, but they had their limits; the only way to *really* learn was to go out into the field. But it was all Mandy had at the moment, so it would have to do. She paid the tender, loaded one of the clips into the gun, and fired on the targets. The gun jerked in her hand – the sound was louder than she had expected, despite the earmuffs she'd been offered – as it fired.

"Hit," the system reported.

"Good," Mandy muttered. The weapon seemed to work fine. "Let's try that again, shall we?"

She fired seven more times, emptying the clip while testing the gun's tolerance. Her tutors had hammered firearms safety into her head, warning her never to treat her weapons lightly. One of them had been fond of horror stories about self-inflicted wounds caused by carelessness with loaded weapons. Later, Mandy had asked Jasmine if the stories were true and the Marine had confirmed them. There were thousands of ways to commit suicide accidentally with a loaded weapon and the Civil Guard had done most of them over the years.

Ignoring a couple of offers – both indecent – from other pirates, she walked out of the firing range and right into Commander Travis, who held up a hand to stop her. Mandy barely knew him as anything other than a distant presence, the XO of *Sword* and one of her superiors. He was a short, rat-faced man with a smile that never quite touched his eyes and an attitude that chilled her, as if he was – in his own way – as insane as Ha.

"You will join me for dinner," he said, flatly. It wasn't a request. "Come with me."

Mandy wanted to bristle, to refuse, but she knew that could prove painful. All of the senior officers had permission to whip their subordinates whenever they felt like it and even though she'd managed to remain untouched since the first day she'd spent on the ship, she knew that could change in an instant. Instead, she followed him mutely, wondering just what he wanted to say to her. Or did he have something else in mind? If she'd given herself to Vane, did Travis think that he could have Mandy too?

Haven was larger than she had realised, with an entire section set aside for the senior officers and those with considerable amounts of money. It reminded her of the wealthier section on Camelot, before the Battle of Camelot and the destruction of the old Council. The thought made her smile humourlessly, as Travis led her into a bar and then into a private compartment, closing the door behind him. Mandy felt a chill running down her spine as she realised that she had nowhere to go. If he wanted her...

"Sit," he ordered, picking up a menu from a slot on the wall. "Order whatever you'd like."

Mandy felt an odd sense that the world was turning surreal as she studied the menu. It could easily have come from a restaurant on Earth, one of the places she'd patronised with her friends before her father had annoyed the authorities. The menu included steak and chips, fish and chips, pies and chips...the owners seemed fond of chips. So were the settlers on Avalon. *Everything* seemed to go with chips.

"I recommend the steak," Travis said, when it became apparent that Mandy couldn't make up her mind. "They bring it in from a farming world and fry it up nicely."

Mandy nodded, feeling her mouth watering. After the ration bars, she would happily have eaten the algae-based sludge that kept the population of Earth alive. Steak and chips was really too much to hope for. Quickly, she nodded and allowed him to use a small intercom to place the order, before sitting down facing her. His dark eyes locked onto her face, something that bothered her more than she would have expected. Most of the pirates didn't bother to look at her *face*.

"Ordered," Travis said. He produced a device from his pocket and put it on the table, between them. "Do you recognise this gadget?"

Mandy shook her head. It was a tiny sphere, no larger than an eyeball, glowing faintly with an eerie green light. The design meant nothing to her.

"The average person calls these things a privacy generator," Travis said, his tone darkly amused. "They're banned in the Empire, of course. If you have nothing to hide, or so the reasoning goes, you don't need to keep your conversations a secret. As you can probably imagine, there is a vast underground market for these devices. The most advanced ones can defeat even the latest bugs devised by Imperial Intelligence and are used to monitor careless chatter when people think they're alone."

His eyes peered into hers. "What we say to each other, here in this chamber, will *not* go any further."

Mandy swallowed, feeling as if the ground was shifting underneath her feet. "Why...?"

Travis smiled. "I suggest you don't mention this conversation to anyone," he said, dryly. "It could be extremely damaging to your health."

There was a *ding* from the wall. Travis stood up, opened a hatch, and produced a large plate of steak and chips. "Yours, I believe," he said, as he passed it to her, before taking the other plate for himself. "Do you understand what I told you?"

"...Yes," Mandy stammered. "Sir, what is going on?"

Travis took a bite of something that looked like fried meat and noodles. "You're new to the crew, but you have to understand that there's no going back," he said. "Whatever you were before you joined us, you're one of us now. And if you want to survive as one of us, you have to blend in and join a network." His lips twitched. "A network like the one I operate."

Mandy took a chip and chewed on it to cover her feelings. It really tasted very good. But then, she told herself, the pirates weren't likely to merely refuse to pay if the food wasn't excellent. They'd be more likely to shoot the cook to encourage the others.

"It's really quite simple," Travis said, into the silence. "You agree to work with me; I give you my protection. Without some protection, young lady, you will eventually be dragged down. You've already survived one attempt at doing just that."

"The man I killed," Mandy said. It was astonishing how quickly she'd accepted what she'd done. "Don't you *care* about his death?"

"There is no shortage of thugs willing to serve as dumb muscle," Travis said. "Right now, the Admiral is recruiting a dozen more to take his place. You, on the other hand, have potential. As a member of my network, you could earn status and power, perhaps even found a network of your own. But on your own..."

He leaned forward. "Sooner or later, someone is going to bring you down," he added. "And then you will be nothing more than the ship's whore."

Mandy shivered. She'd understood, but she hadn't really wanted to face it. But who could blame her? All of a sudden, she understood why

Jasmine had been so scathing about some of the cultures she'd seen as a Marine. Their unlucky inhabitants were shaped by the society they inhabited – and if their society refused to admit the rule of law, they ended up with the rule of the strong. Kill or be killed.

"Very well," she said, carefully. Common sense said that she should see what other offers there might be before committing herself, but she suspected that there wouldn't be *any* other offers on the table. "What are you offering me?"

"You get a step up from engineering to tactical," Travis said. "And you work for me directly. And you spy on Vane."

Mandy flushed, which made him grin. "Do you really think the entire ship hasn't noticed that you're sleeping with him?"

"No," she admitted. "Why do you want me to spy on him?"

Travis gave her a long considering look. "Do you always ask so many questions?"

Mandy pasted a smile on her face. "How do you expect me to work for you properly if I don't know what's going on?"

"True," Travis agreed. He took a piece of meat off his plate and chewed on it before speaking again. "Vane is part of the Captain's personal network – why do you think he gets such a free hand in the engineering compartment? Weakening his position strengthens the position of the engineering second, who happens to be part of *my* network. If the Admiral should happen to believe that Vane is incompetent, or wasting time and resources, the Captain will have no choice but to give him an airlock promotion."

Put him out the airlock, Mandy translated, mentally.

She suspected she understood how Travis intended to operate. Take over enough parts of the ship, through putting his people in the right places, and he might be able to seize control of *Sword* – and then either replace the Admiral, or be anointed as the new Captain. It made her wonder why the Admiral or the Captain didn't simply replace him, before she realised that they would spark off an internal mutiny simply by trying. Removing the head of a patronage network – for that was what it was – would destroy everyone who was *part* of that network. They'd have to fight, if only out of self-defence.

Travis finished eating his meal and looked over at her. "I won't ask again," he said. "If you don't want to join me, you can continue on your own, sleeping with Vane and trying to avoid the rest of the crew. But sooner or later, you *will* run out of luck and that will be the end of you. Those who stand on their own have no friends nor family."

"I understand," Mandy said. "I will join you."

"Good," Travis said. He reached into his pocket and pulled out a privacy generator, just like the one he'd placed on the table. "This one is for you."

Mandy took it in surprise. "On the ship, use it whenever you talk to any of my people – or me," Travis explained. "Try not to use it if you're alone, because that can arouse suspicions – the Admiral might object, strongly. Or when you're with Vane. The Captain keeps an eye on him and he might realise that you have one too."

"Oh," Mandy said. She felt her face turning red. "I…"

"The Captain probably isn't interested in watching your couplings," Travis said. "Just as well, as I am sure that Vane uses his own when he's with you. But still…try to avoid using it unless there's no other choice."

He stood up, "I'll pay for the dinner," he said. "Order dessert, if you would like."

Mandy hesitated as he reached for the privacy generator. "A question," she said. "How do I know I can trust you?"

Travis snorted. "If you learn nothing else from me, learn this," he said. "There isn't a person on the ship, or this asteroid, who will do anything unless there's something in it for him. I don't benefit by betraying you, so I'm not going to bother. We can help each other, which should be enough to keep us both loyal."

He smiled. "And if you *are* planning to betray me, rest assured that I have precautions in place," he added. "You won't even begin to betray me before I kill you."

Chapter
Twenty-Six

> Q-ship: general term for a warship rigged up to look like a merchantman, or built on a merchantman hull. Commonly used during the Unification Wars to sneak into orbit of enemy worlds and start firing; later, with the growth of interstellar piracy, used to lure pirates into point-blank range before opening fire. Advantages; stealth and surprise. Disadvantages: bulky, unwieldy and often inflexible.
>
> -Jane's Fighting Starships

"You and your bright ideas," Joe said.

"The Colonel said that it was a great idea," Blake protested, as they scrambled over the freighter's hull. "And the intelligence girl *loved* it."

"That's because the intelligence officers have never met an idea for sneaking around and spying on people that they didn't like," Joe pointed out. "Whatever happened to charging in, blowing the shit out of everything that moved and then screaming questions at the wreckage?"

"It went along with the rest of the Empire," Jasmine reminded him. There would be no replacement for the dead Marines, or anyone else they lost on Avalon. She had wondered, after the wake, if one day the company would be whittled down to a handful of Marines, with no hope of rebuilding their strength. "We don't have superior firepower right now."

The freighter they'd pulled from orbit around Elysium had been designed to transport goods across the galaxy, not engage in fights with warships. But no mercenary company would travel in an unarmed ship – mercenary companies made enemies and an unarmed ship would be a sitting duck – and so the Marines were bolting various weapons to the craft's hull. Doing it in Phase Space was tricky – and scary, even for the Marines – but there was no choice. Once they'd handled Crawford, they would have to go on to the pirate base.

"I never thought that I would miss the Navy," Blake admitted, as they struggled to put a missile pod in the right place. "All those fleet officers, drinking coffee while we slogged through the mud, reluctant to bring their ships into engagement range for fear that they would get their pretty hulls scratched…I never thought I'd miss them. A single squadron could probably trash everything the Admiral has in a single fight."

"But pirates never try to put up a stand-up fight," Joe said, tartly. He finished bolting the pod to the hull and ran an activation program. The missile pod came to life, linked into the modified computer network on the freighter, and announced that it was ready for operations. "They normally run from anything that looks like a warship."

Jasmine shook her head as she looked down at the pod. It was massive, larger than the Marines, carrying five missiles primed for simultaneous launch. Normally, missile pods would be deployed from starships to give them some additional punch in the first salvos, but the freighter simply wasn't designed to carry the pods in its hold. Bolting them to the hull was a compromise solution, one that was far from ideal. Once the missiles were launched, the remainder of the pod became nothing more than dead weight.

But Joe was right. Hunting pirates with regular warships was like looking for needles in haystacks, with the added disadvantage that the needle might be trying to hide. In the glory days of the Empire, the Imperial Navy had provided escorts to convoys moving along the Rim, daring the pirates to face the warships protecting them. But now, with the Imperial Navy pulled out of the outer sectors, there would be few – if any – escorts for the remaining freighters. The pirates could prey on them to their hearts' content.

But that will eventually kill interstellar shipping completely, Jasmine thought. Once, merchantmen had been able to claim the cost of buying a new ship from their insurance companies, although the premiums had been incredibly expensive. Now, though, there would be no insurance companies along the Rim – and few shipyards to rebuild the lost freighters. The Admiral and his men might wind up killing the goose that laid the golden eggs. They were so used to having plenty of targets to prey on that they might wipe them all out.

Or maybe he was smarter than that. One of the Professor's lectures had once compared government to a protection racket, in which the victim was offered the choice between paying protection – taxes – or being harassed by the criminals. Maybe the Admiral would start demanding protection money from merchantmen, offering to allow them to go on their way in exchange for the cash. Why not? It would almost certainly be cheaper than losing the whole freighter. Of course, the merchantmen might just decide to give up. Government couldn't easily encourage free enterprise, but it could strangle it in its cradle. The Empire's history had proven that more than once.

She looked up and out towards the bubble surrounding the ship. Phase Space was dark, far darker than normal space. It was impossible to escape the feeling that they were all alone in the dark, completely isolated from the rest of the universe. There was no shortage of legends about strange sightings in Phase Space, of weird alien monsters that were glimpsed briefly in the darkness, none of which had ever been substantiated. Jasmine didn't believe the stories – she knew no one who did – but she could see why they might have spread. Phase Space was eerie, even to the Marines. The sense that it wasn't a human place was overwhelming.

"Just one more pulsar to put in place," Joe said, cheerfully. "And then we can go rest!"

"Lazy bastard," Blake said, as he headed over to the cargo hatch. "Or did you mean you were going to keep trying to chat up the volunteers?"

Jasmine followed him over, rolling her eyes. They'd managed to find hundreds of volunteers with genuine space experience on Elysium and a number had been willing to serve on the unnamed freighter or the *Dancing Fool* rather than go directly to Avalon. Captain Stevenson had been delighted, apparently. The new crewmen had allowed her to get her ship into fighting trim, fixing most of the problems the pirates had left behind. Preparing the freighter to serve as a Q-ship, however, was a different task.

"They were very keen to chat to me, I'll have you know," Joe insisted, firmly. One of the volunteers was a young red-headed girl, who would have been badly mistreated by the pirates if they'd ever taken her alive. "The redhead's eyes just shone with lust."

Blake snorted. "And yet somehow she *didn't* wind up in your bunk on the first day," he said. "I think you have Optimist's Selective Understanding Syndrome."

"I didn't notice you having any more luck," Joe said. "And to think you spent time boasting to her about your enhanced cock."

"How was I to know," Blake demanded, "that she knew that the Slaughterhouse doesn't have to enhance our balls?"

Jasmine snickered, despite herself. "Common sense?"

"Overrated," Joe said. "I think she just got tired of Blake's bragging."

"Honestly," Jasmine said, as she pulled the pulsar cannon out of the hold and passed it to Blake. "All the bandits would have to do is march a naked whore around the edge of the FOB and you lot would go running after her with your tongues hanging out."

"Nah, that wouldn't work," Blake said. "If you ask me, Lieutenant, it's the same in fighting as it is in fucking. It's not what you have so much as what you do with it."

There was a long pause as they floated the cannon over to the weapons mount. "I suppose that makes sense," Joe said, finally. "But think how nice it would be to have a lot of it *and* know what to do with it."

"It is great," Blake said. He laughed. "Or were we still talking about fighting?"

"Giggle, giggle, giggle," Jasmine said. "I think your career as a comic is not going to take off unless you come up with some better lines."

The banter paused as they fixed the pulsar to the weapons mount and then hooked up the power conduits. That was a weakness in the design, Jasmine had been told, but it was one they couldn't fix without a proper shipyard. A warship had hardened power conduits, at least two fusion reactors and a dozen power cells for emergency operations. The freighter had precisely one fusion reactor and no power cells. If they lost main power, for any reason at all, they'd be dead in space. And if enemy weapons started bombarding the hullmetal, they'd be likely to cause brownouts even if they didn't penetrate the hull.

And who are you trying to kid? She asked herself. *Of course they're going to burn through the hull.*

"It could be worse," Joe said, as they started to head back to the hatch. There were regulations about how long anyone could work in vacuum, or Phase Space, and they were pushing the limits. A mistake that would cause nothing but embarrassment on a planetary surface could be lethal in the unforgiving environment of outer space. "He could be the reincarnation of the Joker."

Jasmine nodded, reluctantly. Marines who picked up nicknames that were recognised outside their units were famous, but often for the wrong reasons. The Joker had been known for cracking 'knock-knock' jokes while using shaped charges or grenades to blow his way into enemy strongholds. And then he'd bought it on Han when he'd blasted his way into a HIED – a house that had been rigged up as a massive improvised explosive device. The jokes had come to an end.

The airlock hissed open, allowing them to access the interior of the starship. Not unlike any military starship, the larger the ship, the smaller the space put aside for the junior crew – and Marines. In theory, a freighter could be operated by five or six people, which was true enough as long as everything went perfectly. It never did, of course, and most freighter commanders preferred to have a much larger crew. Jasmine had been told that warships did the same, with the crew largely given make-work until they were actually needed to handle damage control. But any Imperial Navy crewman would pick up a great deal of experience very quickly.

She caught sight of two of the volunteers as they removed their helmets and returned the vacuum suits to the rack, after checking them carefully for damage. Once, Jasmine had hated the endless checking and rechecking that was part of a Marine's life, but a very brief exposure to vacuum as part of her training had cured her of that. Everything had to be in perfect shape, or clearly marked as damaged, or it might kill someone. Even in Phase Space, where a ship was effectively untouchable, the standards had to be maintained. There was no shortage of stories about starships suffering catastrophic damage between the stars and being forced to limp home on sublight drives.

And plenty of ships have simply vanished too, she thought, remembering the sole rediscovery of a ship that had been lost hundreds of years ago. It had been sheer chance, they'd been told, that a starship had stumbled across the missing ship; normally, no one ever dropped out of Phase Space in interstellar space. The crew of the ship had been astonished to pick up a large object near their position and had investigated, only to discover that the object was a battleship from the Unification Wars, believed lost with all hands. Later, the ship had been left in interstellar space as a memorial. It had been a popular tourist destination for a few years.

But it was the images recorded by the first boarding party that had stuck in her mind. Cold vacuum had held the battleship in stasis, freezing the bodies of the crew where they'd died and preserving much of the equipment. The boarding party had downloaded the logs, which had recorded the final months of the *Defiance*, and then left the ship for the follow-up team to salvage, if they thought it was worth the effort. *Defiance* had suffered a series of freak disasters that had ended up with the ship drifting through interstellar space, leaking air. The end had come swiftly.

"We need to run," Blake grumbled, as they made their way to their quarters. "There just isn't room on this ship."

Normally, the platoon would share a compartment, or barracks on the ground. The platoon that slept together fought together, or so the Corps said, a statement with enough unfortunate implications to start fights between Marines, regular soldiers and Civil Guardsmen. But the freighter, as yet unnamed, simply didn't have the room. Instead, Jasmine had had to split up the platoon, three to a compartment – and they were still cramped. She hoped that everyone could sleep properly, as absurd as it seemed. There was something very reassuring about knowing that her comrades were right next to her, if the base were to be attacked in the middle of the night.

"Then we do press-ups instead," Jasmine said, firmly. "Or we load simulations into our suits and practice them."

"Without hurting ourselves this time," Joe added. "That was damn embarrassing last time."

Jasmine nodded. It was possible to become too wrapped up in the simulation and actually try to move, which could result in crashing into bulkheads or ceilings that didn't exist in the simulated world. The holographic chambers on the Slaughterhouse were much better, even if the scenario designers were notorious bastards who delighted in trying to put together impossible problems for the Marines. But it would be years before they saw the Slaughterhouse again, if they ever did. God alone knew what was happening thousands of light years away.

She checked her communicator, confirming that the Colonel hadn't sent them any specific orders, and then grinned at her subordinates.

"Time to don the suits," she ordered. They'd worked their way through all of the formal scenarios – several times, when they hadn't been actually deploying on Avalon – but there was a randomiser built into the system. The computers weren't very smart, certainly not as smart as the computer geeks had promised, yet they could be unpredictable. "Let's go prove ourselves again."

Edward crept down a long corridor, weapon in hand. In the distance, he could hear the sound of someone screaming and, behind him, the sound of weapons being fired. He reached a door and braced himself, unhooking a grenade with one hand before peering through the gap, seeing a handful of bodies lying on the ground. Their throats had been cut by one group of insurgents or another, he realised, as he slipped through the door, keeping his finger on his rifle's trigger. And they'd been raped and tortured first.

He felt sick. The Slaughterhouse had prepared the Marines as best as it could, but actually seeing evidence of man's inhumanity to man sickened him. What had the murdered people – all young teenagers – done to deserve death? Looking at them, it was easy to tell that they fell into one of Han's ethnic groups, presumably killed by one of the others as part of their attempt to cleanse their planet. The insurgents had beaten back the Empire's military and wiped out most of the Civil Guard. Now, the stresses that the planet's former rulers had encouraged to keep themselves in power had finally turned to violence. Han was ripping itself apart.

Edward heard someone screaming for help, only a few doors away. Carefully, relying on the sound to mask his approach, he slipped back into the corridor and down to the door, peering into the room. The girl on the table couldn't have been more than twelve; even with the genetic alterations the founders of Han had programmed into their people, she definitely looked as if she hadn't started to mature yet. But that didn't matter to the people holding her, torturing her, raping her…

The rifle jerked in Edward's hands as he fired, blowing an insurgent's head off. He moved from target to target before they could react, until the entire party had been eliminated. Edward was moving forward before the last of the bodies could even hit the ground, only to discover that he was too late. The girl gave a last despairing gurgle and expired. Perhaps advanced medical treatment could save her, but there would be none. Edward himself wouldn't be trying to make it back to the Empire's lines on foot if there was any sort of combat evacuation capability on Han. The last update he'd received had warned that the insurgents had HVMs and were using them on anything that flew…

He looked down at the girl's face, frozen in death…

…And snapped awake. He wasn't on Han; he was in his cabin on the unnamed freighter. The girl was long dead, along with hundreds of thousands of others, murdered in the frenzy of inter-ethnic tension that had been unleashed on Han. And her ethnic group had been just as guilty, Edward knew. There hadn't been a single group that had resisted the urge to try to clear out a living space for itself. The slaughter had been unimaginable.

Damn it, he thought, wiping sweat from his brow. It had been years since he'd dreamed of Han. The Marine Corps had never been quite sure if dreaming of past horrors was a good thing or not; he'd certainly never reported it to senior authority. God alone knew what they would have made of it.

But Han wasn't the only world in the Empire with ethnic tensions. Edward hadn't understood why, with thousands of empty worlds opening for settlement every year, the Empire had planted groups that hated each other on the same worlds. Later, he'd decided that it was deliberate, that the hatred shared by those groups prevented them from uniting against their true oppressors. Finally, he'd realised that the Empire simply didn't care.

And now the Empire was dying.

We're going to have to do better, he thought, as he stood up. *Whatever it takes, we're going to have to do better.*

CHAPTER
TWENTY-SEVEN

It is often asked why, when the pirates are so desperate for skilled manpower of almost any sort, Imperial Intelligence isn't very effective in introducing spies into their networks. The answer is, unfortunately, very simple. Before they accept someone completely, the pirates demand a show of commitment, one that involves doing something that will be considered a crime by the Empire. Put simply, all senior pirates have blood on their hands.

The agent might be asked to kill a helpless victim, or bombard a planet. Either way, they will be forever tainted by their act. And for those who aren't agents, who haven't steeled themselves to commit a dreadful act, the act can sever all ties with their old life.

-Edward E. Smith, Professor of Sociology. *Pirates and their Lives.*

Sword spent barely three days at Haven before cutting loose and heading back into interstellar space. Mandy had found herself ordered back to the ship after the first day by Vane and forced to assist the pirates in installing new equipment they'd bought on Haven into the starship, including a device Vane identified as a military-grade sensor suite cannibalised from a modern Imperial Navy starship. Thankfully, Vane had been so exhausted by working seventeen hours a day on refitting parts of the ship that he hadn't pushed her into doing anything with him, even though they shared the same bed.

Most of the new crewmembers, as Travis had hinted, were nothing more than thugs, utterly unskilled in anything apart from violence. Mandy gave them a wide berth, preferring to eat her meals in Vane's cabin or in the tubes, even though she had a suspicion that the internal monitoring network worked better than she'd thought. Maybe that was how the Admiral kept control of his crew, she thought, or maybe his entire network depended on him and him alone. Anyone who killed him might inherit *Sword*, but they wouldn't inherit his empire.

It was five days after departure when Travis found her in the engineering compartment. "Come with me," he ordered, bluntly. "Now."

Mandy pocketed her tools – she'd taken to carrying some of them on her belt, intending to use them as weapons if she lost the gun – and followed him through the ship's passageways into a smaller compartment. It was bare, apart from a single console in the centre of the room. Mandy realised, as he motioned for her to sit down in front of the console, that it was designed for training exercises. It looked cruder than some of the equipment she'd worked with on Avalon, but one thing she *had* learned from the pirates was that crude didn't necessarily mean useless. Travis tapped a switch and the console came to life, displaying a tactical scenario. *Sword* was heading towards its target, a single armed freighter.

"Take control of tactical," he ordered, briskly. "I want you to capture that ship."

The Imperial Navy, Mandy had been told, had worked hard to make its systems idiot-proof. When she'd asked Jasmine about it, the Marine had pointed out that some idiots could be very smart indeed, or at least imaginative. The console in front of her was simple, leaving most of the trickier calculations to the computers; indeed, a proper battle with a warship would leave the tactical officer issuing basic directions and putting everything else in the hands of the computers. A human mind just couldn't react fast enough to handle the little details.

Even so, she found herself struggling with the console. She had never realised how much actual work went into being a tactical officer; the officer had to handle everything from weapons selection to actually setting the parameters for the engagement. Use the wrong missiles and the target might be destroyed, instead of being crippled...and then, the pirates rarely *wanted* to even cripple their target. A ship that couldn't move was one that had to be looted and abandoned, rather than being used to haul its cargo to an asteroid base. In the end, Mandy accidentally blew the target ship into a ball of plasma.

"Dear me," Travis remarked. "That wasn't good, was it?"

Mandy barely sensed his motion before the neural whip cracked across her back. It couldn't have touched her for more than a second or two, but the pain tore through her mind and left her unable to do anything, apart from screaming. She slumped across the console, wondering what would happen to her next, if Travis would decide that she wasn't worth protecting after all, or…? He put his hand on her shoulder and pulled her back upright, roughly.

"Stop crying and start again," he ordered. "Bring up the tutorial this time."

Mandy gave him a resentful look and did as he suggested. She should have realised that there was a tutorial system built into the training simulation; she'd certainly seen them before on Avalon. They might have been programmed by someone who thought that an irritating female voice was key to getting the best out of someone, but they were complete and comprehensive. Carefully, she followed instructions and managed to capture the ship on the second try.

"Not too bad," Travis said. He tapped a switch, bringing up a second scenario. "You will keep working on these, one by one, for the next four days. Once you have completed the entire course, you can leave this compartment. Don't worry about disappointing Vane; he knows that you're going to be sleeping here until you complete the course. I'm sure that you will consider that a bad thing."

Mandy flushed. Sleeping in the bare compartment – although there was no bunk, not even a pile of bedding – would be infinitely preferable to sleeping with Vane. Travis laughed at her expression and headed over to the hatch, pointing out the hatch that led to the washroom, where someone had left a small pile of ration bars. She'd remembered Jasmine joking about someone trying to save time on Earth by placing the washroom right next to the mess. The joke didn't seem so funny now.

Travis opened the hatch and stepped through it. Mandy tested it and discovered, not entirely to her surprise, that it was locked. The pirates clearly believed in forcing people to undergo the test, or die trying. It was quite possible that was exactly what would happen, she decided, as she checked the ration bars. Assuming she was careful, she should have enough food for five to six days, by which time she had better be qualified – or else starve. Looking back at the console, she guessed that Travis had probably installed some monitoring software. Jasmine had complained about Civil Guardsmen who weren't smart or knowledgeable enough to realise that their systems had been hacked; the pirates, Mandy suspected, would be just the same. But she lacked the knowledge to take advantage of it.

But you can learn, she told herself, as she sat back in front of the console. *And then you can see what you can do.*

The simulations rapidly blurred together as she worked her way through them, one by one. They started as simple exercises – capture the target ship – and went on to others, practicing combat against actual warships. Most of those exercises ended in disaster, leaving Mandy despairing of learning anything, at least until she realised that the point of the simulation might have been to teach her that *Sword* should not try to fight a genuine warship, manned by genuine military crewmen. But if the Admiral was serious about building his own empire, sooner or later he *would* have to fight other military forces. The Imperial Navy might be crumbling, but there were planets with their own self-defence forces. Surely, they would fight...

Hours later, she nibbled one of the ration bars and took a nap, lying on the hard metal floor. She awoke five hours later, washed her face with cold water and stumbled back to the console. Again, the simulations started to blur together, forcing her to think through the haze of tiredness that had enveloped her brain. And to think she'd complained about the exams on Earth! She'd never realised that she'd learned nothing useful – or disruptive – until she'd been forced to move to Avalon.

The thought made her scowl as she completed yet another simulation. No one had ever punished her on Earth, certainly not her teachers; it seemed that almost any behaviour was tolerated, as long as it didn't bring the Empire itself into question. And she'd been lucky to go to a high-class college...some of the stories she'd heard on Avalon, from people who had been less lucky, had been hair-raising. There were schools on Earth that were nothing more than criminal training grounds, where violence, rape and murder were common. Whatever else could be said about Avalon, now that the old Council had been disposed, it didn't tolerate such crap from its children. Perhaps the Empire would have done better if it had known better than to show so much forbearance. But it hadn't shown any to her father…

She caught herself drifting off at the console and forced herself to complete the simulation, before going back to sleep. Her dreams were full of starships hunting and being hunted, snapping her awake with the unshakable conviction that someone was in the room with her, watching her. Mandy glanced around, drawing her gun, but saw no one. Slowly, she checked the washroom before going back to the hatch and confirming that it was still locked. It had to have been nothing more than a nightmare…

Two days passed before the console proclaimed that she was ready to take the test. By then, Mandy felt too tired to function, even though she'd managed to get several hours of sleep a day. Even working for Vane, watching her back all the time, hadn't been so stressful. Perhaps it was deliberate, to force her to develop her skills, or perhaps it was just a side-effect of studying so hard. In the end, it hardly mattered. She *needed* Travis's support – and that meant satisfying him.

I guess I should be grateful that he doesn't want my body, she decided, as she started the test. *That would be worse…*

The console froze the moment she completed the test, leaving her unsure if she'd passed or failed. Mandy stood up, wondering what she should do now. She'd eaten the last of the ration bars before starting the test; if she'd failed, perhaps Travis would just leave her in the room to starve. It seemed unlikely – the pirates needed engineers as much as they needed tactical officers – but she had a feeling that Travis wasn't entirely sane. But then, the same could be said of all the other pirates. She was still mulling it over when the hatch opened, revealing Travis.

"Congratulations," he said, as the hatch hissed closed. "You passed."

Mandy couldn't help yawning. "Welcome to the tactical staff," Travis added, dryly. "Get something to eat, then go back to your cabin and sleep for at least twelve hours. You're going to be on duty afterwards."

Reluctantly, Mandy obeyed. The word must have gone round the ship, because apart from a handful of leers there were no indecent suggestions from the rest of the crew – or perhaps it was just the presence of a handful of new sex slaves who'd been purchased on Haven. Mandy guessed that the girls had been kidnapped from an isolated colony or simply taken off a captured starship – or, perhaps, sold by their families into slavery. It was a hard life along the Rim, she'd been told, and it was possible that *someone* might decide that selling his daughter was the solution to his problems. Mandy had never really realised how lucky she'd been to have her family, as dysfunctional as it was; her father would never have considered selling her into slavery. Even her mother would have balked at the thought.

She looked away from the girls as she ate, knowing that she couldn't do anything for them. Their mere presence was a reminder that failure would result in a fate worse than death, for her and anyone else who failed their superior officer. Her back itched where she'd been whipped – it didn't *feel* as if she'd spent four days locked in the testing compartment – as she ate her food. It turned out that promoted crewmen got better rations than the average newcomer to the pirate crew. Mandy guessed, as she stood up and walked back to her cabin, that it was a reward for good work, something for the juniors to want as they climbed up the ladder.

Her cabin was just as she had left it, untouched since she'd moved into Vane's bed. She closed the hatch behind her, lay down on the bunk and closed her eyes. Sleep came almost instantly, but when she awoke she felt as if she'd barely slept at all. At first, she wasn't even sure why she'd been woken, until she felt a faint quiver running through the hull. *Sword* had dropped out of phase drive and returned to normal space.

Glancing at her watch, she realised that she was due on the bridge in forty minutes. Desperately scrambling to her feet, she opened the locker and discovered, to her surprise, that someone had left her a whole new shipsuit. She pulled it out and inspected it, shaking her head in relief. It might be tight enough to show off the shape of her breasts and thighs, but it wasn't torn, exposing her bare skin. A mask, just like the one she'd used on the RockRat ship, hung on its belt. If *Sword* was hulled – and she wouldn't have bet her life on the internal airlocks working properly – she might have a chance to survive.

I guess they think I'm a valuable crewmember now, she thought, as she placed the gun on her belt. The downside of the new shipsuit was that it was harder to hide the knife, all she had to remind her of Michael. She hadn't even seen him since they'd docked at Haven. *Joy.*

Shaking her head, she walked to the dining hall, had a quick breakfast and then walked up to the bridge. The compartment had originally been on the list of sections she wasn't allowed to visit, but now the guard just stood aside and allowed her into Officer Country. Unsurprisingly, the Admiral and his officers had better cabins than anyone else – and their own personal sex slaves. The hatches were unmarked, leaving her wondering which one belonged to Travis, before she finally reached the hatch leading onto the bridge. It hissed open when she touched the access panel, revealing a large compartment strewn with consoles like the one she'd used to train on. The chairs, she'd heard from Vane, were rigged. If someone displeased the Captain, or the Admiral, they could just push a button and run thousands of volts through their body, killing them instantly. She was rather surprised to notice that the bridge crew were not chained to their seats.

In the centre of the compartment, there were two giant throne-like chairs, one slightly larger than the other. The Admiral was seated on it, smiling faintly as he studied the holographic display in front of him. In the other, the Captain was glancing from crewman to crewman, scowling fiercely at his underlings. His face was twisted and scarred; both of his eyes had been replaced by implants that glowed with an eerie red light. And his body, Mandy realised as he stood up and loomed over her, had been enhanced, very crudely. She could see the artificial muscles rippling under his skin as he moved.

"You will take the tactical console," he said. His voice was underlain with an unpleasant buzzing sound, as if he'd had his voice box replaced with a computer voder. The way his head moved, Mandy was left wondering if he'd had his skull replaced with a metal protective sheath, making it very hard to kill him. "Prepare yourself for operations."

The previous tactical officer looked relieved when Mandy was pushed over to his console. Mandy couldn't really blame him; by any definition, working under someone who could kill you at the push of a button had to be stressful. *She* suddenly wished to be back in Vane's bed, or working in engineering. It had to be less dangerous than serving as part of the bridge crew. But there was no choice. She sat down, brought up the tactical display and studied it quickly. Unsurprisingly, *Sword* didn't seem to have a full weapons load. Or maybe certain systems were locked out to her.

"We are lurking in this system for a target," the previous officer informed her. "There's a limited amount of in-system traffic, but we're waiting for bigger prey."

"Thank you," Mandy said. She honestly couldn't think of anything else to say. "I'll deal with it."

He gave her an odd look and quit the bridge, no doubt heading to the compartment housing the slaves. The Captain returned to his chair and waited. Mandy hesitated, expecting orders, but none came. It took her a moment to realise why. They were waiting for their target.

Jasmine had once told her that military operations were often 'hurry up and wait,' but Mandy hadn't realised that was true of piracy too. Keeping her expression as blank as possible, she started pulling up what data she could from the console, only to discover that someone had gutted the system. She could discover plenty of information about the star system they were currently occupying, but nothing about its actual location – or where the ship might be going next. It struck her as odd, until she realised that the pirates wouldn't want to tell just *anyone* where their bases were hidden. The Imperial Navy might find out and then destroy them.

Bringing up a tactical puzzle, she started to work her way through it. If nothing else, she could use her time productively. Perhaps they'd see it as a sign of her being willing to work for them, without reserve. The more they trusted her, the better. Or so she told herself.

CHAPTER TWENTY-EIGHT

It is easy for us to stand up and condemn people who do things that we don't like – and indeed, in many cases, there is no reason for the act beyond simple evil. But it is important to remember that many atrocities are rooted in history, even if it does boil down to; they did this to us last year, so we do it to them now. But we actually did it to them two years ago, which is why they did it to us one year ago…

Even on a more personal level, people can be pushed into doing things they would never normally do, if the stakes are high enough. It is astonishing how easy it becomes to justify stealing, or murder, or any other form of criminal act, if vital interests appear threatened. And once that line is crossed, crossing it again becomes much easier.

Marines must recall that they are pressured so hard in the Slaughterhouse to ensure that they don't break in the field. Civilians rarely have that level of fortitude.

-Major-General Thomas Kratman (Ret), *A Civilian's Guide to the Terran Marine Corps.*

"We just picked up a brief message from our agent on the planet," the communications officer reported. "The freighter is preparing to depart."

"Finally," the Captain said. "Admiral?"

"The orders stand," the Admiral said. "We will intercept them when they are well clear of the planet."

Mandy listened, keeping her eyes on the tactical console. *Sword* had been in the system for nearly three hours, just waiting. At such a distance from the planet, it was unlikely that anyone would pick up a hint of their presence, but the Captain apparently hadn't wanted to take chances. All sensors were stepped down to the bare minimum and every entertainment device on the ship had been turned off, just in case. Mandy suspected that the precautions were excessive, but the Admiral couldn't really afford a public defeat, or even embarrassment. It might convince others to stand up to him.

The system itself was apparently more developed than Avalon, which had left her wondering why no one had mentioned it to her in training. Her access to the ship's passive sensors was limited, but there were definitely radio sources on three different planets and a multitude of interplanetary craft moving between them. It looked like a major colony world, perhaps one older than Avalon, rather than a newly-established system. She found herself wondering just where they were – closer to the Empire's collapsing borders, perhaps – but there was no way to find out. Her console had been locked out from the star charts.

She'd wondered just how the pirates found targets if the interstellar economy was collapsing, before realising that some parts of the sector were trying to keep it going. They *needed* an influx of parts and supplies, either from the Empire or from isolated worlds with a manufacturing capability. The tramp freighters weren't anything like as efficient as the ships operated by the big corporations, but they were all the sector had until places like Avalon started building their own ships. And if the Admiral was building his own empire, Avalon would need a fleet of its own too. If it survived the Admiral's first grab for the system…

The Admiral hadn't bothered to interrogate her about Avalon, something that puzzled her. Had he decided that the Marines were too tough to fight, or had he had other plans for the system? Or had he already occupied Avalon? Mandy recalled the selfish brat she'd been and shuddered, realising that she'd started to slip back towards being completely self-centred. It had honestly never occurred to her to worry about what had been happening on Avalon while she'd been a pirate prisoner, and then a crewwoman. For all she knew, the system had been occupied and Colonel Stalker and his men were dead.

She was still mulling over the thought when her console chimed. A small red dot had left the planet and was heading towards the inner edge of the Phase Limit. Mandy didn't understand the Phase Drive – very few people did, she'd been told – but she did understand that the Phase Limit was defined by the gravity field surrounding stars, and kinked by the presence of large planets in orbit around their parent star. Any Phase Limit was, therefore, somewhat imprecise, which was why civilian craft preferred to go STL some distance from where the limit should block their advance. Running right into the Phase Limit at FTL speeds could result in, at best, a very rough return to normal space. Quite a number of ships had been reported lost, presumably after getting their coordinates wrong and hitting the limit.

"She's putting on a great deal of acceleration," the sensor officer reported.

"Well, give chase," the Captain ordered. "There's nothing near the planet that can help them."

Mandy winced inwardly as *Sword* started to move. Their target had been lucky, but not lucky enough to escape, even though the pirates were now committed to a stern chase. Their only real hope was to get across the Phase Limit and escape into Phase Space, but she didn't need to look at the console to know that was impossible. The freighter would be run down well short of the Phase Limit.

But they kept going, trying desperately to stay ahead as long as they could. It puzzled Mandy, until she recalled the state of the average pirate starship. If they were forced to run their drives on full power for too long, it was just possible that something would break, making it impossible for them to continue the chase. But she knew that Vane was a good engineer, no matter how much she hated him, and she was grimly certain that the drives would hold out long enough to catch their target.

All of the entertainments she'd seen on Earth had suggested that space was full of places to hide. Nebulas, the atmosphere of various gas giants, entire asteroid fields…the real universe wasn't like that, not really. The thickest asteroid field she'd ever seen was still wide enough to allow half the Imperial Navy to fly through without seriously risking a ship. No, the only way to hide was to cut drives and pretend to be a hole in space, but the pirates would have no difficulty in calculating where the ship had to be hiding. Gas jets might have been undetectable, yet they also lacked the power to move the freighter far enough to avoid detection by the time the pirate ship arrived.

Briefly, she considered trying to do something, but what? If she started to draw her gun, she knew that the Admiral's guards – and the enhanced Captain – would kill her before she had it out of the holster. She'd be dead and they'd just keep going, running the freighter down before it could escape. Maybe there was something she could do with the tactical options…no, there was nothing, at least not without revealing her hand. And then they would kill her and someone else would operate the console as they completed the interception. All she could do was watch, and pray that something occurred to save the helpless freighter.

But nothing happened. "Entering extreme weapons range now," the helmsman reported, gleefully. Mandy winced as the tactical console activated automatically, allowing her to target the fleeing ship. "Close interception in twenty-seven minutes, assuming constant course and speed."

"Of course," the Captain said, rather dryly. Mandy realised that the helmsman was trying to impress him – and that the Captain wasn't falling for it. "Tactical, prepare to fire a warning shot."

Mandy swallowed. Typing in the command was easy, of course, but she couldn't quite grasp the fact that she was about to fire on a fleeing starship. Surely there was something she could do, apart from obeying orders…but there was nothing. She finished inputting the commands and looked up at the Captain, fighting to keep her face expressionless. If he saw the struggle inside her mind…

"Missile locked, sir," she reported. Maybe she could convince the warhead to detonate inside the launch tube…no, it was a standard HE warhead, rather than a nuke. All she'd do was take out the weapons rack and little else. Besides, overriding the safeties on the warhead was beyond her skill. She thought desperately, but she couldn't think of a solution. All she could do was obey. "Ready to fire on your command."

The Captain smiled, his half-metal face twisting unpleasantly. "Then by all means," he ordered, "fire."

Mandy pushed the switch. *Sword* barely shivered as the missile blasted free of the launch tube and raced ahead of the starship, heading right towards the freighter. Mandy found herself praying that the target ship carried some form of point defence, but there was nothing, not even an attempt to use a civilian sensor suite to produce improvised ECM signals. The missile slipped past its target, almost close enough to scratch the paint, and exploded ahead of the fleeing freighter. They couldn't have missed the proof that *Sword* could now fire into their hull.

"They're starting evasive patterns," the sensor officer reported. On the display, the ship was starting to zigzag back and forth. It was a brave effort, Mandy knew, but it was futile. The seeker heads on the missiles wouldn't be thrown off the scent by such basic manoeuvres. Maybe, if they'd had weapons slipped into their hull…but there was nothing. "Captain?"

The Captain keyed a switch on his console. "Attention," he said. "This is *Sword*. You are ordered to cut your drives and surrender your vessel. Refusal to obey will result in certain death; I repeat, refusal to obey will result in certain death. You have two minutes to comply."

Mandy watched as the range continued to close. The freighter crew had to *know* they were doomed, but they kept struggling anyway. She couldn't help, but admire them for their determination, even though it was futile. But then, the pirates would probably take any sign of resistance, or attempting to escape, as an excuse for pillaging the ship and raping the crew. The Admiral might want survivors to pressgang into his ship's crew, but even he would have difficulty restraining the psychopaths he'd hired as soldiers. Some of the tales Mandy had overheard had chilled her to the bone.

"Prepare a laser warhead," the Captain ordered. "Target their drive section."

Mandy blinked, although she shouldn't really have been surprised. Taking out the drive unit would bring the freighter to a halt, allowing the pirates to board and storm her without difficulty. But it also meant that the Admiral wouldn't be able to take the ship somewhere else and press it into service. Whatever the freighter carried would have to be transferred to *Sword* before she left the unnamed system.

Unless they decide to try to tow her through Phase Space, she thought, grimly. It was theoretically possible, but only very skilled crews would risk trying. Expanding the Phase Field that far would be immensely draining on the ship's resources and if it collapsed, it might wreck both ships. No, it was far more likely that the freighter would be looted and then abandoned. Perhaps the inhabitants of this system would be able to recover and repair her.

"Missile ready," she said. A laser warhead used a nuclear bomb to generate an immensely powerful pulse of energy, which stabbed deep into its target's vitals. It was also likely to cripple, rather than destroy, it's target. She found herself wondering if she could *accidentally* destroy the ship – better dead than raped and murdered – but it would be difficult to devise a convincing mistake. And besides, they'd kill her a moment later. "Captain?"

The Captain smiled. "Fire," he ordered. "Now."

Mandy keyed the command into the console. A moment later, the second missile launched and roared towards its target, which was continuing to zigzag through space. That was a mistake on their part, Mandy realised, although it didn't really make much difference to the outcome. Every time they zigzagged, they lost a little extra ground to their pursuer. This time, with a missile closing in on them, they twisted desperately, to no avail. The missile detonated, driving a pulse of laser energy into their drive. A moment later, their drive field started to flicker and fail.

It looked bloodless on the display. Mandy realised in horror that it was easy to forget that it would be far from bloodless on the target ship. Their drive section seemed to have been badly damaged, perhaps destroyed; they'd have crewmen fighting desperately for survival, if anyone had survived in the rear of the ship. The fact that their drive field hadn't simply vanished suggested that *someone* was still alive, trying to shut the drive field down carefully rather than risk a complete collapse. It might have caused the compensators to fail too, killing the entire crew instantly.

"Their drive system has failed," the sensor officer reported, gleefully. "The drive section is completely fucked."

"Cut our own drives," the Captain ordered. Mandy hadn't really dared to hope that they'd overshoot the target and have to waste time circling around before boarding the derelict ship. He keyed his own console. "Attention; prepare to receive boarders…"

"You son of a bitch," a female voice snapped. "Nine of my crew are dead, killed! Jack was *nine*!"

Mandy blanched, fighting hard to control her expression. She'd killed a *child*? But why should that have been a surprise? She'd known that the RockRats kept their children on their asteroids, along with many other spacers. They considered a life in space to be far superior to living planetside; besides, there were fewer interfering meddlers in space. Mandy felt sick, right to her very heart. She'd killed a child. Maybe she'd been following orders, but that didn't matter. She'd killed a child…

"Prepare to be boarded," the Captain said. "I won't ask again."

He broke the connection and snickered. "Launch the assault shuttles," he ordered. "Pass the word; they are to be taken alive, if possible."

Mandy raised her eyes and looked around the compartment. No one else seemed shocked, or even surprised. Indeed, some of the crew were grinning, as if they'd just scored a victory of some kind. She looked back down at the console before anyone could notice her face, trying to keep herself from crying. What could she do now? Avalon would never want her back…

But you should have known, she told herself, savagely. *You utter fool. Didn't you think they'd want you to get blood on your hands*?

She watched, blinking away tears, as the assault shuttles screamed towards their target. It was hopeless; they'd board, they'd storm…and then they'd amuse themselves with the crew. The Captain had ordered them to take the crew alive, but Mandy had seen enough on the ship to know just what horrors it was possible to survive…it was almost a relief when the console pinged, reporting the launch of a lifepod. Perhaps some of the crew would survive. A second followed, a moment later, leaving the ship abandoned. The first assault shuttle docked, allowing the assault team to board the freighter.

"They fled, sir," the leader reported. "And they wiped the main computer before they left."

"Really," the Admiral purred. "Did they think that would delay us for long?"

Mandy tried to think about it, despite the growing ache in her soul. Wiping a ship's computer was enough to make it useless, at least until a replacement program could be uploaded. It was quite possible to add in a virus as well, just to make life interesting for the salvage crews, although it might not be enough to prevent them refitting the ship. Standard procedure was to install a replacement system if possible, preventing any little surprises from ruining the ship's future career.

The lifepods drifted further away from the two starships, their distress beacons screaming for help. Mandy knew that it would be hours, at best, before any help arrived; she rather doubted that the Admiral would waste time picking them up. Once *Sword* was gone, an interplanetary ship could be diverted to rescue them. There were several ships in the system that should be capable of carrying out a recovery mission. Grimly, she looked away, wondering what the hell she was going to do now. Even if she did managed to stick a knife in the Admiral's back, she knew that Avalon wouldn't want her back. Maybe she should just find a way to blow the ship and kill herself in the process.

"We've secured the cargo, sir," the assault team leader reported, finally. "It's what we were led to expect."

Mandy frowned, inwardly. No one had told her what they were stealing, but it had to be something important and rare to make all this effort worthwhile. She watched as the shuttles returned to *Sword*, carrying with them…something. The Admiral seemed to be excited, she decided, and he smiled openly as soon as the shuttles docked. Maybe they could escape back into Phase Space now…

The Admiral turned back to her. "Target the lifepods," he ordered. Mandy froze, staring at him in absolute disbelief. What possible good did it to do to fire on the lifepods, to slaughter the remains of a brave crew. "Take them out. Now."

Mandy couldn't move. The thought was appalling, terrifying. But his hand was hovering over the button that would kill her, if he pressed it… she asked herself if she could get off the chair in time, maybe even kill him…no, she knew that there was no hope. If she fought now, she died for nothing. They'd wipe out the lifepods after they killed her.

"Now," the Admiral repeated. There was a hint of impatience in his voice. "Deal with them."

Mandy's finger came down on the button. The lifepods weren't armoured; they were designed to be as light as possible. Bursts of plasma fire tore through them as if they were made of paper. The distress beacons emitted one last squawk and fell silent.

"Take us back over the Phase Limit," the Admiral ordered. He didn't seem to care about her distress, or even about the remains of the dead crew left behind. "It's time to go home."

CHAPTER TWENTY-NINE

What we didn't know at the time was that the Admiral's plans were actually quite well advanced – and, to some extent, he had already moved on to the 'government' stage. Put simply, he had already started to charge planets and starship crews taxes – in reality, protection money. The operation was simple and self-sustaining; in order to avoid bombardment, planetary governments would collaborate, which would in turn force them to become dependent upon the Admiral's mercenaries to prop up their power. Acts of terrorism, such as the death of Captain Lawson and her entire crew in the Draco System, merely illustrated the choice facing the rest of the sector; death or submission.

Unlike the Empire, however, the Admiral had no capital known to the rest of the sector. Accordingly, even those who wanted to fight found it impossible to actually bring their weapons to bear on him. In a sense, the Admiral had mastered insurgency warfare in space.

- Professor Leo Caesius, *The Perilous Dawn* (unpublished).

"They don't seem to have established an OBS system here," Kitty commented, as the three ships slipped into the Crawford System. "There isn't even an orbital station."

Edward shrugged. "I suppose it would defeat the purpose of being hidden if there was a big station orbiting the planet," he pointed out. Kitty was on *Dancing Fool's* bridge; he was on the Q-ship's bridge, no doubt to her relief. "There's no sign of any orbital presence at all?"

"Nothing that we can detect," Kitty said. "The system appears to be clean."

"Good," Edward said. "Push the remotes in closer and let's see what we have."

Crawford had been a dying system long before the black colonists had arrived. Evolution was a hit-and-miss process and it wasn't unknown for something to evolve that disrupted the ecological balance so far that it never recovered. Indeed, there were people – the radical Greens, in particular – who believed that humanity had done just that on Earth. Crawford had evolved no intelligent race, making the ecological collapse utterly unavoidable. According to the survey team, who had looked the planet over seventy years ago, the only remaining water was in reservoirs below the surface and the only surviving plant life were those who had grown their roots deep enough to reach it.

Returning the planet to a habitable state wouldn't have been that difficult, they'd concluded. An infusion of water, taken from the asteroids drifting in the system, and the introduction of Earth-native plants and animals should have worked, although it would have taken upwards of two hundred years. It would be a slow process, but cheaper and easier than Mars, or the other worlds the Empire had terraformed in its glory days. But Crawford was right on the edge of the Rim, without anything to attract investors. The planet had simply been left alone until the black colonists had arrived.

Edward wondered, absently, what they'd been thinking. A high-tech society was easy to detect from orbit, unless they buried everything deep beneath the ground. Most black colonies on planets were low-tech, emitting nothing that might betray their presence, but the settlers on Crawford *needed* high-tech to survive. They couldn't hope to remain undetected once the Empire started expanding into the sector; at the very least, they'd have to pay huge fines for claim-jumping and then start paying taxes to the Empire. Or did they believe that the Empire was on the verge of collapse? Perhaps they'd planned to slowly build up their society as the Empire withdrew from the Rim.

If so, they'd been right. But they hadn't anticipated the Admiral.

"One settlement, right where we were told to look," Kitty said, as the remotes reported back. "It looks like a prefabricated camp, Colonel, not a proper settlement. The Admiral's men, keeping an eye on the system for him."

Edward keyed his communicator. "Shuttle one, prepare to launch," he ordered. He would have preferred to have his Marines in assault shuttles, but the pirates would be expecting heavy-lift shuttles carrying vast pallets of foodstuffs. "They don't seem to suspect anything."

His lips twitched. Even if they *did* suspect something, what were they going to do about it? They had no heavy weapons, nothing that could reach up and touch the starships – and there were no other ships in the system, as far as they could tell. The Marines would overrun the pirate base within seconds, taking them all prisoner, and then Edward could talk to the locals while they prepared the Q-ship for its first proper operation. And ask them why they hadn't set up local farms of their own. They wouldn't be in such a bad position if they'd started growing algae-based foodstuffs for themselves.

But it didn't really matter, he knew. Once the pirates had taken control of the high orbitals, Crawford would have been helpless. It would have been a choice between fighting the pirates and being killed, or bending over for them. Edward couldn't really blame them for choosing to collaborate. It was one thing to fight to the death when you were alone, but another when entire families were at stake.

"Picking up a signal from the ground," Kitty reported. "They're confirming our codes, sir."

Edward grinned. The pirates on the supply ship had sung like canaries, once they'd realised the danger of being left on Elysium. He'd worried that one of them would have given them a false code, despite the lie detectors; pirates had been known to give their junior officers incorrect information, just to make it harder for them to stick a knife in their superior's back.

"Launch the first shuttle," he ordered. "Go."

The heavy-lift shuttle had clearly seen better days. Jasmine heard the hull creaking alarmingly as the shuttle dropped into the planet's atmosphere and headed towards the pirate base. Unlike a Marine shuttle, there were no sensors on the hull for her to access, leaving her sitting inside her armour worrying about what would happen if the pirates detected them too soon.

A Marine shuttle was armoured, but the heavy-lift shuttle was all engine and cargo hold. It wouldn't withstand a blast that a Marine shuttle would shrug off long enough for the Marines to be ejected out to safety.

"Picking up a low-level beacon," the pilot called. "They're guiding us into land."

"Right where they want us," Blake muttered. He looked over at Jasmine and smiled. "Just think about the expression on their faces when we come boiling out of the shuttle."

"Just think about all the heavy weapons they might be pointing at the hatch," Joe said. They were all tense, all feeling claustrophobic inside the heavy shuttle. "Or just think about what hostages they might have on the surface."

Not again, Jasmine thought, pleadingly. The briefing had stated that most of the black colony was underground, a wise precaution on a world where winds blew with gale force over the remains of a once-proud ecosystem. She'd read the report from the original survey team, who'd concluded that the winds would have to be tamed before the planet could be settled properly. They would tear through any normal settlement, leaving it devastated. It wouldn't be the first time some planet had been too dangerous to settle easily, if the Empire hadn't had a population it wanted to dump somewhere away from Earth. Instead, they'd just left Crawford to die, allowing the black colonists to move in and settle the planet.

"At least it isn't another Ripley," Harris pointed out, dryly. "*That* wasn't fun at all."

Jasmine smiled, humourlessly. Ripley had been settled for two years when the planet had suddenly gone silent, with two supply ships reported overdue. A company of Marines had been dispatched to investigate, only to discover that the original survey team had missed thousands of lethal creatures that hibernated deep under the ground. The creatures had woken up, burrowed their way to the surface and attacked the colonists, who had been completely unprepared for their arrival. They'd been wiped out – and even the heavily-armed Marines had had problems keeping themselves alive. Right now, the entire planet was quarantined, although that hadn't stopped hunters from trying to pit themselves against the creatures. Most of them didn't come back.

The shuttle shuddered as a gust of wind struck it. "Just coming into land," the pilot reported. "There's no sign of anything suspicious, boss. Just a handful of buildings and a couple of people waiting for us."

"Here we go," Jasmine said, as she stood up. The shuttle had come to a hover, slowly lowering itself to the ground. "Stunners only, at first. Take them all down and then we can interrogate them at leisure."

The hatch cracked open, allowing the planet's atmosphere to leak into the shuttle. Jasmine's suit reported that it was breathable, but very dry, almost completely dead. The survey team had suggested that eventually the planet's atmosphere would stop being breathable, although it was possible that the ecology would evolve something that would help stabilise the planet's atmosphere. Or, for that matter, that an infusion of plants from Earth or something genetically-engineered for Crawford would save the planet. Blake stepped forward as the hatch opened wide and jumped out of the shuttle. The two pirates had no time to react before he stunned them both.

Jasmine barked a command and the Marines streamed out of the shuttle. The settlement was tiny, just as the remotes had suggested; a handful of prefabricated buildings and a single ex-Imperial Navy shuttlecraft, sitting on a hard patch of ground. Jasmine detailed three Marines to take the shuttle as she led two more towards the first building, kicking the door open to reveal a handful of men sleeping on the floor. They had no time to react either; Jasmine swept the stunner over them, knocking them all out. She took a moment to check that they were really out of it before moving on to the next target. Some of their smarter opponents, having prepped themselves against stun bolts, had the wit to pretend to be stunned and then crawl off when the Marines moved on to the next target. But no one here looked ready for the sudden attack.

"I've raided Civil Guard bases that were better defended than this," Blake said, as he cleared a second building. "They weren't expecting us at all."

"We had all the right codes," Jasmine reminded him. The third building was completely empty, without either people or supplies. "Would *we* be ready for attack if a shuttle landed, having passed all of the code-checks?"

"We were on Han," Blake said. "The Civil Guard wasn't. Poor bastards."

Seven minutes after they landed, Jasmine felt that she could pronounce the base secure. Thirty-two pirates had been taken prisoner; they were secured and dumped in the empty building until the interrogation teams could start working on them. A small arsenal of weapons and equipment was secured, all ex-Imperial military gear. The pirates had clearly intended to hold their base for as long as possible, if the locals turned on them. But then, they hadn't even taken basic precautions like setting up a fence or a minefield. Maybe they'd just intended to intimidate the locals into surrender.

The wind was growing stronger as the next flight of shuttles landed. Captain Stalker had given orders to bring along the supplies from Elysium, in the hopes of using them to bargain with the locals. Jasmine wondered, absently, where the locals actually *were*. She'd expected to find some of them in the base, but the pirates hadn't even had sex slaves. *That* was downright un-pirate behaviour. It was weird, to say the least.

"Maybe they were all homosexual," Joe suggested, when she said that out loud. "Or maybe they just managed to dispose of all their slaves before we caught them."

"We would have seen the bodies," Harris pointed out. "And if they had known that we were hostile, why didn't they fire on us as we came in to land?"

Jasmine nodded. Besides, the pirates couldn't dispose of their slaves on the theory that an incoming shuttle *might* be carrying Marines, or they wouldn't have any slaves left afterwards. Maybe Joe was right, although it was unlikely that *all* the pirates were homosexual, or maybe they were missing something. Or…

"I've got movement," Blake snapped, through the network. "One mounted person, riding a neo-camel, coming in from the west."

"Hiding under the storm," Harris commented. A single rider, masked by the growing sandstorm, might pass unnoticed. Using animals instead of powered vehicles was common on colony worlds, if only because the animals required less maintenance. And a neo-camel, a genetically-modified beast from Earth, would be ideal for Crawford. "Any weapons?"

"None that I can see," Blake reported. "You want us to snatch him?"

"I think we should try to talk first," Jasmine said, practically. Snatching someone, no matter how necessary, tended to create a bad first impression. "I'm going out there. Cover me."

Warnings flashed up in her HUD as she left the base behind, heading towards the oncoming storm. The sensors revealed the local, holding position near the base waiting for her. Jasmine looked at the sandstorm and shivered inwardly; without the sensors on the suit, it would be very easy for her to get lost in the desert and start wandering in circles. They'd been shown how easy it was to get lost on the Slaughterhouse…

The local was wearing a flowing robe and a mask that covered his face. Jasmine saw no weapons, but that didn't mean that he was unarmed. Bracing herself, she cracked her helmet and allowed him to see her face, despite the heat and the grains of sand in the air. Crawford smelt odd – every planet had its own smell – but she pushed it aside.

"Lieutenant Yamane, Terran Marine Corps," she said. She held out an armoured hand, wondering if he would take it. Very few people would willingly shake hands with someone in powered combat armour. One slight mistake and their hand would be crushed to powder. "We came to liberate your world."

The local removed his own mask, revealing a weather-beaten face. "Jack," he said, simply. "And may I say that this is the first time I have *ever* been pleased to see the Empire?"

"They landed several months ago," Jack explained, once they were in one of the buildings the pirates had set up. "Told us that they were in charge now and gave us a list of components they wanted us to produce. If we refused…well, they held the high orbitals and were quite prepared to drop KEWs on us. We couldn't see a way to beat them."

Edward nodded, unsurprised. The story was always the same, after all. "I quite understand," he said. "But we're working on picking the Admiral's operation apart right now."

"That's good to know," Jack said. He hesitated. "How much will we have to pay?"

It took Edward a moment to realise what he meant. Jack hadn't realised what had happened to the Empire, or why the Admiral's forces had been so blatant. He thought that the Empire had sent the Marines to liberate Crawford and then incorporate it into the sector government, like other discovered black colonies. But the sector government was *gone*…

"Nothing," Edward said, and started to explain. "The Empire has withdrawn from the sector."

Jack's face shifted rapidly as he tried to come to terms with what he was being told. The Empire had been far from perfect, yet it had handled law and order in the sector, protecting planets against pirates and raiders. Now, there was nothing left to maintain order, apart from a company of Marines and whatever support they could scrape up from the rest of the sector. The black colonists had just gotten a lesson in why they needed the Empire – and the Empire was no longer in a position to help them. They would have to look after themselves.

"Shit," Jack said, finally. "They could come back at any time."

"Not for several months, at the very least," Edward said. "They didn't get a message out to the Admiral, so he won't know that anything has gone wrong. What did they have you building for them and when did they pick it up?"

"Starship components," Jack admitted. "We set up a full industrial base on this world, under the ground. The founders had the idea that we could develop and then declare ourselves to the Empire as a world that could stand up for itself. But we weren't ready for even a single pirate ship."

Edward shrugged. Who knew what would have happened if the Empire hadn't withdrawn from the sector? If Crawford had had something to bargain with, the Empire might have been willing to accept it as a class-one colony world, rather than as a helpless supplicant. But the Empire was gone and the point was moot.

"They placed quite a large order last time," Jack continued. "And they said they wanted them in five months."

"Plenty of time," Edward said, slowly. "Did they bring you supplies too?"

"Yeah," Jack said. "And they brought us a number of skilled technicians from other colony worlds. Other than that, they left us alone as long as we obeyed."

"Clever bastard," Edward muttered, thinking of the admiral. Looting, raping and burning tended to make enemies – and collaboration difficult. Instead, the Admiral had effectively isolated Crawford, treating them almost decently in exchange for cooperation. *That*, he suspected, explained why the pirate guards had had no slaves to tend to their needs. "We have someone on our ship who needs to talk to your leaders."

The Professor could make Crawford the same offer as he'd made Elysium; they could join Avalon and as many other worlds as would join in a new alliance. Crawford had a lot to offer, including a small but capable manufacturing base. Added to everything Avalon had built over six months, it would be very helpful. They might be able to hasten the starship construction program.

Because we're going to need it, Edward thought, grimly. *How long do we have before the Admiral realises that we weren't occupied by his men?*

CHAPTER THIRTY

One should never underestimate the human ability to rationalise the worst of atrocities. The Holocaust, the Final War, the Bombardment of Sigma Alpha, the Han Purges…all were justified by those who chose to commit them. Their logic was flawed and utterly inhuman, but it was believed. Nor is this solely operative on a large-scale. Humans can justify and rationalise almost anything to themselves.

We are told that stealing is wrong, yet it is easy to rationalise the act. Stealing isn't stealing if one is trying to feed a starving child, for example, or stealing isn't really stealing when the victim has so much that they will never notice the loss. Or murder isn't really murder if the victim deserved to die. How easy is it, therefore, for even the most moral person to fall under the spell of the pirate society? On one hand, death or worse; on the other, acceptance, even a kind of camaraderie. How many people would remain 'moral' when forced into such a society?

-Edward E. Smith, Professor of Sociology. *Pirates and their Lives*.

Mandy lay in her cabin, staring up at the ceiling.

She'd killed. It wasn't the first time she'd killed, but her first victim had deserved to die. He would have forced himself on her and left her a broken shadow of herself, if he hadn't killed her after he'd had his fun. He'd deserved to die. But the crew of the freighter had been guilty of nothing more than trying to keep themselves away from the pirate ship. How had *they* deserved to die?

Her dreams had tormented her for days. She'd dreamed of being onboard the lifepods when the pirate ship had destroyed them, leaving dead bodies drifting through space for the rest of eternity. Perhaps there had been children onboard the pods, watching helplessly as their skins crisped into fire before merciful death came for them, or perhaps the children were already dead, killed when she had fired into the freighter's drive section. Her nightmares gave the victims – her victims – the faces of her friends and family, people she'd known. Mandy had snapped awake, covered in sweat, knowing that the nightmare was far from over. She had killed innocent people.

She looked down at her hands as she swung her legs over the bunk, feeling a faint quivering running through the deck. There was no visible blood on them, naturally, but she knew that she was a murderess and worse. She tried to tell herself that it was better that they died quickly, rather than being thrown to the pirate crew where they would be literally raped to death, but it failed to convince herself. Carefully, as another quiver ran through the ship, she stumbled into the washroom and splashed water on her face. The sweat might be washed clean, yet the blood would never fade away.

The hatch opened. Mandy let out a squeak and grabbed frantically for something to cover herself. Travis entered, glanced at her without bothering to conceal where his eyes were wandering, and then waited patiently for her to wrap the blanket around herself. He didn't look happy, but Mandy found it hard to care. Maybe she should just find an airlock and throw herself into space. It was no less than she deserved.

"Sir," she said, finally. Travis had never shown any interest in her sexually, but maybe that was about to change. "I was just…"

Travis brushed her excuses aside. "We have arrived in an isolated star system," he said. "The Admiral is going to meet with certain allies of his. I need you to spy on them."

Mandy blinked. "Allies?"

"Yes," Travis said, without giving her any more information. "You have access to the tubes. You will get into a position where you can listen to them, without being detected. I strongly suggest that you don't get caught."

"No," Mandy agreed. If the Admiral was keeping something a secret from Travis – and perhaps from the Captain as well – he'd kill her to keep the secret to himself. And Mandy was probably the most expendable of Travis's patronage network. If she was caught, Travis would deny all knowledge while she was executed. "That would be bad."

There didn't seem to be any alternative to pulling on her shipsuit in front of him, so she dressed reluctantly, wondering if he would try something. Vane hadn't called her in the two days since she'd become a murderess, leaving her to wonder if his interest was dying away. But that was a good thing, wasn't it? She'd once read a book about a seductress who'd tricked a horde of villains into killing themselves, but she knew that *she* couldn't do that. How could she, when any of the pirate crew could gain access to the sex slaves on the lower decks and use them however they wanted?

"Keep the privacy generator on as soon as you enter the tubes," Travis ordered. He passed her a code-key, followed by a pen and notebook. "They'll have their own privacy generators running, naturally, but you can still *hear*, if you're close enough. That code-key should let you into the right compartment without being spotted. I'll want it back afterwards."

Mandy gazed down at it, wondering if she dared make a copy before returning it to him. The XO had permission to go almost anywhere on the ship, except perhaps for the Admiral's private quarters. If she could copy the code embedded in the key – and it was a fairly simple process – she would have that access too. And who knew what she could do with it? She'd *have* to make a copy, she told herself, even though it was risky. Luckily, one code-key looked very much like another – and she had been given one by Vane, for her engineering work.

"I understand," she said, nervously. "I won't let you down."

Travis smiled at her. "Of course you won't," he said. "You need me more than I need you."

There was no entrance to the tubes in Mandy's cabin, unfortunately. Many of the starships she'd studied had been honeycombed with tubes, but the pirates had sealed up a number of access points to make it harder for their prisoners to escape. Instead, she allowed Travis to lead her down to a nearby storage compartment, which had an entrance to the tubes hidden behind stacks of boxes. Mandy had checked the boxes days ago, when she'd been given more freedom to roam the ship, only to discover that they contained ration bars and cans of flavoured water. The Admiral clearly wasn't taking any chances with his food supply.

"Good luck," Travis said, as Mandy opened the hatch with the code-key. "Remember, don't get caught."

Mandy climbed into the tube and crawled up it, wincing as he banged the hatch shut behind her. Taking a moment to orientate herself, she started to head directly for the section the Admiral used for his private meetings, a section that had been barred to her since she'd started working for Vane. It took nearly thirty minutes to crawl through the tubes until she reached the sealed hatch, partly because she'd had to avoid another worker inside the network. She had no idea if he was someone else who had been press-ganged, or another willing volunteer, so she kept her distance. Besides, what might he try to do if he caught her in the tubes alone?

The sealed hatch was unmarked. Bracing herself, Mandy slid the code-key into the slot and breathed a sigh of relief when it clicked open. The hatches on the RockRat ships didn't have locks – they trusted their own people – but Imperial Navy starships had all kinds of security precautions to deter intruders. If there had been something wrong with the code-key, the security system might have run a few thousand volts through her, or merely stunned her long enough for the security officers to investigate. Instead, she crawled into the isolated section and grimaced at the smell. No one had been doing any maintenance in the compartment and it showed.

Forcing herself to breathe through her mouth, Mandy kept going, eventually hearing the sound of voices ahead of her. The Admiral and his staff used the tubes to get around without being seen – just like Mandy herself – and naturally there were several access points within his private section. She felt her privacy generator vibrate as it sensed the presence of other privacy fields, just before she almost yelped in shock as a cockroach scuttled through the tube ahead of her. Fighting down the urge to be sick, Mandy watched it go, cursing the little creatures under her breath. Nothing short of venting the entire ship would eradicate cockroaches, or rats, or all the other creatures that managed to breed on starships. Even the RockRats had problems dealing with them.

Carefully, she crawled up to a point where she could hear clearly and then pulled the notepad out of her back pocket. It was a simple solution to the problem of being unable to use a recorder, she decided; Travis was evidently smarter than she'd realised. But then, he was the XO of *Sword* and a prime target for assassination by anyone who wanted his job. If he wasn't extremely cunning, he'd have been killed long ago.

"…Reports suggest that nine more planets have accepted our terms," the Admiral said. He sounded more…composed than usual, much to Mandy's surprise. "They can't contribute much, as yet, but they will remain part of the empire."

"But few of them have any industrial base at all," a new voice said. It was female, Mandy realised in shock, and sounded as if she was firmly in command. "The real prizes will be harder to take."

"Avalon should already be under control," the Admiral said. "Once we have the cloudscoop working at full capacity, we should be able to bring the others to heel without having to fight. Without HE3, their economies will grind to a halt."

"Unless they build their own cloudscoops," a third voice said. This one was masculine, sounding surprisingly disinterested. "It isn't as if the concept is a difficult one to master."

"They'd need to build up the infrastructure first," the Admiral reminded him. "The Empire wasn't keen on helping any of the Rim worlds gain energy independence – Avalon only received a cloudscoop after the ADC paid the Sector Governor massive bribes. At the very least, assuming a stage-two industrial base, it would take five years to produce a new cloudscoop – and besides, it would be a sitting target."

"As the skimmer-ships have been," the woman said. "And you shut down Gonzalez nicely."

"Serve the bitch right for thinking that she can establish an independent network," the Admiral said, sharply. "Her freighter was disabled and her crew were killed. And the components she was trying to smuggle to somewhere outside our control were captured. We will forward them to another sector and put them to use for us."

Mandy kept scribbling down notes, but her mind was elsewhere. Who was Gonzalez? The person whose freighter she'd crippled, whose lifepods she'd destroyed? Or was it something completely different. And the Admiral had claimed that Avalon was securely under their control… was that true? If so, Mandy was truly alone in the universe…

"Overall, however, the plan is working perfectly," the Admiral said, into the silence. "The sector will soon be under our complete control."

"Unless the Empire comes back in force," the man said. "Are we sure that they won't attempt to return to the sector?"

"The last intelligence reports suggested civil war breaking out in several sectors closer to the core," the Admiral said. He sounded rather irked, as if he'd said it before and resented having to say it again. "A number of over-mighty Sector Governors have started to move independently of the Empire, while the Imperial Navy is being torn apart by faction-fighting. There is little hope of the Childe Roland being able to reassert control, not with the Grand Senate holding all the cards."

"As if he could," the woman sneered. "The Emperor has been a spoiled brat since the day he assumed the Throne."

Mandy felt her heartbeat racing. The Childe Roland – the Emperor of Man – was even younger than her, having assumed the Throne after his father had been assassinated. But he was too young to rule and the Grand Senate had effectively assumed what remained of the Emperor's powers. Mandy's father had once commented that the odds were heavily against the Childe Roland ever reaching his majority, even if he hadn't been such a spoilt brat. The Grand Senate was hardly going to surrender meekly to the teenage Emperor. It was much more likely that they'd arrange an assassination and then pass the Throne to someone more controllable. Or maybe one of the Grand Senators would try to make himself Emperor.

They knew almost nothing of what had happened in the Empire, since the day they'd been told that the Empire was leaving the sector. Mandy looked down at the notes she'd taken and shivered. Colonel Stalker needed to know what was happening, if he was still alive. If the Admiral had taken Avalon…just for a moment, she understood the frustration that had gripped her father. The Empire's slow collapse into chaos was beyond their ability to stop, no matter how hard they fought.

"It may not matter," the Admiral pointed out. "We expect successor states to start declaring themselves within the next two years – five at the most. By then, we need to be in a position to hold this sector against all comers, or the ultimate plan will fail. If we can't stand up to one of the successors, we will rapidly lose our independence."

"True," the woman agreed. "And with the Empire gone, the successor states will operate with more independence."

There was a long pause. "So we continue with the plan," the man said. "Admiral, are you sure that you can keep your crews under control?"

"They will obey as long as they are rewarded for their services," the Admiral said. "Using the scum of the galaxy as crewmen has its risks, but we can keep them under control long enough to complete part one of the plan. After that, we can kill the useless ones."

He snorted. "There's a report that places a handful of Terran Marines on Avalon," he added. "I gave orders for them to be taken alive, if possible. We're going to need men like that in the future, not thugs."

"Risky," the man mused. "Could you really trust them?"

"Without the Empire, they would have no choice," the Admiral said. "They could either help us stabilise the sector or watch it fall into chaos."

"I shall hope that you are right," the woman said. "We will leave the time and place of the next meeting at the dead drop. Good luck, Admiral."

Mandy realised that they were departing and crawled back up the tube, wincing again as she caught sight of rat droppings on the hatch. The code-key worked again, allowing her back into the main tube network; quickly, she headed down towards one of the little workshops Vane and his engineers had established in the network. There was a small collection of tools there, including one that should allow her to make a copy of the code-key. If it failed – and if it damaged the code-key – she would have to lie to Travis and hope that he believed her. If not…

She pushed the thought aside as she entered the workshop and straightened up, glancing down at her shipsuit. It was covered in dirt and grime from the isolated tubes – and it was starting to smell. Cursing under her breath, Mandy started to work on the code-key, praying silently that it would work properly. Thankfully, most of the thugs the pirates used as dumb muscle couldn't have operated a computer, let alone understood what was actually happening inside the machine. Travis might well be smarter, or at least more knowledgeable, but he hadn't managed to secure the device. Mandy breathed a sigh of relief as she copied the access permissions to a blank wafer and then to another code-key. She tested it on the way out of the compartment and it worked perfectly.

Travis caught up with her just as she was about to enter the shower compartment. Mandy passed him the old code-key and the notepad without comment, knowing that he would probably want to ask her questions about what she'd overhead. Instead, he allowed her to shower and dry off before leading her to his cabin and interrogating her at length. He particularly wanted to know the identities of the two people who had visited the Admiral, but they had never used any names.

"So he's planning to betray us afterwards," Travis mused. He didn't seem to doubt her word, Mandy realised. Did he think she was completely his now? "That's interesting."

Mandy watched the thoughts playing over his face, wishing that she knew how to read minds properly. Jasmine seemed to do it pretty well, somehow. Travis probably wanted to strike first, to remove the Admiral before the Admiral could remove them, leaving him with the problem of ensuring that the Admiral hadn't left any unpleasant surprises for his successor after he was killed. Mandy had no doubt that the Admiral would have taken precautions against assassination.

She could understand why he might want to rid himself of the pirates. Most of them were useless for anything other than extreme violence. They would be liabilities once he'd established a proper government; they might force civilians into desperate resistance, rather than acceptance. But when did he intend to move? And how much of the pirate world did he actually control?

And who was backing him?

"Cuddle up to Vane," Travis ordered, finally. "If anyone will know, it will be the Chief Engineer. And then I have something else I want you to do."

"Yes, sir," Mandy said. She had an idea of her own now. "I live to serve."

CHAPTER THIRTY-ONE

All warfare is based on deception. Battles have been won or lost because one side successfully deceived the other into making mistakes, or into misunderstanding what they were seeing. Sometimes it is as simple as convincing the enemy that there is a full division bearing down on them – when in reality there is nothing more than a single company – and sometimes it is far more complex than that. Deception may not sit well with us, but it is a vitally important part of warfare.

Marines are therefore encouraged to deceive the enemy as much as possible. Surprise is, after all, the most deadly weapon known to man.

-Major-General Thomas Kratman (Ret), *A Civilian's Guide to the Terran Marine Corps.*

"I look like a fucking movie star," Jasmine muttered, looking at the mirror. "Are you *sure* that this is what the well-dressed mercenary is wearing?"

The uniforms they'd captured from Garth's men were at least a size too small for her, tight enough that she'd had to take needle and thread to it to allow her to move properly. Even so, it was tight enough to press up her breasts – and cut low enough to reveal more flesh than she'd ever been comfortable showing outside the shower. She would almost have preferred to fight naked. It also showed off her muscles, which was part of the point, but that wasn't much of a consolation.

"Garth's men swear to it," Blake said, as he donned his own uniform. If anything, his outfit revealed more flesh than hers. "Remember, we have to make an impression on the bastards."

"And we can't do that by wearing normal uniforms," Jasmine agreed, sourly. "Damn it."

Marine Corps uniforms would draw a reaction, all right, but it wasn't the one they wanted. Instead, they were posing as former Black Watchmen. The unit had earned countless battle honours as part of the Imperial Army, but it had lost the battle of the budget and the former soldiers had been unceremoniously dumped onto the job market. Jasmine wouldn't have been surprised to discover that a number of Watchmen had become mercenaries. The job market wasn't kind to former soldiers, or anyone else these days. Jasmine just hoped they didn't run into any real Watchmen on the pirate base, or their covers would be seriously threatened. Bad comedy programs aside, it was difficult for an outsider to pose as a member of any military unit; they'd be ignorant of all the little traditions that each unit had developed for itself.

"Make sure you are familiar with your background," she reminded Blake. "*Someone* is bound to start asking questions."

She glanced down at the ID card they'd put together and hoped it would fool anyone who scanned it. Her card stated that her name was Jennifer, close enough to Jasmine for her to react normally when it was used. According to the file the intelligence officers had spliced together, she'd been tossed out of the Black Watch for extreme violence, before signing up with a low-level mercenary company and serving with them closer to the core. There *had* been a major snafu on Gamma Prime several months before Stalker's Stalkers had been exiled to Avalon, with a large number of mercenary units involved. It would make perfect sense for the company to flee to the Rim after being tainted with involvement in that particular disaster.

"Just remember to stick to the script," Colonel Stalker said as he strode into the room. He was going with them, despite objections from the Command Sergeant and just about everyone else. "We're a light assault unit who have trained and fought together for several years. We don't want them thinking that they can split us up."

Jasmine nodded. Mercenary units ranged from reasonably competent to outright disasters waiting to happen. The former worked better when left as a unit; the latter needed to be broken up and the better officers and men distributed to other units. She'd read through all of the interrogation reports and they'd suggested that the Admiral's men were in a strong position to bargain, not least because they controlled much of the HE3 in the sector. The last thing they wanted was to have the Admiral's staff trying to split them up.

She checked her weapon as the Q-ship – now formally named the *Spider* – headed towards the asteroid base. Pineapple wasn't really a pirate settlement, although the distinction might have been lost on the Imperial Navy if it had ever come knocking. The base was quasi-legal, part of a chain of settlements that led from legal planets to hidden colonies and pirate bases along the Rim – and, naturally, almost completely lawless. It was the perfect place for mercenaries and other volunteers to contact the Admiral, or anyone else who might want to hire them. Once, Imperial Intelligence would have maintained a post on the asteroid. Now, Jasmine suspected that the post had been abandoned, the spies left out in the cold.

Or maybe they went native, she thought, grimly. It wasn't unknown for spies and other deep-cover agents to go native, to lose themselves in the persona they were forced to adopt to remain undiscovered. Marines considered themselves immune to it, but Jasmine had a feeling that it had never truly been tested. How well would she do if she was sent – alone – to blend into a network of Cracker bases? Or even the bandits?

"They seem to have accepted our IFF codes without demur," Lieutenant Faulkner reported from the bridge. "And they've sent us instructions to a docking port."

Jasmine watched through the ship's sensors as the asteroid came into view. It looked like a giant red pineapple – she assumed that was where the name came from – with long struts reaching out of its solid core to grasp at incoming starships. There were more ships than she'd expected docked to the base, including a handful of starships that had clearly once belonged to the Imperial Navy. They'd been meant to be refitted before being sold to civilians, with all of their weapons and sensors stripped down to civilian-grade, but Jasmine had seen enough starships like them to know that they were often left armed. The Imperial Navy had too many corrupt officials working in the bureaucracy.

She hefted her weapon as the ship docked. Unlike more normal stations, there was no trickle of power from the asteroid's fusion reactors, or supply of HE3 waiting to be pumped onboard. Pineapple was clearly receiving HE3 from somewhere, probably from the gas giant orbiting on the other side of the primary star. Given enough industrial capacity, they could certainly produce cloud-skimmers even if producing a whole cloud-scoop was beyond them. Besides, they would have little choice. Without a steady supply of fuel, the asteroid would eventually grow cold and die. There was nowhere else to go in the system.

"Follow me," Colonel Stalker ordered. "And just remember that you're supposed to be mercenaries."

The hatch opened and Jasmine stepped out, into a long passageway leading down to the asteroid's shell. It didn't take much training to know that the design was inefficient but very secure. The asteroid's command staff would have plenty of time to see their new arrivals before they reached the secondary airlock. Jasmine fought down the sense of vulnerability as they walked down the passageway, tasting the faint scent of overused filters in the atmosphere, as well as a faint sense that the balance between oxygen and nitrogen wasn't perfect. It was clear that Pineapple was falling on hard times.

Colonel Stalker reached the hatch, which opened as they approached. Any normal settled asteroid would have an immigration department, checking all new arrivals and carrying out bio-scans, but Pineapple seemed to have nothing. Jasmine exchanged glances with Blake, who looked equally puzzled. Pineapple might be run by a semi-independent syndicate, yet even they should worry about the possibility of contamination. Or were they just proving that their services were offered anonymously? There would be no record of who came to the asteroid – or if they ever left.

Inside, the passageways ran down into a set of massive caves, dug out of the rock. Jasmine had worked her way through simulations of Marines storming asteroid settlements; this one was little different, at least as far as she could tell. There were hundreds of stalls with thousands of people, the scum of the galaxy, moving between them, buying and selling as the fancy took them. One glance at the stalls told her that most of the merchandise had been stolen.

She felt a hand at her pocket and snatched downwards, automatically. A young boy, barely entering his teens, stared up at her, one hand gripping the wallet she'd been given on *Spider*. Jasmine took it back, squeezed his hand hard enough to hurt for several days without causing permanent damage, and shoved him away. No one paid any attention to the brief exchange; the asteroid played host to hundreds of people with no hope at all. Jasmine felt a moment of pity, before recalling that the pickpocket had probably robbed hundreds of people. But did he have any choice?

Blake leaned closer to her. "Better watch your back," he muttered. "We have been attracting attention."

Jasmine nodded. In truth, she wasn't surprised.

Edward scanned through the various communications channels on the asteroid, using his implants to access processor nodes and upload queries into the network. Unlike a more standard asteroid – or planetary settlement – Pineapple seemed to have a dozen different networks, all competing to share a very limited customer base. The basics were free – that was true everywhere, apart from Earth – but anything more advanced required a fee. Still, it was relatively easy to locate a middleman; Edward had been sure that there would be one on Pineapple. There was *always* a middleman.

He noticed that they had picked up a tail as they made their way out of the market and into the more secure part of the station. It was evident that the more organised smugglers and mercenaries had their own offices, mainly to ensure privacy while they discussed their operations with prospective customers. A place like Pineapple was as private as one could get, outside of a secure room on Earth; the operators would take a dim view of anyone trying to spy on their clients. Edward found the right door, nodded briefly to his two escorts, and knocked on the hatch. A moment later, it hissed open, revealing a small office.

Edward wasn't too surprised when he saw the middleman. He was short, wearing a suit and tie that seemed out of place on Pineapple. The man didn't look very dangerous at all, but no one would dare touch him, not when some very powerful and dangerous people owed him favours. Middlemen put certain people in touch with other people and pocketed the fees, all without getting blood on their hands. The best of them could find almost anything a client could want, if the money was right.

"You're Ward," the middleman said. He didn't bother to give his name. "You came onboard from *Spider*."

"Yes," Edward said, flatly. The middleman would have his own code inserted into the asteroid's multiple computer network. For a person who made a living by trading services and information, it was a must. "We're looking for work."

"I see," the middleman said. "Not familiar with this sector, are you?"

"No," Edward confirmed. Mercenaries from the sector would know who to contact, without the middleman. But refugees from another sector...? They'd *need* someone to point them in the right direction. "We just arrived from Sector 012."

"Very interesting," the middleman said without inflection. Sector 012 was very close to Earth, one of the oldest settled regions in the galaxy. "And what, exactly, do you bring to the table?"

Edward smiled. "We're a light assault unit, optimised for space assaults," he said. The Marine equipment would be a dead giveaway – most of their suits could only be obtained from the Slaughterhouse – but they'd recovered enough equipment from Garth to display to the middleman, or anyone else. "Thirty-two of us, counting the ship's crew, and armed."

"Not a large unit, then," the middleman said, in the same bland monotone. "Are you capable?"

"Yes," Edward said. The minuteman lifted a single eyebrow. Edward produced a datachip and dropped it on the desk. "Our battle honours."

He watched as the middleman plugged it into an isolated datapad and scanned it quickly. The intelligence staff had taken days to craft an identity that was reasonably believable, although Edward wasn't sure how long it would stand up to a careful check. At least they'd have to send word to Sector 012 to confirm their suspicions, if something didn't hold together perfectly. That would take months, if it was possible at all. But if the middleman was suspicious, he'd just make sure that they never got any further. His reputation would be at stake.

"An impressive list," he said, finally. "But you were never in overall command?"

"We operated independently," Edward confirmed. Few mercenaries were ever happy operating under someone else's direction, even on the strategic level. They'd be very reluctant to accept tactical or operational orders from anyone else. "We didn't want to be swallowed up in the overall operation."

"And you wanted to be able to back out, if necessary," the middleman said. Edward didn't bother to try to deny it. "I can't fault your paranoia."

Edward nodded. The operation on Gamma Prime hadn't been *quite* as bad as the uprising on Han, but it had been disastrous for the mercenary companies the founding corporations had hired to put down the revolt. They hadn't realised just how desperate the rebels were, or how savagely they were prepared to fight – and the managing director appointed by the corporations had thought himself a military genius. The operation had come close to failing completely by the time the Imperial Army stepped in…and, the last Edward had heard, there was still a low-level war being waged on Gamma Prime. But that had been almost a year ago.

"Well, I'd have to show your resume to a few recruiters, but I think I can find work for you," the middleman said. He looked up at Edward. "What do you have to offer?"

Edward looked back at him. "I assume that Imperial Credits are worthless here?"

"I'm afraid so, unless you want a completely ruinous rate of exchange from a moneychanger," the middleman said. "There are some people who are stockpiling credits in hopes of the Empire returning to this sector, or taking them back to the Core Worlds, but they're not offering very high rates. What else do you have?"

Edward produced another datachip. Thankfully, Kitty had had some experience of dealing on semi-independent asteroids and she'd produced a list of items they might be able to offer in barter. Weapons and equipment were out – Edward had vetoed that firmly – but they did have some foodstuffs left over from Elysium. They'd been rebranded as coming from further into the Core, although Edward doubted that anyone would ask any questions. Fresh beef, lamb, pork or chicken would go a long way on the asteroid.

"Two hundred beefsteaks?" The middleman asked. "Where did you get them?"

"Picked them up before we left and dumped them into a stasis box," Edward said. Maybe someone was going to ask questions after all. "We were all thoroughly sick of ration bars."

"Hard to blame you," the middleman commented. "I can sell these for you, taking a cut for myself. Or you can give me fifty of the beefsteaks and sell the rest yourself. You'd find that the meat would go quite some distance if you let me sell it."

Edward pretended to consider it. On one hand, the middleman would probably know where to go to get the best price. But on the *other* hand, he'd have ample opportunity to cheat them. He might not cheat them too badly – he depended upon repeat customers – but it went against the grain to allow anyone to cheat him at all.

"That would save time," he said. "How big a cut do you want?"

"Thirty percent," the middleman said. Edward snorted. "Very well; twenty percent."

"We have a list of supplies we need," Edward said. He produced a third datachip and passed it to the middleman. "Get us these supplies, and some spending money, and a few other things, and we won't quibble over what else you make for yourself."

The middleman studied it thoughtfully. Edward had put the list together carefully, naming things they needed as well as things they didn't need, but wanted to know if they could be obtained on Pineapple. HE3 was top of the list, along with a handful of weapons and ammunition supplies. And the name of a reputable information broker.

"Hans is the best information broker on the station," the middleman said. "He charges highly, but he never shares any information on his clients with anyone. Beyond that…"

He finished studying the list. "I can get all of these for you, in exchange for all of the meat you have," he concluded. "Do we have a deal?"

Edward took his hand and shook it firmly. He disliked dealing with middlemen; they made a profit out of blood and suffering, while keeping their own hands clean. The bureaucrats who ran the Supply Service on Earth, as savage a bunch of leeches as any other form of lower life, were preferable to the middlemen. But there was no choice.

"We have a deal," he confirmed. "Have the supplies sent to our ship, along with the details of our job."

"I will have the recruiter contact you," the middleman said. "A pleasure doing business with you, Colonel Ward."

"Yes," Edward agreed. Later, once the Admiral was defeated, Pineapple would be cleaned up by the Marines. The middleman would spend the rest of his life on a penal colony. "A pleasure."

CHAPTER THIRTY-TWO

Information is very much the second most deadly weapon in warfare. It can be something as simple as knowing when and where the enemy plans to advance, or knowing just what the enemy actually wants to do. Gathering intelligence, therefore, is a top priority of the Marine Corps and all Marines are thoroughly schooled in the vital importance of securing as much as possible. Marines are almost always outnumbered on the field of battle. It is intelligence that allows them to fight smarter than their opponents.
-Major-General Thomas Kratman (Ret), *A Civilian's Guide to the Terran Marine Corps.*

The information broker had a whole suite of rooms to herself, Edward was unsurprised to discover, along with a small army of enhanced guards. Information brokers were rarely popular; indeed, he would have been surprised to encounter one on an asteroid owned completely by a pirate gang. They sold information on anyone and anything, to anyone with the money; Edward had never heard of one of them having the scruples to avoid selling information, even when it risked lives. But they were almost always reliable. An information broker who lied, or was revealed to have verified information that was useless, would rapidly go out of business.

He allowed the guards to search him, leaving most of his weapons with his two escorts, before he was shown into the broker's office. Unlike the middleman's office, it was decorated with all sorts of trinkets, all designed to display the broker's wealth. One particular set of statuettes, Edward noticed with some amusement, had been designed by a con artist, who'd claimed that they'd been pulled from the ruins of a long-dead alien civilisation. The con had been revealed very quickly, but the artwork had remained surprisingly popular – and thousands of copies had been produced. In the darkness, the artefacts glowed with a faint yet unmistakable light.

The broker herself was a tall woman, with black hair tied back in a severe bun and a pair of spectacles balanced on her nose. A successful information broker would be more than wealthy enough to afford an eye-correction operation, so the spectacles were part of her appearance – and probably rigged to allow her to see beyond the normal range of human eyesight. It was easy enough to read a person's emotions by studying their body temperature, or measuring their heartbeat. Edward knew biofeedback techniques to make that difficult, but using them would also be revealing.

"The middleman has forwarded credit for you to use," the information broker said. She had a crisp precise voice, one that brooked no doubt or uncertainty. "You may call me Bachman. What questions would you like answered, Colonel Ward?"

Edward nodded, shortly. He wasn't surprised that she knew his false name. The last report from *Spider* had warned him that the ship's computer had been pinged a dozen times, probably by information brokers and the recruitment officers. So far, no one had managed to hack into it, or to pull out anything beyond the fictitious resume they'd put together for the mercenary group, but Edward suspected that it would be just a matter of time. Knowledge was power, after all, and anyone who got to it first would be in a position to use it for their own advantage.

He smiled. "I want a guarantee that whatever we ask goes no further, Miss Bachman," he said. "I assume you can do that for us?"

Bachman smiled back. "Confidentiality is part of the service," she assured him. "If you want exclusive access, on the other hand, that will cost you."

"Good," Edward said. Bachman was probably telling the truth – her reputation wouldn't survive if she started passing on information about her clients – and he'd already planned to take a calculated risk. "We have been looking for people who might be interested in our services. Tell me about the Admiral."

Bachman made a show of considering the question. Like every other information broker Edward had met, she would store most of her knowledge in her mind, where it couldn't be hacked or altered by her rivals. She'd probably had treatment to enhance her memory if she hadn't risked using implants. And Edward would have been surprised if she hadn't been asked about the Admiral before. Mercenaries liked knowing as much as they could about their employer *before* they signed the contract.

"He claims to be a pirate commander," Bachman said, finally. "Probably ex-Imperial Navy, or so I have been told, although I have been unable to verify that factoid. In the last nine months, he has built up a respectable fleet of pirate ships and has been using them to take control of part of the sector. Most of his rivals have ended up dead or forced into his organisation. The absence of the Empire is having a serious effect on the local pirate gangs."

Edward concealed his amusement. Before the Empire had withdrawn from the sector, a large pirate gang was quite likely to fracture, with one faction trying to betray the rest to the Empire. A pirate flotilla would rarely consist of more than three or four ships. Now, however, the Admiral could control a much larger fleet if he chose, probably through a mixture of threats and promises. It would be simple enough to rig a starship with a nuke that would vaporise the ship if the crew set off on their own.

"He spends most of his time on his flagship," Bachman added. "The closest thing he has to a main base is Haven, an asteroid only a few days flight from here. What else would you like to know?"

"It sounds as if he would have plenty of gainful employment for us," Edward said, mildly. "How much else do you have on him?"

"Bits and pieces," Bachman admitted. "The Admiral is good at concealing his movements, or his intentions. I can give you a list of planets under his control, but it may already be outdated. Or I can tell you who else has signed on with him."

"That would be very helpful," Edward said. The second question was less important, yet they needed to know. "Are there truly no remnants of the Empire's military in this sector?"

"Apparently, there's a handful of Marines on Avalon," Bachman said. "No one has been to the system to investigate, however, so they may have been withdrawn with the rest of the Empire's military. There's also a report of a heavy cruiser left in the sector, but it hasn't been confirmed and may be just wishful thinking on their part. I can give you a complete breakdown of the rumours if you would like."

Edward nodded. The one question he wanted to ask was the one he couldn't; what did Bachman know about the inner sectors. But they claimed to have come from the Core Worlds and if they asked about something they should already know, it would definitely arouse suspicions. Indeed, Edward was surprised that Bachman hadn't offered to trade information on the Core Worlds for information on the Admiral. She would probably profit hugely from such information.

Unless they don't want to know, he told himself thoughtfully. *They might prefer to forget that the Empire ever existed.*

Bachman reached for a terminal and tapped it. A moment later, a single datachip was pushed out of the device, which Bachman picked up and passed to Edward. "Your data," she said, simply. "Everything on that chip is either verified, or clearly marked as unsubstantiated. There is also a list of other services I can provide, should you be interested. Your men may wish to get laid, right? I could put you in touch with the best slave dealers…"

"No, thank you," Edward said, firmly. Inwardly, he felt sick. Slavery was epidemic along the Rim – or something that was effectively slavery, in all apart from name – and it didn't take any imagination to know what Bachman had in mind. "We really need employment first."

"The Admiral has a good reputation for paying his men," Bachman told him. "Good luck."

Edward was still scowling as he walked out of her office. Mercenaries needed to be paid to fight, something that bothered the professional soldier in him. It was true that the Civil Guard had the same attitude, but even they wouldn't put down their guns because the pay was a day or two overdue. On the other hand, he had to admit, the Civil Guard often grew disgruntled if pay was delayed or stolen by their superior officers. Edward had seen units where their COs pocketed all the wages, or taxed their subordinates for imaginary services. Unsurprisingly, those units rarely bothered to put up a fight when the rebels rose up against them, if they weren't already themselves responsible for the revolt by mistreating the local population.

There was a message from the middleman waiting for him, he discovered as he checked the local communications network. Apparently, he had managed to link Edward and his men to a suitable recruiting officer; would Edward like to come meet the man? Edward pocketed the chip – it would be checked carefully for unpleasant surprises before the intelligence officers went to work on it – and allowed his two escorts to lead him back to the middleman's office. This time, it seemed, they were expected. The middleman came outside to greet them personally.

Inside, the recruiting officer was sitting on a chair, studying Edward thoughtfully. He didn't look very impressive, unlike the Marines Edward recalled from the day he'd first walked into the Recruiting Station on Earth. It was easy to forget that the Marines who manned the station were actually quite senior members of the organisation, and that their first impressions of a prospective recruit could make or break a career. The Admiral's recruiting officer, on the other hand, was overweight, smoking a cigarette that was tinted with a narcotic drug. His fingers twitched uncontrollably while he spoke.

"I read your resume," he said. His voice was thin, almost oily. "You have a very impressive team. I sure hope that you can live up to your boasting."

Edward nodded, keeping his expression under firm control. If he spoke like that to every mercenary who happened to visit the Pineapple, it was a miracle that he was still alive. The resume had been prepared carefully, showing off their skills while trying to avoid anything that might scream *Marine*. There *were* a handful of Marines who had gone bad, Edward knew, but claiming to be an entire ship of them would raise suspicions.

"Glad to hear it," the recruiting officer said. He held out one stubby hand. "You may call me Ollie."

His hand felt oily to the touch. "You do not appear to be in a good position to bargain," Ollie continued. Edward wondered absently if he gave this treatment to everyone, or only to people who couldn't go elsewhere. Officially, *Spider* barely had the fuel to make it to the next star system, where they would be stranded without HE3. "Here is the standard mercenary contract. Read it and then sign on the dotted line."

Edward took the sheet of paper and scanned it quickly. The Empire had worked hard to regulate mercenary groups, at times stepping in to squash groups that went too far to the dark side. It wasn't too surprising; anyone who fought for money alone might switch sides if given a better offer, or start a fight with their employers if the pay was late. Normal procedure was to place their pay in escrow, where it couldn't be retrieved by anyone until the terms of the contract were met. The Admiral, on the other hand, had the power to dictate terms – and was willing to use it.

The contract stated that they would be paid a small retainer as long as they were signed up with the Admiral, but payment for any operations would be withheld until the operation was completed – and would be reduced if the unit was forced into surrender by the enemy. *That* wasn't too uncommon, particularly if mercenaries were fighting on both sides of the conflict, although there was no prohibition against taking up service with the other side. Edward found himself wondering if the Admiral was overconfident, or if he had a surprise or two up his sleeves. No wonder Garth had been prepared to quietly gather information on the Admiral's operations. The Admiral had effectively dictated terms to his subordinates.

"Right," Edward said. He asked the obvious question. "What about HE3 supplies?"

"Fuel will be provided for operations you conduct on our behalf," Ollie explained. "You will also be charged a cheaper rate as long as you are accepting our retainer. However, should you wish to leave our service, you will be charged the standard rate."

Which might be very high, Edward thought. They still didn't know where the Admiral was getting his HE3. He turned the page and skimmed through the various other clauses, noting that the Admiral was being something of a cheapskate. There were no death benefits for the mercenaries, nothing for their families if they died on the Admiral's service – and only one bonus, awarded when the mission was completed. Standard contracts offered bonuses for every contact with enemy forces.

He read the final page quickly, scowling. The Admiral wouldn't be providing anything beyond basic ammunition; everything else would have to come out of their retainer. It was easy to see that the Admiral wanted to keep his people on a very short leash, just to limit their ability to cause trouble for him elsewhere. Edward had to admit that he had a point – bored and underpaid mercenaries tended to cause mayhem in bars – but it would alienate his supporters. And some of the equipment specialist units needed was very expensive.

"That's the contract," Ollie said, when Edward pointed that out. "I was under the impression that you *had* equipment."

"Equipment wears out," Edward said, wondering how Ollie managed to live on an asteroid without knowing that. Anything, from a gun to a suit of powered combat armour, could wear out without constant maintenance. He resorted to what was effectively baby talk to get the point across. "If we lose our advanced gear, we become less mobile, less capable of doing what you want."

"I'm sure that something could be arranged," Ollie said, finally. "Are you going to sign the contract or not?"

Edward scowled, but made a show of signing his false name. "There," he said. "Where do you want us to go?"

"I shall be accompanying you on your ship," Ollie said. "The coordinates will have to be uploaded into your navigational computer and then wiped, once we have arrived at our destination. Your men must not be allowed to know where we are going. It is a simple security precaution, covered in Clause Thirteen."

"Yeah," Edward growled. It wasn't hard to pretend to be annoyed; hell, *anyone* would be annoyed at Clause Thirteen. If nothing else, it made it harder to catch up with the Admiral to extract revenge for non-payment of debts. There wouldn't be any escrow in this sector for years to come. "When do you want to leave?"

"I have documents to bring," Ollie informed him. "And you will require HE3. Shall we leave in two hours? I will make the arrangements for your ship to be refuelled."

He took one copy of the contract and passed it to Edward, placing the other copy in a secure briefcase. Edward eyed it thoughtfully, quietly confident that one of his intelligence officers could crack into the briefcase without triggering the security device that would flash the entire contents to dust and ash. He shook hands again and left the room, carrying the contract with him. As he knew Ollie would expect, he headed right back to the ship, followed by his two escorts.

"Scan us," he ordered, as soon as they entered the airlock. "Are we clean?"

"You got stung, *twelve* times," Gwendolyn said, as she ran a scanner over his body. "One of the bugs appeared to be non-functional – I'm not sure why – but the others are busy chirping away to whoever planted them on you." She scanned the other two Marines quickly. "Nine bugs on you two. Someone really wanted to keep an eye on us."

Blake Coleman scowled as the bugs were removed and destroyed, one by one. "The pirates?"

"Could be anyone," Edward said. The bugs were so tiny that they were completely invisible to the naked eye. "Anyone who walks onto one of those asteroids might be targeted. Knowledge is power, after all."

He passed the chip Bachman had given him to the intelligence officers and then walked through the ship, making sure that there was nothing that gave away their true nature as Terran Marines. The combat suits had been modified slightly, enough to make them unrecognisable by anyone short of an expert, and he hadn't had the impression that Ollie was an expert in anything other than bargaining from a commanding position. It was a risk, but one they would have to run. There was no other choice.

Ollie came onboard two hours later, wearing a shipsuit that looked to have been specially tailored to hide his bulk. Edward contrived to give him a sanitized tour of the ship while they undocked from Pineapple and headed towards the Phase Limit, waiting for the moment they could give him access to the navigational computer. Unlike a standard model, this one was rigged to save every command loaded into it, without revealing that it was doing so unless someone had the right codes. Ollie didn't seem to notice anything; he just inputted the coordinates as the ship prepared to jump into Phase Space.

Edward pushed a stunner against the man's neck and he collapsed to the deck. "Move him down to the interrogation chamber," he ordered, as he checked the coordinates. They were for a red star, three light years away. The perfect spot for a pirate base. "Let's see what he has to tell us."

Chapter
THIRTY-THREE

There is a theory that the largest group that can operate effectively is 100 people. If any larger, the group becomes factionalised very quickly, with the various different factions often working at cross-purposes. An army, for example, may have the same overall objectives, but different factions may have different ideas about how best to achieve those objectives. This can often become confusing, even nightmarish. An army's supply officers, for example, may see their objectives being keeping those supplies, rather than distributing them to the units that need the supplies.

And if regular military units, or civilian businesses, have problems with factions, what do you think the average pirate gang must be like?

-Edward E. Smith, Professor of Sociology. *Pirates and their Lives*.

"The Admiral has backers," Vane had said. "He tells us nothing about them."

Mandy looked down at his sleeping form and shook her head. Vane might be a competent engineer – no, he had to be a genius to keep *Sword* running as well as she did – but he seemed to lack curiosity. Or maybe it was simple self-preservation. The Admiral wouldn't be too happy if Vane started asking questions; he might even see fit to rid himself of his Chief Engineer, no matter how competent he was. Mandy wondered, absently, if the Admiral had someone who could take Vane's place. Without a skilled engineer, the ship would come apart very quickly.

She swung her legs over the side of the bunk and stood up, feeling cold air blowing across her body. Naked, she padded over to the Engineer's desk and stared down at the papers there, hoping that she would see something she could use – or trade to Travis to convince him that she was worth keeping under his protection. But there was nothing, apart from a list of spare parts that were running short, mainly military-grade equipment. Apparently it was running out all over the Rim.

Taking a quick glance at Vane to ensure that he was still asleep – she'd worked hard to tire him earlier – she opened one of the drawers and looked inside. Vane had placed a small pistol in the drawer, along with a selection of specialist ammunition, and a device Mandy didn't recognise. After a brief examination, which left her no wiser, she closed the drawer and opened the next one. This one held a set of deck plans for a starship; a quick look revealed that they weren't for *Sword*. The notes beside the plans, written in Vane's crabby handwriting, classed the new ship as an improved light cruiser. Mandy looked back at Vane's sleeping form, feeling an odd spurt of admiration. She'd never realised that he designed starships in his spare time.

Shaking her head, she closed the drawer quietly and walked into the washroom. As a senior officer, Vane was entitled to his own shower – and, naturally, he'd kept it in perfect condition. Mandy turned on the water, waited for it to run warm, and then stepped under the flow, washing away the sweat that had congealed on her body. Vane wouldn't be expecting to find her in the room when he woke up; Mandy had been given other duties now that she was a full member of the pirate crew. She finished scrubbing her body, stepped out of the shower and looked at herself in the mirror. And recoiled.

Her face had grown thin, she realised, and her eyes looked harder than she recalled. Perhaps it was the poor eating or the constant fear, but she looked ghastly. But what did she deserve? She was a murderess, someone who fitted in with the pirate crew. There was no hope of returning home. Looking away from the mirror, she stepped out into the main room and picked her shipsuit off the deck. Vane didn't seem to care for slow foreplay. He just wanted her to strip before he started pawing at her.

She pulled the shipsuit on, took one final look at his slumbering form, and walked out of the cabin. Vane had his quarters near the engineering compartment, just so he'd be close if something happened to his beloved engines. Mandy looked around as she entered the passageway, saw no one standing there, and started to walk down towards the supply compartments. The heavy hatches were sealed, only open to senior officers, but Mandy had a copy of a code-key. She found herself praying as she stopped outside the hatch and pressed the code-key into the slot, knowing that she was dead if something had gone wrong. A moment later, just long enough for her to feel the first tinge of panic, the hatch slid open in front of her, revealing a darkened chamber. Carefully, she walked inside.

The compartment was massive, crammed with boxes of supplies. Mandy had discovered that the pirates didn't bother with manifests, unlike the RockRats or the Imperial Navy. They could have buried just about anything in the supply compartments and forgotten about it, particularly if it wouldn't bring them any money. Mandy looked around until she found what she was looking for – a small collection of mining explosives, taking from a captured freighter before she'd joined the crew – and inspected it. The devices looked simple enough; attach the trigger, key in the right code to the detonator, and the explosives would detonate. There didn't seem to be any elaborate safety precautions. Quickly, Mandy dropped a dozen explosive packs and detonators into a box, followed rapidly by a handful of tools she suspected would come in handy. And then she walked out of the compartment, hearing her own heartbeat pounding in her ears.

No one questioned her as she closed the hatch behind her and walked down to the nearest tube access point. Few of the pirates bothered to question what their fellows were doing, even if it looked dangerous. She still had sweat trickling down her back when she climbed into the tube, pushing the box of explosive charges ahead of her. Inside the tube, it seemed warmer than she expected, but there was no sign of anyone else. She scrambled forward until she reached one of the little nooks and crannies she'd been using as a place to rest and hide, stashing the detonators in a hiding place. Even if someone happened to stumble into the tiny section, they'd have real problems finding the detonators unless they searched everywhere.

They're not going to do that, she told herself firmly, as she sat down until her heartbeat returned to normal. She'd done the most dangerous part of the plan already – and it was unlikely that anyone would notice that the detonators were missing. *No one will find them.*

Forcing herself to stand up, she headed for the tube and scrambled back into the network, coming out as close to the bridge as she could. She was meant to go on duty in thirty minutes, even though there was no chance of *Sword* stumbling across a target in Phase Space. And then Travis had something else for her to do.

She saw Ha from a distance as she pulled herself out of the tube and headed for the bridge. The young psychopath didn't notice her, not least because he was occupied with a naked girl he was dragging around on a leash. Mandy felt a spurt of pity for the girl – that could be her – before she deliberately forced herself to look away. There was nothing she could do for the helpless captives on the ship, not now. All she could do was continue with her plan and pray that she managed to cripple the ship at the right time.

There was no sign of the Admiral as she stepped onto the bridge, but she was very aware of the Captain's mechanical eyes following her as she relieved the previous tactical officer and took his seat. Unsurprisingly, there was nothing to do but more simulations, so she worked her way through them one by one. Travis had told her that the pirates had modified a standard Imperial Navy training simulation for their own use, allowing the crew to practice against a far higher calibre of opponent than they were used to facing. She was still aware of the Captain watching her as the hours dragged on, until she was finally relieved by another officer. As she left, she saw the Captain looking at her, his eyes glowing faintly. Did he suspect something? Or was he merely enjoying the chance to look at her body?

Travis met her outside the bridge, his thin lips pulled up into a smile. "Come with me," he ordered, turning to head back down the passageway. Mandy scowled, but obeyed; she didn't have any other choice. Travis stopped outside a sealed hatch and tapped a code into a hidden panel, rather than using the code-key Mandy had copied. "This compartment is ours."

Mandy blinked. "Ours?"

"Everyone who works for me," Travis clarified. Mandy allowed herself an inwards sigh of relief. Vane pawing at her was quite bad enough.

Travis pointed her to a chair in front of a table and placed a box of equipment in front of her. "I need you to work on this communications gear."

Mandy opened the box and peered inside. The communications units looked primitive, certainly when compared to the wristcoms she'd seen on Earth, or the implanted communicators used by the Marines. She guessed they'd been produced by one of the colony worlds along the Rim, or maybe a black colony, although there was no way to be sure. A quick glance revealed that the builders hadn't bothered to work much advanced technology into the primitive handsets. They looked surprisingly clunky to her eyes.

"I picked up several hundred of them," Travis explained. "I want you to repair as many as you can, using equipment cannibalised from the others, and then set them up so they operate on an isolated frequency. Do you understand me?"

"Not quite," Mandy said. "An isolated frequency?"

"I do not want anyone else to be able to hack into the signals," Travis said, patiently. "If someone doesn't have a handset, I don't want them to be able to hear us."

Mandy frowned, considering. Repairing the devices wouldn't be difficult, as long as she had enough spare parts; the problem would be in rendering the signal undetectable. Marine communications units automatically encrypted signals sent by the Marines, but they could still be detected. But not all the time, according to Jasmine. Unfortunately, she hadn't given Mandy any details as to *how* it worked.

"I think the signals would be picked up by the ship's internal network," she said, slowly. The RockRats had certainly monitored their own interior – and she assumed that was true of the Imperial Navy too. "I *could* add in an encryption unit, if you have any…"

"You could certainly find them on Haven," Travis said, confirming her suspicion that they were heading back to the asteroid base. "I don't want anyone to know about this, unless there is no other choice."

Mandy smiled, inwardly. Travis wanted a private communications network…it could only mean that he was preparing his coup against the Captain. And if she helped him, who knew what he'd give her as a reward.

And it was an opportunity, she was sure of that. If only she knew how to exploit it properly.

"I'd need at least forty of them," Mandy said. It had been months since she'd looked at such primitive gear, but she'd been forced to pick up a great deal of practical experience very quickly. Besides, working on the communications devices would keep her mind off other things. "How long do I have?"

"As long as it takes," Travis said. "You will come to this cabin every day after your shift in the bridge, and work on the devices. Don't worry about your other duties. You are to finish this first."

"Yes, sir," Mandy said. It was irritating – she'd wanted to start hiding the detonators around the ship – but Travis wasn't giving her a choice. "I'll start at once."

"See that you do," Travis said. "And come up with a list of what you'll need from Haven. I might have to call in some favours to obtain the materials for you."

Mandy nodded and opened the box properly, picking up the first communicator and opening it with a sonic screwdriver. Inside, it was just about what she had expected, a handful of components welded together, designed to pick up the user's voice and relay it through the airwaves to a receiver. It took several minutes of careful prodding before she realised how to change the frequencies, leaving her wondering why the designers hadn't wanted to make it obvious. Could it be that they'd intended the users to have almost no access to the device's higher functions? Absently, she wondered who had built them and why. The pirates couldn't have made more restrictive devices if they'd tried.

Fixing them wasn't easy; wherever they'd been stored, they had been allowed to decay. For every communicator that was in working order, there were three that required careful work before they could be deemed usable. The main problem was the batteries – which were surprisingly primitive compared to what Mandy knew to be possible – and she had to work carefully to fix them. Quite a few proved to be completely beyond repair. If she'd had time, she was sure that she could put together something better out of spare parts, but Travis hadn't given her any time. Besides, she didn't think she wanted to go too far in helping him.

The problem of how to make the signals undetectable continued to puzzle her as she stopped for evening dinner, followed by sleep. No matter how she fiddled with the devices, the signals were *always* detectable, even when it was nothing more than a simple carrier wave. It was possible, she decided, to cheat by programming the ship's internal security network to simply ignore the signals, but she doubted that Travis would have that sort of access. And he was hardly going to ask the Captain to program the computers to ignore his private communications network.

It took three days to get most of the devices into working order, but she still had no solution to the problem of making the signals undetectable. Travis proclaimed himself pleased with what she had done and promised to obtain the encryption systems as soon as possible, yet Mandy wasn't happy. Like it or not, she had tied herself to Travis and if his plan went wrong, she would be taken down in the fallout. She was still mulling over the problem when he sent her back to resume her maintenance duties, where it hit her. There *was* an obvious solution to the problem after all.

"Vane doesn't trust the onboard communications network," she explained to Travis. "It's very wise of him because the network is badly degraded, even with all the work we've been doing lately to repair it. Sometimes we get false reports of damaged components and sometimes damaged components are simply not reported to us. So Vane rigged up a set of independent reporting systems, which signal him if there's a real problem. The main computer is programmed to ignore those pulses because otherwise the alerts would keep going off."

Travis nodded, impatiently. "I can program the communications devices to work on the same frequency," Mandy explained. "With a little fiddling, I can even ensure that they ignore the emergency alerts; they won't have the right header to activate the network. You could send all the signals you liked and no one would be any the wiser."

"Good work," Travis said. "What happens if someone makes an independent check? Or wouldn't Vane notice if there are more signals on his emergency network?"

Mandy shook her head. "The system Vane rigged up only accepts messages with the right header, messages from the independent reporting systems," she said. "Our messages simply won't register. If we modify our own headers, *his* messages won't register on our system either."

Travis smiled. "And no one would realise what we were doing," he said. "How long would it take you to match the frequencies?"

"Only a few minutes for each device," Mandy assured him. She had something else in mind too; with a little careful work, she should be able to record every message Travis and his men sent through the network. And if he let her work on the encryption, she'd be able to decode them too. She had no idea what she'd *do* with the information, but it was a start. "When do you want me to get started?"

"Now," Travis said. He looked over at her and frowned. "We'll be at Haven in two days, unless we have to divert to somewhere else. I'll get you the encryption devices then and you can install them."

Mandy nodded as she returned to the workroom and started to work. Travis seemed to be in a hurry, which was interesting. Was he planning to move quickly? The longer he waited, the greater the chance that someone would get cold feet and betray him to the Admiral – and the Admiral might take a dim view of Travis attempting to assassinate the Captain. Mandy considered the possibilities thoughtfully, wondering how best she could twist them to her advantage. Travis hadn't introduced her to anyone else in his circle, but judging from the number of communications devices he had to have quite a following. But then, a small team, armed to the teeth, could take an entire ship.

She contemplated the possibilities as she worked her way through the devices. Travis was untrustworthy, she knew, and once he'd finished with her she would become expendable. He might realise just how badly she'd taken it when she'd killed helpless innocents; he might well decide that she was no longer required, once he was Captain. Or he might find another position for her.

But I won't stay here, she told herself firmly. *I want to go home.*

CHAPTER THIRTY-FOUR

> In many ways, pirate society is a dark mirror of the Empire's. Sure, there are no social welfare programs to help the downtrodden, but there is work for those who are willing to work, even if the pay isn't great. Indeed, one can live for quite a long time on the Rim without ever being seduced into piracy – or living an illicit life. The dangers, however, can be extreme. There is no law along the Rim, but what they make for themselves.
> -Edward E. Smith, Professor of Sociology. *Pirates and their Lives.*

"Mandy!"

Mandy turned in shock. She'd decided to visit Haven when the ship docked because the alternative was spending time with Vane, but she hadn't expected to run into a friend there. Indeed, she realised with a flicker of guilt, she'd barely thought about Michael after he'd been dumped on the asteroid. She hadn't even considered asking Travis to bring him back onto the ship.

Michael looked…thinner than she remembered. His face was lined, but otherwise he looked healthier than Mandy herself. Part of her wanted to run, before he sensed the blood she had on her hands; part of her wanted to hug him and forget everything else in his arms. He stopped in front of her, looking down into her eyes, his face twisted between delight and fear. Did he know what she had become?

"Michael," she said, feeling her knees buckle. How *could* she not have anticipated this meeting? "Can we go somewhere for a drink?"

Michael nodded and led her into a small bar, with a handful of privacy cubicles at the rear. Mandy ordered drinks for them both and carried them into the cubicle, locking the door and placing the privacy generator on the table. She was sure that nothing they were going to say to each other should be heard by anyone else. God alone knew what Michael would make of the new her. He was a reminder that she'd once been…a potential engineer, working for Avalon's planned navy. Now, she was just a pirate bitch.

"You look dreadful," Michael said, as he sat down. "What happened to you?"

Mandy hesitated, finding herself tongue-tied. Did he know what she'd done to secure his release, rather than a quick departure through an airlock? What would he think of her if he knew the truth? The memories came back to her and she swallowed hard, trying to keep herself from throwing up. She'd sold herself to Vane to save her boyfriend's life and he'd hate her if he ever found out the truth.

"They keep me busy," she said, finally. She couldn't tell him everything. "This is the first time we have returned to Haven."

She looked over at him. "What have *you* been doing with yourself?"

"Surviving," Michael said, grimly. He held up a bracelet wrapped around his wrist. It showed a timer, counting down the seconds to zero. There were ninety-four hours to go, if Mandy was reading it correctly. It looked a very simple device. "You know they charge for oxygen here?"

Mandy's eyes opened wide. Oxygen was easy to produce; hell, most starships used a form of genetically-engineered grass to help cleanse the atmosphere. She'd never heard of anyone *charging* for oxygen, or everything else that went into a human-compatible atmosphere, at least outside the early days of the Mars Terraforming Project. But modern technology made it unnecessary.

"Anyone who stays here as a permanent resident gets one of these," Michael said. "You buy a week's worth of oxygen at a time. If you run out, you get pitched out the airlock or sold as a slave, depending on your appearance. As you can see" – he touched the side of his face – "no one would actually buy me."

"Oh," Mandy said, quietly. She didn't want to know, but she had to ask. "What…what have you being doing to keep yourself alive?"

"I've been working as a bouncer, mostly," Michael admitted. "Plenty of nightclubs here have problems with rowdy crews on leave from pirate ships, so there's always work for people willing to risk life and limb in the defence of the owner's property." He shrugged. "I'd hoped I could buy passage out of here, but apparently I'm not allowed to leave the asteroid."

He looked over at her. "I haven't been able to find a way to send a message to Avalon either," he added. "Have you had any more luck?"

Mandy felt a crushing sense of guilt as she shook her head. She hadn't found a way to get a message off, or even escape *Sword*. Maybe she could jump ship at Haven…no, eventually she'd be classed as a permanent resident and forced to work to breathe, let alone to eat. And besides, there was her plan…if she managed to get it to work. Seeing Michael was a reminder that there was something to live for after all.

"No," she admitted, feeling tears forming in her eyes. She took a quick swig of her glass, before wiping her eyes. "I haven't been able to find a way to send a message home."

"Don't cry," Michael said, quickly. Like most teenage boys, he was useless at dealing with emotional girls. "We'll get out of this somehow."

Mandy snorted. Michael hadn't got blood on his hands. It was possible that Colonel Stalker would have some very hard questions for him, but there shouldn't be anything preventing him from going back to Avalon and rejoining the Knights. Mandy, on the other hand, had killed, and become part of a pirate patronage network. There would be no mercy for her…

But what do you deserve? A voice asked, at the back of her head. *Stop feeling sorry for yourself and think!*

"I don't know how," she muttered, finally. Part of her just wanted to give up. The rest of her wanted to try to take *Sword* with her. She was sure that the heavy cruiser was unique in the sector, certainly in the Admiral's fleet, or he wouldn't have needed to bother playing games with protection rackets. "Do *you* see any way out of this?"

Michael shook his head. "There will be a chance," he said, as he squeezed her shoulder. "Do you make more money than I do?"

"Probably," Mandy said. Or maybe not. *She* wouldn't have cared to be a bouncer on Haven, particularly one who dealt with drunken pirate crews. "What do you want to do with the money?"

"Buy weapons," Michael said, promptly. "Maybe we could hijack a starship."

Mandy considered it, briefly. "I don't think we could fly one alone," she said, reluctantly. Even the smallest spacecraft needed at least five crewmen to operate it. And a starship would need at least twenty crewmen. "Even if we did, where would we go?"

"There'd be a navigational computer on the ship," Michael pointed out. "Avalon's coordinates are hardly a secret."

"Unless they encrypted the database before docking," Mandy countered. There were just too many problems in the plan, even though she had to admit that it might be the best hope they had. "Do you think you can recruit others?"

"The slaves are kept under careful control," Michael said. "I'm not sure who else I can trust among the permanent residents."

Mandy grimaced. She'd seen some of the slaves on *Sword*. Some of them were so badly mistreated that they flinched at everything, but they weren't the worst. *They* were the girls who had had something done to their brains, something that had rendered them little more than living meat, barely capable of doing anything more complex than lying back with their legs spread. If the other girls hadn't taken care of them, they would have wasted away through starvation. No, they couldn't recruit help from the slaves. And who else was going to be prepared to help them?

"But I don't think that time is on our side," Michael added, grimly. "There's been some muttering about Avalon recently."

Mandy shivered. "Avalon?"

"It seems that the Admiral detailed a ship to occupy the planet," Michael said. He grinned, suddenly. "Apparently, the ship is overdue."

Mandy stared at him. "Overdue?"

"So I have been told," Michael said. "Not that I would gamble on the bastards having the ability to keep schedules, but..."

He shrugged. "You do know what this means?"

Mandy nodded, thoughtfully. A pirate ship had tried to take Avalon and been destroyed. She cautioned herself against being too hopeful – the pirates might have suffered a drive failure, or maybe they'd simply decided to rebel against the Admiral – but it was still a pleasant thought. But the Admiral's whole scheme depended on people being too afraid to stand up to him. If the Marines – and she was sure that the Marines had been involved – had destroyed a pirate ship, the Admiral would need to make an example of them to scare anyone who might have been thinking about revolt. And besides, he would still need the cloudscoop.

"If we assume the best," she said, looking down at the privacy generator and hoping that Travis was right, "how are they going to find us here?"

Michael looked down at the table. "I don't know," he admitted. "Everything I've heard suggests that the coordinates for this base are secret. Even some of the spacers I've met in bars don't know where they are. It could be a long wait before they get here."

"The Admiral will go to Avalon and attack," Mandy said, with complete certainty. She felt new hope flaring through her breast as she considered the possibilities. Maybe, just maybe, she could do something for the planet that would convince them to overlook what she'd done while trapped on *Sword*. "Maybe I should try and smuggle you on board."

"I think that would be asking for trouble," Michael said. "They already chose to reject me, remember?"

Mandy lowered her eyes, reluctantly. He was right.

"You have to see what you can do," Michael said, firmly. "Mandy, everything could depend on you."

"I know," Mandy admitted. The Marines didn't have a heavy cruiser – and the Admiral wouldn't be overconfident. If something had happened to the first ship, he'd be very careful in how he approached Avalon. "I didn't need the pressure."

Michael leaned forward and kissed her on the lips. Mandy felt herself flinching away, remembering the feeling of Vane's body pressed on her, in her. She was no longer the person who had dated Michael, no longer the person who had been happy to share pleasure with him in the RockRat garden. The grim despondency, almost depression, had penetrated her entire soul. If she had been a man, she wasn't sure if she could have performed in Vane's bed – or anyone else's, for that matter.

"I'm sorry," she said, standing up. She couldn't tolerate his presence, or the reminder of better times in the past, any longer. "I'll see you when I next come to Haven."

"Mandy," Michael said, softly. "Our homeworld is under threat."

"I know that," Mandy snapped at him. He was right. It didn't make it any easier to bear. "Don't you think I know that?"

She picked up the privacy generator and held her finger over the switch. "I'll see you the next time I am here," she said, sharply. "Goodbye, Michael."

Mandy felt his eyes watching her as she strode out of the bar and joined the throng of residents and spacers on shore leave as they sought enjoyment and relaxation for themselves. The guilt was almost overwhelming – he had to be wondering if she'd been seduced completely by the pirate lifestyle – but she hadn't been able to stay with him for a moment longer. He'd been trapped on an asteroid where he had to work merely to breathe – and yet he'd remembered his duty far better than she had. But he'd been a soldier and Mandy was merely an engineer.

Brat, she told herself, sharply. *Useless spoilt brat.*

Lost in her thoughts, she wandered through the asteroid, only stopping when she heard the sound of loud music ahead of her. People were dancing in a large room, spacers dancing with girls from the asteroid, bumping and grinding together as they swayed to the beat. Mandy felt an odd sense of *déjà vu* as she remembered dancing like that herself, back when she'd been young and foolish. The spacers were pirates – or, at the very least, people who operated on the far side of the law – but they looked completely carefree as they danced with the girls. One of them, she couldn't help noticing, had his hand halfway up a girl's skirt, clutching her buttocks as they spun around the dance floor. Another seemed so drunk that it was a miracle he could even stand upright.

It was tempting to just walk in and throw herself into the dance. But she couldn't; even if she'd been back on Avalon, she was no longer the carefree girl who had indulged herself with nary a thought for the possible consequences. Shaking her head, she walked away, catching sight of a line of girls waiting for possible clients. Mandy wondered, bitterly, if Michael had ever indulged himself, before asking herself if it really mattered. After everything she'd done, what claim did she have on him?

The next compartment offered electronic simulation, either through induction contacts or direct implantation. Mandy shivered, remembering how many of her classmates on Earth had used simulation to lose themselves in a world of never-ending pleasure. Somehow, it was one delight she'd never sampled for herself; the addicts had chilled her to the bone when she'd seen them for the first time. They lost interest in everything save the current running through their brains. Mandy had watched them growing thinner and thinner, unwilling to eat or drink even to save their lives, until the day they'd vanished from class. It was possible, she'd been told, to break an addiction to electronic simulation, but it required a vast amount of willpower. She'd never seen any of the addicts again.

Now, she found herself wondering if she should go in and have an implant stuck in her head. It would be so easy to lose herself, to ignore whatever happened to her body in the tidal waves of pleasure, to forget everything that had ever once mattered to her. She could do it – Travis had given her a considerable bonus as a reward for her work – but it would be the ultimate defeat, the ultimate surrender. *Jasmine* would never have surrendered. Mandy could do no less. Besides, if Michael was right, she would soon have an opportunity to avenge herself on the Admiral and his servants.

Shaking her head, she started to walk back through the stalls. Some of them were tempting, selling foodstuffs from various colony worlds, all more interesting than the ration bars on *Sword*. Others were selling thoroughly illegal drugs, or at least, drugs that were illegal in the Empire. There was no law on Haven save what the asteroid's administrators made. And none of them cared for the Empire's regulations. She could buy something that would send her into a whirlwind of pleasure, if she was prepared to accept the crashing low after the drug-induced high. The electronic simulation implant would be less harmful, if she was prepared to surrender to its control.

She stopped in front of one counter, looking down at the handful of gray capsules lying on the middle of a grass cabinet. They weren't ordinary drugs; indeed, she was surprised to see them at all. Jasmine had told her about *Boost* when talking about her training, explaining that *Boost* give the user boosted strength, speed and pain resistance, as long as it lasted. Afterwards, the user collapsed, barely able to keep going until his or her body had recovered from the experience. Jasmine had been talking about the dangers in chemical courage – a boosted person might make mistakes, simply through not having time to think – but Mandy could see some advantages to taking the drug. She looked over at the seller and asked the price. It was high, but not as high as she had feared.

"One capsule," she said, finally. It came with a standard medical injector tab, used to inject medicine into a person's bloodstream. The pirates used it for drug abuse, although the Captain had strict rules concerning anyone foolish enough to abuse drugs while on duty. "And do you have a cleanser?"

"No," the dealer said. "I checked the drug" – the pirates wouldn't bother to file complaints if they thought they were cheated – "and it's sealed, as fresh as the day it was produced. One injection and you'll be faster and stronger until the drug wears off."

Mandy nodded, thoughtfully. Jasmine hadn't been very clear on how long *Boost* actually lasted, while there was nothing on the capsule to tell her. It probably depended on factors like body weight, muscle and energy reserves…she made a mental note to try to look it up in the manuals the pirates had collected in their travels. The Admiral seemed to love information; Mandy had heard some pirates bragging about vacuuming every last scrap of information out of a captured ship and receiving a bonus for it. There would probably be something she could use in the files.

She yelped as she felt a hand fall on her buttocks and spun around, one hand reaching for the pistol on her belt. Ha stood there, smiling his disturbing smile. Mandy shivered inwardly and hoped to hell that it didn't show on her face. Show someone like Ha any weakness and he'd walk all over her. Or decide that raping her might be a good way to pass the time. Or…there seemed to be no limit to his depravity. Some of the rumours she'd heard had been awful, even by pirate standards. When they wanted to scare each other, they told stories about Ha.

"The Admiral wishes to see you," Ha said. He took her by the hand and pulled her forward, speaking in a mockingly childish voice. It sent shivers down Mandy's spine, steeling her resolve. Whatever else happened, Ha had to die before he could harm anyone else. *"Someone's* been a bad girl."

Chapter
Thirty-Five

It was inevitable that the Admiral would eventually realise that the ship he'd sent to Avalon – the ship that became the Dancing Fool – had failed in its mission. Perversely, the Admiral's very reluctance to stay in one spot made it harder for him to hear of the failure, a problem aided by the fact that pirates were often reluctant to pass bad news on to their superior. As always, the problems of coordinating anything across interstellar distances made running his network difficult even for him.

But our luck ran out eventually.

- Professor Leo Caesius, *The Perilous Dawn* (unpublished).

He can't know everything, Mandy told herself, as Ha pulled her towards the airlock. *If he did, I would be dead by now. He wouldn't have let me go to Haven if he knew the truth.*

Her thoughts ran in circles. What did the Admiral know? Did he want to interrogate her about the work she'd done for Travis? Or had he actually noticed the missing detonators? Or…she gasped as Ha pinched her bottom, giggling disconcertingly as the airlock opened, laughing at her. Maybe he knew that she was walking to her death. Bracing herself, Mandy walked faster, trying to leave him behind. It didn't work.

There were four guards in front of the Admiral's cabin, who removed her gun and knife before carrying out a surprisingly professional search. Feeling naked and defenceless, Mandy stepped through the hatch and into the Admiral's quarters. He was standing in the centre of the room, studying a hologram of a blue-green world that Mandy had no difficulty in recognising as Avalon. She felt a twinge of homesickness as she came to a halt and waited, facing the Admiral. It was funny how quickly Avalon had become home, once she'd resigned herself to spending the rest of her life along the Rim.

"I sent two ships to Avalon," the Admiral said, still studying the hologram. "One kidnapped you and your friends, and then left the system; the other had orders to secure the high orbitals and take control of the planet. That ship is several weeks overdue."

Mandy remembered what Michael had told her and fought to keep her face expressionless. Michael had been right; *something* had happened to the pirate ship…and the Admiral clearly assumed that it had been enemy action. It was possible that *something* had gone badly wrong with the ship's drives, destroying it – but even the pirate maintenance wasn't that bad. No, Mandy had to agree with the Admiral. The ship he'd sent to Avalon had been destroyed by the Marines.

"That is inconvenient," the Admiral continued. "I require Avalon for my plans to go ahead."

"Yes, sir," Mandy said. She'd picked up enough to know that the pirates had access to black colonies that operated cloud-skimmers, but cloud-skimming couldn't produce anything like as much HE3 as a single cloudscoop. A steady source of fuel would secure the Admiral's position and allow his industrial base to expand rapidly. "How may I be of service?"

The Admiral turned to face her. "It is clear that Avalon is defended," he said, flatly. "You will tell me everything about those defences."

Mandy hesitated. "I was only a lowly engineer," she temporised. The hell of it was that she probably knew more than any of her classmates, if only because of listening when her father and Colonel Stalker planned the future. "They didn't tell me everything."

"Tell me what you know," the Admiral ordered. "How many starships do they have?"

"None," Mandy said. It had certainly been true when she'd left. The largest ship in the system had been an interplanetary barge used for mining asteroids. Even the RockRats hadn't had their own starships. "Avalon was completely cut off from the Empire."

The Admiral didn't seem to believe her. "The system has a cloudscoop and no starships?"

"None," Mandy confirmed. She was tempted to lie, to claim that the Imperial Navy had stationed an entire task force in the system, but the Admiral would almost certainly have other sources of information. God alone knew what had happened to the others who had been kidnapped at the same time as herself; it was quite possible that some of them were still alive, ready to be interrogated. "It's a long story."

The Admiral peered at her, so Mandy told him everything about the Avalon Development Corporation's plans for the sector. She half-expected the Admiral to tell her to stop, but instead he listened carefully, even when she dropped into the boring economic details that had brought the ADC's plans crashing to a halt. It dawned on her a moment later that the Admiral was genuinely interested, for his own reasons. His empire couldn't suffer the same disaster or it would fall into ruin.

"They should have invested in tankers as well," the Admiral said, when she'd finished. Thanks to her father, she could explain it in great detail. "Right now, they will have very real problems getting the fuel from Avalon to somewhere it's needed."

Mandy nodded. The cloudscoop produced vastly more fuel than Avalon actually needed, at least for the moment. Even the Sol System, home to the largest industrial base in the known galaxy, had only a dozen cloudscoops to feed its economy. Given time, the expansion plans for Avalon would call for using more and more fuel, but it would take decades before they needed to invest in a second cloudscoop. By then, they might even be able to build it.

"Tell me about the planet's defenders," the Admiral ordered, breaking into her thoughts. "Tell me about the Marines."

"I don't have much to do with them," Mandy lied. If he'd spoken to someone else, would that person have known that there was a Marine she looked up to as a big sister? Or that she'd met a handful of other Marines? "I spent most of the Battle of Camelot hiding in the basement, fearing for my life. The only time I actually saw the Marines was during transfers through orbit station or once at the inauguration of the new government."

The Admiral studied her. "But what have you heard? How many of them are there?"

"I'm not sure," Mandy claimed. It wasn't entirely a lie; she'd never been sure of the difference between a full Marine and one of their auxiliaries. "I think there was supposed to be at least a hundred of them, but civilians like myself were never allowed on Castle Rock."

"So there could be more," the Admiral mused. "And what about the Civil Guard?"

"Largely disbanded," Mandy said. "From what I heard, most of the good Civil Guardsmen were folded over into the Knights of Avalon, the new army, while the bad ones were dishonourably discharged and told to earn a living somewhere else. But I never had very much to do with the military."

She felt sweat running down her back as the Admiral considered it. If he knew that Michael had been a Knight, that he was on the asteroid… he'd grab her former boyfriend and interrogate him. And that might reveal all sorts of things, starting with the fact that Mandy hadn't been entirely truthful when she'd been talking about the Marines. No, she couldn't risk him interrogating Michael. She'd just have to pray that the Admiral never realised that there was someone else he could question.

The Admiral tossed a series of questions at her, mostly ones that no one outside the military could answer. Mandy didn't know what weapons were used by the Marines, or the Knights of Avalon; the only weapons she could talk about were the ones she'd been taught to use as part of her training. The Admiral wasn't too impressed when Mandy downplayed her skills with a pistol, although aiming a pistol accurately wasn't as easy as the movies made it look. She'd been much better with a rifle, but she thought that was true of almost everyone.

"They didn't have me working as their quartermaster," she protested, when he started asking how many powered combat suits the Marines had brought with them. How was she supposed to know that? She'd certainly never asked Jasmine – and her friend would probably have refused to tell her if she *had* asked. "The only logistics work I did was preparing for hikes over the countryside to train us for something."

"That must have been fun," the Admiral said. His eyes narrowed. "Did you intend to go into the military?"

"It was part of a general fitness course," Mandy explained. And to hammer the fundamentals of self-reliance into their heads, something they hadn't realised at the start. They'd only discovered the truth when they'd discovered how easy it was to forget something simple, but important – toilet paper, for example. In space, such a mistake could easily prove fatal. "They didn't want us to go into orbit until we were healthy."

"How wise of them," the Admiral agreed, dryly. "Space is no place for those who cannot take care of themselves."

Mandy shivered. She'd seen a handful of fat people on Haven, but most of the asteroid's population had been young and reasonably healthy. Given what Michael had told her about oxygen rationing, it was probable that the older members of the population died off as soon as they lost the ability to work. The whole concept was horrifying; no wonder the pirates were so ruthless. Death and the threat of death was their constant companion. Her own grandparents had been kept alive on Earth, right up until the point her father had been forced out of work. They'd died soon afterwards.

He changed tack, leaning forward to stare into her eyes. "Tell me about the planet's government," he ordered. "How does it work?"

Mandy swallowed, thinking hard. She couldn't think of any way in which the information could hurt Avalon, but what if she was wrong? The Admiral was obviously planning a return to Avalon in force, taking a small fleet along to secure the system. What if he drew something from her information that he could use to beat the planet into submission? But she couldn't think of any way the information might make taking the planet easier.

"There are twenty-one districts on the planet," she said. Maybe she could confuse him, just slightly. "Each district elects one member to the Avalon Council, which has overall authority on the planet. They also have local councils which have responsibility for local affairs; they have twenty-one members too, just like the planetary council. Councillors have to have lived within their district for the last five years prior to being elected and cannot serve again once they've had a five-year term in office. They're also supposed to spend at least three days a week listening to the people who elected them."

If the Admiral considered her information to be useless, he didn't show it. "It sounds fairly simple," he said, finally. "What happened to the old Council?"

Mandy blinked in shock, trying hard to hide her reaction. Her father had once suggested that the old Council had had contacts from off-world, but nothing – as far as she knew – had ever been proven. The Crackers had bought weapons from off-world, too. Had the Admiral's mysterious backers been meddling in Avalon's affairs long before the Empire withdrew from the sector? Or was she merely drawing the wrong conclusion from incomplete intelligence?

"They were corrupt bastards," she said, finally. "I believe that most of them were exiled to a prison island, along with some bandits whom they'd tried to exploit. The islands don't get visited afterwards, not by anyone. They could still be alive…"

"Or killed by their former allies," the Admiral said. "A death sentence, really. Did any of the old Council survive the war?"

"I think there were a couple who were genuinely honest," Mandy admitted. For once, she cursed herself for not paying attention to politics. Earth's elections were meaningless; Avalon's were actually quite important. It was possible for the population to elect someone who actually gave a damn about their interests. "But I don't think they managed to get elected to the new Council."

The Admiral stroked his chin, thoughtfully. Mandy wondered what he was thinking – and what he knew about the Council's links to off-world organisations. Her father probably knew everything the Empire knew about off-world groups that might wish Avalon ill, but she hadn't ever thought to ask him about them. In hindsight, she should have spent more time listening to her father – and perhaps reading his banned book. Maybe there was a copy somewhere on Haven. It was easy to pirate books, or music recordings, or videos. There were only a handful of interstellar celebrities because it was very hard to outrun the bootleggers.

She answered the rest of his questions as best as she could, although she honestly didn't understand how he expected her to know certain details. Yes, the Marines were based on Castle Rock, but she didn't know the locations of their other bases, or anything about the bases used by the Knights of Avalon. The big garrisons that had once surrounded Camelot had been largely dismantled or turned over for civilian use, now that there was no longer any need to maintain a security cordon around the city.

"And the population has plenty of guns," the Admiral mused. "Does your family own guns?"

Mandy hesitated. Thankfully, he didn't seem to know who her father actually *was*...

"Mom would never allow it," she said, finally. "She was afraid of what might happen."

Earth's citizens had been taught to fear weapons for centuries, along with most of the population of the Core Worlds. As absurd as it seemed, an armed man in a building had the same effect as a savage tiger bent on eating human prey. She had never even *seen* a gun, let alone touched it, until she'd been exiled to Avalon, where guns had been freely available. The old Council had worked hard to ban weapons – fearing a revolt against their rule – but it had been almost useless. And the new Council believed that everyone should own at least one gun.

It was astonishing – and terrifying – to realise just how deep the propaganda had sunk into her mind. When she'd first gone to the firing range, she'd been scared to even *look* at the weapons, for fear that they might go off. Later, she'd still had problems holding the weapon, or standing near some of her classmates, particularly the more idiotic ones who had waved guns around as if merely holding a weapon made them invincible. The tutors hadn't hesitated to discipline those idiots; it had taken longer to cure Mandy of the fear that had made it hard for her to learn how to shoot. At least she'd listened to the lectures on basic safety. One of her classmates had managed to shoot himself in the leg while drawing his pistol.

"It might be impossible to occupy the surface," the Admiral said. "But we don't really care about the planet's surface."

Mandy nodded, thinking hard. Gun ownership hadn't saved the farmers who had been targeted by the bandits; they couldn't afford to maintain an armed guard while tending their fields. It didn't help that the Civil Guard had had orders to confiscate all unregistered weapons – which was most of them – although the Guardsmen had generally ignored the order. The Admiral could make his demands and bombard the entire planet from orbit if his demands were refused. No assault rifle could target a starship in orbit. The very thought was absurd.

She still didn't know how many ships the Admiral had under his control, but *Sword* was a heavy cruiser, powerful enough to blast its way into orbit without raising a sweat. Indeed, unless the Marines had had something powerful concealed in orbit, occupying the high orbitals wouldn't be very difficult at all. And then Avalon would be his, along with the cloud-scoop, the true prize. He could use the demand for fuel to keep the sector under control, without ever needing to use his forces to crush resistance.

"You may return to your duties," the Admiral said, dismissing the hologram of the planet. "We will be departing for Avalon in two days, once we have assembled the squadron. You will remain on the ship; I may have more questions for you. Luckily, there is no shortage of maintenance work that needs to be done."

"Yes, sir," Mandy said.

She felt a moment of relief as she stepped out of his quarters and recovered her weapons; he didn't know what she'd been planning. But what he *had* called her for was worse. She had no idea how far they were from Avalon, which meant that she had to assume the worst and move fast. The half-formed plan she'd created to cripple the ship would have to suffice.

"The Admiral must have liked your excuses," Ha said, with a leer. He started to follow her down the passageway, his eyes trailing slime all over her rear. "I thought you were a dead bitch for sure."

"Thank you," Mandy said tightly, as her caught up with her. She saw his smile and shuddered. Why did the Admiral tolerate him? But the answer to *that* question was obvious. Ha was perfectly suited to life on a pirate ship. "This bitch has work to do."

"What a pity," Ha said. "I had thought we might find some time in the recreational tubes."

Mandy felt sick as his hand stroked her bottom. Nothing, not even Vane's fumbling, had ever felt so repulsive. Travis's protection clearly had limits. She wanted to brush his hand away, but she didn't dare. Ha's victims were often damaged beyond the ability of the pirate doctor to deal with them. Besides, the rumours surrounding the doctor were even worse than the rumours surrounding Ha.

"The Admiral ordered, so I shall obey," she said, and hoped it would be enough. "He wants me to be busy."

"He always does," Ha said. He gave her a mocking bow. "Have fun, my darling."

Mandy waited until he was gone before sagging in relief. That had been too close. Far too close.

And God alone knew how much time she had left before *Sword* reached Avalon.

CHAPTER
THIRTY-SIX

It is said – truly – that no battle plan ever survives contact with the enemy. That is not too surprising. The enemy may not do what you expect him to do, therefore throwing your plan off before it can be completed. It can be disastrous if a battle plan relies on the enemy doing a single specific response, because the enemy might not do what you want him to do. And continuing to try to implement the plan after the enemy has reacted incorrectly can only cause confusion.

Therefore, one must learn to balance pre-combat planning with initiative, as the plan may go wrong from the start. The intelligence might be wrong, the enemy might be too smart or too dumb to do what you want him to do, there might be a missing factor…in short, prior planning can only go so far.

-Major-General Thomas Kratman (Ret), A *Civilian's Guide to the Terran Marine Corps.*

"You fucking *traitor*!"

Edward allowed himself a smile as Ollie glared at him. They'd stunned the recruiting officer as soon as *Spider* and the other ships had dropped into Phase Space, allowing the combat medics a chance to scan his body and remove a number of implants with interesting functions. The anti-interrogation implant couldn't be removed, unfortunately, but Ollie no longer had the hidden surprises he'd depended upon to keep himself alive. He wasn't taking it very well.

"I am Colonel Stalker, Terran Marine Corps," he said, and waited for Ollie to finish spluttering his outrage. Somehow, a man who dealt in treachery rarely expected to find himself on the receiving end. Edward had seen enough of the Admiral's handiwork to refuse to feel sorry for the bastard. "You are our prisoner."

"This isn't legal," Ollie protested. "The Empire abandoned our sector! You have no jurisdiction here."

"Interesting argument," Edward said, and pretended to consider it. "I suppose that your master's argument is that might makes right. Here you are, strapped to a chair, a helpless prisoner…I'd say that I certainly had the might. Wouldn't you?"

He studied Ollie thoughtfully. The recruiting officer didn't look to be a fanatic, thankfully; fanatics weren't good for anything but suicide attacks. Besides, loyalty to one's superior was rare among the pirates and he doubted that the Admiral could have changed that in a hurry. Ollie would probably crack, if pushed the right way. And besides, he'd already given them the location of the Admiral's main base. His only hope for survival was throwing himself on Edward's mercy.

"I've been here before," Edward said, flatly. "You have an implant that makes it hard to interrogate you. Yes, we could take you to the lab and see if we can beat it, this time. But we already have the information we really need, so we don't have to waste time doing that. We can just hand you over to the Admiral, should we have to come to terms with him."

Ollie stared at Edward. "The Admiral would *never* make a deal with you," he snapped. "And why would you make a deal with him?"

Edward smiled, coldly. "It stands to reason that we could help each other," he pointed out, smoothly. "We have the cloudscoop – and we've rigged it to blow if the Admiral tries to capture it. But we could offer to trade him fuel in exchange for equipment we desperately need…he might even be happier with us sitting on the cloudscoop, rather than someone who might prove untrustworthy. Do you think he might take that bargain?"

"You have got to be joking," Ollie protested. "You're the *Marines*."

"You think the Admiral would be the first person we had to deal with?" Edward asked. "We've had to hold our noses before while coming to terms with certain people and groups. We can do the same for the Admiral."

His eyes narrowed. "And we can offer him *you*," he added. "I'm sure the Admiral would be pleased to see you."

Ollie looked down at the deck as that sank in. The Admiral would not be pleased to hear how Ollie had betrayed his base. Ollie would die horribly, just to provide an object lesson for anyone else who might grow careless. Edward certainly *intended* to reveal what had happened after they'd completed their operation, just to force the pirates to be more paranoid when they hired mercenaries. Ollie would be a dead man anywhere, apart from a penal island on Avalon. He would have no choice but to bargain with the Marines.

"I won't waste your time," Edward said. "You can tell us everything you know about the Admiral and, in exchange, we will ensure that you spend the rest of your life somewhere nicely isolated from the rest of the universe. The Admiral will be told that you were executed – there will even be a very convincing body, should he wish to see one. Or you can wait here until we come to terms with the Admiral and you're handed over to him as part of the deal."

He paused. "I once saw recordings of what happened to a guy who betrayed a pirate chieftain," he added. He kept his voice light, almost casual. "The man was forced to swallow Slicer eggs from Deben, which hatched in his stomach and the little insects began to eat their way out of his flesh. It's how they breed, you see; the mother dies when her children eat their way out of her womb and burrow their way into the open air. But they can eat human flesh too. I could probably dig up the recording if you want."

Ollie looked up at him. "You give me your word you'll protect me?"

"You'll spend the rest of your life somewhere safe and isolated," Edward assured him. "But it comes with a price. You lie to us, or try to mislead us, and we will consider the deal off. My interrogators will have a great many questions for you. You will answer them all, as completely as possible. One lie and…"

"I get the point," Ollie said. "One lie and you kill me yourself."

"Smart boy," Edward said. He turned and headed for the hatch. "The interrogators are on their way."

"Haven asteroid," Gwendolyn said, two days later. "The nerve centre of the Admiral's operations."

Edward had wondered about that. Ollie had been a fount of information which, when added to the information he'd purchased on the Pineapple, painted a very worrying picture. There were suggestions that the Admiral had had help from another faction, one with access to a considerable tech base. As far as they knew, no world in the sector should be able to provide the Admiral with such support, but there might well be a hidden black colony that was secretly backing the Admiral. Or it could be a faction within the Empire itself, making a grab for power now that the Imperial Navy had been withdrawn. There were too many possibilities and not enough answers.

"According to our friend, Haven is designed to be completely concealed from view," Gwendolyn continued. The Marines watched with interest as she rotated the holographic representation, although they knew not to trust it too far. It had been put together from Ollie's information and couldn't be considered precise. "Most starships dock by flying into the crater here" – she tapped one end of the asteroid – "and either docking or landing inside the asteroid. The whole system is rather unsafe, but very secure. Once inside, their drives are completely shut down, rendering them undetectable. According to our friend, the landing bay is large enough to take a couple of battleships."

Edward had his doubts about that too. The design was badly flawed from a tactical perspective; it would be easy for a single ship to trap the docked ships inside the asteroid. Haven had to be colossal even to accommodate all of those ships, while he couldn't imagine any Captain being happy parking his ship inside a rocky trap. The Admiral had to have one hell of a reputation to convince his subordinates to go along with it. Haven would turn into a death trap if the Imperial Navy ever came calling.

"Past the docking cave, there's a large section that is comparable to other independent asteroid settlements," Gwendolyn continued. She wouldn't normally give a briefing, but it was important to remind everyone that their information was very imprecise. "This section holds stalls, food outlets and everything else pirates might need when on shore leave. Naturally, this includes prostitutes and sex slaves; according to Ollie, most of them are on long-term contracts rather than actually being kidnapped from the nearest colony world, so don't take them lightly.

"After that, there's a large habitation section for mercenaries and pirates when they're not on their ships, followed by the asteroid's administration and educational section. The Admiral has apparently been creating a bureaucracy—"

"Now we *know* he's evil," Blake Coleman muttered.

"—and using them to collect data on his conquests," Gwendolyn continued, ignoring the interruption. "At the moment, it seems a little slapdash, but if we combine the data we collected on Elysium and Crawford with the information we pulled out of Ollie, it looks as if the Admiral is slowly constructing a more effective system. They were collecting data on trained manpower on Elysium; Crawford received several hundred unwilling immigrants from four other colony worlds, all of whom were told to get on the ships or get shot. Surprisingly, the Admiral allowed them to take their families as well."

Edward frowned, considering the thought. The Empire had been moving trained manpower around for centuries, simply because there was always a shortage of genuinely competent engineers, computer programmers, construction experts and every other speciality the Empire needed desperately. Allowing them to take their families was simple common sense; it kept them happy and often moved their families into better accommodation. But there simply weren't enough experts to maintain Earth, let alone the rest of the Core Worlds. Edward had seen the models of what would happen when Earth finally collapsed. It wasn't going to be pleasant.

The Admiral, unlike the Grand Senate, seemed to recognise his weaknesses – and was trying to deal with them. From what Ollie had admitted, he wasn't just rounding up everyone with some level of technical knowledge; he was actively trying to train up new engineers and other experts. Youngsters with little to look forward to beyond a lifetime spent looking at the rear end of a mule, were being offered the chance to train as engineers instead. Most of them would become nothing more than competent personnel, but a handful would be brilliant, truly understanding what they were doing. It was another worrying sign that the Admiral was far more than just a simple pirate leader. His dreams of empire might come true.

"We don't know what level of defences might have been mounted on the asteroid," Gwendolyn admitted. "Ollie was apparently kept in the dark about that, unsurprisingly. He had no need to know. Given the difficulties in defending a stationary target against a well-armed mobile force, it's possible that the pirates simply didn't bother to install weapons on the hull. However, we *cannot* take that for granted. It's quite possible that they installed enough weapons to delay the Imperial Navy while the pirate commanders made their escape."

Edward stepped forward as Gwendolyn finished her part of the briefing. "We have the codes from Ollie that should allow us to enter the main cave and dock inside the asteroid," he said. "*Dancing Fool* will accompany us under cloak, hidden from their view. Unfortunately, once we dock we are supposed to be inspected carefully before being accepted into the Admiral's service. Our deception will be uncovered the moment they insist on seeing Ollie."

He'd tried to game out a scenario where they posed as mercenaries long enough to get into the asteroid without fighting, but too much could go wrong, even if the pirates didn't have any suspicions at all. Instead…

"As soon as we dock," he continued, "First and Third Platoons will stream into the asteroid, stunning everyone they encounter. The objective will be to capture the asteroid's command centre before they can do anything drastic like blowing themselves up. We don't know how much resistance we will face, but most of the pirates won't expect anything from us, apart from a quick trip out the nearest airlock. Expect desperate resistance and watch your backs. They know the asteroid far better than we do.

"Fourth Platoon will occupy the main airlock shaft and attempt to secure as many docked ships as possible. We don't know how many there will be on Haven, so we may have to break Fourth Platoon down into fire teams to secure the ships. In the event of there being too many ships for us to take easily, we will have to call on the volunteers to help secure the airlocks while Fourth Platoon takes the ships."

He scowled, noticing that most of the Marines shared his concerns. Crawford had loaned him a number of volunteers, men who wanted to fight the pirates, but they weren't anything like as well trained as the

Marines. Edward would have preferred a Civil Guard unit, if he'd been given the choice. Fighting in an asteroid was nothing like fighting on a planet's surface, even though it did bear similarities to street-fighting. But then, MOUT – Military Operations in Urban Terrain – had always been bloody. The buildings could cancel out many of the advantages enjoyed by the Marines.

"*Dancing Fool* will decloak as soon as the attack begins and move to engage any ship that attempts to escape the asteroid," Edward concluded. "Ideally, we want all of those ships intact, but we do not want them leaving. If worst come to worst, we may also need *Dancing Fool* to provide fire support."

He looked around the compartment. "Any questions?"

As always, there were a handful of questions; Marines were encouraged to use their brains and consider everything carefully. Edward had never been able to understand why the Civil Guard was so keen on blind obedience, although he had to admit that it wasn't possible to pause a battle just so the soldiers could question their orders. But the Marines knew better than to do it in the midst of a battle. He remembered being lectured for doing that at OCS as *everyone* had tried to impress the Drill Instructors with their tactical skill.

"Get some sleep," he ordered, finally. "We arrive at Haven tomorrow at 1900."

They'd go over the operation again as they approached Haven, just to make sure that they had the most up-to-date information. Ollie was proving a gold mine for the intelligence officers, who were taking turns to bounce questions off him and demand answers. If nothing else, they were starting to see how the Admiral was slowly taking control of the entire sector. Edward would have felt a twinge of admiration if he hadn't been condoning all sorts of atrocities to convince helpless colonies to submit to his rule.

He watched as the Marines filed out of the compartment. God, he was proud of them. The mission would be risky, easily the most dangerous operation Edward had ever planned, perhaps even as hair-raising as the recovery operation that had been mounted on Han. But then, they'd had the Imperial Navy to provide fire support and plenty of Civil Guard units in reserve. Here, there were just twenty-eight Marines and forty volunteers with questionable skills. At least they were enthusiastic.

But enthusiasm can only go so far on the battlefield, he reminded himself. The fanatics on Han had been enthusiastic, of course. They'd charged the Marines, seemingly unaware that human wave tactics just gave the Marines more to shoot at. But then, they'd overrun bases when the defenders had literally run out of ammunition. A thousand Han fanatics had died for each Marine, but the loss rate had been in their favour. It was a sickening thought, yet it had to be faced. Who knew *what* the pirates, desperate to escape, would do?

"You need some sleep too," Gwendolyn reminded him. "Everyone needs to be fresh tomorrow."

Edward nodded, sourly. "You get some sleep too," he ordered. Gwendolyn would be attached to Fourth Platoon, along with a number of auxiliaries to boost Lieutenant Faulkner's strength. He might well have the most dangerous part of the operation under his command. "You're going into combat tomorrow."

"You might be fighting too," Gwendolyn pointed out. "What happens if they manage to muster a counter-attack?"

"We would be in some trouble," Edward agreed. Standard procedure was to deploy at least a full company of Marines to attack an asteroid base, if the base was deemed worth taking. If not, the Imperial Navy would launch nuclear missiles at it from a safe distance and watch as the asteroid shattered, destroying the pirate settlement. *His* force was going to be badly overstretched. "We're going to have to raise more space-capable troopers in the future."

He thought, briefly, of Michael Volpe. Edward had hoped that the young man – and the rest of his platoon – would become the core of a new space-capable unit. But Michael Volpe was missing, presumed dead, and the rest of his unit had been withdrawn to Avalon. They'd have to start again from scratch.

"Or see what the other worlds can provide us," Gwendolyn pointed out. "There were quite a few Special Forces operatives who went to colony worlds along the Rim. Some of them would probably be willing to return to service."

Edward nodded. The Empire liked sending its former SF operatives to the Rim. Their training was very useful when it came to survival on hostile planets, as well as allowing them to start training up new soldiers to guard the settlements. Avalon hadn't had many – if any – because of the ADC's long-term plans for the future, but there were other worlds in the sector. Elysium certainly had quite a few.

"If we win," he said, quietly. But he couldn't allow himself any more doubt. "Once we win."

Shaking his head, he headed for his bunk. Gwendolyn was right. He *did* need to sleep.

Tomorrow was going to be a very busy day.

CHAPTER
THIRTY-SEVEN

No soldier likes being caught in restrictive terrain. Half of the great battles of history have been won or lost because one side was caught on bad ground. But operations on asteroid settlements are conducted in very restricted terrain indeed. The invading force is often ignorant of the asteroid's interior layout, the number of defenders, their weapons…and almost everything else an attacking force would like to know.

On the other hand, once an asteroid settlement comes under attack, its fall is just a matter of time.

-Major-General Thomas Kratman (Ret), *A Civilian's Guide to the Terran Marine Corps.*

"And you're sure that these will work?"

Mandy nodded as Travis looked down at the communicators, doubtfully. It had taken hours to splice the encryption systems into the communicators, but Mandy was rather pleased with her success. A series of checks had revealed that the communicators were effectively undetectable by the ship's internal network, while the encryption would be very difficult to break in a meaningful timeframe. Mandy's best guess was that it would take months, at the very least, for even the most advanced decryption system in the galaxy to break the code, barring a massive stroke of luck.

"Just make sure that everyone knows not to lose theirs," she said, briskly. "I couldn't install anything to lock out someone who isn't on our side."

She'd half-hoped that Travis would give her a complete list of his faction, but he hadn't been that stupid. Chances were that he'd established a network of cells, each one unaware of the identities of anyone belonging to the others. It was simple security – and it made it harder for his subordinates to plot to unseat him. The Captain would have his own faction, Mandy knew, as would the Admiral. It made her wonder how the pirates coughed without someone taking it as a sign to start something violent.

"Pity," Travis said. "But only my people will know which code to use. Anyone else will be shit out of luck."

He stood up and headed for the hatch. "We're due to take on more mercenaries this afternoon," he added, as he paused in front of the solid metal airlock. "I believe that Vane would like some help ensuring that the life support is up to the task of keeping them alive."

Mandy winced as Travis departed, the hatch closing behind him. Over the last two days, the Admiral had been putting together the force he intended to throw at Avalon. There were at least four heavy transport ships, two light combatants and *Sword* herself, which would be carrying a small army of mercenaries. The pirate crew had been grumbling at being forced to share cabins with their fellow pirates, but no one dared object too loudly, not when the Admiral's guards were a constant reminder of his power. They had already made an example of a pirate who had thrown a spanner at one of the mercenaries.

Shaking her head, she picked up her terminal and glanced down at it, silently grateful for the manuals the pirates had stolen from countless freighters and colony worlds. Few people really realised what went on inside a computer processor, or how easy it was to customise a device to suit one's requirements. Mandy had been given the terminal to monitor the computer nodes they'd installed to improve the starship's performance, but it hadn't taken her long to turn it into a detonator for the explosive packs she'd stolen. Or so she hoped. There had been no way to test it completely. The signal the terminal produced *did* span the entire ship, so it *should* work…

The thought kept nagging at her as she left Travis' private stateroom and headed for the tubes. They were still largely empty, despite the presence of the mercenaries; Mandy could make her way down to engineering without being seen. Vane had grumbled to her in bed that they were over-stressing the life support, which had struck Mandy as amusing when she'd looked it up afterwards. The Imperial Navy massively over-engineered the life support on their capital ships, assuming that they might have to rescue colonists or transport troops at any moment. In theory, *Sword* should have had no problems transporting two complete battalions of mercenaries.

But Vane was probably right, Mandy knew. The pirates had over-stressed the life support units in the past, which struck her as either igno-rance or stupidity. They *had* to know that without the life support they would have no air to breathe, but they didn't seem to care. Now that the crew had suddenly tripled, Vane and his team had to work desperately on the life support and pray that it held until they reached Avalon. *Anything could happen in transit and most of the potential disasters ended with the ship never being seen again.*

She climbed out of the tube and headed into engineering. No one paid any attention to her now; after what she'd done, after the people she'd killed, she was part of the crew. A handful of new recruits from the aster-oid were standing in front of the fusion core, being lectured by Vane on the need to keep the starship clean at all times. At least she was no longer cleaning the tubes, Mandy told herself, and shivered as she realised just how far she'd fallen. It was impossible to avoid realising that Stockholm Syndrome was taking hold of her mind.

Just remember what you have in mind, she told herself, as Vane fin-ished his lecture. With so many new people on the ship, the newcomers would have to work in teams, rather than being isolated from everyone else. *And think about what you owe the dead.*

"We transmitted our IFF and Ollie's codes," Gwendolyn said as *Spider* made its way towards Haven. "So far, we have received no response."

Edward nodded, unsurprised. Haven was very well hidden, even by the standard set by pirate bases and black colonies. Orbiting a dull red dwarf, the asteroid was emitting nothing that the passive sensors could detect, not even a faint trickle of radiation. The system itself had nothing to recommend it, even to the RockRats; a handful of asteroids, a single isolated comet and a useless star. There was little point in anyone settling the system unless they had something to hide.

The Imperial Navy was supposed to regularly inspect such star systems, but it was an impossible task. There were *thousands* of similar stars within the Empire's borders, even after it had started to collapse. Inspecting them all thoroughly would take years; a simple fly-though the Haven System would be unlikely to pick up anything suggesting that the system played host to a pirate base. Edward could almost admire the Admiral's concept; a hidden capital would be difficult for *anyone* to find and destroy.

"Keep us heading in on the right course," Edward ordered, grimly. Ollie had admitted that all starships heading to Haven had to come in on a single trajectory, or they would be assumed hostile. He hadn't been able to say what would happen to any hostile ship, but Edward had assumed the worst. "And keep the laser link to *Dancing Fool* active."

He watched grimly as the tiny cluster of asteroids came closer. It was very rare to encounter a star with no companions, or a planet or asteroid drifting through interstellar space. Millions of years had drawn the asteroids closer together before they settled into stable orbits – or perhaps that had been outside intervention. Haven might have been a black colony before the Admiral had taken control of it for his own purposes. It would certainly explain the interior docking cave and the obsession with secrecy.

"Picking up a single laser transmission," Delacroix said, sharply. She'd transferred over from the *Dancing Fool* to serve as *Spider's* XO, as well as operating the sensor console. "They're demanding specific access codes."

Edward took a breath. If Ollie had lied to them – or had been misled himself – they were about to find out. "Transmit the codes," he ordered. He looked over at the display and frowned. "Is the laser coming from Haven itself?"

"No," Delacroix reported. "It seems to be coming from a smaller asteroid, orbiting three hundred kilometres from Haven."

Gwendolyn glanced over at Edward. "Another base?"

"It could be an asteroid fortress," Delacroix admitted. "Or it could simply be an asteroid with a laser communications system mounted on the rock."

Her console chimed. "They're sending us another trajectory," she added. "They want us to pass very close to that asteroid as we head down to Haven."

"Move us in," Edward ordered. The alternative was breaking off and trying to storm the asteroid from the outside. It might work, but it would be very costly. Besides, the pirates would be alerted the minute *Spider* moved off her assigned trajectory. "Carefully, now."

The second asteroid loomed up on the display, far larger than the light freighter they'd converted into a Q-ship. Edward studied it through the passive sensors, looking for signs that the pirates had burrowed into the rock and mounted weapons to surprise unwary visitors. Asteroid fortresses were far from unknown in the Empire, although they posed their own problems for defence planners. A single hit with a nuke could send one of them drifting out of orbit, down to the planet below. The heavy rock that provided shielding against missiles would rapidly become a liability when the asteroid hit the planet and devastated it. Edward had seen recordings of asteroid impacts during the Unification Wars and they'd always killed millions of innocent colonists.

"I'm not picking up any active sensors," Delacroix reported. "If they've armed the asteroid, I cannot pick up any evidence…"

Edward scowled. Heading into an asteroid base, with a potential threat at his back…it wasn't an ideal situation. Perhaps he should order *Dancing Fool* to fire on the asteroid with nukes the moment the shit hit the fan. It might be a colossal overreaction, but it was the only way to be sure. He keyed his console, sending the orders through the laser link to the light cruiser, wondering just how many other asteroids might have their own surprises. The Admiral could have had *years* to prepare his base for operations.

"Keep an eye on it," he ordered, finally. "Is there anything coming from Haven at all?"

"Not a peep," Delacroix confirmed. "That's some very good shielding woven through that rock."

Haven was a long asteroid, reminding Edward of an uncooked potato spinning slowly through space. One end had been marred by an impact thousands of years in the past, providing a perfect place for the pirates to dig into the rock and conceal their landing bay; the other end looked rocky and unsafe. Edward recalled the first training operations they'd carried out in space and scowled. Fighting on an asteroid's surface could be incredibly difficult for people who weren't used to operating in less than standard gravity. There was even a story about a Marine who'd evaded an enemy cruiser by keeping the bulk of an asteroid between himself and the hunting ship.

Even up close, there were few hints that someone had set up a base inside the asteroid. There were no worker bees buzzing around, no starships making their way to and from the dockyard, not even a hint of radio chatter. The passive sensors didn't even pick up any waste heat from the asteroid. Edward made a mental note to have the asteroid studied carefully after they took it, if they managed to take it intact. It was possible that they might have to hunt down other bases and knowing how the pirates hid might give them clues to locating others. Or maybe they'd just have to depend on having other strokes of luck.

"They're telling us to get into the docking cave," Delacroix reported. She broke off as the docking cave started to open in front of them. "My God."

Edward couldn't disagree. The standard procedure for space docks – and shipyards – was to allow the starships to dock outside the station. It was a great deal easier to dock a starship like that, as well as eject it out into space if something went badly wrong. The pirates, on the other hand, had hollowed out part of the asteroid and turned it into an immense docking cave. Edward watched in disbelief as the asteroid opened, revealing a handful of freighters inside the huge structure. It was so vast that even a bulk freighter fitted in without problems.

"The docking crews will have nightmares," Gwendolyn said, quietly. "If people have problems in an orbital shipyard, what will they have here?"

"True," Edward agreed. "They'll all have nightmares."

From the point of view of someone standing on the rocky surface below them, the giant starships would be hovering in the air, high over their heads. The entire bay was completely without gravity – the crew would probably have to use magnetic boots to get around – but the eye would still be fooled. If the vast shipyards orbiting Mars and Jupiter had to regularly rotate their dockworkers, what would happen in Haven?

He felt his eyes opening wide as he saw the light freighters on the landing pad below them, all parked out in the vacuum. The crews would be forced to don spacesuits just to board the asteroid, he realised, unless there was a bus that transported them from their ship to the airlock. Edward wondered just how much influence the Admiral had to force crews to put themselves in such a vulnerable position, before realising that he held a tight grip on the HE3 supplies. A crew that refused to cooperate could be simply stranded until they saw reason. If he ever got his hands on the cloudscoop, Edward knew, he'd extend the same system to the rest of the sector.

"Keep updating the HUD plans," he ordered. Most of the ships appeared to be shut down completely, which meant that they were probably deserted. Fourth Platoon could take the airlock complex – it was starting to come into view – and then hold it as a chokepoint. The pirates would have to go through them to get to their ships. "Are there any warships in the cave?"

"Just a single destroyer, *Cadbury*-class," Delacroix said. "The ship appears to be in the middle of a refit, Colonel."

Edward nodded. The *Cadbury*-class had been good ships in their day, but that had been centuries ago. Their hulls would still be good; everything else would need to be replaced before the pirates would have a halfway respectable ship under their control. It was yet another sign of the sheer scale of the Admiral's ambitions. Most pirate gangs couldn't hope to refit starships on their own. They tended to be dependent upon black colonies and shipyards that were happy to take bribes and not ask too many questions.

"Mark it down for later attention," he ordered. Judging from the number of open compartments in her hull, the destroyer was nowhere near ready to return to service. Still, they'd keep an eye on her. If her weapons were active, she could tear *Spider* apart. "Do we have any better interior diagrams?"

Gwendolyn tapped the display. "We have airlocks here, here and here," she said. "Big ships like ours seem to be expected to dock at this section" – she tapped a location where four other freighters were docked – "and it looks as if they are preparing to extend a docking tube."

Edward scowled. Being trapped in a docking tube could prove disastrous for his platoons – and he didn't dare run any more risks than were strictly necessary. "Alert First Platoon," he ordered. "They are to depart through the starboard airlock and head directly for the docking complex; we'll use a mining laser to burn a path into the metal. Third Platoon can backstop them; Fourth Platoon can fly down to the lower airlocks."

His scowl deepened. "You will take the auxiliaries to secure the docking tube," he added. "Once secure, you can move forward and join up with Fourth Platoon."

"And you're going to stay here," Gwendolyn said firmly. "*Someone* has to be capable of seeing the overall picture."

Edward nodded, tiredly. As far as he could tell, his two assault forces were going to be widely separated, at least until they managed to secure the entire docking complex. According to Ollie, the pirates had worked in a few chokepoints of their own, although Edward knew better than to take everything Ollie told him for granted. If he'd been the Admiral, he would definitely have given Ollie some misleading information just to confuse anyone who came after him.

"Pass the orders," he said. Carefully, he studied the main docking complex. It didn't look to be built out of hullmetal; a single laser sweep should be enough to open a gap for the Marines, with the added advantage of depressurising the inner complex. The pirates would be rushing around looking for safety gear rather than trying to engage the Marines. "We launch in two minutes."

"They're ordering us to prepare to be boarded," Delacroix reported, as the docking tube started to extend towards *Spider*. No one seemed to be waiting in the semi-transparent tube, but that wasn't too surprising. "The inspector wants our entire crew – and Ollie – waiting for him when he boards our ship.

Edward's lips twitched. "I'm afraid he's going to be disappointed," he said. He took personal control of the laser cannon and swung it around to target the docking complex. It looked to be a fairly standard installation, he decided; the pirates had probably stolen it from a supply convoy for a new colony. Several convoys had gone missing in the days before the Imperial Navy had abandoned the sector completely. "Weapon locked on target."

He checked with the rest of the Marines, making sure that they were in position, and then tapped a switch. "Firing…*now!*"

CHAPTER THIRTY-EIGHT

The great weakness of pirate society is that there is actually very little holding it together but force – or the threat of force. There is no camaraderie among the pirates – certainly not outside very small groups – and every pirate firmly believes that he has to look after himself first and foremost. Once the limited cohesion is shattered, therefore, the pirates often become unable to offer meaningful resistance.
-Edward E. Smith, Professor of Sociology. *Pirates and their Lives.*

"Go!"

Jasmine grinned as she launched herself from the airlock and flashed towards the pirate complex, propelled by her suit's onboard drive. Ahead of her, she saw the complex glowing red and melting where the ship's laser burned through the metal, the laser beam invisible to her eyes but clear to her suit's sensors. Of all the ways to go, dying because she'd accidentally steered herself *into* the beam's path would be the worst, so she kept a careful eye on it as atmosphere began to stream out of the complex. A moment later, the first handful of pirates were propelled outwards, launched on trajectories that might blow them completely out of the asteroid. It wouldn't really matter. They'd be dead a long time before they reached the hatch.

An explosion billowed out of the complex as the laser beam burned through something ahead of them, cutting off as the Marines flew through the breach. The remaining pirates were struggling desperately for life, unable to offer any resistance; Jasmine stunned them rapidly, even though it would probably kill them. They didn't have the manpower to risk leaving enemies behind them.

"Launch drones," she ordered, as the Marines spread out. The atmosphere was dropping rapidly, suggesting that airlocks were closing ahead of them. That wasn't too surprising; unless the pirates had neglected all safety precautions – which was a distinct possibility – they'd have the ability to seal off a hull breach very quickly. "Find the way into the main complex."

"Got it," Blake reported, as they fanned out. The atmosphere was almost completely gone now, ensuring that anyone without a suit would suffocate to death. "One airlock, leading onwards into the complex."

Jasmine smiled, grimly. "Get it open," she ordered. If possible, they'd try to leave the airlock in place. The Colonel did want prisoners, after all, and venting the entire asteroid would slaughter the population. "And get the drones moving past it."

She checked her HUD as Blake went to work. The pirate communications network seemed to have come to life, screaming in outrage. There were hundreds of messages, all encrypted, bouncing from node to node. Jasmine guessed that the pirates were trying to organise resistance to the Marines, although they would find that tricky. Fourth Platoon was heading to a different part of the complex and the pirates would have some difficulty trying to decide which attack was the main thrust. They might not realise that *both* attacks were deadly serious.

The intelligence staff were trying to hack into the pirate network, but it was proving slow going. Unsurprisingly, the network wasn't a standard one and large sections were locked out to everyone without the right passwords. Given time, Jasmine was sure, they'd crack into the network, but there was no way to know if they'd succeed in time to be useful. The Marines would have to press on and hope for the best. Jasmine watched as Blake finally managed to open the airlock and stepped inside, followed by two more Marines. The airlock hissed shut behind him.

"The second hatch is opening now," he reported. There was a long pause, just long enough for Jasmine to start worrying. "We cleared the welcoming committee, boss. None of them had protective suits."

"Or even proper weapons," Joe added. "What the fuck were they thinking?"

Jasmine smiled as she moved the rest of the platoon through the chokepoint and ordered the drones to start flying ahead of the Marines, mapping out the pirate complex. It was possible that the pirates would deploy countermeasures, if they realised that the drones were spying on them for the advancing enemy force, but if the Marines were lucky the pirates would have no time to check for their presence. The handful of guards hadn't had a chance, she knew; Blake had been right. They hadn't been armed with anything that could scratch powered combat armour.

"They'll have armed mercenaries further ahead," she reminded the platoon as they advanced down the corridor. "Don't get cocky."

The drones located a number of pirates running for their lives, rather than trying to put up a fight. If someone was trying to coordinate a resistance, they weren't doing a very good job. Instead, they seemed to be trying to seal off the spaceport complex entirely. It wouldn't have been a bad tactic on an orbiting space station or shipyard, but it was actually pointless on Haven. The section couldn't be blown free and then destroyed from a safe distance.

"I'm always cocky," Blake said, quickly. He paused, long enough to glance through a half-opened hatch and fire a pair of stun bursts into the room, stunning two pirates who had been trying to hide. "And brave, and bold, and…"

"And don't we just know it," Joe countered. He paused as a set of red icons appeared on the HUD. "Boss, I think we have trouble."

Jasmine nodded as she accessed the live feed from the drones. A set of heavily-armed mercenaries had finally made their appearance, wearing powered combat armour of their own. It wouldn't be entirely comparable to Marine armour, but under the circumstances that wouldn't matter. Besides, one didn't need armour to kill Marines, just a weapon that could burn through armour. Unless she was very much mistaken, those mercenaries were carrying heavy plasma rifles. They were probably carrying HE grenades as well.

"Switch to plasma rifles," she ordered. The mercenaries were setting up a position in a chokepoint, gambling that the Marines would have to come to them. There was no point in using stun weapons, not when their targets were wearing armour of their own. Even light armour could neutralise stun bolts. "We'll fire a round of grenades into the chamber first, and then follow up with a charge."

She braced herself as they rounded the corner, scanning rapidly for enemy drones. There were none, but the pirates probably didn't need them to track the Marines. Most asteroid settlements were riddled with internal sensors and they didn't dare assume that Haven was any different. The pirate communications network was, if anything, only babbling louder, although there was still no way to even guess at what the pirates were saying. Colonel Stalker's broadcast was trying to override the network, offering life to anyone who surrendered. Jasmine wasn't sure how many pirates would take the offer. They'd have to suspect that it was a trap.

Maybe executing every pirate we caught wasn't a good idea, she thought, sourly. But she'd seen recordings of the wreckage pirates left in their wake. How could anyone blame the Empire's population for demanding the death penalty for pirate scum? But now it was making it hard to convince the bastards that they'd be allowed to surrender. She switched back to the HUD and scowled as she realised that more pirates were preparing themselves, just past the spaceport complex. They were probably praying desperately that the mercenaries would be enough to stop the Marines.

Ahead of them, there was a large storage compartment, crammed with metal crates. The mercenaries had taken up position in the compartment, preparing themselves to engage the Marines as soon as they appeared. All things considered, Jasmine decided, it wasn't a bad ambush site, but only if the intended target didn't know that the mercenaries were lying in wait. She muttered orders and three Marines stepped forward, switching their grenade launchers to rapid fire. HE blasts were unlikely to actually kill the armoured mercenaries unless they exploded right on top of their armour, but they'd be very disconcerting.

"Fire," she ordered.

The Marines fired nine grenades, one after the other. Explosions ripped through the crates, filling the air with flying shrapnel; the mercenaries, just for a few seconds, were unable to mount a resistance. Blake led the charge forward, filling the air with brilliant white bursts of plasma, relying on the drones for targeting information. Four mercenaries died before they knew what had hit them; the remainder scrambled backwards, firing back towards the Marines. The great weakness of plasma weapons was that it was impossible to conceal where the bursts were coming from; every time someone fired, other combatants fired back in their direction. Jasmine snapped orders and additional grenades were fired at the mercenaries. The explosions knocked them about, just before the Marines finished them off. There were no survivors.

She checked the bodies quickly, making sure that they were actually dead. Their leaders hadn't invested in proper suits, she realised, although there was no way to tell if that was a matter of choice or necessity. A Marine suit was designed to keep its wearer alive, if possible; there were designs that could even fight or flee on their own. The mercenaries wore very basic armour, designed to do nothing more than provide limited protection. None of them had survived the brief firefight.

"Moving onwards," she reported, back to Colonel Stalker. She knew how he must be feeling, trapped on *Spider* as his Marines assaulted the pirate base. "Drones report heavier resistance up ahead."

The spaceport was sealed off from the main complex by a set of heavy-duty airlocks. Someone had been thinking, Jasmine realised, and destroyed the control processors that would normally have opened the airlocks, processors that the Marines could have hijacked and overridden to make it easier to assault the base. On the other hand, the airlocks themselves might be secure, but the surrounding rock wasn't so strong. The Marines placed explosive charges on the rock and stepped back, detonating the charges a moment later. Jasmine allowed herself a tight smile as the Marines advanced, watching carefully for further ambushes. The pathway into the heart of Haven lay open.

Her HUD blinked up warnings as it analysed the atmosphere. Normally, asteroids had very clean atmospheres, but this asteroid had a surprising amount of contaminants in the air. Most of them were fairly harmless; a couple were addictive, if breathed in for long enough. Jasmine found herself wondering if the asteroid's owners had deliberately designed the air to be addictive, before deciding that the levels were too low to cause addiction unless someone spent *years* on the asteroid. It was much more likely that she was picking up residue left behind by illegal drug use. After piracy, drug abuse was a very minor charge to throw at the unhappy inhabitants.

"Try not to breathe the air," she said, as the platoon advanced carefully. "You never know what you might catch."

The first of the massive caves lay open in front of them, crammed with stalls and completely deserted. A handful of stalls seemed to have been stripped bare, the remainder had been abandoned; it didn't take a genius to guess that the stripped stalls had sold weapons. The whole scene reminded her of the markets on Avalon, the ones that had operated on a semi-illegal basis before the first Council had been overthrown, where one could buy almost anything if one had the cash. There were stalls selling ladies' underwear, spare parts for starships and even a handful of paper books. The pirates, Jasmine decided, had some pretty weird priorities.

"I think they just sell whatever they have," Harris said, when Jasmine made that observation out loud. "You can sell anything, even shit, if you find the right buyer."

"Blake should be in the money then," Joe said. "He's *full* of shit. And farts."

"Those are my specialised antipersonnel weapons," Blake said, quickly. "I am an *expert* with antipersonnel weapons."

"It's the friendly fire people complain about," Joe mock-protested. "I think you'd better stop eating those meals at the cheap diner. No more curried eggs for you."

Jasmine rolled her eyes. "The drones are having difficulty penetrating their way into the second cave," she reminded them, sharply. Banter was all very well, but they were in the middle of a combat zone. "Besides, your shit belongs to the Marine Corps."

"We should look into this," Joe said. "How much do you think we'd get paid if we tried to sell genuine Marine shit…?"

The banter cut off as a stream of pirates appeared at the far end of the cave, opening fire with automatic weapons and plasma rifles. Jasmine dived to the deck, switching rapidly to her grenade launcher as the stalls were ripped apart by streams of bullets and firing two grenades at the nearest pirates. Most of them weren't wearing armour, or carrying plasma weapons; she had a feeling that they'd been pushed into attacking by people who *were* wearing armour. It was quite possible that they were intended to serve as a human wave, overrunning the Marines through sheer weight of numbers. Or that their superiors were using their deaths to buy them time to escape.

She smiled as the explosions tore through the pirate ranks, killing or injuring most of the advancing horde. The Marines took advantage of the sudden pause to take up firing positions, whereupon they poured fire into the pirates, who very rapidly dissolved into a mob. They might have assumed that the stalls would provide some cover, but anyone with any real combat experience would know better. Bullets and plasma pulses would go through the stalls like knives through butter. They hadn't bothered to build them from anything tough enough to stand up to a beating. But then, why would they have bothered?

"Blake, Joe; switch to stunners, wide beam," she ordered. Very few of the pirates were wearing any form of protection, apart from a handful of pieces of obsolete body armour that had probably come from the Civil Guard. *They* were rarely given powered combat armour, largely because their budgets couldn't afford it. And Jasmine wouldn't have trusted Civil Guardsmen in armour anyway. "Stun as many of them as you can."

The remainder of the platoon held fire as stun beams played out over the pirates, sending them falling to the ground. Anyone who stayed upright after being hit with a stun bolt was shot down quickly; the Marines knew better than to take chances with someone who might be boosted or wearing concealed armour. Jasmine walked forward carefully, watching for pirates who were still twitching after being stunned, and motioned for two of the Marines to advance into the second cave. They were greeted by a hail of fire from a handful of pirates who had paused to set up a better ambush.

"They're pretty firmly dug in, boss," Blake reported. "The drones just aren't getting through."

Jasmine scowled. The pirates had built what looked like a settlement inside the second cave, with a hundred different buildings, each one a potential ambush point. A pair of bodies – both girls – lay on the ground, leaving her wondering just what had happened to them. Slaves, trying to escape? Or pirates who'd been trying to surrender? Or simple victims of misdirected fire? Politicians might believe otherwise, but accidents happened in wartime, some of them tragic. But they were genuine accidents.

For a moment, she considered her options. Could they outflank the enemy? It didn't seem possible; all routes further into the asteroid ran through the second cave. The drones had found a handful of maintenance tubes, but their armour was too bulky to allow them to use the tubes, at least without stripping off their protection. Jasmine thought about it for a long moment before deciding that it was too risky, even for Marines. They didn't dare risk being caught unprotected if the pirates vented the asteroid.

This is why they pay you the big bucks, she told herself. She could ask the Colonel for orders, but that would be an abdication of responsibility. *Jasmine* was the woman on the spot, with a firm grasp of the tactical situation – or at least the *best* grasp. She couldn't go running to the Colonel for instructions every time she ran into trouble.

"Switch to plasma grenades," she ordered reluctantly. Using heavy firepower in a confined space was always dangerous, not least because there were almost certainly innocent victims in the second cave. But heavy firepower was their only hope of cutting through the pirate position without risking too many lives. "I want one grenade inside each of those structures, as soon as we burst into the compartment. Let them all burn."

There were brief acknowledgements from the Marines. Plasma grenades set fire to almost anything, from wood to human flesh. Jasmine had seen them used on Han, when the Marines had almost been overrun by human waves; she remembered watching insurgents screaming as white flames burned through their bodies, running around desperately before the flames mercifully killed them. Nothing could have saved their lives.

The weapons weren't – technically – banned, but almost every military formation in the Empire was reluctant to use them unless there was no other choice. It was her decision, but she knew she'd face some hard questions from the Colonel afterwards.

"Get ready," she ordered, as the Marines fanned out. The drones made a breakthrough and reported that there were at least fifty pirates lying in wait. God alone knew how many people were living on the asteroid. Haven was easily big enough to support a population of over several thousand pirates. There were asteroids in the Sol System that held over a hundred thousand inhabitants. "Now!"

The grenades were fired as the Marines ran forward, detonating inside the structures. A moment later, white-hot flames flared through the buildings, tearing through the ambush at terrifying speed. Jasmine saw one of the structures tipping as its supports gave way, before crashing down in a sheet of flame. The pirates hiding inside the building hadn't stood a chance.

"Onwards," she snapped. "Take them at a run!"

CHAPTER THIRTY-NINE

While the officer on the spot is in the best position to understand the tactical realities, it is the officer in overall command who is in the best position to understand the strategic realities. It is his responsibility to determine, for example, if fighting a particular battle is a good idea, or if the Marines should withdraw without contacting the enemy. This may seem perverse, but it is true that a victorious but expensive battle can actually cost the overall war.

This is not a comfortable position. The temptation to micromanage is overpowering.

-Major-General Thomas Kratman (Ret), *A Civilian's Guide to the Terran Marine Corps.*

"Fourth Platoon reports that they have secured the spaceport complex," Delacroix reported. "So far, they are not meeting any organised resistance. Fire teams are heading out to secure the ships."

"Start moving the volunteers down there," Edward ordered. They'd had to load the volunteers onto shuttles, which carried its own risks, but there was no choice. They didn't have armour for them all, even if they'd been trained in using it. "And keep adding new drones to the network."

He looked back at the display, fighting down the urge to issue orders to his subordinate commanders. No wonder that so many Generals and Admirals gave in to the temptation to micromanage their forces, he realised; they were ultimately responsible for the success or failure of their operations. And it was easy to forget that he *couldn't* see everything through the drones, or the direct feeds from the combat suits. He could have believed that he knew more than the person on the ground, if he hadn't been put through exercises intended to convince him that he didn't. OCS' instructors had been scathing on the subject of micromanaging troops. The Civil Guard officers didn't get such lectures, which might explain why they were so prone to trying to micromanage from a distance.

The operation seemed to be going well, although he knew that overconfidence was a weakness and nothing was truly secure until after the fighting had stopped. First Platoon was cutting its way towards the heart of the enemy base, while Third Platoon had secured the docking complex and Fourth Platoon was securing the smaller ships. The pirates didn't seem to have any significant internal defences, although he could see why they hadn't bothered to add them to their asteroid base. Once discovered, the base's fall was just a matter of time. The pirates were fighting desperately, no doubt hoping that they could overrun the Marines, reach their ships and make their escape. It wasn't going to happen.

"Signal from Captain Stevenson," Delacroix reported. "*Dancing Fool* has hit the suspicious asteroid with two nukes. If there was anything there, it isn't there now."

Edward's lips twitched. "Order her to move up to Haven and prepare to fire on targets if necessary," he ordered, shortly. If nothing else, *Dancing Fool* could blockade the asteroid or fire nukes into the docking bay. Haven was massive, but few asteroid settlements could resist nukes detonating inside their habitation caves. But that would mean the loss of his entire force. "And now that our cover is blown, she can launch remotes too. I want this entire cluster scanned for signs of life."

He turned back to the display, watching helplessly as First Platoon blasted its way through an ambush and continued towards the core of the pirate base. There was nothing he could do, one way or another, to influence the outcome, apart from ordering Third Platoon to advance forward, now that drones and remotes had secured the docking complex. The handful of ships in dock weren't likely to pose a problem, but the Marines would secure them just in case he was wrong. And then he could detail Third to move up in support of First.

"*Dancing Fool* reports that there appears to be a secondary docking cave at the far end of the asteroid," Delacroix said, sharply. "At least one ship inside, probably a destroyer…"

"Order Captain Stevenson to intercept her," Edward ordered. If the pirates managed to get an armed starship into the battle, the outcome could easily be disastrous. "She is cleared to engage with extreme force."

"Understood," Delacroix said. "Extreme force is now authorised."

They watched grimly as the light cruiser moved to intercept the new pirate vessel. Edward guessed that the Admiral's senior staff had boarded the ship, as she didn't seem inclined to stick around and fight. If *Dancing Fool* hadn't been in position to intercept, she would have raced off to the Phase Limit and vanished. Instead, the light cruiser sent a surrender demand and then opened fire. The pirate ship returned fire, but she didn't have the throw weight to pose a threat to the light cruiser. Two minutes later, a missile struck her hull and she vanished in a white-hot flare of radioactive plasma.

"Pirate ship destroyed," Delacroix reported. "*Dancing Fool* reports that just before her destruction, she beamed an omnidirectional signal out across the system."

Edward leaned forward. "Saying what?"

"Unknown," Delacroix said. "It appears to be a single word, rather than an encrypted message or compressed transmission. The intended recipient probably knows what it means."

Edward nodded. Marines had specific codewords for certain situations, particularly situations where it would be unwise to speak too clearly. No outsider would know what they meant, even if the codewords were sent without encryption. Any report that began with a statement that everything was absolutely peachy meant that the sender was under duress, warning the other Marines not to run into a trap. And any report that included the word 'ghost' meant that the situation was beyond salvaging and the Marines in combat had to be abandoned, with no attempt at a rescue. Edward had never heard of it being used outside exercises.

"Tell me," he said, "have they picked up any traces of anything else in the system?"

"No," Delacroix said. "But if someone was lying doggo, they wouldn't pick up *anything*."

"Yeah," Edward muttered.

It was common sense. A starship or automated station could be hiding along the Phase Limit, just waiting for the next pirate ship to arrive. When it did, the crew would be warned that Haven was no longer safe and that they should head somewhere else. They'd look, of course, but he knew better than to assume they'd find any watching ship or station. A star system was an immense place to hide something.

He sat back and forced himself to relax. The die was cast. All he could do now was watch, and pray that the Marines could bring it off. Again.

"We have a team of men in spacesuits, emerging from the far airlock," Delacroix reported, suddenly. "I think they're planning to outflank Fourth Platoon."

"Target them with the laser, and then melt that airlock," Edward ordered. The pirates had to be getting desperate. They *knew* that *Spider* was armed. "And then warn Lieutenant Faulkner that he may be getting visitors."

Jasmine fired constantly as the Marines ran through the burning holocaust. A handful of pirates had survived long enough to open fire on the Marines; others were screaming in pain, burned so badly that they couldn't hope to survive without immediate medical assistance. The Marines shot them rapidly – they were mercy kills, she told herself – as they pushed onwards, cutting through the remains of the ambush. Most of the pirates had been killed in the first seconds after the plasma grenades had detonated.

"The flames are going to be a problem," Blake observed as they reached the edge of the cave. A new set of airlocks barred their way, but resistance was crumbling and no one had bothered to seal them. "They'll destroy everything."

"They can't burn the rock," Jasmine reminded him. The flames were already cooling, although there were still flashes of blinding white light where they burned through the containment chambers of plasma rifles dropped by the pirates. "If worst comes to worst, we can vent the asteroid and put the fire out that way."

She lifted her rifle as they stepped into the network of corridors and chamber that made up the rest of the asteroid. According to Ollie, there were hundreds of tiny offices and shops belonging to pirates and their backers who didn't feel like being in the open. Jasmine wouldn't have been too surprised to discover that Haven had its own network of information brokers, as well as the Admiral's newborn civil service. Ideally, she knew, they had to take them all alive. Interrogating them might lead the Marines to other pirate bases. The drones kept updating her HUD as they flashed ahead, pointing out rooms where people were cowering, trying to hide from the Marines. There was no sign of any further resistance.

The Marines kept advancing, pausing only to stun everyone they encountered in the network of corridors. Jasmine watched carefully, sure that the penny was about to fall. The pirate chiefs might have been trying to escape – somehow, she wasn't surprised that they would desert their allies – but they would have left people in charge of organising resistance, surely? Or was it every man for himself now? There was no point in taking chances, so they pressed on carefully, watching for signs of trouble. But nothing happened as they reached the sealed airlocks leading into the very heart of the asteroid.

"Heavy fuckers," Blake commented, as they paused long enough to regroup. "You want to bet that there's an ambush on the far side?"

"No," Jasmine said, dryly. It *was* the obvious tactic; the Marines would have to fit through a very small gap while the pirates could pour fire on them from concealed positions. They'd have to use grenades to clear the compartment, which could mean damaging equipment they desperately needed to preserve. "Rig the charges and bring that fucker down."

Blake slapped explosive charges on the airlock as the rest of the Marines retreated to a safe distance, taking advantage of the moment of comparative peace to check their weapons and swap out ammunition clips. Jasmine smiled as Blake ran to join them, seconds before the charges exploded, blowing the hatch off its hinges and slamming it forward into the compartment. If anyone happened to be caught by the hatch, they'd be badly injured even if they were wearing combat armour. The Marines ran afterwards, using drones to locate and target a handful of pirates who had lurked in ambush. There were fewer than Jasmine had expected.

Her suit reported a communications channel opening. "Attention, Marines," an unfamiliar voice said. "We would like to deal."

Jasmine felt her eyes narrowing. A genuine offer to surrender – or an attempt to buy time? But why would they bother trying to buy time? The only thing they could do if they wanted to thwart the Marines was to blow the asteroid themselves, which would be suicide. They could have done it by now if that was what they'd had in mind.

"Surrender," she said. Colonel Stalker had issued orders that surrenders would be accepted, after all. The pirates would get to keep their lives, if not much else. They couldn't do any real harm on a penal island. "Surrender and you get to live."

There was a long pause. "And why should we surrender when all we have to look forward to is a penal colony?"

Jasmine used her hands to motion the Marines forward, watching as the drones flashed ahead of her. There were negotiators who could build up rapports with pirates or kidnappers, but that wasn't *her* speciality. She'd been trained to kill people and break things, not to pretend to be a friend to the scum of the universe. But then, they probably wouldn't believe honeyed words.

"We're going to storm our way through your position," she said, flatly. "There is no way out for you. The worst you can do is blow up the asteroid and believe me, that isn't going to save your lives. And we came here knowing that we might be killed in action. The fear of death doesn't slow us down."

She smiled, coldly. "No one is coming to save you," she added. "The Admiral won't risk bringing his fleet here to engage us. Even if he does, we'd blow the asteroid ourselves rather than let him recover it. You are trapped – and if you keep fighting, we will eventually kill you all and destroy the asteroid. There's no way out.

"If you surrender, you get to keep your lives."

The pirate didn't reply immediately. Jasmine took advantage of the pause to update Colonel Stalker, checking to see if she should offer the pirates anything other than bare survival. The Colonel seemed quite happy to allow her to continue the negotiations, but ordered her to keep advancing gingerly at the same time. Jasmine was quite happy to comply. The more pirates they stunned, the stronger their bargaining position would be. Their enemies hadn't even thought to demand a hold in place while they argued.

A handful of pirates appeared at the far end of the corridor, their hands held high in the air. The Marines beckoned them forward, pushed them into a compartment and then stunned them, leaving them lying on the deck until the post-battle teams could round them up. They couldn't risk leaving them awake, not when there was no time to secure the prisoners and make sure that they were unarmed. And still there was nothing from the pirates.

Jasmine found herself wondering just what was happening in their command centre. Some of them would want to surrender, to accept permanent exile to a penal colony; others would be so horrified at the thought of losing access to space that they might prefer to die. It was even possible that they'd started shooting at each other as the bonds binding them together frayed and snapped. Those who wanted to surrender might gun down those who wanted to fight to the bitter end. Or so she hoped. If it went the other way, the Marines might find themselves inside a giant bomb.

The channel reopened a second later. "We had to…discuss your offer," a different voice said. "We'd like to surrender."

"A wise decision," Jasmine said, calmly. "Order your men to put down their weapons and await us. They will all be stunned for transport to the holding ship. If there is any further resistance, or if we see anyone with a weapon, we will open fire. After that, unlock your command network. We want full access to your computers. Do you understand me?"

"Yes," the pirate said. There was a long pause. "We're passing the orders to surrender now."

Jasmine nodded, although she knew better than to assume that *everyone* would obey the command to surrender. The Crackers had been remarkably disciplined for an insurgency movement, although *they* had effectively won most of what they wanted from the government in exchange for an end to hostilities. Other insurgencies had fragmented after winning, or after being forced into surrender; it wasn't uncommon for splinter groups to keep fighting in hopes of winning more concessions, or because they couldn't abide peacetime. And it only took one idiot, determined to go out in a blaze of glory, to get his former comrades slaughtered. Surrenders were always tricky, particularly when dealing with pirates and others who knew that they would never be released from POW camps and returned to civilised society.

The Marines advanced forward, carefully. Most of the pirates had obeyed orders, although a handful seemed to be trying to retreat, only to be stunned before they could get out of firing range. They looked a sorry lot, Jasmine decided, as the Marines reached the airlock leading into the command centre. The airlock was open and a pair of bodies lay in front of it, one with a knife in his back. Jasmine checked the other one, realised that he'd been shot in the head, and then entered the command centre.

It was surprisingly similar to the ones she'd trained on, although most of the equipment seemed to have come from a dozen different sources. The asteroid's command crew gazed at the Marines resentfully, just before they were stunned into helplessness. They'd be somewhere secure, probably on one of the captured freighters, before they woke up.

"See if you can get into their network from here," she ordered. "They may not have unlocked it properly."

She watched Joe take one of the seats as the rest of the Marines checked the interior of the command centre. A handful of cabins seemed to be intended for the staff, as well as a kitchen and a set of washrooms. Two of the cabins held girls who seemed both relieved and fearful to see the Marines, almost certainly long-term captives and slaves. They'd be held separately from the rest of the prisoners until they could be interrogated, and then…Jasmine didn't know *what* would happen to them afterwards. They might be offered a chance to build a new life on Avalon, but would they really fit in?

"The network is open," Joe reported. "The intelligence staff are taking control now."

Jasmine nodded. With the network under their control, any remaining pirates could be hunted down, wherever they tried to hide. Most of them seemed to be obeying the order to surrender, or clustering into nooks and crannies in the vain hope the Marines would miss them. And one pirate was actually heading towards the command centre. Jasmine muttered orders and Blake moved to intercept him, just in case he had suicidal ambitions. They hadn't found anything that looked like a self-destruct system, but those were rarely attached to open command networks in any case.

"Boss," Blake said, suddenly. "I think you need to meet this one."

"Coming," Jasmine said, in some surprise. She walked out of the command centre and down to where Blake was waiting, his rifle covering the pirate. "Why...?"

And then she recognised the young man. They'd met before, back during the war.

"Michael?" She demanded. "What the fuck are you doing here?"

CHAPTER FORTY

> The operation doesn't end when the fighting finally comes to a halt. Each victory must be followed by an attempt to build on the success to produce more success. Prisoners must be identified and interrogated; buildings and structures must be searched for useful data…in short, every effort must be made to exploit the victory. Failure to do so can be costly.
> —Major-General Thomas Kratman (Ret), *A Civilian's Guide to the Terran Marine Corps.*

It had been months since Edward had last met Michael Volpe.

They'd first met when the young man had taken the oath that would eventually lead him into the Knights of Avalon, and again when he'd been given a medal for his performance during the final battles of the war. Edward remembered him as a strong young man, healthy and fit thanks to a combination of military food and heavy exercise, one of the best candidates for the space-capable operations unit he'd hoped to produce from the Knights. And then the pirates had attacked and Edward had assumed that he'd died, along with the other victims. No one had ever found a body.

Now, Michael looked thin and alarmingly pale. The presence of the two armed and armoured Marines – Gwendolyn had refused to allow Edward anywhere near Michael unless the young man was restrained and escorted – couldn't account for it all. Michael knew that he might be held to account for everything he'd done on the pirate base. Edward had already resolved to listen with an open mind instead of leaping to judgement. God alone knew what Michael had gone through since he'd been kidnapped from the RockRat ship.

"Start at the beginning," he ordered. "What happened to you?"

He listened as Michael told his story, starting with the kidnap and continuing to describe how he'd been booted off the Admiral's ship and forced to serve as a bouncer on the pirate asteroid to stay alive. Edward found himself believing most of the story; it wasn't uncommon for the pirates to abandon useless hostages on their bases, knowing that most of them would never manage to make it home. And they clearly hadn't realised that Michael had had any military training, or they would simply have killed him out of hand. Michael admitted that he'd been stumped to find a way home when the Marines had invaded Haven.

"Luckily for you," Edward commented. Given time, the pirates would eventually have corrupted Michael and anyone else who fell into their clutches. "What happened to the others?"

"They killed some," Michael said. "And they kept Mandy on the Admiral's ship."

Edward felt a complex mixture of relief and pity. Relief that the Professor's daughter was alive; pity that she would probably have been turned into a sex slave as the price for keeping her life. Or…he listened grimly as Michael explained that the pirates had put her to work as an engineer. Mandy had shown promise, he recalled from the reports he'd read months ago; the pirates would have pushed her into working for them or being thrown to the crew to be raped. It was hard to blame her for choosing to collaborate with the pirates.

"She's changed, sir," Michael reported. "I last saw her five days ago and she wasn't the same person at all."

He broke off. "Sir, they're planning to attack Avalon!"

Edward stared at him. "Explain," he ordered, finally. Had they gone through everything only to be too late to save their world? "What do you mean?"

"The ship they sent to occupy Avalon didn't report back," Michael said. "The Admiral was gathering a vast army of mercenaries and planning to return to the planet. He was still assembling his forces when you arrived."

"That might explain why there was so little resistance," Gwendolyn sent over the private communications channel. "And why they were so eager to snap up every mercenary unit they could locate."

"Probably," Edward sent back. Had the Admiral already set out to invade Avalon? There was no way to know. He looked directly at Michael as he asked the next question. "What sort of ships does he have under his command?"

Michael hesitated. "The only ones I know about are a heavy cruiser and a handful of destroyers and transports," he said. "But I always had the impression that he kept his fleet distributed around the sector, rather than concentrating it in one place. I don't know for sure."

Edward scowled. A single heavy cruiser in decent condition would be more than a match for the tiny fleet he'd assembled. Indeed, it could obliterate every ship they'd captured on Haven in a stand-up battle. Chances were that the pirate ship *wouldn't* be in good condition – pirate ships rarely were – but it wasn't something he could count on. And he was desperately short of crewmen for the ships he did have. They *had* recovered a number of slaves and press-ganged workers from Haven, yet he knew better than to trust them without reservation.

This would be a great moment for the Imperial Navy to return, he thought, but he knew it wasn't going to happen. *How the hell do we stop him?*

"The interrogators are going to go through everything that happened to you," he said to Michael. "It won't be a very pleasant experience, I'm afraid, but we need to know everything you know. After that…welcome home."

He watched as the Marines escorted Michael out of the hatch, to the compartment the intelligence staff had converted into an interrogation chamber. It was impossible not to feel sorry for Michael; whatever else happened, the young man would never be the same again. There was no way he could simply be returned to his unit; he'd probably need some form of counselling. Edward had never placed much faith in the psychologists, particularly the civilian ones who knew nothing about the military, but Michael would definitely need help. Others, liberated from pirate bases, had committed suicide soon afterwards.

"Poor bastard," Gwendolyn commented. She scowled. "Do you think we can take on an entire heavy cruiser and escorts?"

"The alternative is surrendering," Edward pointed out. Taking out the heavy cruiser would be difficult, but perhaps not impossible. If nothing else, they could always try to ram her with one of the captured transports. "Contact Colonel Stevenson; I need to talk to her immediately."

"Of course," Gwendolyn said. She reached for her communicator and then stopped. "What do you want done with the prisoners?"

"Move the important ones to *Spider* for the interrogators," Edward ordered. "Everyone else can go into the life support bubbles – segregated, of course. We'll come back and pick them up after we save Avalon."

He shook his head as he took the communicator. "Get the other ships ready to go as quickly as possible," he added, "and tell the crews to take any ship-mounted weapons the pirates might have left hanging around. There's no point in staying here if we can't defend Avalon, so rig the asteroid to blow if someone tries to get in without the right codes. Do the same for the bubbles. One way or the other, we'll be rid of one problem."

The communicator buzzed in his hand. "Kitty," Edward said as Gwendolyn left the compartment. "We've had bad news."

There had been no time to relax since they'd secured Haven. Jasmine and First Platoon had spent the two hours after the fighting dragging stunned prisoners to the inflatable bubbles the crewmen were rigging up to serve as temporary prisons. It wasn't a perfect solution, but it was unlikely that the prisoners would be able to do more than kill each other while they were trapped in the bubbles. The other platoons had to work on the captured starships and start moving them out into open space, while keeping a close eye on the engineers and crewmen the pirates had captured and put to work. No one knew for sure if they could be trusted or not.

The order to return to *Spider* was a relief; the entire platoon was thoroughly exhausted. Marines were trained to just keep going – one part of their training had involved an endless march, where the recruits had reached each waypoint only to be told that they had to walk another ten miles – but tiredness always dimmed their edge. Jasmine would have seriously considered calling in and requesting relief if there was any relief to be had. As it was, she knew that all of the Marines would be pushing their limits.

"Catch a shower and a change," Colonel Stalker ordered as they boarded the Q-ship. "All Marines are to report to the briefing compartment in thirty minutes."

"Something must have gone wrong," Blake commented, as they reached their quarters. Thankfully, there was no shortage of water on the Q-ship, even if they did have to share showers. "You think they know where the Admiral is?"

"No idea," Joe commented. "Just remember to bag up your shit for profit…"

"Oh, shut up," Blake said crossly. "Or I'll stuff it into your sleeping bag."

"Get washed, the pair of you," Jasmine snapped. The bickering was threatening to get out of hand. "We don't want to be late."

She stripped down and stepped into the shower, washing the sweat from her body, and then stepped back out of the shower. It had been a long time since she'd been bothered by the fact she was naked in front of her fellow Marines, something that wasn't going to change just because she'd been promoted. No one paid any attention as she got dressed, pulling on a clean set of BDUs. None of them wanted to be late for the briefing.

The sound of the ship's drives grew louder as they mustered outside the cabins and then headed down to the briefing compartment. *Spider* was moving, heading out of the asteroid and back into open space. It wouldn't be the first time they'd turned around and headed elsewhere because they'd stumbled across some vitally important piece of intelligence that had to be exploited quickly, but she had a feeling that this was something more important than knowing where the Admiral would be in a few hours. Besides, they would normally have spent days working their way through Haven, vacuuming up every scrap of usable intelligence. And instead they were practically deserting the asteroid!

A hologram floated in the middle of the compartment, showing a small flotilla of starships accompanying *Spider* and *Dancing Fool*. Jasmine had heard that Fourth Platoon had managed to capture a number of ships, but it hadn't been quite real until she'd seen the display. Nine heavy freighters, one converted escort ship and a pair of corvettes…they'd give the Marines some additional firepower to protect Avalon, as well as the other worlds in the sector. And, whatever else happened, taking them from the Admiral weakened his forces significantly.

"Stand at ease," Command Sergeant Patterson ordered. She nodded to the display. "As you can see, we picked up a number of working starships on Haven."

"Good for us," Rifleman Singh of Fourth Platoon said, just loudly enough to be heard by everyone in the compartment. "We kicked ass."

"Up yours," Blake said. "We captured the base."

Colonel Stalker cleared his throat loudly and silence fell. "Unfortunately, we also managed to pick up some intelligence on the Admiral's next planned move," he said. "He intends to move on Avalon with a quite considerable force."

Jasmine winced, inwardly. They'd all known that the Admiral would realise sooner or later that his grand plan to capture Avalon had failed spectacularly, but they'd hoped that they were operating within his decision loop. If they'd managed to take Haven *before* the Admiral had realised that his ship had failed, they might have succeeded in keeping him off-balance until it was too late. Instead, it looked as though Avalon was still in terrible danger.

"We don't have a complete breakdown of his fleet," Patterson said, softly. "We believe that it consists of one heavy cruiser and a handful of light escorts – and at least five heavy transport ships, carrying a large army of mercenaries. The figures we have been given suggest upwards of twenty thousand mercenaries have been recruited by the Admiral, although we have no idea how many of them are actually experienced soldiers."

"It does seem a large figure," Jasmine said, without thinking. "*Twenty thousand?*"

"It does indeed," Colonel Stalker agreed dryly.

Jasmine flushed, and then pushed the reaction aside. Offhand, she couldn't recall ever hearing of a mercenary unit larger than two or three battalions, roughly three thousand men. Supporting a larger force was difficult without the infrastructure the Marines or the Imperial Army had built up over the centuries, with fleets of heavy transports and combat support arms, something that few mercenary forces could operate. Hell, even the Civil Guard had problems when it was ordered to send regiments from one world to another.

Coming to think of it, were there even twenty thousand mercenaries in the *sector*? There was no shortage of work for mercenaries along the Rim, but still…twenty thousand seemed very large. But even if most of them were new recruits from colonies that had been brought into the Admiral's pocket empire, they'd be enough to give Avalon's defenders a very hard fight. Assuming the Admiral could support them, of course. He probably assumed that he could make Avalon support the troops.

She scowled at the thought. With the bandits effectively destroyed and the Crackers part of the government, Avalon had been enjoying a boom in food production. The planet probably *could* support an additional twenty thousand uninvited guests, at least for a while. And resistance would be very difficult if the Admiral commanded the high orbitals.

"That gives us a major problem," Colonel Stalker said. "We have to head back to Avalon – now – and pray that we beat the Admiral there. He will almost certainly guess where we came from and he'll need a major victory, unless he wants to admit that his dreams of building an empire are doomed. And if that happens, one of his subordinates will probably stick a knife in his back. If he takes the cloudscoop intact, he can still make his play for empire."

He looked around the compartment, his gaze moving from Marine to Marine. "We are going into battle against very long odds," he added. "But it is a battle we have to win. If we fail, this sector will become overrun with barbarism. We must not fail. We *will not fail*."

His voice hardened. "It will take twelve days to reach Avalon from here," he said. "Once we're in Phase Space, get some rest; we'll start preparing combat scenarios tomorrow. Dismissed!"

Jasmine turned to go, only to be stopped by a hand falling on her shoulder. "Stay here a moment," Colonel Stalker ordered. "We need to chat."

The remainder of the Marines filed out, no doubt wondering if Jasmine was being held back so the Colonel could yell at her in private.

One advantage of being promoted, Jasmine had been told during the private lessons she'd received from the other lieutenants, was that you were never dressed down in front of the lower ranks. Apparently, it was considered bad for discipline to see one's seniors in trouble. On the other hand, lieutenants didn't get to wash away mistakes with several hundred press-ups or a few nights of KP.

"Sit down," the Colonel ordered, as the hatch closed behind the final Marine. "Michael Volpe gave us some news that you will want to hear."

Jasmine felt her heart jump before he confirmed her thoughts. "Mandy seems to be still alive," he said, softly. "But she's on one of the pirate ships."

"Shit," Jasmine said. Relief warred with fear in her heart. Relief that Mandy was alive – and that she wasn't in trouble; fear for the girl's future. Mandy was young and beautiful. Being trapped on a pirate ship must have seemed an early exposure to hell. "Sir, can we save her?"

"I don't know," Colonel Stalker admitted. "We're in enough trouble without planning a rescue mission as well. I don't think that the Admiral will surrender as easily as his asteroid crew. And she might be… *contaminated*."

Jasmine grimaced. Mandy would have spent nearly two months on the pirate vessel, living alongside the pirate crewmen. Stockholm Syndrome was a very real possibility, particularly if she had had to work with some of the pirates to protect herself from the rest. Jasmine could just imagine a senior pirate offering Mandy protection in exchange for sex, or whatever other services a perverted pirate could want. Pirates never seemed to want anything wholesome…

The thought nagged at her mind. If they recovered Mandy, what sort of person would she have become?

It doesn't matter, part of her mind insisted. *She'd be alive.*

But the rest of her mind wondered if Mandy would be better off dead.

"You have to remember that civilians are never pushed to the limit," her Drill Instructor had told them, after yet another gruelling eight-hour march. "You are drilled endlessly here to toughen you both physically and mentally. Civilians do not have that training and most of them couldn't hack it if they did. Their minds can be broken under sudden intense stress."

The rest of the lecture had been chilling. Why did men and women stay in abusive relationships? Or serve under dictators who'd execute them for saying the wrong thing at the wrong time? Or accept direction from religious leaders who didn't believe in God?

"Their minds are warped – rather, they warp themselves – to make their treatment bearable," her Drill Instructor had said flatly. "A person can become used to anything, even repeated rape and abuse, if it becomes the new normal. This is part of the human condition, but it must be beaten out of you. Marines must never snap under the pressure…"

Jasmine shivered as she took her leave. If they did recover Mandy, and she would hope for the best, what would her friend have become?

CHAPTER
FORTY-ONE

One major advantage of a standard military, even a standard civilisation, is that it can absorb defeat and keep going. To some extent, it can even recover from a crushing defeat, assuming it isn't broken up and annexed by the enemy. The pirate society, on the other hand, embodies the old saw about victory having a thousand fathers, but defeat being an orphan. Or, more practically, defeat being the sole responsibility of the person in charge.

Unsurprisingly, pirate commanders who face defeat – and survive the experience – have to fight to stay alive, let alone in command.

-Edward E. Smith, Professor of Sociology. *Pirates and their Lives.*

Mandy held her hands firmly at her side as the Admiral's guards pushed her – and a dozen other crewmen – into a large compartment. They hadn't told her why they'd grabbed her or the others; she'd wondered if the Admiral was making a pre-emptive strike on Travis' faction simply because she couldn't think of any other explanation. If they'd found the charges, which was a distant possibility, they would surely have grabbed her alone.

Unless they didn't know it was me, she thought, as she saw the Admiral waiting at one end of the compartment. He looked grim, she realised, as if something had gone badly wrong. Maybe the life support systems had started to fail after all...no, she would have heard of that through Vane or the other engineering crewmen. They'd certainly made her work hard to keep the life support systems in working order, even though the ship was crammed with additional bodies. The Admiral stepped forward and Mandy focused on him, wondering what he was about to say.

"Haven has been attacked," the Admiral said, each word heavy with menace. Mandy stared at him. Attacked? By whom? She'd racked her brains trying to think of a way to get a message out and she hadn't succeeded. Had Michael succeeded – or had the Admiral suffered a colossal stroke of bad luck? "The base was attacked by the Marine Corps."

A dull muttering ran through the compartment, many of the pirates looking fearful. Mandy could understand their feelings; the Marines were their natural enemy, the force that hunted them down and raided pirate bases. And yet, she didn't understand where the Marines had come from… no, she was being silly. They *had* to be Colonel Stalker's Marines, from Avalon. As far as she knew, there were no other Marines – or Imperial Navy starships – left in the sector. But how had they travelled from Avalon to Haven?

They captured the Admiral's starship, she thought, feeling a flash of brilliant amusement - and delight. Even *she* knew that boarding a starship wasn't easy; the pirates had to have screwed up by the numbers to allow the Marines to board. *No wonder the bloody ship was overdue!*

"This may seem like a disaster," the Admiral said, when the muttering died away. "Many of you will wonder if we should run for our lives, fleeing to another sector where there are no Marines. But this is far from the end. We are building a new empire out here and a single defeat will not stop us.

"We planned to invade Avalon," he added. "We are still going there, in force. The planet will fall to us and the Marines will be destroyed with overwhelming firepower. They are tough, and very capable, but we have more starships than they can possibly have. We will smash their defences, land on their planet and occupy it, along with their cloudscoop. Those who refuse to serve will be exterminated."

There was a coldness running through his voice that sent shivers down Mandy's spine. The Admiral was completely ruthless, willing to do whatever it took to establish his empire. If he was prepared to work with pirates – who looted, raped and burned their way access entire sectors – he was prepared to destroy entire planets if they tried to resist him. Avalon might have the Marines, but otherwise its defences were critically weak. Mandy couldn't see *how* the Marines could beat the small flotilla the Admiral had assembled.

But they do have an ally, she told herself, firmly. *Me.*

"But there is another matter I wish to bring to your attention," the Admiral said. "Commander Gaston was a trusted member of my council. He was given rewards – money, girls, power – in exchange for his loyal services. But after the news of Haven's fall reached him, he decided that he was best served by launching a coup against me, a coup that failed spectacularly. I have eyes and ears everywhere and I knew about his plan before he could even command his people to start moving."

He tapped his wristcom and a hatch opened, revealing a handful of guards and prisoners. Mandy barely knew Commander Gaston – he was one of Travis' rivals, she knew – but she didn't recognise the broken bloody mass pushed forward by the guards. They'd worked him over savagely, she realised, breaking bones and cutting his skin merely to create an awful object lesson. The rest of his faction didn't seem to have been treated any better. They looked as though they would fall apart the moment the guards let go of them.

"I am in command of this ship," the Admiral said. "I am in command of this fleet. The empire I am building is *mine*. None of you know enough to take it over, even if you could unseat me. The best that would happen is that you would gain control of a handful of starships while the rest of the empire falls into rubble. You would be in command, but you would have less than you had while serving under me."

There was a long chilling pause. Mandy understood what he was trying to tell them, all right; they *needed* him if they wanted to be part of a new empire, with power that no normal pirate commander could hope to hold. The Admiral – and his mysterious backers – knew how the empire worked, knew the location of all of the bases, knew which planets were firmly under control and which ones should be allowed a degree of independence…anyone else would effectively have to start again from scratch.

But maybe that wasn't what the pirates wanted. Travis had spoken of wanting independence, of wanting a command of his own. The Empire gave its Captains vast latitude, but even they had been bound by a framework of laws and regulations. Pirates, on the other hand, were truly free; they could do whatever they liked regardless of law and morality. And many of the black colonies along the Rim had been settled by people who wanted to be independent of the Empire and its laws.

The Admiral picked up Gaston by the neck and held him, before squeezing hard. Blood spurted out of his body as his neck was crushed, splattering on the deck just before the Admiral let go of his body. It fell to the deck and lay there, unmoving. No one could have survived that, Mandy decided, at least without immediate medical attention. Gaston wasn't going to get anything of the sort. The Admiral had killed him, after he'd been tortured, to make a point to his remaining officers and crew. Attempting to overthrow him would be very dangerous.

"*That*," the Admiral hissed, "is what will happen to all those who try to overthrow me."

Mandy felt her legs weakening and fought hard to hold herself together as the Admiral wiped the blood from his hand. She'd thought herself used to horror, but watching a man's neck get crushed – and ripped open – was something new. The Admiral had to be enhanced in some way, she guessed, just like the Marines. She didn't think that any normal man could have crushed a neck so completely. Or maybe they could. Michael had once told her that there was a Civil Guardsman so strong that he could pick up a LAV with his bare hands. She pushed the thought aside as the guards started to order them all out of the compartment. No doubt the Admiral intended to execute the rest of the prisoners in front of other crewmen.

There was no time to go back to her cabin and collapse. Vane had kept her working hard, along with the rest of the engineering crew, something that would be all the more important now that the Admiral was taking *Sword* into battle. Mandy was privately worried that one of the engineers would stumble across the hidden charges, even though she'd worked hard to ensure that they were concealed from all but the most thorough inspection. Their hiding places shouldn't need further repair work – she'd done a good job at fixing any decay after placing the charges in position – yet Vane was monomaniacal on getting the ship ready for battle. He must have heard about what had happened to Haven long before the rest of the crew.

After working on engineering tasks for an hour, she found herself press-ganged into helping prepare the missile tubes for immediate use. The Admiral had ordered that the starship's weapons be kept in good condition, regardless of what happened to the rest of the ship, but Vane wanted to swap out a number of components to ensure that there were no problems when *Sword* went into battle. Mandy had never quite realised how large shipkiller missiles were until she'd actually seen one in the tubes – even the smallest were twenty metres long – and moving them through the ship was difficult, even with mobile tractors to help. She spent some time inspecting the warheads and wondering if she could convince one to detonate inside the ship, but it still seemed futile. The pirates might skimp on safety everywhere else, yet they took good care of their warheads.

"Twelve days to Avalon," Vane informed her, when she finally reported back to engineering. There was no point in trying to delay. Pirates who slacked off were treated to a dose of the neural whip by their superiors – and she knew that Vane would have no hesitation in whipping her if he felt that she was underperforming. "We want the ship to be ready for anything by then."

The hours seemed to blur together as she worked on the ship's interior. By the time Vane sent her and a handful of others off to eat, she felt too exhausted to do anything other than collapse back into her bunk and go to sleep. But she had to eat; the dining compartment was crammed with mercenaries, all pushing and shoving at each other and the pirate crew. Their commanders were running from group to group, breaking up fights with a savage venom, snapping at their men when they refused to listen for more than a few seconds. Mandy couldn't help but be reminded of the food fights they'd had at the technical college, back when she'd been far more innocent of how the universe worked. And yet the mercenaries and the pirates were armed to the teeth. She snatched up a plate of gruel, a handful of ration bars and a bottle of juice before fleeing back to her cabin. Just after she left the compartment, she heard the sounds of fighting as the men finally snapped.

There was no rule against having food in her cabin, at least not on the pirate ship. Part of the reason the pirates had such unhealthy ships was because they ate and crapped everywhere, even though it risked their lives as well as damaging the ship itself. But most pirates had at least a limited amount of genetic engineering spliced into their bodies, giving them the enhanced immune systems that helped humanity to settle any number of colony worlds. It was rare to encounter a disease that could spread from a new colony world's biosphere into humanity, but it had happened – and some of those events had been disastrous. These days, the Empire ensured that all colonists were given at least some enhancements to make it harder for them to catch a disease.

But that is going to change, she told herself, as she ate her meal. The Empire was breaking down; the services it had provided, good or bad, would no longer be available to the human race. It seemed absurd to imagine disease ravaging the sector in the wake of the Empire's departure, but it was a possibility. Somehow, she doubted that the Admiral's empire would be interested in providing the same services. Attempting to provide vast social services to its inhabitants – at least those on the Core Worlds – had been a major contributing factor to the Empire's decline.

Once she'd finished the food, she picked up the communicator she'd taken from Travis and hooked it to her terminal. She'd told the XO that the remainder of the communicators had been broken beyond repair, only useful for being cannibalised for spare parts, but one of them was still in full working order. Travis might not have told her the encryption code he was using to speak to his faction, yet she'd managed to piggyback her communicator onto the rest. She would be able to identify everyone carrying one of his communicators, as well as monitoring his signals and determining the panic signal. Unsurprisingly, after the Admiral had made such a horrific example of Gaston, Travis had set a panic signal for his faction. If sent, they were to drop everything and mutiny against the Admiral.

Mandy made a careful note of the signal on her terminal and then checked that the detonation signal was ready to be sent. Part of her was tempted to send the signal now, ensuring that *Sword* would be lost forever in interstellar space, but she didn't quite dare. Her plan for escaping the ship was dangerous – and it would only be workable once she was in the Avalon System. Otherwise, she might as well sit back and wait for the Admiral's crew to rape her to death before they ran out of supplies and died themselves.

Glancing at her bunk, she sighed out loud before picking herself up and heading for the hatch. Dinner break was almost over and she'd been told to go straight back to engineering, rather than catch some sleep. Vane was handing out very limited stimulants for his crew, but Mandy had already decided to refuse them. Stimulants gave the user a burst of energy; they also tended to make the user overconfident and inclined to boast. The last thing she needed was to confidently discourse on her the entire plan to her shocked co-workers…

Outside, the Admiral's guards seemed to have restored order in the dining compartment. A long line of mercenaries and pirate crewmen were outside in the passageway, kneeling with their hands on their heads. A number looked beaten, suggesting that the Admiral's guards had been quite savage with them when they'd refused to stop fighting. Judging from the angry discussion between a number of mercenary commanders, the guards might have overstepped their bounds. Mandy found herself wondering if the tension would lead to outright civil war on *Sword* as she walked past the mercenaries, feeling their eyes boring into the back of her head. They'd been given the use of the ship's sex slaves, but there just weren't enough of them to keep the mercenaries occupied.

Vane met her as she entered engineering. "Do you know anything about powered combat armour?"

"Nothing," Mandy said, not entirely truthfully. She knew quite a bit from Jasmine about how the suits were used, but she had never been taught how to maintain them. In theory, the Marines were meant to do their own maintenance. "I do know how to maintain a spacesuit."

"There are suits that need to be fixed," Vane informed her. He sounded pissed; his crew were meant to be maintaining the ship, not helping the mercenaries ready themselves for battle. "Apparently, they were meant to be sent to Haven for repair before the asteroid was attacked. The Admiral is not happy."

Mandy wasn't surprised. Organising any sort of large-scale military operation, according to Jasmine, was a great deal harder than it looked… and the Marines normally didn't have to worry about losing their bases while they planned their operations. No doubt the mercenary commander had planned on using Haven's facilities, only to see that base captured or destroyed by the Marines. Maybe they'd rescued Michael…she found herself hoping that they'd saved his life. And Michael could have told them where the Admiral was going with his fleet.

"I can do my best," she offered. She *had* to show eagerness; she *had* to pretend to be a willing part of the crew. But how long would it be before the facade became reality? "If they're as simple as spacesuits…"

"They're not," Vane said, tartly. He paused, considering. "Go relieve Abdul; Abdul has experience with combat suits. I didn't want to pull him away from the sensor nodes, but the mercenaries need their suits ASAP."

His gaze suddenly narrowed and focused on her eyes. "And I want you to tell your patron that you'll be needed here when the fighting begins," he added. "This ship will take damage and most of the crew will be absolutely useless when it comes to damage control. You will be needed here."

"Yes, sir," Mandy said. *That*, at least, was a relief. She'd been worried that Travis would make her serve on the bridge when *Sword* entered the Avalon system and opened fire. But Vane was right; there were more tactical officers than engineers. "Shouldn't we be telling them what to do?"

Vane eyed her, crossly. "What sort of stupid idea is that?"

Mandy nodded and headed out of the compartment, as quickly as she could. It had been a mistake, one that might nag at Vane until he checked on her work; the pirates *never* shared information with anyone who didn't really need it. Knowledge was power – and that worked for engineering knowledge as well as anything else.

Twelve days to Avalon, she thought, grimly. *Am I really going to last that long?*

CHAPTER
FORTY-TWO

It is astonishing how much the prospect of hanging concentrates a person's mind. Unfortunately, as a long-forgotten philosopher noted, it tends to concentrate a person's mind on the fact that it is in a body which is going to be hanged. That, in many ways, sums up the attitude of the Avalon Council to the news that their planet was about to be attacked a second time...

...However, being made of tougher stuff than the last Council, they didn't seriously consider the possibility of surrender. Instead, they prepared to fight.

- Professor Leo Caesius, *The Perilous Dawn* (unpublished).

"We could do with a bigger fleet," Gaby observed. "You couldn't capture a battleship or two, could you?"

Edward had to smile. "A battleship squadron would be quite beyond our ability to support," he pointed out dryly. "And besides, the Imperial Navy is always nervous about scratching the paint on their beloved capital ships. It's cruisers and destroyers that do most of the real work in the Empire."

He sat back, silently grateful that he'd had a chance to rest while *Spider*, *Dancing Fool* and the other captured starships had made their way back to Avalon. And that he was speaking to Gaby alone, as the remainder of the Council had dispersed over Avalon, along with much of the city's population. They'd get a full report on the meeting, but so far they hadn't decided – unlike the Grand Senate – that the most important task for the military was giving the politicians endless briefings.

"And no hope of getting any of those too, unless we build them for ourselves," Gaby observed. "What made the Empire so damn determined to abandon us?"

Edward shook his head, tiredly. In the end, the reasons behind the Empire's withdrawal hardly mattered. All that mattered was saving Avalon, protecting her population and eventually building up a new polity that could protect the entire sector. They had delegates from Elysium and Crawford on Avalon now, talking to the Council and trying to prepare a framework for something that might take the place of the Empire, at least until the Empire returned to the Rim. But if they failed to defeat the Admiral, it would become completely moot. The Admiral would establish his own order and…

…And then what?

Revolution wasn't easy; the Crackers had held most of the advantages in their war, at least before the Marines had arrived, and they hadn't been able to defeat the Civil Guard. But if they had succeeded, what would have happened? Edward had seen revolutionary movements that had managed to establish reasonably good governance, but they were in the minority. It was far more likely that the rebels would fragment, turn on each other and eventually fall into dictatorship. The Empire had a habit of falling back, allowing the new government's internal dynamic to rip it apart, and then return in force, once the population had realised why they needed the Empire. What would happen if the Admiral secured his rule over the entire sector?

It was possible that the Admiral would throw himself into decadence and allow the new empire to decay far more rapidly than *the* Empire, or perhaps he would turn into a strong leader, making the starships run on time. But historical cases where rebels proved to be good at rebuilding were very rare. Building a strong and permanent edifice required some degree of cooperation from the population, and gaining active cooperation required not holding them down too savagely. It often required some degree of power-sharing. Could the Admiral do that?

"They couldn't afford it any longer," he said, returning to the original question. The cost of patrolling the Rim and maintaining squadrons of starships and naval bases had been immense, although nowhere near as high as the costs of maintaining the Empire's fraying social security network. "They decided to cut their losses and withdraw from the Rim."

He smiled, rather thinly. "Without it, you wouldn't be here," he reminded her. "Be grateful."

"And neither would the Admiral," Gaby countered. "Who could be backing him?"

Edward had given the matter some thought, but he'd had to reluctantly concede that there were too many suspects. There were black colonies out past the Rim who would want to prevent the growth of any new power in the wake of the Empire's departure; they'd certainly have a motive for backing the Admiral. And then there were factions further into the Empire who might want to use the Admiral as a cat's paw. And then there were Grand Senators who might want to prevent the rise of a new multi-system power along the Rim.

It seemed paranoid, but Edward had seen at first-hand just how the Grand Senate put its own interests ahead of the Empire's general wellbeing. They had refused to pay for the military force needed to keep order, while trying to hamper the growth of independent planetary self-defence forces that might have been able to fill the gap. And they'd allowed the Civil Guard to become a corrupt organisation, riddled with patronage, that preyed on the population it was meant to be defending. Who knew what else they might do, just to keep all power firmly concentrated in their hands?

"We may never know, unless we take him alive and convince him to talk," Edward admitted. "But that might prove tricky."

"I know," Gaby said. "Are you sure you can hold the system?"

Edward shook his head. The Admiral would have a very definite advantage in firepower, unless he held off for several months – and Edward rather doubted that they would get that lucky. Kitty Stevenson and a handful of others with naval experience had put together a plan for defending the system, but she'd warned that it was too complex for its own good. Most naval operations consisted of finding a target the enemy had to defend and charging right at it, forcing the enemy to engage on unfavourable terms. If the Admiral just charged at Avalon, they were going to be in some trouble.

"But we won't surrender," Gaby said, flatly. "The Council is determined on that, whatever else happens. So are the RockRats."

She looked up at him. "How long do we have?"

"Unknown," Edward admitted. "There's no way to know until he drops out of Phase Space."

According to the interrogations, the Admiral had been assembling his fleet a handful of light years from Haven when Edward's Marines had attacked the asteroid. Assuming that word had gone out the moment the Marines had revealed themselves – the worst possible case – the Admiral could be within hours of Avalon now. Edward had even worried that the Admiral would *beat* them to Avalon, although that had seemed unlikely. The heavy transports he'd brought to haul his mercenaries couldn't travel as fast as his warships.

But the thought had haunted him until they'd returned to discover that Avalon was still independent.

Gaby smiled. "So we can only wait," she said. She looked up at him and her smile grew wider. "Would you care to join me for dinner?"

Edward blinked. "I have too much to do," he admitted, reluctantly. He *had* to be back in orbit when the Admiral arrived. This time, he was *not* going to be in the rear, issuing commands from a safe distance. "But after the battle, why not?"

Gaby's smile grew wider. "Why not indeed?"

"We've been rigging up the captured ships with missile pods," Kitty Stevenson reported, two hours later. Every engineer in the system – and everyone else with even the slightest piece of experience in space operations – had been working frantically since the first reports of the oncoming storm had arrived. "We've also been scattering them in orbit around Avalon, tied into the command network. It should give the Admiral a nasty surprise."

Edward nodded. Military starships rarely used missile pods; towing them dampened the ship's acceleration to the point where their presence was obvious to even the most dim-witted enemy sensor officer. But with the transports, such considerations were hardly important. There was no way they could match the Admiral's speed if he decided to go for a long-range missile duel. They'd just have to place themselves between the Admiral and his target.

"The RockRats have been preparing their transports for war too," Kitty added. "They're damn near impossible to detect except at very close range, but they're far too slow. If the Admiral doesn't react as we hope, they're going to be out of place. We're actually planning to deploy some of them from the freighters, using them as makeshift carriers. It might help us to land a few more blows."

She scowled, looking down at her display. "We've run the simulations," she admitted. "It depends on the assumptions we put into the simulation matrix, but the good guys lose more often than they win. If we had any hope of reinforcements, I'd tell you to retreat now and come back with a few battleships."

"It won't happen," Edward said. "What about the cloudscoop?"

Kitty made a face, as if she'd bitten into something sour. "Our best guess is that the Admiral will go for Avalon first," she said. "He'll detect our little fleet as soon as he arrives; he can't risk leaving us in his rear. Besides, if he can force the planet to surrender, he'd get the command codes for the cloudscoop and ensure that we remove the nukes. And there'd be less chance of accidentally destroying something he desperately needs."

"Yeah," Edward said. "But we cannot allow him to take it intact."

Without the cloudscoop, the Admiral would have real problems keeping what remained of his empire operational. Presumably he could make up the shortfall through cloud-skimming, yet it wouldn't really be enough to allow expansion. Edward hadn't discussed it with Gaby, or anyone else, but he'd already determined to destroy the cloudscoop rather than risk allowing it to fall into the Admiral's hands. It would be his final service to the Empire.

The Admiral would be furious, he knew. It was quite possible that he'd take it out on Avalon, bombarding the planet from orbit or landing his troops – even though Avalon's population was armed to the teeth.

And yet there was no choice, not really. Allowing the Admiral and his backers to build their own empire could only lead to a new threat pressing against the Empire's borders. Edward had made life-or-death decisions before, but this was different. He'd come to love Avalon in the months since the Cracker War had come to an end. Everything they'd built would be lost if the Admiral took his rage and frustration out on the planet.

There's no choice, he told himself, and hoped that he was right. *There's no choice at all.*

"Our command datanet is weak," Kitty admitted. "Given time, we could probably put together a proper network, but we don't have time. We really need a year or two, Colonel."

"I know," Edward said. Given a year, Avalon could start producing her own destroyers, perhaps even light cruisers. Without the Empire's carefully-regulated plans for industrial development getting in the way, Avalon could advance by leaps and bounds – assuming, of course, that they survived the coming war. "But we don't have a year."

"We're having to route everything through the *Dancing Fool*," Kitty admitted. "If they have a skilled tactical officer on the other side, he's likely to realise it even though we have been preparing all sorts of deceptions to hide the truth. And once they blow away the light cruiser, the rest of the flotilla will be broken into independent units."

She looked up at him. "We could take out the transports in our first strike," she offered. "If he lost all of his mercenaries…"

Edward shook his head. "He'd either bombard the planet or retreat until he can recruit more," he said. The Admiral wouldn't have any real problems rounding up more unskilled manpower. According to the interrogations, the Admiral had ten other colony worlds under his control, all forced to pay homage to his empire. He'd be short of trained leaders, but somehow Edward doubted that would bother him. "Besides, I'd like to take the mercenaries alive, if possible."

Kitty smiled. "More labourers for the work camps?"

"Perhaps," Edward said. He didn't trust mercenaries, if only because their only real loyalties were to their pay-checks, but they could come in handy. It depended on just what units the Admiral had pulled into his service. "Not that it really matters right now. We have to stop the Admiral or lose everything."

"I was told not to approach the Professor," Jasmine said as she inspected her armoured combat suit. "Did you get similar orders?"

"You're actually a family friend," Lieutenant Faulkner pointed out. "But seriously – do you think the Colonel had a choice?"

Jasmine considered it. Part of her knew what the Professor had to be going through ever since he'd heard that his daughter was missing, presumed dead. Telling him that Mandy was alive would make him feel better, but it would be a cruel joke if Mandy died in the coming battle for Avalon. Or if she'd contaminated herself so far that she had to face the full weight of Imperial law, rather than being considered an innocent victim who had been kidnapped and press-ganged into service. It might be better if the Professor never realised that Mandy had survived the attack on the RockRat transport that had started the new conflict.

But it just didn't feel *right*.

"I don't know," she admitted. "Does OCS teach you to make decisions like that?"

"I think it's a function of being the sole authority for hundreds of light years," Faulkner said after a long moment. "Back on Earth, the problem would be handed over to the local authorities and we wouldn't have to worry about it. The Corps wouldn't be responsible for informing the civilians of anything. But here…there's too many different problems for the Colonel to handle. And he's on his own."

Jasmine understood. The Marine Corps was trained to delegate responsibility as much as possible; a Captain would command a company, but expect his Lieutenants to command the platoons. As always, the person on the spot knew more about what was going on than the person at the rear – although, to be fair, most Captains led their men into battle. But then, operations that involved more than a couple of Marine companies were commanded by a Colonel or a Major. And there would be a specific staff to work with the civilians, should it be necessary.

"I see," she said, finally. "But I don't like it."

She ran a testing diagnostic through the suit and relaxed when it returned a long string of green lights. Marine combat suits were tough, designed to keep going even when damaged, but they'd been taught always to keep them in prime condition. There were enough horror stories about what happened when suits were left unchecked for too long to keep their minds focused on maintaining the suits. Or, for that matter, what happened when a damaged spacesuit was left in the rack for an unwary person to wear as they went outside the ship's hull. Space was utterly unforgiving of mistakes, even more so than the battlefield.

In their *copious* spare time at the Slaughterhouse, the Marines had been expected to read. Many of the books had been manuals and memoirs written by various Marines, but a handful had been stories that illustrated the points the Drill Instructors were trying to hammer into their heads. One of them – banned elsewhere in the Empire, for reasons Jasmine had never understood – starred a young girl who had stowed away on a spacecraft heading for a colony world, trying to visit her brother. But she hadn't known that the spacecraft was carrying a desperately needed vaccine for the colony, or that her presence would mean that the spacecraft would never make its destination unless the pilot put her out into space. There had been no choice, according to the writer – and the physical laws of the universe. The girl hadn't meant to cause a problem and she certainly hadn't been *evil*, but she had had to die for the sake of everyone else.

Afterwards, the Instructor had summed up the moral of the story for the recruits. "Stupid people die in space," he'd said. "Check everything. Check everything *twice*."

"That's life," Faulkner said, as he opened his suit to remove a power cell. "You are not expected to like every order you're given. But you *are* expected to understand the reasoning behind it as well as carrying it out."

He gave her a droll smile. "If it's any consolation, everyone goes through the same period of self-doubt," he added. "Just hope that Mandy will return to her father, largely unscathed by her experience. And if that isn't possible, hope that she dies quickly rather than facing trial for her deeds as a pirate."

Jasmine gave him a sharp look. "*That* isn't very reassuring," she pointed out. "What happens if she does have to face trial?"

"I was on Skaro when the local commander decided to be reassuring to the Civil Guard," Faulkner said. "He told them that the enemy rebels only numbered a couple of hundred idiots with nothing more dangerous than bolt-action rifles. They went into battle with great enthusiasm, only to discover that there were over a *thousand* rebels, armed with modern weaponry. They had their asses kicked by the enemy position and we had to go in and clean up the mess."

He smiled as he picked up a sonic screwdriver. "You're not in this business to be reassuring," he said, dryly. "If that's what you want, you might as well listen to the news broadcasts from Earth. They're *designed* to be reassuring."

"And lie through their teeth," Jasmine said. After Han, she'd looked at what the population of Earth had been told about the savage fighting. They'd been told that it was nothing more than a mere brushfire, with only a handful of deaths. "I take your point."

"Good," Faulkner said. "Back to work, I'm afraid. I don't know how much time we have left."

CHAPTER FORTY-THREE

> The ultimate objective of an attacking force is to slip into attack range undetected. This is easier than it may seem; unless the system has a whole network of satellites assembled along the Phase Limit, it is quite easy to miss a starship – or an entire fleet – dropping out of Phase Space. And once their arrival has gone undetected, they can slip into the system, confident that they won't be spotted until it is too late.
>
> -Admiral Darrin Webster, *Basic Naval Tactics (34th Edition).*

Mandy jerked awake as the klaxon echoed through the entire ship, feeling oddly disoriented. Vane had ordered his entire staff to get at least twelve hours of rest before they entered the Avalon system, only to catch Mandy a moment later and order her to his bed. She had wanted to refuse – the last thing she wanted was Vane pawing at her – but she hadn't really had a choice. Who knew what would have happened if she'd refused?

She pulled herself out of his bed and started to dress, grimly aware that he was watching her as she donned the basic underwear she'd been given by the pirate quartermaster. They should have at least an hour before the ship crossed the Phase Limit and entered the Avalon System; thankfully, Vane didn't seem like some of her former boyfriends, who would have had a specific use for that time in mind. Instead, he sat up and swung his legs out onto the deck himself, waddling naked towards the washroom. Mandy took advantage of his absence to finish pulling on her shipsuit, check the communicator and terminal, and exit through the hatch, heading for the dining compartment. They'd been cautioned to be sure they ate something before they arrived at Avalon.

The sense of heady excitement was spreading through the ship as the pirates gathered in the dining compartment, where stewards were handing out ration bars – and chocolate, stored in a stasis pod for this very moment. Mandy took two of the chocolate bars for herself, along with five standard ration bars. They might taste awful, but the pirate commanders were right; they *did* need to eat while they were engaging Avalon's defenders. A battle in space could take hours before one side emerged as the clear winner. And it would take hours before they even entered firing range.

Leaving the dining compartment, still nibbling on one of the ration bars, she strolled back down to engineering, where the rest of the crew were gathering. Vane had promised to hand out assignments at the last moment, if only because he'd been rotating his crewmen too hard over the last few days and he wanted a chance to see who would be best placed where. So far, no one seemed to have discovered the charges, but Mandy couldn't help feeling nervous. There was too much that could go wrong...

"I want one third of you to remain here," Vane ordered. "We can expect them to be trying to take out our drives, stranding us in the Avalon System. If the drive system comes under attack, we may need to repair it in a hurry." He tapped the display and rotated it so that they could see. "The next group will be stationed near the weapons systems. If something goes wrong there, we will have to repair it as quickly as possible. Everyone else will be scattered throughout the hull, ready to intervene at crucial points. Keep your communicators with you at all times; if there is a crisis, I expect you to respond to it at once."

His eyes narrowed. "I also want you to ensure that you have full safety gear with you at all times," he added. "You know exactly how reliable the internal airlocks are – and besides, you might have to work in the vacuum. Do you understand me?"

There was no disagreement, so he started parcelling out the engineers. Mandy had hoped that she would be assigned to one of the rotating groups, but instead she was ordered to remain in engineering with Vane and a dozen others. She couldn't tell if Vane was trying to do her a favour – engineering was one of the best-protected parts of the ship – or if he merely wanted her with him. So far, he hadn't pulled her away from her duties for a quick and unwelcome fuck, but there was always a first time. But instead, she told herself as she picked up the safety gear, being in engineering would make it easier for her to monitor the progress of the battle.

Unsurprisingly, Vane started running them through damage control drills as soon as the others had dispersed to their combat stations. Mandy had never had to do damage control work in practice, but the basic idea was comparable to what she'd already been doing; removing damaged components and replacing them as quickly as possible. This time, however, the damage might be more serious and not limited to a single section. *Sword* was heavily armoured, but a single bomb-pumped laser would burn through the hull and wreak havoc inside the ship. The internal armour wasn't anything like as strong as the exterior hullmetal.

"This should be fun," Gary said. Mandy glanced over at him, wondering why Vane tolerated the young man. He'd apparently joined up because he wanted to get away from a pointless life on a pointless colony world, or so he'd told her while trying to lure her into bed. Mandy had refused and he'd seemed to accept it, for the moment. It made him better than the vast majority of the pirate crews. "I've never gone into battle before."

Mandy winced, remembering the people she'd killed. Gary hadn't done anything like that; he was just a new recruit. He didn't even know that it was Mandy's homeworld that they were about to attack. She swallowed the words that came to mind – there was no point in provoking a fight now – and looked over at the timer. They would return to normal space in fifteen minutes, right along the edge of the Phase Limit.

"You wanted excitement," Mandy said, finally. Gary would probably end up becoming a loyal little pirate, seduced by what looked like a wonderful lifestyle. "I hope you enjoy it."

"I'm sure I shall," Gary said, with a grin. "Hey, after this, do you want to celebrate with me? Some of the girls are happy to do it with other girls."

Mandy felt sick. Gary had been subjected to a concentrated seduction as soon as he joined the crew. When he wasn't working, he could play games or spend time with the best of the sex slaves, the girls who were actually paid for their services. Life would be good for him and he didn't even have to get blood on his hands, not yet. When the time came, he'd probably do it willingly, without ever bothering to think of what it really meant. He'd slip into atrocities soon afterwards, becoming just the type of person the Admiral wanted. And he might even be less unstable than the average pirate. A replacement for those the Admiral could never hope to control permanently, perhaps.

"No, thank you," she said, tartly. Vane was quite bad enough – and besides, she'd never been attracted to other women, even though she'd been tempted to experiment while she'd been on Earth. It had been what just about everyone did there. "Besides, you really don't want to mess with the woman your superior is fucking."

The look on Gary's face suggested that he wanted to do just that. Mandy kept her own expression blank, wondering if he was insane – or too ignorant to understand the dangers involved in effectively cuckolding a senior pirate under his very nose. Even Travis, the XO, hadn't tried to seduce her, or take her away from Vane. Apart from Ha, who was of questionable sanity, no one else had tried to rape her since she'd started sleeping with Vane.

But one way or another, it was about to become moot.

She wondered, absently, what Travis was planning – if anything. Would he try to overthrow the Admiral before they engaged the Marines on Avalon, or was he keeping his head down, remembering what had happened to Gaston? There was no way to know, she told herself; she'd just have to remember her plan and stick with it. And pray to God that the pirates didn't realise what she was doing until it was too late.

Ravenna watched as the tiny drones impacted on the comet, slowly burrowing their way deep into the heart of the icy snowball. As she had expected, its interior was a loose collection of ice, dust and rocky particles, just right for the RockRat requirements. The comet would be slowly tipped into the inner system, where it would be mined for water and everything else the RockRats needed. No one who lived permanently on a planet could truly appreciate how easy it was to live in space.

Like most RockRats, Ravenna was a little agoraphobic, unable to tolerate the kind of population densities the dirty-feet on planets considered normal. She spent most of her life alone on her starship, part of a community and yet rarely touching other RockRats; she never talked to anyone else if it could be avoided. Alone, her ship had no difficulty in supporting her life for as long as necessary. After she died, the automated systems would send it back to the asteroid settlements, where another RockRat would take her place. Some RockRats destroyed their ships when they died, but Ravenna had always found that to be a crude custom. Just because one could no longer use one's properly didn't mean that *no one* could use it.

She scowled as the console started to bleep, indicating the presence of a starship dropping out of Phase Space. It was always a problem for her when starships arrived; their crews sometimes wanted to be friendly, particularly when they realised that she spent most of her time absolutely naked. Didn't they realise that no one became a comet-hunter through love for her fellow human beings? But at least they were preferable to the fools on Earth that objected to mining the asteroids, gas giants and comets. *They* were too stupid to realise that without off-world resources, Earth would be dead within a week.

The console bleeped again, indicating the presence of *nine* starships, one of them very definitely a heavy cruiser. Ravenna made a face, remembering the message she'd been sent a few months ago by the RockRats who lived in the inner system; *they* wanted her to keep an eye out for incoming starships. Part of her simply didn't care – what could dirty-feet affairs have to do with the RockRats – but the rest of her knew that she had a certain duty to her society. Reluctantly, she powered up the transmitter and started beaming a message towards the inner system, just before powering down the remainder of her ship. It was just possible that the newcomers would mistake her for a piece of asteroid debris drifting along the edge of the system.

They didn't seem interested in scanning for potential threats, she decided, a moment later. Instead of trying to hide, they powered up their drives and started to head into the inner system, faster than Ravenna's little spacecraft could hope to travel. But not fast enough to get there before her warning reached the RockRats. *They* could decide if they wanted to pass the alert to the dirty-feet or not. Shaking her head, Ravenna watched the ships go, noting that five of them were wallowing, almost certainly overloaded. The dirty-feet had so much and yet they wanted to steal more?

Idiots, she thought, dismissing them from her mind. Whatever war the dirty-feet were fighting was no concern of hers. One day, the RockRats told themselves, the dirty-feet would tear themselves apart, leaving the universe for those who were truly civilised. What was the point of fighting when there was enough in the universe for everyone?

Edward knew what it meant the moment his buzzer rang, waking him from a fitful sleep. "Report," he ordered, keying his wristcom. "What do we have?"

"A warning passed from one of the RockRats," Kitty reported. "Nine starships dropped out of Phase Space, heading into the inner system. One heavy cruiser, three destroyers and five overloaded transports. I think the Admiral is having problems with his staff."

Edward nodded in wry amusement. Unless they were designed for the military – and sometimes not even then – transports were slow lumbering targets that couldn't even shoot back. Standard practice in the Imperial Navy was to send the warships ahead to clear all resistance out of the way before the transports approached the planet, which had the added advantage that the transports could drop back into Phase Space if the fighting went badly and the Imperial Navy had to withdraw and wait for reinforcements. But if the Admiral had left the mercenaries at the edge of the system, they might be tempted to make a run for it. Instead, he was keeping them under his guns.

"That should slow him down," Edward said. There was no way that those transports would be able to match the speed of his heavy cruiser, let alone the destroyers. The Admiral would have to know that the defenders would have *hours* to prepare once he arrived in the system. And he didn't even seem to be trying to hide. "Pass the alert to the other units."

"Already done," Kitty said. "I told them not to come to full alert just yet. We'd only tire our people for nothing."

"Good thinking," Edward said. He'd met a few Imperial Navy officers who treated their crews – and the Marines – as just more pieces of interchangeable material. No military force, even the Marines, could remain permanently on alert. Their edge would wear away a long time before the enemy made its appearance. "Did the RockRats send anything else?"

"Apparently, they forwarded everything they received," Kitty said. She shrugged. "I don't think they'd lie about this."

Edward nodded. There were factions in the Imperial Navy that disliked and distrusted the RockRats, and part of the Grand Senate wanted to bring them firmly into the Empire. But it wasn't going to happen; the RockRats rarely fought, but they were very good at hiding. The entire Empire was infested with hidden settlements, ones that rarely bothered to have anything to do with the ones they called dirty-feet. It was easy to imagine the RockRats cheering the collapse of the Empire…

…But they also knew that the Admiral would be much less tolerant of their independence than the Empire. Or, for that matter, Avalon – and the planned association of worlds.

"Keep watching for them," he ordered. Now that the Admiral was heading in-system, it was difficult to track him until he reached the inner system. It wouldn't be too hard for him to alter course and come in at Avalon from an unexpected direction. "He might try something sneaky."

"Not with those transports," Kitty assured him. "Those bastards will be detectable light-hours from the planet."

"Unless he changes his mind," Edward said. He took his seat and studied the display, feeling time ticking by slowly. "On a direct course, how long do we have?"

"Seven hours," Kitty said. She tapped a switch, bringing up the projected course. "It cannot be taken for granted, Colonel."

"Of course not," Edward said. The Admiral could have changed course the moment he was well away from the RockRat ship, if he'd known he'd been detected. There was no way to know for sure. "Keep monitoring the stars."

Edward linked into the planetary communications network, watching as Avalon prepared for the attack. Thankfully, Camelot and most of the major cities had been nearly evacuated before the first starship had entered orbit and the population had been warned not to return. The handful who *had* been allowed to go home – mostly those working in the planet's growing complex of factories – were being evacuated now. Long before the Admiral arrived in orbit, the planet would have effectively gone dark.

He wouldn't have any trouble locating the cities through orbital observation, Edward knew, but destroying them would be pointless. Most of the equipment and facilities the Marines had built up over the months since their arrival had been concealed. The Admiral could devastate the planet – there was no way to stop him if he took out the defending fleet – but he would never be able to occupy it, unless he wanted a constant insurgency. There were far more weapons on the surface now than there had been during the Cracker War.

Edward felt an odd spurt of sympathy for the naval officers he'd known. Handling a battle in space was very different from handling one on the ground, or even a relatively complex operation like storming an asteroid. The enemy could come from anywhere – and, if he were careful enough, could sneak up on the defending fleet. Edward knew better than to assume that the Admiral didn't know anything about their location; it was difficult, almost impossible, to conceal *all* of their precautions. They could only hope that the sensor decoys would catch him by surprise.

A console started to chime. "Got them," Kitty announced. A set of red icons appeared on the display. "Two hours to contact, Colonel; they're holding a fairly standard convoy escort formation. And they could stop the transports if they tried to run too."

"Launch probes," Edward ordered. There was no point in trying to conceal the fact that they'd detected the enemy ships. He doubted the Admiral would be credulous enough to believe that he'd remained undetected. Anyone who'd sweated his way through Imperial Navy training simulations would probably know better. "And warn the planet. Whatever happens here will determine the future of this sector for a very long time."

He settled back in his seat and waited.

CHAPTER FORTY-FOUR

As a general rule, the bigger the starship, the lower the rate of acceleration and manoeuvrability it possesses. To compensate for this, heavier starships carry heavier armour, more missile launchers and plenty of point defence weapons. The sheer weight of armour on a battleship should not be underestimated; even without the gravity shields, it is capable of standing off a nuclear blast...

...Accordingly, standard tactics involve using heavier ships against heavier ships, with smaller vessels serving as light supports. When this balance isn't present, the results can be disastrous.

-Admiral Darrin Webster, *Basic Naval Tactics* (34th Edition).

Mandy took a moment to glance at the terminal, after checking that Gary was safely asleep. The long crawl towards Avalon had given them a chance to rest, even though she hadn't been able to actually *sleep*. Instead, she'd watched through the ship's sensors as *Sword* advanced on the planet – and the small flotilla assembling itself to block the cruiser's path. The Marines had clearly been busy...

"Attention all hands," the Admiral's voice said, echoing through the intercom. "We are about to engage the enemy. All hands, prepare for combat operations."

Mandy returned the terminal to her belt as Gary jerked awake, eyes flickering around as if he expected the enemy to materialise out of nowhere. From what he'd said, he didn't have any realistic ideas about what fighting would be actually like. Did he expect the Marines to *teleport* onboard *Sword*? Mandy half-wished they could, but even the Empire's science had never been able to produce a teleporter.

"This is it?" Gary asked. "We're about to fight?"

"Yes," Mandy said, tiredly. She'd studied *Sword's* specifications as well as helped to keep her in fighting trim; she *knew* what sort of firepower the ship carried. *Sword* might not be a battleship, but she carried more missiles than the entire defending fleet put together. The Marines and their allies were going to be heavily outgunned, unless Mandy's plan worked. "We're about to fight."

She looked over as Vane's head popped out of a hatch. "Stay here," he ordered, flatly. "And make sure you wear your goddamned spacesuits."

Gary scowled after the engineer as he vanished down the passageway, making a final tour of the engineering compartment before the missiles started flying. *He* hadn't been very keen on wearing his suit, demanding to know why they had to wear it when they were hours away from Avalon and any conceivable danger. Mandy hadn't bothered to argue. If the ship did take heavy damage, it would be better for the planet's defenders if the pirate crew didn't bother to wear shipsuits, let alone heavier protection.

"Asshole," Gary said. He looked over at Mandy. "What does he have that I don't?"

"Rank," Mandy said, simply. She leaned over and keyed the console, bringing up a display of what was happening outside the ship. "What else does he need?"

Gary followed her gaze. "I thought there could only be a handful of ships at most," he said, in surprise. "How many ships are there on the display?"

"Fifty," Mandy said, equally surprised. "They…"

Her voice trailed off. The ships couldn't *all* be real.

"The decoys are away," Kitty said, softly. "They should be seeing fifty warships."

Edward nodded. The pirates wouldn't be fooled; they would *know* that those fifty ships couldn't be real. But they'd have to separate the real ships out from the sensor ghosts and that was going to be difficult, particularly when the missile pods opened fire. It might even convince them that the fifty ships *were* real after all, at least until they failed to fire a second salvo. Would it be enough to convince the Admiral to retreat?

"They're continuing to advance," Kitty added, after a moment. She looked over at him. "Request permission to open fire, Colonel."

"Granted," Edward said. There had been too many times in his career where they'd had to wait for the enemy to fire the first shot. This time, at least, they *knew* the Admiral had hostile intent. "Fire at will."

Kitty keyed a switch. "All ships, fire at will," she ordered. "I say again, all ships; fire at will."

The missile pods opened fire, launching their missiles towards the heavy cruiser. From the pirate point of view, the ghost ships, the ships they knew couldn't be real, had just unleashed a salvo of impossible missiles. It was possible, Kitty had pointed out during the planning sessions, that they'd assume that the missiles were sensor ghosts themselves and ignore them until they got into attack range, even though it would be extremely difficult to produce fake missiles. A moment later, the enemy ship returned fire, unleashing a vast spread of missiles towards the defending fleet. Most of them were heading towards the sensor decoys, Edward noticed with some relief; the remainder had locked on to real targets. Their next barrage would be far more focused.

"Point defence network active, targeting incoming missiles," Delacroix reported. "Missiles appear to be standard design; no ECM detected…"

Edward wasn't surprised. Pirates rarely had access to the more specialised warheads designed by the Imperial Navy, let alone the technicians needed to maintain them and the sensor experts trained to make best use of the equipment. Not that it really mattered, he knew; high-explosive or nuclear-tipped warheads would tear his little fleet apart, no matter what tricks they deployed. And once his ships opened fire with their point defence, the pirates would have no difficulty separating out the real ships from the sensor ghosts. The sensor ghosts carried no point defence.

On the display, the pirate ships opened fire with their own point defence, trying to take out as many missiles as they could before they closed to attack range. Edward scowled; the pirates obviously didn't have a command network of their own, but they made up for it with sheer firepower. *And* the heavy cruiser could generate a formidable gravity shield... thankfully, they couldn't even *begin* to shield their entire hull, but it would give them some extra protection. Only three warheads made it through to strike at the pirate hull...

"Three hits," Delacroix reported. "No serious damage."

Edward winced. The pirate missiles were tearing into his fleet. Two of the converted freighters, ships that had never been designed to stand in the line of fire, were blown away before their crews could abandon ship. A third took a direct hit that destroyed her drive section, leaving her drifting helplessly through space. One more took minor damage that would cripple her if she tried to run, leaving her staggering towards the enemy ship leaking plasma from her rear section. It looked as though his last battle was also going to be his shortest.

"Continue firing," he ordered. Their next salvo was going to be much smaller – and the pirates would no longer be distracted by the sensor ghosts. "And warn the RockRats to prepare to engage."

The pirate ship picked up speed as she launched a second salvo, heading right towards the defenders and daring them to stop her. Edward suspected that he knew what had been going through the Admiral's mind; he'd made a slow approach, just to give himself a chance to escape if it turned out that the defenders had too much firepower for him to win. But now he had the measure of his foes he was advancing rapidly, forcing them to engage him at close range, where his missiles batteries would tear them apart.

"The RockRats are ready," Kitty said. Their tiny ships couldn't hope to match a starship, but the Admiral was obligingly coming right to them. "They want cover from our remaining sensor decoys."

"Use them," Edward ordered. He understood the reluctance to deploy all of their advanced and expensive hardware in the battle, but if they lost this fight it wouldn't matter if they saved the equipment or not. Besides, he didn't want to leave it as a prize for the Admiral. "And wish them luck."

The RockRats had used very primitive technology to build most of their interplanetary craft, choosing to use rockets and gas jets rather than drive fields or fusion drives. Edward had found their reluctance to move at any pace but their own rather maddening, yet he had to admit that it had its advantages. Their worker bugs were slow – they couldn't hope to keep up with the starships – but they were almost completely undetectable. And the Admiral was about to impale himself on them.

Producing nukes and bomb-pumped lasers was easy, if one had the right technology and patience. Edward had known that the RockRats pulled uranium and minerals out of the asteroids they mined, but he hadn't realised just how *much* they'd stored over the years. If Avalon had felt like pressing the RockRats, as the Empire had tried over the years, the resulting war might have gone very badly for the planet. As it was, the RockRats had ended up their allies against a common foe. Their worker bugs each carried one bomb-pumped laser and the enemy ship had come too close to their position.

Edward smiled as the RockRats opened fire. Each worker bug had only one shot, but from the pirates' point of view the blasts had to come out of nowhere. Some were wasted on the gravity shield, but most of them stabbed into the pirate ship's hull. Edward knew that the ship was heavily armoured – and the interior was armoured too – yet the blasts had to have done some damage. He just hoped that it would be enough.

"The pirate destroyers are lashing out," Delacroix reported, as the heavy cruiser slowed alarmingly. "They're firing on everything that *might* be a RockRat ship…"

"Move to cover them," Edward ordered. The RockRat ships couldn't even stand up to a single pulsar hit. Their only hope was remaining undetected long enough to break contact and escape. "Damage report on the heavy cruiser?"

"Uncertain," Delacroix said, after a long moment. "She took several nasty hits, sir, but I don't think that any will have proved fatal. The drive section wasn't hit, as far as I can tell, and I don't think their internal network will have been compromised…at least, one of *ours* wouldn't be compromised."

Edward nodded. He'd hoped that the generally shoddy state of pirate maintenance would have made it harder for the ship to survive the battle. It was quite possible that their command network wouldn't have the ability to reroute itself around damaged components, but it seemed that the

Admiral actually *did* understand the value of basic maintenance. Quite how he managed to keep his crew working on it was a mystery – most pirate crews didn't have the discipline to do work that was second nature to the Imperial Navy – yet it didn't really matter. All that mattered was that the Admiral might still win the battle.

"Enemy ship appears to have lost four missile tubes and a handful of point defence nodes," Delacroix added. "At least, they're not firing any longer."

"It may not matter," Kitty said quietly. "They *still* have more tubes than our entire fleet."

Her voice sharpened. "Incoming fire," she snapped. "All hands, brace for impact…"

Dancing Fool shook violently as a nuke detonated far too close to the ship's hull. Edward hung on to his chair for dear life, feeling strangely helpless as the gravity field flickered and faded before snapping completely out of existence. Red icons flared to life on the main console, warning of heavy damage to the ship's upper hull, a second before one of the consoles exploded, blowing the operator right across the bridge.

"Damage…" Kitty coughed, clearing her throat before she started again. "Damage report?"

"Major damage to upper hull," Delacroix said, poking her console. The bridge hatch opened, revealing a pair of combat medics who hurried over to the stunned console operator. "One of the fusion cores is gone; the other is fluctuating badly. Drive power is at thirty percent and dropping. Internal network is badly compromised…we're going to need weeks in the yard, at the very least."

"We don't have weeks," Kitty snapped. She glared down at the console beside her chair. "All Category-B personnel; abandon ship. I say again, all Category-B personnel abandon ship."

Edward opened his mouth, but she spoke over him. "This ship is a sitting duck," she said, sharply. "Our drives have been crippled. The next salvo will finish us off."

Her voice hardened. "Colonel, go to one of the lifepods," she added. "There should be enough drive power left to *ram* the pirate ship. Let's see them survive that!"

"You're going to be needed," Edward said, grimly. But she was right. *Dancing Fool* had been crippled; her only defence was that the pirates might assume that she was completely helpless, no longer worth bothering with. "Kitty…"

"*Go*," Kitty ordered. She smiled, rather dryly. "I do plan to abandon ship with the Category-A crew once we have locked the ship onto her new course. Now, *go*!"

———

Sword rocked violently as laser beams stabbed deep into the hull, but none of the damage seemed to be fatal. Vane and his crew had worked miracles, at least by pirate standards; the ship seemed to have enough resilience to just keep going, even if the damage looked bad. As long as they didn't lose the drives or the weapons, they could continue to advance on the planet. And they were tearing through the remaining defenders. There only seemed to be a handful of ships left…

"That's another one," Gary proclaimed. They'd been told to stay in engineering, so he was watching the display as Mandy sat in the corner, one hand toying with the terminal on her belt. "They took her out!"

Mandy glared at him, remembering what she'd gone through when the pirates had attacked the RockRat transport. The damaged ships would have become nightmares, their crews struggling to survive and find their way to the lifepods, picking through interiors that had suddenly become unfamiliar – and lethal. Maybe it would be kinder to destroy a ship completely, rather than damage it; the crew would not have time to realise what had happened before they died.

But there was no more time. She'd hoped for privacy, hoped that Vane would send her somewhere she could slip into the tubes and hide, yet it wasn't going to happen. There was no more time to hesitate. Either she acted now or she surrendered completely and became a pirate…

Pulling the terminal off her belt, she keyed in the code that activated the transmitter. If she'd failed, if they'd found the detonators…but they hadn't. Vane would have organised a search of the entire ship if they'd found one of the detonators; the Admiral would have interrogated everyone who might have had access to the storage rooms. But she wasn't *meant* to have access to the stores…for all she knew, the Admiral had discovered the detonators and blamed them on Gaston. Maybe *that* was why he'd tried to launch his coup.

Gary looked over at her as she keyed in the final code. "What are you doing?"

"Checking something," Mandy said, absently. Would Gary realise that she wasn't meant to use a terminal on duty, certainly when not checking specific components? "Keep an eye on the enemy."

She keyed in the final code and pushed the trigger. There was a long pause, just long enough for her to worry that something had gone badly wrong, followed by a dull explosion in the distance. Seconds later, the lighting failed completely, leaving the compartment plunged into darkness. Even the consoles that should have kept them apprised of the ship's status had failed. An Imperial Navy starship had emergency lighting systems that were disconnected from the main power network, but the pirates hadn't bothered to keep them properly maintained. Given how much else there was to do on the ship, Mandy could understand that… but it was going to cost them.

Gary started to splutter. "What…what happened?"

Mandy pulled her goggles out of her belt and donned them rapidly, pulling them over her eyes. They were designed for use in darkness, allowing her to see without carrying a source of light. There hadn't been time to practice using them, but they seemed to be simple enough; Gary was starting to panic, unsurprisingly. The battle had suddenly become nightmarish for him.

"This ship is under attack," Mandy said. "What exactly did you think was happening?"

She ignored his sputters as she pulled the communicator out of her belt, keying the switch that sent Travis' emergency signal. His faction would take it as their cue to start launching a coup, turning on their fellows and trying to take the ship's vital compartments. Vane was a skilled engineer and it was possible that he might manage to restore power, but not if several pirates were trying to capture engineering. Jasmine had told her stories of just how confusing a battle could be if there were several different factions involved; here, there would be at least two factions, perhaps more. Mandy smiled darkly as she drew the pistol from her belt. In the darkness, Gary wouldn't be able to see her at all.

"I...I don't know what to do," Gary said.

"Die," Mandy snarled, and pulled the trigger. The gun jerked in her hand, but the shot was perfect. Gary stumbled backward and fell on the deck, blood pooling around his prone form.

Mandy swallowed the urge to laugh as she started to run. Vane's crews would all have their own goggles, as would the Admiral's troops. And it wouldn't take them long to work out what had happened to their ship. *Sword* felt oddly silent around her – the noise produced by the life support system was gone – but it wouldn't be long before the fighting began in earnest. And if they caught her...

She slowed as she reached the engineering compartment, where Vane was trying to organise his crew, reminding them not to panic. Mandy smirked inwardly, knowing that advice wouldn't be followed by everyone. Most of the crew and the mercenaries would have been plunged into absolute darkness. Feeling oddly calm, she lifted her pistol and shot Vane, before firing into the crowd of engineering crewmen and forcing them to dive for cover.

And then she turned and fled.

CHAPTER FORTY-FIVE

It is rare to try to board a ship in the midst of a fleet action. Normally, the crippled ships would be called upon to surrender and then destroyed if surrender wasn't forthcoming. In the event of such a boarding action being necessary, it can be very risky. Even a handful of point defence systems can rip apart a boarding party before they managed to dock their shuttles, or land on the hull.
-Admiral Darrin Webster, *Basic Naval Tactics* (34th Edition).

"They lost power?"

"So it would seem," Lieutenant Faulkner said. "We're moving in now."

It could be a trap, Jasmine thought. The Marines had been in their shuttles, ready for a last-ditch gambit of trying to board the enemy cruiser. They'd known that it was effectively suicide – the cruiser would have no difficulty detecting them as they closed in – but they'd been ready. And now the enemy ship seemed to have lost power. With Colonel Stalker out of contact, Faulkner was in command…and he was right. They couldn't let this opportunity slip past.

The shuttle lurched into life and sped towards the stricken ship, running an evasive pattern just in case the two remaining pirate destroyers managed to engage them. With the heavy cruiser suddenly out of commission, the pirate ships had found themselves outgunned; Jasmine wasn't too surprised to see them break off and start to run for the Phase Limit. The mercenary transports had been abandoned.

"Negative incoming fire," the pilot reported. "They're not even tracking us."

Jasmine nodded. They *must* have scored a lucky hit, she decided; one of the bomb-pumped lasers must have cut something vitally important. No one in their right mind would let Marine shuttles get so close, certainly not close enough to start launching Marines out of the hatch and down to the enemy hull. Once the Marines were in space, hitting them would be a great deal harder.

"Someone must have spectacularly bad timing when it comes to launching a coup," Blake suggested. "That looks like internal damage to me."

Jasmine shrugged. "Prepare for ejection," she ordered. The Marines braced themselves. "Now!"

Mandy could hear the shouting – and shooting – as she ran from engineering, looking desperately for the nearest entrance to the tubes. Someone seemed to be firing a heavy machine gun up ahead, although she couldn't tell what – if anything – they were actually targeting. She couldn't hear anything from behind her, but if the engineers managed to rig up a makeshift communications network they'd be able to tell the Admiral what had happened. It was a relief when she managed to climb into the tubes and relax, before starting to crawl up the passageway. A moment later, the gravity failed completely.

Keep moving, she told herself. The tubes were *designed* to make it easier to move around without gravity. There was plenty of handholds to use to pull herself up through the tube network. Pausing in a workspace, she glanced down at the communicator and smiled as she saw a number of messages being exchanged between the various members of Travis' faction. No doubt they were trying to organise themselves, now that they were committed to victory or a horrible death.

Switching to the terminal, she checked the internal network, sighing in relief as she realised it had gone down completely. She'd worried about that – Vane had insisted on building multiple redundancies into the system – but all of his precautions seemed to have failed. The Admiral and his officers would be relying on independent communications systems to pass messages from deck to deck. She didn't dare assume that he wouldn't have his own set of communicators – if Travis had, the Admiral certainly would – but it wouldn't be easy to coordinate everything. Besides, the Marines would be coming.

She flinched as she heard someone making their way down the tubes towards her. There was no way to know if they were searching for her or if they were merely trying to hide, but as they came closer she heard their breathing and shuddered in recognition. Only one person breathed like that, as far as she knew; Ha. The Admiral might have sent him to kill her, or he might have decided that he was going to have his fun anyway...

"Oh, *Mandy*," Ha called. His voice echoed in the tubes, sending chills down her spine. "You've been a *very* bad girl..."

Mandy shuddered again. There was something in his voice that kept her rooted to the spot, a primal terror that seemed impossible to overcome. She *knew* that he was going to torture her, to prolong her suffering as much as he could, before finally killing her...and yet it was so hard to move. All the stories she'd heard about him echoed through her mind. Ha was a complete psychopath, willing to do absolutely anything to anyone. And loyal to the Admiral, who gave him such freedom to indulge himself.

No, she told herself, as she reached into her belt. The drug injector was where she'd hidden it, ready for emergency use. She pushed it against her neck and pressed down hard on the tab. There was a sharp prick as the drug rushed into her system, followed by a sudden wave of nervous energy. It was suddenly very hard to stand still and wait for Ha, moving in what looked like slow motion, to enter the chamber. His face was twisted into a sinister smile, one hand gripping a short knife. And it was suddenly the easiest thing in the world to lash out and knock the knife out of his hand.

Ha spun backwards as Mandy punched him, knocking into the bulkhead and banging his head on the cold metal. His face looked shocked as Mandy hurled herself onto him, feeling a rage of energy burning right through her body. Ha couldn't react in time to stop her slamming punch after punch into his face, and then into his neck. Mandy was barely aware of anything but the need to kill him, to end his life as savagely as she could. By the time the drug started to fade away, Ha had been battered into a pulp.

Mandy stared down at her hands and shuddered. She had been so lost in the drug that she hadn't realised that she'd damaged herself, or that he'd managed to kick her in the chest. The sheer sense of power the drug had given her was fading away, slowly becoming a crushing despondency that left her floating in the middle of the compartment, unable to care enough to move. And yet she knew she had to move. Ha wasn't the only one who would be looking for her.

Jasmine guided her suit down towards the gash in the ship's hull, plunging right into the interior of the heavy cruiser. The bomb-pumped lasers had burned through the hull, but it seemed that the internal safety systems had been working after all, or else the entire ship would have vented. Jasmine brought up the ship diagrams in her HUD and led her platoon towards the nearest access point, knowing that the rest of the Marines would head to their own targets. A quick burst of plasma fire cut their way into the ship's interior, cracking open the airlock. Jasmine pulled herself to one side as a stream of atmosphere rocketed out, carrying a number of pirates into the vacuum of space.

"They seem to be fighting each other," Joe commented, as two pirates, locked together by hatred, tumbled out past them and into the darkness. "Someone definitely mounted a coup."

"I told you so," Blake said. "Lieutenant?"

"Onwards," Jasmine ordered. Her HUD projected the quickest path to the bridge in front of her eyes. "We have to secure the ship before they can restore main power."

The interior of the pirate ship was rapidly becoming a nightmare. Some pirates had thought to wear shipsuits and carry masks, others hadn't bothered with any protection at all. Jasmine could understand what they were feeling – the heavy protective gear was uncomfortable, as well as hot when worn on a planetary surface – but it was foolish. Any tendencies she'd had that way had been hammered out of her at the Slaughterhouse. One sniff of irritation gas and you never wanted another one.

Joe was right, she decided, as they cut their way through the next internal airlock. The pirates were definitely fighting each other, while the mercenaries were just trying to stay alive. A report from Lieutenant Faulkner's platoon, heading to engineering, stated that a number of mercenaries had surrendered, rather than try to fight any further. Admittedly, only a fool would try to fight in a wrecked starship, but it was odd. Maybe the mercenaries had been promised an easy victory and had decided to surrender when it had become clear that victory was *not* going to be easy, or even attainable.

Her suits sensors reported that only a handful of communicators were still operating, sending messages around the ship. They must have lost the internal communications network as well, she decided, although she couldn't understand why they hadn't handed out independent communicators to their crewmen. The Imperial Navy, aware of the dangers of losing the main network, ensured that *everyone* had an independent system…but the pirates probably feared what would happen if the crew could talk freely. Right now, however, it made it hard to coordinate a resistance.

"We've broken into engineering," Faulkner said. "Not much resistance; I think they killed half of their staff before we arrived. No clue what actually caused the power loss yet."

Jasmine nodded as Blake and Joe took point, advancing towards Officer Country. If the pirates were going to make a stand, here was where they'd make it…but as far as she could tell, there was nothing in their path, apart from a handful of dead bodies. One of them looked to be illegally boosted, with the massive muscles and puny frame of the incomplete treatments that had leaked out to the Rim; the others looked to be normal humans. And they'd all killed each other…

She glanced up as a figure exploded out of nowhere, throwing himself on Blake. The newcomer didn't seem to be wearing a mask, but he seemed to have no difficulty operating even in the reduced atmosphere. A Cobra, Jasmine realised, as he punched and kicked at Blake's armour with augmented strength. Blake just couldn't move fast enough to grab the Cobra before he moved again, even though the Cobra couldn't break through his armour. Joe lunged forward, slammed into Blake and sent him flying forward, just before spraying the Cobra with a wide-angle stun beam. The Cobra was boosted to prevent stun beams from knocking him out, but he staggered, just long enough to allow Blake to catch him. A moment later, Blake's armoured fist crushed the Cobra's neck.

"Got him," Blake said. "I *knew* I could take one of them."

"Take him without your armour," Joe said. "And what about my stunner?"

"Get into the bridge," Jasmine ordered, before they could start arguing properly. "Hurry."

The pirates had once had a guardpost outside the bridge, she realised, as the Marines approached the hatch. Now, they'd ripped themselves apart; judging from the damage and where the bodies had fallen, there had been at least three different factions. Two men appeared to have survived, both struggling for breath as the atmosphere faded away into nothingness. Jasmine nodded to Joe, who stunned them both and then placed masks on their faces. They should remain alive long enough for the follow-up teams to drag them to a POW camp.

"The hatch is sealed," Joe reported, flatly. "Blake?"

Blake stepped forward, slapping charges on the hatch as the other Marines took cover. There was a brilliant flare of white light, followed by the hatch collapsing inward. Blake and Joe ran forward, weapons raised, and stopped. Jasmine followed them, carefully, and swore. The entire bridge had been devastated by an explosion. Looking at the damage, it seemed to have been centred on the command chair. Everyone in the compartment was dead.

"The bridge has been destroyed," she reported. "The Admiral may be dead."

The briefing had suggested that *someone* was backing the Admiral, presumably the same person who had somehow set up a factory for producing Cobras. Maybe the Cobra who had attacked them had wanted to delay the Marines long enough to destroy the evidence. But why not destroy the entire ship?

She shook her head. That wasn't her concern. "Orders, Lieutenant?"

"We're talking the mercenary transports into surrendering now," Faulkner said. "Once they're secure, we'll have reinforcements brought up to the cruiser and we can start pulling the prisoners out of the ship. The drones are reporting that a number of pirates are still alive."

"Understood," Jasmine said. She hoped that Mandy was still alive, but there was no way to know. They'd just have to search the ship to account for all the bodies. "We'll stay on alert here."

Mandy pulled herself through the tubes, noticing that the atmosphere was slowly starting to fade away completely. Her charges shouldn't have caused a hull breach, but it was possible that she'd accidentally wrecked one of the interior airlocks. Or that the Marines had boarded the ship and were venting it to kill most of the pirates before they could mount a defence.

Her entire body felt heavy, almost completely helpless. If she hadn't been in zero-gravity, she suspected that she wouldn't have been able to move at all. As it was, she had to think about each step, about each handhold she gripped to pull herself forward. She reached the end of the tubes without quite realising it. The shuttlebay was right in front of her, crammed – at least in theory – with the assault shuttles the Admiral had planned to drop on Avalon. Instead, she could hide there until the Marines found her.

The hatch cracked open, revealing the shuttlebay. Unsurprisingly, a number of shuttles had been tossed around by the impacts – and the main hatch looked cracked, threatening to allow the atmosphere to slowly leak out of the compartment. Mandy frowned – something about the hatch looked wrong, but she couldn't get her addled mind to process it – before pulling herself completely out of the hatch. The shuttles were tough. Even if they had been banged up, their crew compartments should still be airtight. And perhaps she could contact the Marines and ask for pickup. She paused outside one of the shuttles and reached for the panel, flipping it open to reveal the keyboard underneath. No one had told her the codes, but Vane had taught her a trick for forcing the hatch to open anyway…

A hand caught her arm and yanked her backwards. Mandy felt suddenly very sick as the compartment spun around her, just before she crashed into the far side of the bulkhead. The combination of the drug's after-effects and the spin was making it hard to think, just as she saw a figure jumping towards her. His hand caught her neck and hauled her up to face him, his eyes glaring down at her. The Admiral didn't look happy.

"You did this," he snarled. Mandy felt his grip tighten on her neck and wondered if she was about to die. After what she'd done, after the innocent people she'd killed, what else did she deserve? "You did this to me!"

Mandy couldn't talk. She was convinced that she could feel her neck slowly cracking under his grip. The Marines were enhanced – it was hard to kill them physically, she'd been told – but she had no such enhancements. And the Admiral was clearly strong enough to break her in two effortlessly. He'd probably been enhanced himself at Haven or another hidden asteroid settlement.

"Don't you know what you've done?" He demanded, as he glared down at her. She had no choice but to meet his gaze, knowing that he intended to kill her. And yet she was helpless. "The empire I sought to build lies in ruins!"

Mandy scrabbled desperately at her belt. The terminal was useless, the communicator was useless…all she could reach with her free hand was the sonic screwdriver. But what could she do with that? Desperately, she pulled it out of her belt as his grip tightened and stabbed it into his chest. He recoiled, just enough for Mandy to break free and kick herself off the wall, throwing herself right towards the far edge of the compartment. The Admiral turned and came after her, pulling himself almost casually through the air. Mandy felt herself choking, as if she'd swallowed something too large for her throat, but there was no time to do anything. She was about to die. All she could do was try to take him with her.

Shuttles could catch fire, she knew, and if that happened the only thing to do was to vent the bay as quickly as possible. The Imperial Navy worked all kinds of safeties into the system to prevent the shuttlebay from being depressurised accidentally, but the pirates hadn't really bothered to maintain the safeties. Mandy heard the Admiral yell something – lost in the roaring sound in her ears – a moment before the emergency charges blew.

The hatch exploded outwards into space, followed rapidly by the atmosphere and most of the debris in the shuttlebay. For a horrified moment, Mandy thought that the Admiral was still in the ship, before he was picked up and flung into space. Despite the shipsuit, the temperature dropped rapidly. It was all she could do to hold on to the bulkhead as the rest of the atmosphere faded away, leaving her floating in vacuum.

There was someone out there, wasn't there? She couldn't tell in the eerie silence that had descended on her. Someone was speaking…was it her long-dead Grandma, or someone she vaguely recalled from Earth, or…her thoughts just faded away into the darkness. The last thing she thought before the darkness claimed her was that she had paid for what she'd done.

CHAPTER
FORTY-SIX

The apparent harshness of Imperial Law is, surprisingly, a weakness. If someone is merely charged with a crime and found guilty, without any examination of the context, it is perhaps unsurprising that few chose to trust the justice of Imperial courts. Or, to paraphrase a saying that predates the Empire, 'if the penalty for being late is death, and the penalty for rebellion is death, and we're already late…why not rebel?'

This shouldn't have been too surprising. The Empire existed to govern hundreds of thousands of worlds. It simply couldn't take note of subtle points, even ones that were supported by common sense. Avalon's new legal system, deliberately isolated from the thousands of years of useless precedents set by the Empire was designed to take such points into account.

Not that I had any personal interest in such matters, of course.

- Professor Leo Caesius, *The Perilous Dawn* (unpublished).

"What a goddamned mess."

Edward nodded. He'd been pulled out of a lifepod to discover that the battle was over, the enemy ship – she had been called *Sword*, apparently – had been captured and the Marines were trying to clear up the mess. Twenty thousand mercenaries and seven hundred pirate crewmen had had to be taken into custody – they'd been left on their transports for the moment, at least until they could be transferred to a POW camp – and the cruiser had to be checked carefully for surprises. There was just too much to do.

The defending fleet had been torn to ribbons. *Dancing Fool* was so badly damaged that she should be scrapped, if they had been able to afford to let go of her so easily. Two freighters had survived the rest of the fighting, along with a handful of RockRat worker bugs. The remainder had been destroyed, taking with them three hundred irreplaceable experts. Edward was already considering press-ganging the remaining pirate engineers into his forces. There seemed to be no other way to rebuild quickly, let alone expand Avalon's industrial base. And *thank God* that *Sword* had never ranged in on the planet.

"You did well," he assured Lieutenant Faulkner. Back home, he would have deserved a chance to command his own company. That wasn't going to happen on Avalon, unless he transferred to the Knights. "And the enemy cruiser?"

"Sabotaged," Faulkner said. "I think we owe Mandy Caesius one hell of a debt."

Edward looked over at him. "They found her?"

"Half-frozen to death, but alive," Faulkner reported. "I understand that Lieutenant Yamane is currently with her. We probably also owe her for tossing the Admiral out into space."

"Probably," Edward agreed. He'd hoped to take the Admiral alive for interrogation, but it was rare to take any form of covert operative alive, not when their implants would kill them as soon as it became clear that the situation was hopeless. "But we do need to interrogate her first."

Faulkner looked worried. "Sir," he said, "she *was* on a pirate ship."

"I know," Edward said. "There's no choice. We need to know what happened before we make our final choice about her future."

"How are you feeling, kid?"

Mandy stared up at a familiar face, hovering over her. She'd thought she was dead; she had been *convinced* that she was dead. The Admiral had been blown out into space and her thoughts had just started to fade away…and now she was in what looked like a medical compartment. She looked up at Jasmine and wondered just what had happened to her.

"Bad," she said, finally. Her head felt thick and useless…and behind it, there was the towering guilt. She might have wrecked *Sword*, but she'd been wrong. The debt she owed the innocent was greater than she could ever pay. "What happened?"

"They found you in the shuttlebay, freezing to death," Jasmine supplied. "So they brought you here, where the medics saved your life. I understand that you crippled *Sword*?"

Mandy blinked. "How did you know?"

"The Admiral ordered the pirates to kill you," Jasmine explained. "We interrogated a handful of them as we were taking them off the ship. They were happy to tell us what happened in the ship's final moments."

"I killed him," Mandy said, slowly. "And I killed others."

It all came tumbling out of her as she cried, finally losing control of herself. Jasmine held her as Mandy confessed everything, starting with working for the pirates, selling herself to Vane to keep Michael alive and finally murdering innocent crewmen on the Admiral's command. And how she'd managed to hide charges throughout the ship, crippling *Sword* as she advanced on Avalon. Jasmine listened, holding her gently, without saying a word. Mandy just *knew* that her friend hated her now, hated her for being so weak. *Jasmine* would have found a way to kill the Admiral before she gained so much blood on her hands…

"You should kill me," she said, finally. "Please. Just end it all."

"Don't be silly," Jasmine said, tartly. For a moment, Mandy remembered their first proper talk – and how it had ended. "You seem to have done very well, not like the other girls on the ship."

Mandy winced. No one had given a damn about the sex slaves. They'd probably died when their compartments vented, or were burned open by bomb-pumped lasers…or maybe the pirates had killed them when it became clear that they were going to lose the battle. Or maybe they'd survived long enough to testify against their captors. She could have asked Jasmine, but in truth she didn't want to know. There was enough blood on her hands.

"I'm afraid you will be interrogated," Jasmine admitted, "once the medic certifies that you can stand it. That *boost* you took wasn't brewed right – did you realise that? It could have easily killed you."

Mandy shook her head. It would have been a relief, in a way.

"Don't worry," Jasmine reassured her. "Whatever else happens, I'll be with you."

It was two days before Colonel Stalker came to see her. Two days, during which she was interrogated under a polygraph and injected with truth drugs. In the end, her memories thankfully blurred together, making the whole experience a hazy dreamlike sensation. And to think that this wasn't a *rigorous* interrogation!

He looked older than Mandy remembered, although perhaps that wasn't surprising. She'd first met him as leader of a small unit of Marines; now, he was effectively the senior military officer in an entire sector, one who had come far too close to defeat. The Colonel nodded politely to her as he took a seat beside her bed, folding his hands on his lap. Mandy felt her blood run cold for a long moment before relaxing. If she was in real trouble, they would have put her in a cell by now.

"We went over everything that happened since you were kidnapped," he said, without preamble. "It was decided that most of the work you did for the pirates you did under duress, therefore you cannot be legally held accountable for it. And what little willing help you did offer was intended to set them up for disaster. Accordingly, there will be no piracy charges filed against you."

Mandy stared at him. "But I deserve them!"

"You were given no choice," Stalker said. He seemed to understand what she meant without asking…naturally, he would have read through all the interrogation transcripts. "If you'd refused to fire on the freighter, the pirates would have killed you and someone else would have fired on the freighter. You would have thrown your life away for *nothing*."

Mandy scowled. She knew that, but she didn't really *believe* it. The guilt would be with her until the day she died. She could rationalise it all she wanted, just like the pirates themselves did, yet it didn't matter. The guilt would always be there.

"I understand that your father and sister want to see you, once we transfer you back down to Avalon," Stalker said, "but I thought we might take a moment to talk about your future."

"My future?" Mandy repeated. She *hadn't* given any thought to her future, not since she'd determined to risk her life wrecking the pirate ship. "What about my future?"

"Thanks to you, *Sword* was captured almost intact," Stalker said. "It will take several months to repair the damage to her hull, but the rest of the ship shouldn't take so long to fix up. On the downside, we cannot really trust any of the engineers we captured, those you left alive. We certainly cannot trust them on a warship."

He leaned forward. "You're the most familiar with her systems," he added. "Would you like to serve on her?"

Mandy hesitated. Part of her wanted to refuse the offer, to crawl back home and hide. She certainly didn't want to go back to the ship that still haunted her nightmares, even if the pirates and their equipment – and their victims – had been cleaned out. But she owed the dead a debt that had to be repaid. If serving on *Sword* – or whatever they called it after the repair job was complete – would make up for some of what she'd done, there was no other choice.

"I have a lot to learn," she admitted. Vane *had* hammered a great deal into her head, but he'd kept some information to himself. "Are you sure you want me?"

"You don't have to choose at once," Stalker said, standing up. "But you do need to find something to do, rather than wallowing in self-pity."

Mandy felt her temper flare. That just wasn't *fair*. "Everything is so easy for you Marines, isn't it?"

Stalker shrugged. "We get pushed to the limits in the Slaughterhouse," he said. "By the time we graduate, there's very little that can faze us. You were dropped right into a nightmare without any prior preparation at all. I think you did very well, under the circumstances."

"I wish I felt that way," Mandy said. "But…"

She hesitated, and then asked the question she hadn't wanted to ask. "What do they think of me?"

"The entire planet knows that you saved them from the pirates," Stalker said. "Not us, not the handful of starships we had to defend ourselves…but you. You're a planetary heroine. They'll probably wind up naming a ship after you."

He walked over to the hatch and then looked back. "You'll be transferred to Avalon within the day and your family can see you then," he added. "Take some time to rest and think about my offer. We still need you."

Mandy watched him go, looking down at her hands. The bloodstains were invisible, but she knew that they were there. They would *always* be there. And the Colonel was right. She could crawl into a hole and hide, or she could do what she could to rebuild her life and make up for her crimes. Shaking her head, she reached for the terminal and started requesting reports on *Sword*. She might as well get started now.

"You do realise that this could probably be considered treason?"

Edward nodded. He hadn't expected Governor Roeder to be happy with what he was suggesting. They had already planned to make alliances with the other worlds in the sector – particularly the ones that had been conquered by the Admiral – but this was taking it a step further. It was a tacit acceptance that the Empire would never return.

"Forming an independent unit, even a local alliance, would go against Imperial law," the Governor added. "And you're planning to take it a great deal further. Are you sure you want to do this?"

"I think so," Edward said. On one hand, the Governor was right; it *was* treason, if the definition of treason was looked at properly. But on the other hand, they'd learned a great deal about the situation in the surrounding sectors by interrogating the pirates and mercenaries. The Empire was effectively gone, at least for several thousand light years. "I think there's no choice."

They hadn't learned much about the Admiral's mysterious backers. Everyone who might have known something – the Admiral, the Captain, his Cobras – was dead. The handful who remained alive simply hadn't known very much and most of what they *had* known consisted of rumours rather than hard data. One of them firmly believed that the Admiral's backers were *alien*, an absurd thought when humanity was alone in the universe. But there was no shortage of rumours about what lay beyond the Rim.

Edward suspected that the truth was a little more mundane. A rogue faction from within the Empire, perhaps, or a black colony, trying to destabilise what remained of the Empire. Or maybe even a RockRat faction. They'd *certainly* have a motive to upset the apple cart. But it didn't matter. The unknowns had lost their agent, yet they remained uncovered. They would have plenty of time to try again.

His plan was simple enough. Right now, the sector had at least thirty worlds that had experienced either near-complete isolation or the heavy hand of the Admiral's attempt at establishing his own union. Once the Marines had dealt with the rest of his forces, those worlds would be invited to join a new union. Elysium and Crawford had already signed up, starting the ball rolling. Individually, few of those worlds could take care of themselves. Collectively, maybe they'd be able to stand against the wave of chaos he knew was coming.

The Empire would not approve. He'd heard that some of the older sectors were starting to opt out of the Empire's economic union, forming their own economic systems that were vastly more efficient – and responsive. Back before they'd left, he'd even heard rumours that the Grand Senate was considering an armed response to such sectors, branding their inhabitants traitors and using the military to crush them. But there was no other choice. The alternative was remaining as an isolated handful of worlds, vulnerable to the first major threat to materialise.

"Very well," the Governor said finally. "And I hope that you're wrong."

Edward nodded. It would be nice to think that the Empire would survive the crisis it was facing, but he suspected that it wouldn't escape this one. The crisis was simply too immense, too far-reaching. Solving it would require the Grand Senate giving up its power and control, accepting a permanent shift in the Empire's nature. But he knew the Grand Senate would never surrender control willingly. They had too many enemies who would wage war on them at the slightest hint of weakness.

"Thank you, Governor," he said. "I hope I'm wrong too."

"You're going to be shipping out again?"

"No rest for the wicked," Jasmine confirmed. "Besides, there are planets still held in thrall by the Admiral's men. We want to deal with them before they realise that the Admiral is gone."

Mandy had been…*clinging* to her over the last two days, although she found it hard to blame the girl. Jasmine's sisters had been very like her when they'd been children, before growing up and moving into boring lives as housewives and mothers. Or so she had heard. It had been nearly a year since she'd received a letter from home. For all she knew, her homeworld had been destroyed in the civil wars Mandy's father had predicted would tear the Empire apart.

"I'll miss you," Mandy admitted. "You'd better come back alive, or I will kill you personally."

Jasmine had to smile. "I've had Sergeants who would happily dig up my corpse just to put me back to work," she said. One of them had had a yell that would wake the dead. He'd died on Han, which had surprised the young Jasmine. She'd found it hard to imagine anything capable of killing him. "I will come back to you."

Mandy hugged her, tightly. "I don't even know what I should say to Michael," she added. "I'm not the girl he fell in love with any longer."

"You're asking *me* for romance advice?" Jasmine asked, dryly. Her love life had never been very exciting, even before she'd graduated from the Slaughterhouse. "What do you *want* to do?"

"I don't know," Mandy said. "Part of me wants to go back to him, to forget everything that happened, and part of me knows that it can never be the same again."

"So," Jasmine said, after a moment, "there's no point in telling you to follow your heart?"

Mandy gave her a sharp look. "My heart wants two different things," she said. "I don't know which way to jump."

"Neither do I," Jasmine said. She considered it for a long moment. "People grow older all the time, Mandy. You're not the person you were when you came to Avalon—"

"You saw to that," Mandy said, one hand rubbing her rear end lightly.

"-And you're not really the same person who was taken onboard the pirate ship," Jasmine continued. "And I'm not the Rifleman who came to Avalon either. We've both had to grow and develop a little and we'll do more in the future."

She smiled, openly. "Take some time, come to terms with who you are now...and then decide if you want to continue the relationship," she advised. "If Michael loves you, he'll understand that – and he will forgive you for selling yourself to save his life. But if he doesn't – and men can be stupid when sex is involved – just move on. You'll have grown apart and that's all right. It happens."

"I know," Mandy said, miserably. "Change isn't easy, is it?"

Jasmine looked up into the darkening sky. The stars were coming out, stars that were part of the Empire – or had been. Sol lay in that direction, she thought, but it was too dim to see with the naked eye. There was no way that anyone would pick up the presence of a technological civilisation at such a distance, or know what was happening there without taking a starship and going to investigate. Anything could be happening towards the Core Worlds and the first they'd know of it would be when the impact washed over Avalon.

The Empire was changing – and Mandy was right. Change was never easy.

End of Book Two

AFTERWORD

When I was a child, my mother would tell me to be sure and brush my teeth. Being as sensible as most boys that age, I didn't really listen to her. The net result, I have to confess, is that I spent too much time sitting on the dentist's chair as he worked on my teeth, inserting more fillings than I care to talk about. Suffice it to say that I learned a lesson about taking care of myself – and if I had learned it sooner, I might have had fewer problems in later life.

As my wife will happily tell anyone who asks, taking care of your health is important. Eating properly, drinking properly, getting a reasonable amount of exercise and seeking medical attention when necessary are all requirements for keeping your body as healthy as possible. Of course, barring the development of some form of rejuvenation treatment, you will grow old and die, along with everyone else on the planet. But you can put that day off as long as possible.

You might be wondering, at this point, what keeping yourself healthy has to do with *The Empire's Corps* series. Read on.

I cannot claim to be a formally-trained historian (neither were Pliny or Thucydides) or a sociologist (I have my doubts about many people who publish extensive texts on the subject). What I do have is a great deal of knowledge about history, human affairs and a rather cynical view of human nature. I rather doubt that any of my conclusions are unique to me; I certainly do not claim any breakthroughs. All I can really do is present them for your consideration and invite your comments, particularly if you disagree with me. I welcome open discussion.

From my studies, I have drawn a simple conclusion; *governments decay*. The process is often invisible at the start, but tends to gain speed over the following years. It also tends to accelerate as government responsibilities grow and governments become less accountable to the population. Put bluntly, the more the government attempts to do, the less able it is to do *anything*.

The Union of Soviet Socialist Republics claimed to rule in the name of the People. In reality, the elite held all of the power, which it used to impose a communist state on Russia. I'm sure that some of the Bolsheviks genuinely believed that they were doing the right thing for the People they ruled, just as I am sure that others (Stalin, in particular) were in it for their own personal power. They still created a police state to seek out enemies, imposed a command economy on Russia and smashed any hope of independence in Eastern Europe. It is one of the many signs of communist failure that the Russians, who could have fed themselves if they had been willing to relax communist control, were forced to buy grain from their arch-enemy the United States of America.

It is no exaggeration to say that communist control strangled the life out of Russia and Eastern Europe. How could a planner in Moscow hope to account for all the variables involved in running a modern (insofar as the USSR could be called modern) economy? Where the West rewarded 'searchers,' people who sought out solutions to problems, the USSR relied on 'planners' – and the 'planners' were simply not up to the task. The system relied upon the people at the top to be able to command the others, rather than attempting to make use of the talents of the entire population. Maybe they did mean well, but it didn't matter. The USSR was doomed right from the start.

The lack of proper feedback only made it worse. People tend to respond to incentives and pressures and the USSR – perversely – rewarded lying, rather than honest reporting and debate. Each of the Five Year Plans was hailed as a success, either by moving the goalposts or – more commonly – lying about the results. The USSR needed to draw accurate feedback from its workers. Instead, those who pointed out that the system was failing were branded 'class enemies' and dispatched to Siberia.

It is common to regard 'fascism' and 'communism' as polar opposites. This is simply inaccurate. Fascism can be summed up as gathering all the power in the government's hands for the government's benefit. As such, it is the logical end result for 'communism', which can be defined as gathering up all the power in the government's hands for the People's benefit. But tell me – who defines benefit? Does it really surprise anyone to know that it's the people at the top?

Unsurprisingly, fascist states also decay. Hitler's Germany shared many of the same flaws as the USSR, including a simple inability to grasp facts on the ground, a refusal to tolerate dissent and a dependence on 'planners' rather than 'searchers'. And, for that matter, attempting to exterminate a very productive part of the German population. Fascist Italy did little better before being overwhelmed by its former ally. Spain avoided involvement in World War Two, but decayed from within, with effects that are still haunting the country today. Saddam's Iraq also decayed, to the point where Saddam was as deluded about the outside world as Hitler.

There are people who preach the virtues of surrendering power to the government, either so that the government can take a hard line or impose socialism. History tells us – every time – that the results are disastrous.

It is tempting to claim that the West – by which I mean Europe, America, Australia and New Zealand – has avoided these problems. Unfortunately, that claim doesn't bear scrutiny either.

I'm going to be blunt about this, because there are things that need to be said and said clearly. The West is decaying too. In the long term, the results threaten to be disastrous.

The basic problem – maybe the core problem, although I suspect that many will disagree – is the rise of what we might as well call the Political Class. It consists of a relatively small number of people who provide a disproportionate percentage of politicians and senior ministers. Those who are tempted to mock this theory might want to consider that the United States had two Presidents drawn from the Bush family (father and son), a former First Lady – Hilary Clinton – who attempted to run for President and a handful of political families that have considerable influence, such as the Kennedy family. Aristocracies from all over the world were often utterly unaware of the problems facing the common folk; it should surprise no one that the Political Class is also growing disconnected from the population.

This doesn't merge well with a second growing trend; the increasing willingness of people to place their trust in the government. Government *cannot* solve your problems for you – and to try will prove disastrous (as it did for the USSR). People want more benefits and hang the financial costs, perhaps assuming that the 'rich' will pay. If something doesn't seem fair, then change the rules – but really, why trust the government to do it? The governments we have in the West really don't know what life is like for ordinary people, or how to run a business, or just how disastrous some laws can be for people without deep pockets to hire lawyers.

An incident from the UK illustrates this nicely. Gordon Brown, then Prime Minister, was stopped and questioned by a member of the public about matters of great importance to her and the rest of the population. Afterwards, he referred to her as a 'bigot', unaware that his microphone was still on. Brown, a man who had been a politician for much of his life, had lost touch with ordinary people. He is hardly the only politician to forget where he'd come from.

Added to this problem is the rise of bureaucracy and unelected officials making laws for the general population. It will not surprise anyone who has worked in a large organisation to know that, as new layers of management are grafted on, general efficiency, common sense and competence falls sharply. The European Union attempts to standardise all kinds of items across the European continent. Unsurprisingly, the results have been disastrous. It is perhaps telling that the EU's finances are in such a mess that auditors have refused to certify them.

Setting targets – Five Year Plans, in effect – was a common trait of the Labour Government under Tony Blair. There is something wonderful about being able to say that – for example – twenty-five percent more patients were handled by the NHS this year than the previous year. However, as the USSR showed, the temptation to cook the books became overwhelming. As the government expanded, so did the paper-pushers, while those who actually did the work were pushed aside. One of the reasons Britain has so many immigrant doctors and nurses is because home-grown medical staff, sick of dealing with the NHS, have preferred to emigrate.

(An alternate example of this are the disasters inflicted upon the Third World by Western 'aid' agencies, few of which actually work with the people they are supposed to *help*, let alone be accountable to the locals.

Instead, 'solutions' are often imposed on the locals from the outside, with predictable results.)

Media manipulation is also a hallmark of the Political Class, forming yet another nail in the West's coffin. One fairly simple example was the attempt by the Blair Government to 'spin' what could only be described as a disaster in Iraq. A more dangerous example was how much of the American Mainstream Media lined up behind President Obama in his recent campaign for re-election. The media is not 'neutral' in any real sense; it quite often spins facts to support one political agenda or another.

This has effects both obvious and dangerously subtle. One is the introduction of a dangerous level of 'political correctness' as an attempt, deliberate or otherwise, to muffle free speech. Those who question Islam have often been branded as racists or bigots, as have those who oppose immigration or (in the US) President Obama. For that matter, when Shahid Malik, a Muslim MP, was caught fiddling his expenses, he promptly accused his critics of racism.

I'm not saying that the members of the Political Class are *evil*. I just think that history suggests that allowing them unrestricted control is asking for disaster.

If this goes on, as Heinlein was fond of asking, what might happen? I don't think I want to find out.

There are plenty of people who don't give a damn. Life is pretty good in the West for the vast majority of people. Even our poor enjoy a lifestyle that is beyond the dreams of the noblemen in the Roman Empire. (My dental problems would be incurable even 100 years ago, as Queen Elizabeth I could testify.) There is a considerable temptation not to get politically active. Why not leave it to the politicians?

The thing is, just like my teeth, government and the country requires constant maintenance to keep it functioning. This could be as simple as voting in every election, or as complex as actually running for election yourself. If you allow the government to drift, it will decay. And you happen to live in the country the decaying government is trying to rule. If you accept, however tacitly, that the government and politicians exist on a different plane to yourself, you are abdicating both the birthright and responsibility of a citizen born to a democratic society. Why should you be politically active? Heinlein put it very well:

> "Because you are needed. Because the task is not hopeless. Democracy is normally in perpetual crisis. It requires the same constant, alert attention to keep it from going to pot that an automobile does when driven through downtown traffic. If you do not yourself pay attention to the driving, year in and year out, the crooks, or scoundrels, or nincompoops will take over the wheel and drive it in a direction you don't fancy, or wreck it completely.
>
> When you pick yourself up out of the wreckage, you and your wife and your kids, don't talk about what "They" did to you. You did it, compatriot, because you preferred to sit in the back seat and snooze. Because you thought your taxes bought you a bus ticket and a guaranteed safe arrival, when all your taxes bought you was a part ownership in a joint enterprise, on a share-the-cost and share-the-driving plan."

Study politics, study history, learn the limits of the possible – and don't let the bastards get away with it. It's not too late to save the West, but it needs YOU. Do you really trust the politicians to put your country's interests first?

And consider this – just because you take no interest in politics, as a very ancient statesman observed, doesn't mean that politics will take no interest in you.

Christopher Nuttall
Kota Kinabalu, 2012

If you liked *No Worse Enemy*, you might like

THE COWARD'S WAY OF WAR

"In today's wars, there are no morals. We believe the worst thieves in the world today and the worst terrorists are the Americans. We do not have to differentiate between military or civilian. As far as we are concerned, they are all targets."

-Osama bin Laden

Sometime in the near future, a dying woman is discovered in New York City – infected with Smallpox. As the disease starts to spread, it is discovered that terrorists have unleashed a biological weapon on the American population – and brought the world to the brink of Armageddon.

Against this backdrop, an extraordinary cast of men and women fight desperately for survival in a world gone mad. Doctor Nicolas Awad struggles desperately to contain and control the outbreak; President Paula Handley struggles to rally the shattered country for war and preserve something of the American way of life. On the streets of New York, Sergeant Al Hattlestad and the NYPD try to keep order and save as many as possible, while survivalist Jim Revells takes his family and tries to hide from the chaos.

But the nightmare has only just begun…

CHAPTER ONE

...Among the many difficulties faced in countering such weapons is that the deployment system – i.e. an infected person, willingly or otherwise – is extremely difficult to detect. No reasonable level of security – up to and including strip and cavity searches – can detect an infected enemy agent. The issue becomes only more complicated when one realises that the infected person may be unaware that he or she is infected and, therefore, will show no sign of guilt or fear when investigated.

-Nicolas Awad

New York, USA
Day 1

"Did you enjoy the flight, sir?"

Ali Mohammad Asiri pasted a smile on his face as he looked up at the flight attendant. He had visited America several times before, yet he would never get used to American women and how they chose to dress. Just looking at the attendant – her nametag read CALLY – made him grimace inside, for it was clear that she had no sense of modesty. If one of Ali's sisters had dared to wear such an outfit in front of a strange man, he would have beaten her into a pulp. The Americans were truly a shameless people.

"Yes, I did, thank you," he said, in fluent English. As much as he wanted to reprove the harlot for her dress sense and her forwardness, he didn't quite dare. The orders had been quite specific and completely beyond question. He was to pretend to be a playboy, one tasting the seductive western world for the first time, and do nothing to attract attention. It was odd that leering at a flight attendant was less likely to attract attention than politely turning his eyes away from her, but orders were orders. Besides, he was skilled at concealing his true thoughts. Growing up with a father who adored the Americans – and the money they brought into the Kingdom – had left him very aware of the possibility of betrayal. "It was an excellent flight."

Cally grinned down at him, apparently unaware of his inner thoughts. "I'll be sure to pass your compliments on to the pilot," she said. It had been a boring flight really, with no excitement beyond a short landing in France before flying on to New York. "Is this your first time in New York, honey?"

Ali winced inwardly at her words. "No," he admitted. He would have preferred to claim ignorance, but there was no way of knowing just who Cally truly worked for or even if she would get curious and check his records. "I visited three times before and enjoyed myself, even though I was a child the first time around."

Cally shrugged and headed off to bother another passenger, leaving Ali to slump into his chair in relief. The passengers were disembarked row by row and herded off the plane and into the flight terminal, many of them heading back to the United States after a holiday or business trip abroad. Even in a time of economic recession, the Americans looked fat and disgustingly healthy compared to some of the fighters he had seen at the training camp, but then the devil was fond of rewarding his servants in this life. It was the afterlife that they had to beware, or so Ali had been taught, back when he had rediscovered his faith. Allah saw all and stood in judgement over it all.

He stood up when the flight attendants waved at him, picking up his small carry-on bag as he moved. There wasn't much in it – increasingly burdensome flight regulations had made it impossible to carry anything useful onto the plane – but he had been warned not to let it out of his sight. The Great Sheikh had made it clear that Ali must not lose his documents, even though he hadn't offered any specific instructions as to the disposal of those documents. Indeed, Ali had no idea why he'd been ordered to take a short holiday to New York City and spend a few days just relaxing and enjoying himself. When he thought about the privations being suffered by the fighters in Afghanistan, Iraq and Pakistan, he felt nothing, but guilt. How could he enjoy himself – insofar as it was possible for a believer to enjoy himself in a sinful city – when his brothers were suffering at the hands of the infidel?

But orders were orders.

Ali remembered – as he followed another female flight attendant – how he'd first met the Great Sheikh. He'd been a young man then, barely aware of the greater world outside his home city, yet bitterly aware of his father's lack of faith. His father worked with infidels, did business with infidels, profited from infidels…and ignored his duties to Islam. The young Ali, more influenced by a strict believing uncle than his father, had wondered if his father had had plans to use the infidel lust for money against them, but as he'd grown older he had come to realise that his father just loved their money. He had grown to manhood aware of his family's shame – and of how his world was slipping away from him – and desperate to change it, somehow.

His uncle had introduced him to a more fundamentalist mosque and it had all grown from there. Ali had thought to go to Pakistan – Iraq wasn't a safe place for believers these days, not with an increasingly effective Iraqi Army wiping out *Jihadi* cells almost as soon as they were formed – but the Great Sheikh had had other ideas. Ali was a young man with an unblemished record, one that would sound no alarms in the American security forces. He could be far more useful elsewhere.

The Great Sheikh himself was a great man. He had fought alongside the great Osama bin Laden before the unleashing of righteous wrath on New York City, over seventeen years ago. Since then, he had fought in Iraq, Pakistan and even Europe before he'd finally been ordered to return to his homeland of Saudi Arabia and start forming new cells for overseas operations. Ali, like many other young men, had been captivated by his words, for they had nothing in their lives to live for. Ali had graduated from university with a degree in Islamic Studies that had proven to be worthless in the real world, while there was no hope of marriage or children. His father had refused to help his believing son any further, after reminding Ali that he had urged him to take a more useful – and sinful – course. Instead, one of his daughters was – against all Islamic precepts – slowly assuming control of the family business. Her husband, a weak man easily dominated by his wife, might have control in name, but in reality it was all hers. It made Ali's blood boil. How could any man be so weak?

"You will do nothing to attract attention," the Great Sheikh had said, the first time Ali had flown to America under his orders. Ali had expected to be contacted while in the United States for a martyrdom operation, but nothing had ever materialised and he'd returned home, half-suspecting that the Great Sheikh would be angry with him. Instead, he'd been thanked and urged to return to his studies, before being sent on a second trip a year later. "You will be a typical sinful lad" – at this point, the Great Sheikh had winked at him – "and pretend to enjoy yourself. You will have no connection with us that anyone can see."

Ali could only assume – as he passed through the security checks – that the Great Sheikh had given him the mission because he knew that Ali wouldn't be tempted by the many temptations of the West. It was sad, but true that many of the fighters had been tempted – and fallen – by alcohol, or drugs, or women. Some of the tales whispered by veterans from many campaigns against the infidel had been horrific, suggesting that they'd embraced sin in all of its many forms. Ali had said that that might explain why they'd lost; how could they expect Allah to bless their mission if they broke His rules? The Great Sheikh had taken a more pragmatic view. If someone was willing to fight the infidel, all such failings could be ignored, at least until the *Dar-ul-Harb* became the *Dar-ul-Islam*, when purity would be the order of the day. Ali longed for such a day, for it would give his life meaning. He didn't fit in with the modern world the Americans and their European lackeys had created.

The security checks took longer than they had the last time, causing him to worry about what the Americans might have found, even though he knew that he was carrying nothing that might implicate him in the cause. He had no banned material, no pamphlets castigating the West and the fallen Muslims who accepted the West's domination of their souls… he didn't even have a copy of the *Qur'an*! He had protested when the Great Sheikh had ordered him to carry only western material, but the Great Sheikh had been insistent. He was to do nothing to attract attention. He was merely a tourist visiting New York City and it had to remain that way.

Eventually, the Americans finished their checks and allowed him to pass through the security barrier and into John F. Kennedy International Airport. It was the busiest international air passenger gateway to the United States, according to the Americans themselves, making it ideal for the network's more undercover purposes. There was no point in trying to sneak in – and perhaps being caught by the Coast Guard – when they could just fly into America perfectly legitimately. It was something, Ali had been told, that made people like him extremely valuable. As a 'clean' man, with nothing to alert the Americans to his true masters, there was no reason for them to delay his entry into their country. Even the growing paranoia about Arabs and Muslims in America couldn't delay his operation. It did help that he had no intention of doing anything in New York City.

Waving goodbye to the TSA agent who had searched his bag, Ali headed down to the taxi rack and climbed into a taxi being driven by a Pakistani immigrant. He was tempted to speak to the man in Arabic, but again, it risked attracting unwanted attention. Instead, he gave the man instructions to head directly to the Marigold Hotel and settled back to enjoy the ride. It always amazed him how orderly American streets were compared to the roads back home, where everyone drove as if their lives depended on it.

New York had a remarkable skyline, even though it was nothing more than a sign of American decadence. It was temping to order the driver to take him to where the Twin Towers had once been – before they had been knocked down by the 9/11 Martyrs – yet he didn't quite dare. The Great Sheikh's instructions had been specific. He was not to do anything that might attract attention and that included visiting the site of 9/11, or any other Islamic site in New York.

The movement had spent a considerable amount of money booking him a suite at the Marigold Hotel, allowing Ali to relax in the lap of luxury. He had to repress another surge of guilt as he paid and tipped the taxi driver, before strolling into the Marigold as if he owned the place – and, with the amount he was paying, the staff were happy to treat him as if he *did* own the hotel. Ali allowed himself to act like a Prince he had seen once, tipping the staff as they showed him to his suite and helped him to unpack. The wink from the maid suggested that she would be willing to go above and beyond the call of duty – in exchange for an additional gratuity, of course – but Ali just wanted to sleep. He dismissed the staff, lay down on the comfortable bed and went to sleep.

When he awoke, several hours later, he felt famished and ordered a plate of food from room service. The suite came with a computer and he logged on to a popular and free email account, sending a single email back home to inform his brothers that he had arrived. The email would pass unnoticed, even by the never-to-be-sufficiently-damned American NSA and its dreaded interception skills, for there was nothing in it that might attract attention. Who would notice – or care about – an email from a newly-arrived tourist to his friends back home? He resisted the temptation to log onto some of the cause's websites – that would definitely have attracted attention – and shut down the computer. There was a knock at the door and a maid appeared with a tray of food, much to Ali's relief. He shook her hand, pressed a tip into her fingers and shoed her out of the room, before settling down to eat. It was still early afternoon in the United States, but it felt much later. The jet lag was kicking in.

After he had eaten his food, he left the hotel and played tourist. New York had plenty of interesting sights to see, even if he had been specifically barred from going anywhere near any Islamic sites. He kept his feelings off his face as he walked through endless museums and art galleries, wondering at all the energy surrounding him. The Americans had no sense of shame or decorum. He spied a pair of Americans wearing Army uniforms and shuddered inside, remembering tales from brothers who had narrowly escaped death at the hands of men wearing similar uniforms. The Americans flaunted their power for all to see.

But then, he told himself, what could one expect from unbelievers? When all one had was the glory of one's own self – instead of the glory of God – why would they not flaunt what they had? The temptations of the mundane world were great, yet the price was agonisingly high. He saw a homosexual couple walking hand in hand and shuddered again, remembering the day when a pair of such sinners had been put to death back home. The Americans seemed to embrace sinners. Tired, he started to make his way back to the hotel, wishing – once again – that the Great Sheikh had given him something more worthy to do. Perhaps, the next time he came, he would have orders to spend his life dearly in reminding the Americans that judgement existed, or perhaps he would be part of a team that would bring the United States to its knees.

He stepped onto the underground and rode for several stations before reaching the one closest to the Marigold. Despite himself, he couldn't avoid feeling a childlike sense of fascination with the transport system, even though the other commuters looked bored or angry. He found himself rubbing shoulders with the American melting pot – Latinos from Mexico and South America, Chinese and Vietnamese immigrants from the Far East, men with skins so dark that they looked as if they had come from Africa – and fought hard to keep the distaste off his face. He reminded himself, again, that it wasn't his duty to question the Great Sheikh and his orders. He would carry them out, even if they made no sense.

Back at the hotel, he had a long bath and then settled into bed for the night. The Great Sheikh had ordered him to play tourist for his entire visit, which meant visiting the American cinemas and watching some of their filthy films and other entertainments, perhaps even visiting some of their dance clubs and dancing…could there be any greater sin? The Great Sheikh had told him that sins committed in the name of Allah, with no actual intention to sin for the sake of sinning, were no sin, yet Ali would have preferred to avoid them. If the Great Sheikh had told him why he was following such absurd orders, it would have been easier, but what he didn't know he couldn't tell. Ali was confident that he could survive an American interrogation, no matter how rigorous, yet others had believed the same.

He rubbed at his forearm as he turned over and switched off the lights. The tiny bump had materialised only a day before he'd boarded the flight in Saudi Arabia, a sign that he'd been bitten by an insect in the night. It didn't really hurt, but it twitched from time to time, reminding him that it was there. Ali pushed the pain aside and ignored it. After what some of the movement had suffered over the years at the hands of the Great Satan and its allies, complaining about an insect bite seemed absurd. Shaking his head at the thought, he closed his eyes and went to sleep. He had a long day ahead of him tomorrow, doing nothing.

There had been over five hundred men and women on the aircraft that had brought Ali to the United States. As darkness fell over the eastern seaboard, many of them returned to their homes in New York or headed onwards to other destinations within the United States. The people he had met on his first day in New York – the flight attendants, the security officers, the taxi driver, and the hotel staff – likewise dispersed themselves over the city, relaxing after a hard day at work. Some went to their homes to sleep; others went to party or to relax with their friends. In the end, it hardly mattered.

None of them – not even Ali, who had carried it to America's shores – knew that the most destructive attack in America's long history had begun. None of them knew that they were carrying the seeds of destruction within them. And, because none of them knew this, none of them took any precautions. The attack spread rapidly across the city and outside, across the United States. An attack on a scale to dwarf Pearl Harbor had begun and no one had even noticed.

But they would.

And soon.

Download a Free Sample from the Chrishanger…

www.chrishanger.net

And then download the full novel as an eBook!

Printed in Great Britain
by Amazon